UNBOUND

Two elebrated novels from
the master of erotic realism

Carroll & Graf Publishers, Inc.
New York

LOINS OF AMON

From a high, pale sky the blinding ring of sun smouldered, quivering back off the hot, white flagstones of the inner courtyard of the temple, drawing moans of nausea from the manacled women as it burned into their naked flesh.

They were spread in grotesque attitudes, kneeling with thighs pulled under them, legs wide apart, wrists tied to iron rings in the flagstones, round their necks another rope pulling their shoulders down to the scorching stone.

In the shade of the surrounding colonnade, the lustful eyes of the young priests bored into the soft folds of unprotected virgin vaginas, as if they would rape the women with a look. But, although their bodies trembled with desire, their loins ached, they made no move. These were

5

the special sacrifice to the god Amon. The instruments of ravishing were the sacred baboons.

Under the merciless weight of the sun the virgin flesh writhed, seeking relief from the heat which was as terrible as rape. Breasts slumped to the ground and rose again sharply as the heat burned the nipples in contact. Hips rotated in a small orbit, trying to hide from the solid-feeling touch of the sun the two revealed portals at the leg junction.

The tortured bodies were slim and soft. They had been chosen by the High Priest from the best in the land. It was he who had had the girls stripped before their parents, had smoothed his hands over the flesh, lingering over the mounds of breasts and buttocks and the moist treasures between the thighs. He had judged them fit for sacrifice and had them brought terrified and screaming to the confinement of the temple.

Now they were quiet but for their moans of pain and shame. It was too late to scream and fight.

The priests devoured the mass revealed intimacy of a dozen women unclothed and extended in a position of submission. For many it was their first witnessing of the annual rite.

As it began to seem to some that they must yield to their emotions, must run and plunge their hands into the untried quicksands of women's core, expose themselves and drive in with a warm relief, there was a tremor of movement at the door of a chamber in the gloom at the edge of the portico.

Into the lighter shade and then into the sunlight several large, fierce-looking baboons were coaxed by a little body of priests.

Left to themselves in the heat of the central court, the

shaggy animals walked around in the sun from which they had been kept for hours, scratched and picked at themselves and regarded the audience—peering at them from the shade of the colonnade—with fierce, inquisitive glances.

They were powerful beasts and for a long time they had been deprived of the female of their species to give an impetus to their appetite for human flesh. Their long, raw organs drooped down to the warm dust as they sat.

They seemed to become increasingly aware of the helpless women spreadeagled at a little distance from them. One of them, walking with that queer awkward gait, already had an erection as if he was well aware of the procedure and was boiling in a fever of anticipation. His penis, as thick as a man's, had the advantage of additional length, as the spectators pointed out, muttering amongst themselves in growing excitement.

Having stalked around in the sun for a while, the animal suddenly squatted down before his audience, rearing his colourful organ into full view as if in a bout of exhibitionism and slight chuckles whispered and echoed amongst the shadows of the pillars.

Then he was up again and stalking warily towards the nearest rearing protrusion of soft hips. Between the stretched roundness of buttocks the sun shone in a warm stream on the exposed cleft.

As the beast extended skinny fingers to feel the unhaired flesh with curiosity, the girl turned a pretty, brown-eyed face towards the direction of the touch, chafing her neck on the rope as she did so.

Her features contorted with horror at the sight of the fierce, dog-like face in which the teeth were already bared.

She seemed to become paralysed with terror, mouth drooping open, eyes wild and set.

7

The baboon's snout moved up her smooth, flawless skin like a man's hand. He sniffed at her feet, her calves, her thighs—and then the unrifled entrance between them. The girl squirmed her buttocks away at the feel of his nose and then he was clámbering onto her, clumsily, in a fierce burst of decision. The girl's lips opened but no sound came out. She was shaking all over and it seemed she might faint.

Lying along her back, fur and raw parts pressed against her warm, soft, human flesh, gripping her tightly with his skinny hands, the beast wriggled, searching for the maidenly treasure as he would have searched on one of his own kind, probing thighs, buttocks, with his long, thick finger of rigid flesh. And then he had found it and torn straight in, unused to human frailties.

The girl uttered a heart-rending scream at last and blood spurted. She tried to rise, straining on the ropes which held her for this outraging of her chastity.

The beast had clasped her in a passionate embrace. His long, furry arms gripped her soft body, encircling her just under her quivering breasts. His thick, powerful legs dug into her thighs as, teeth bared, he thundered into her to the accompaniment of animal chatterings of passion.

The girl's head sank to the dusty stone as tears gushed from her eyes. She squirmed her bottom from side to side, but the ropes at her ankles prevented any effective evasion and the bare patches on the buttocks of the animal jerked in and out at his engrossed audience with increasing fury. His strong limbs were crushing the girl as his ruggedly raw penis moved in and he searched in his savage, animal way to lose it entirely in her depths.

The girl began to moan. Sand from the floor of the court

had dusted the tears on her face as she grovelled on all fours, like an animal herself.

Saliva drooled from between the beast's teeth as the thrusting flesh between his back legs was gradually engulfed in the slim, soft passage of the virgin sacrifice, splitting it, broadening it. His toes made indents in the girl's body as the savage surgings rocked his shaggy frame, weight pressing on her and through her in an almost human, but more savage than human intercourse.

All around in the dark colonnades the audience was jostling and staring, moving to get a better view. In other parts of the court the remaining prostrate women looked on, eyes fixed and horrified as they waited for the inevitable duplication of the scene at their own posteriors. Some were soon mounted and eventually the whole, sundrenched square was heaving in a broken, demoniacal rhythm, alive with contorted figures of disappearing virginity, of bestial rape en masse and without struggle.

The pioneer was producing strange, savage grunting in his throat, writhing and twisting furiously on the girl's arched back, clasping her so tightly around her body that she panted, gasping for breath while the gulf between her legs was completely subdued, broken, pillaged, filled to the hilt.

The animal's powerful chest heaved, small, hairy hips jerking with incredibly rapid motion at the thrustout buttocks of the girl. Swifter, swifter, while stirrings at the loins could be detected under the tunics of the watching priests.

His raw organ shot redly into view and then embedded itself inside the girl again at an increasingly rapid speed. His skinny fingers dug her so that she cried out with the pain. The animal was grunting furiously as if with a great,

9

painful effort. And then with a savage, barking cry which brought fresh tears of shame and misery from the girl's eyes, the creature stiffened against her, withdrew and stiffened several times over.

After his hot, animal lust had shot into the depths of the girl, he clambered slowly, awkwardly off her soft body and wandered away, leaving the crushed heap heaving with sobs, unable still, to escape from the ungainly, shameful position of offering.

The audience had moved out from the porticoes, searching for better, closer views and they surrounded the rapidly jerking humps of flesh, staring from all angles at the ravishing, but not getting too close. A baboon could be a fierce enemy in fighting for its property.

One animal had, accidentally, and with great difficulty squirmed his organ into the backside of his victim and was enlarging the inflamed aperture with short, powerful strokes as the girl screamed at each thrust. She was marked down for later initiation.

Soon the sacred courtyard was filled with the slumped forms of ravished women, sobbing on their breasts, carrying between their legs the pain of the obscene friction, and in their loins, the unleashed loads of unfruitful sperm.

They were allowed to lie, burning and miserable for a few moments of recovery and then a word was uttered by the High Priest and the younger priests unabashedly rushed to take the places of the scattered baboons, scrambling to have the woman whose anus had been penetrated, wanting to be the first to initiate her.

The High Priest stood watching the scene of passion for some time and then he turned to the Pharaoh, also a gloating witness of the carnality.

"There are some, as yet untouched in the inner chamber if my Lord so desires," he said.

Ramses smiled with satisfaction.

"I will have a look at them," he said.

He walked away passing through the huddled, groaning pairs braving the fierce sun for the sake of satiation. The High Priest watched him go with a faint smile on his lips.

Leaning against a pillar some yards away in the shade, Prince Ineni coldly considered the High Priest. The scene of sacrifice had aroused in him the sadistic feelings of a warrior, but his feelings were directed against the priesthood. On the next day, the ravaged bodies of the beautiful girls who had suffered such punishment today, would be flung to the crocodiles in the Nile in the final tribute to Amon. It was thus that not only the finest daughters, but the finest sons of Egypt were despatched to the other land. For the High Priest was jealous of his power.

Feeling eyes upon him, the High Priest turned and gazed at Ineni for a moment.

"You have enjoyed the spectacle brother?" he mocked.

Ineni's views on the worth-whileness of sacrifice were well-known. That was why the High Priest used his influence with the Pharaoh to summon the prince as a witness on every possible occasion.

"I have enjoyed things more," Ineni replied, dark eyes cold and hard before the gaze of the High Priest.

"The amount of sacrifice is to be increased," the latter jibed with a sneer. "The number of virgins and young men is to be doubled. Amon is a great god and he demands further satisfaction."

"It will be pleasing news for your young priests," Ineni replied.

11

The High Priest's eyes flickered at the hardly veiled insult.

"It is the decree of the Pharaoh," he said. "You would not say that the decree is unwise?"

Ineni checked his impulse to insult. This evil sapper of Egypt's strength frequently invited him to spoken treason, waiting like a sacred cobra to dart in triumph to the kill.

"Our Lord's word is the Law," he replied.

"Yes-yes." The High Priest's eyes gleamed. "One must not forget His word is the Law."

Ineni was turning away, but the High Priest's gloating was not yet finished.

"I am told that in a few days you leave to subdue the rebellious towns of the northern empire," he said. "Our thoughts will go with you. May you return with much treasure and many captives for the Pharaoh's pleasure."

"I shall do my best for Egypt," Ineni replied.

Ineni turned and walked away through the court and the massive archway, leaving in his wake the coldly triumphant smile of the High Priest and the fading passion of his younger breed of satellites.

Through the next courtyard he passed under the covert glances of the priest guard. They knew him as an enemy and in the unearthly quiet between the great, gloomy porticoes which flanked the couryard, he felt that a spear might plunge into his back at any step.

But he walked on calmly with slow deliberation. The priests were too wise to employ such an obvious means of liquidating a rebel.

The great cedarwood door was swung back for his exit and he moved out into the hot, open desert between the great portal statues of Ramses, breathing with relief. The great door slammed shut behind him, closing in the corrup-

tion around which the people of Egypt clothed such mystery and fear.

Ineni mounted his horse and rode through the desert away from the massive, squatting shape of the temple. It seemed to him, as he glanced back, like a great, carnal vulture, picking flesh from the bones of a dying Egypt.

In the nearby outskirts of Memphis, Ineni slowed to a walk through the fields of cotton and maize in which the peasants were toiling. Many of them nude, men and women together, the women, big-breasted and muscular, these were the people who provided Egypt with the wealth it had acquired. They and the great nourishing Nile in conjunction. And what happened to the wealth? Ineni's lips pursed as he rode. It went into the temples; food, handicrafts, quarried resources, all went into the temples as rich endowments to the dead who needed nourishment in their after life. There in the temples it served to let the priests grow fat and powerful. Under the sheltering name of the god Amon, while the vast empire which had stretched to the ends of the earth, from the dark unknown places of Nubia to the Tigris in the north, was crumbling, the priests grew fat on the wealth which was Egypt's.

Bigger than the Pharaoh's were their herds, bigger than his their land and corn, bigger than his the hoards of gold and silver that adorned the temples. And while the priests wallowed in the plenty, the excess their sacred power had brought them, the people starved, the Pharaoh yielded.

Breaking again into a gallop, long muscles bunched and tense, fine eyes blazing, Ineni gave vent in the fury of speed to his feelings.

He thought with hatred of Ramses' weakness. Were they not both descended from Ramses II whose name had resounded with a strong ring through the camps of the

13

Hittites? And where was the empire now, where the strength of the Pharaoh? The glory that was Egypt's?

Ramses was weak, a tool of the priests. Yet not so weak that he was unable to act, as he recognised the growing power and popularity of Ineni in his position as governor of Heliopolis so close to the seat of power at Memphis. There he had built up a name for strength and justice which had made him the idol of his people.

On the urging of the priests, Ineni had been withdrawn from his local throne and brought into the circles of the court at Memphis where he could better be surveyed. It had been rumoured that he had a claim to the throne which the people would be willing to support if revolt came. And it was known that Ineni had no love for the priests. And that he was a strong and forthright man.

Ineni's steed took him at powerful raking speed, in spite of the sun, through the trees and canals and the cluttered, poverty-stricken outskirts where in crowded quarters, worse by far than the makeshift camps of the marching army, the poor groaned and existed and often died with their pleas to the Pharaoh and the Gods echoing in vain.

In his new surroundings, Ineni had found many friends and admirers and at their permanent seat at Thebes, far south in the valley, the priests had watched with misgiving.

Now they had played their last card. The Pharaoh had ordered his prince to take a small, inadequate army into a suicide trap. In the name of the Pharaoh, nominal emperor of the northern lands, Ineni was to march his men—no more than 3,000 with chariotry—across the mighty eastern desert, infested with fierce, bellicose Bedouin tribes and into Palestine and Syria to subdue a number of recalcitrant vassal cities behind which the awful weight of the Hittite thousands was almost openly in support.

In return for the death of their enemy, the priests of Amon were prepared to fling a handful of men against the Hittite hordes and take, in the almost certain annihilation of the tiny army, a shattering blow to Egypt's waning prestige. Perhaps, even, to risk the invasion of the valley. It was a sorry prospect and Ineni shuddered at the thought of Egypt under the yoke.

Cantering now, he emerged from the partitioned hovels of the poor into the spaced temples and palaces of the Gods and the rich to the north of the city.

It was here, looking out over the placid stretch of the Nile that his own villa and gardens had been built. His villa was beautiful; wall-surrounded, shaded with trees and shrubbery, laced with walks and arbours.

Ineni liked to live well—but he did not hoard wealth. He gave to the poor and encouraged them to reap the benefit of their own labours when they came under his jurisdiction. Would that he had jurisdiction over all, in the place of Ramses and the priests. He would build new homes for the peasants at the cost of the useless glut of temples with which the priests were dotting the plain of Thebes. He would see that the peasants received the stocks of food, which at present endowed the temples to line the fat bellies of the priests. But what hope now?

At the gates of his villa he dismounted, leaving his servants to tend to the horse.

His mind flickered back to the sexual events of the afternoon. He was not out of sympathy with the initiation rites, but to kill so many beautiful maidens was not, he felt sure, to fulfil the wishes of Amon, who would surely want his people to be as happy and powerful as possible.

He might, himself, have selected a woman had it not been in such proximity to the priests. But, anyway, his

own harem was sufficient to provide him with the sexual variety he needed.

It was true that tomorrow he would have to begin preparations for the long trek from the Delta, through the arid eastern desert. Tonight he would indulge.

In the cool shade of his villa, Ineni dined with his three favourite concubines. Two were slim, soft-eyed Egyptians, the other a strong, large-boned woman who had been brought back from early campaigns in Palestine. Her firm, fierce features made a passionate contrast with the soft submission of the others.

Ineni sat on a small stool of ebony, the women at his feet on rugs while the food was served. The meal was rich: fish which Ineni had caught himself in the swamps of the Delta, poultry, bread and cakes, several kinds of fruit and strong cool wines. The women, voluptuous in their long, close-fitting robes, were sad at the imminent departure of their lord, their eyes deep and thoughtful as the dancing girls appeared at the end of the meal.

The dancing girls, as usual, were without any covering. Trained from infancy, their bodies were as supple as papyrus stems and as lacking in any superfluity to spoil their graceful symmetry. Their bodies swayed and twirled, breasts, buttocks trembling lightly at the rapidity of movement, lack of hair at their thigh junctions making them seem even more nude as the slim folds of flesh between their legs tautened and relaxed with their dancing steps.

They moved in fluid patterns close to Ineni so that none of their charms were hidden. The slight, fleshy tensions of their bottoms as they moved, the silken ripple of their thighs, the unconcealed thrustings of their crotches, all in an overwhelmingly close intimacy.

Ineni felt the hot tension in his loins, the power and heat

16

stirring and throbbing there. He stretched out his hand and caressed the long, smooth neck of one of the Egyptian women, his hand stroking gently over her soft, velvet skin, the firm bone of her jaw. She turned towards him and, reaching up from the floor, gently moved her hand under the hem of his tunic, rubbing his calf softly, stroking its muscular hairiness. Under his tunic, his penis was bulging powerfully now, pulsing and hugely fierce and the woman's hand crept up under the garment, slipping over the hairy joint of his knee and on, inexorably up the broad, bulging thigh. Eyes still on the dancers, Ineni slipped the straps of her robe from her shoulders and with a wriggle of her slim torso, she had eased it from off her breasts so that it flopped in a fringe around her waist.

He looked down at her for the first time, at the smooth, brown expanse of shoulder sweeping down into hills of breasts, coppery and ripe. His hand slipped down between the mounds and then out across a breast, savoring it with every pore of his skin, cupping the great nipple.

Her nostrils dilated and with a swift movement, her hand had covered the last inch of thigh and she was drawing long, cool fingers over the relaxed pendants of his testicles, stroking them gently, their rough, hairy surfaces, with electric finger tips.

As volcanoes seemed to simmer in the fat, rigid length of his penis, her hand twitched and seemed to pounce upon its heat, grasping it gently with a sudden foreign touch which made him gasp.

A swift sign from Ineni and the dancing girls sidled off and he was left alone with his three companions. With a sinuous ripple of movement, the woman had slithered out of her robe altogether, revealing soft, fleshy hips which raised themselves, now, towards her lord.

17

Her hand quietly massaged his thick, hard rod as her two companions rose silently, stripped off their robes in turn and began gently to remove Ineni's tunic. It unswathed from his powerful, muscular shoulders, revealing his broad rugged chest, downed with curling black hair and then pulled away from his hips for the massive organ—in powerful proportion with his body—to soar into view. The Palestinian unbuckled his under belt which contained his daggers and placed it near. She unstrapped his sandals, too, her eyes fiercely, eagerly, devouring his strong, potent genitals as she did so.

With his Egyptian maintaining her squeezing hold on his raging tool, Ineni stood up and moved with the women to a great bed of cushions in one corner of the room.

There he sank luxuriously onto his back, a woman each side of him and one at his feet. His hands reached out on either side and fondled breasts and buttocks, navels and smooth, round bellies, while soft hands stirred on his thighs, drew spidery patterns over his testicles, jerked gently and surely on his massive upstanding tool.

His eyes closed, unseeing, while his hands traced paths on thighs as smooth as ivory, felt the lush flesh of portals between legs, entered gently and probed the soft, moist, opening recesses.

From below, between his wide-stretched legs, the strong Palestinian moved up to run her lips up the long, bulging length of bursting rigidity and then to descend her mouth voraciously on it, swallowing it in a soft clinging swamp of lips and tongue.

Ineni jerked his slim, dark hips from the cushions in an involuntary stiffening as the lips, masters for their brief period, sucked without respite, without quarter.

It was as if the base of his penis was striving to go on a

18

hard journey, to reach the far point, where the bulging knob which formed a culminating cudgel was sensitively pulsing, growing redder and more feverish.

His hands gripped the flesh of the women at his sides in handfuls, drew them to him so that they could join their lips to his in fierce abandon, shooting moist tongues, synchronising a tension at the lips with the tension binding his loins like the strong, unrelenting swaths of cloth which bound his ancestors as they were carried in state to their mortuary tombs.

Breath gasping into the mouths of the women who pressed themselves alternately down on his contorted features, Ineni felt his hips writhing, stirring, swaying themselves as if with lives of their own and he thought: my mind is helpless. If the High Priest entered now with a spear to despatch me to the Gods, I should be unable to move to defend myself.

And then even the thought was lost and only the sensation was left, so that his loins, his whole lower body seemed to be swimming in a vast sea of painful sensation so that there was nothing else of him; only the sensation was real.

The seemingly disembodied lips, the mouth, the throat were eating him, trying to draw the whole of him into the aching, yearning body of the Palestinian. He could distinguish no external detail of touch. Doubtless her teeth were there, gnawing gently, her tongue was there licking and twining, her lips, pressing, sucking, but no detail was clear, only the great vacuum of suction drawing all the juices of his body down to the point.

His hands clasped and unclasped on the flesh of the women at his sides. They presented to him breasts which they wanted to feel crushed in his big, strong hands and

then buttocks so that he could grasp the orbs in his iron fingers.

At his loins the sucking was a great, great pain, working furiously like a possessed thing and then his lips were opened as if by a magic force, sounds like unknown, instinctive prayers were sucked from his throat and his loins were jerking up and down, round and up so that the suction was almost displaced in his fury. And the powerful, yearning forces of his body were being drawn from deep inside to the extremity of his spouting, reaching, taut penis-mace. His head was hot, his mouth working, gasping and a great flood, seeming equal to the Nile potential at the rainy season was building, building in his bowels, higher and higher, more and more powerful and potent until it had reached breaking point at which the dams would break; and then with a great rushing noise from his throat the dam had broken and the flood waters were surging in a mighty cataract out of his penis and into the raping source of suction.

The lips, the mouth, worked and swallowed as if his seed was some hallowed offering which gave strength. All his shooting sperm was ravenously swallowed in the gorge of the woman whose own face contorted and twisted in the pain and fury of it.

And then after what seemed an interminable pain, the flood water had ebbed and stilled, his hands had relaxed from the flesh they had enclosed on each side, penis deflated, swung back limply on his thighs while the swallowing mouth had sunk to his mass of genitals and buried itself there, motionless, spent.

For some time all four lay there, still, recovering. Later the women brought wine and fruit and a bowl in which to wash.

Sitting and lying on the cushions they showed no impatience, just waited quietly and certainly for their lord to need them.

Freshly wined and rested, Ineni noticed his penis, long, limp, stretching in warm, ruddy idleness on his strong thighs. Even limp it bulged and the thin veins stood out in mature fullness. As he looked at it, it seemed to stir as if his gaze embarrassed it, made it aware that now was no time to relax.

He drew the Palestinian woman over to him, pressing her along his body, so that he could feel her full-boned, full-fleshed strength throbbing in heat against him. She responded fiercely, thrusting her big breasts into his chest so that he could feel the nipples cutting like pointed buttons into his skin.

She wrapped her arms tightly around his body and he felt his penis lift in a quick, forced movement, impelled by the recognition of her passion.

Feeling it thrusting at her, the woman wrapped her long, firm thighs around it, enclosing it, pressing it until it hurt with the pressure.

Ineni began to move backwards and forwards against her, rubbing his organ against the velvet flesh of her thighs while the breath shot in little delicate snorts down her nostrils.

He motioned with his eyes to the other women, doting over them and one of them lay down behind him so that he could feel her breasts pressing into his back, her soft, cushioning belly enveloping his buttocks, while her fingers stroked his hips and his sides. The other knelt over him, stroking the backs of his knees, his thighs as he squirmed.

Crushed against him, the Palestinian wormed her leg junction down to his probing rod, scrambling it, with her

21

thighs, up so that it rested against the lips of her vagina. There she wriggled it into place, wrapping one leg over Ineni and hesitated, drawing in her breath.

As she paused, with a quick, stabbing up-movement, he had seared into her with one swift, punishing stroke and she gasped and cried out. The other two watched voraciously, pressing themselves close to Ineni's moving warmth.

Cradling him into her chasm, the woman gently eased herself towards him, a gentle pressure, a hint which he could take or reject. With an inward smile, Ineni accepted and swayed over onto his back. The woman pivoted up, squatting over him, astride him, knees on the ground on either side of his hips. There, gazing down at him with fierce eyes full of passion, she rose and slumped on his stem, rose and slumped, contracting her strong hips so that the muscular action clamped her passage tightly around his rearing penis, relaxed and clamped tightly again.

Ineni tightened his buttocks, thrusting his hips off the ground, feeling the jingling at his genitals. The woman spread her thighs, so that, sliding up and down, she soon contained the whole massive tower in her gaping aperture. Her head, paler than those of her two companions, sagged on her neck and then tautened again in passion so that a vein stood out at the side of her throat with the fury of the exertion. Her mouth opened and closed in the mute desperation to which the bursting plunder of her body had reduced her, long hair swayed and swished over her shoulders.

Reaching up, Ineni grasped her swaying, flopping breasts, crumpling them harshly so that hoarse grunts were drawn from the woman's throat. Her strong-boned face swept down to his for a brief moment, brushing a kiss and then swayed up again as she plunged like a fierce arab steed into the heart of the sexual vortex.

The other women had drawn back, confessing, mutely, an admiration for the woman's superiority. Their turn—a softer, more submissive turn, would come later. For the moment they watched, dark, deep eyes inscrutable, all-devouring.

Reaching down and behind her as she bucked on him, the Palestinian caressed Ineni's testicles, massaging them with the lightest of touches. The backward stretching made her body toss precariously on Ineni's hips as he jerked with greater and greater rapidity. She seemed to be riding a wild horse, desperately trying to stay unseated. Her hips descended with greater and greater force as if each time she were collapsing on the downward stroke—only to revive just in time and draw herself up on the great shaft again.

Ineni, tensing upwards and ever upwards, felt the gripping of his loins as if a mighty hand were reaching in and tearing at his entrails, a close, squeezed feeling which made him clasp the woman's waist and ram her down on his organ with all his strength. And the hand was squeezing, squeezing as if pus were to be squeezed from a pimple. And the woman's passage was wide and penetrated, her mouth open in a great O, eyes wide and bulging. The sqeezing was becoming unbearable. The pimple must break. It was hurting, killing and then with a great bursting the skin had broken, the pimple disintegrated in painful cascades to the accompaniment of the woman's long, passion-filled wail.

The women were tender and grateful. It was their life. Ineni was wined and bathed again. They all partook. And then the other favourites of the harem were treated—with slight variations—in similar fashion. It was well into the

23

night before Ineni was able to sleep. And then he slept as one dead.

The next two days, Ineni's time was wholly taken up with the preparation of his expedition. His forces were far from the best available. For appearance's sake he had been given a nucleus of tried veterans. For the remainder, his contingent comprised Nubian and Libyan mercenaries, whose loyalty was always questionable and whose discipline faded in face of spoil for the plunder.

Food and equipment for the campaign were loaded onto the tough, serviceable, little donkeys, the officers rode horses or horse-drawn chariots, the men would walk, carrying their weapons ever at the ready.

So it was, that with Prince Ineni at the head, leading the army on his fine white horse, that the forces of the Pharaoh started once more for Asia, for the hostile lands of the north, which so often had been conquered and forced to recognise his sovereignty. But what a paltry army!

The people who had lined the route to cheer their hero were silent, cheers choked in their throats at the realization of the meagreness of the company. The Pharaoh could still have mustered 20,000 men—and he would have needed them against the Hittite swarms.

On the broad road from Memphis to Heliopolis the peasants thronged the roadside, leaving their fields to watch as their ancestors had watched, the splendid strength of their land passing in battle array. Along this same road Thutmose III had led his glorious thousands who had followed their king as he forged, with his own strong leadership, an empire which had covered the earth, so that the very mention of the Pharaoh's name had struck fear into the hearts of his vassals and not a city had been late with the annual tribute.

With thoughts of the old days, even of Ramses II, whose personal valour had saved Asia for Egypt, the old men in the crowds were silent. Was this all that Egypt could do?

At Heliopolis, old seat of his power. Ineni was greeted with cheers, but here, too, the cheers faded into a sad and horrified watching as the motley force of mercenaries marched through the town. To what avail was their prince's personal strength when the Pharaoh had allowed him so little support? Could one brave lion face a thousand wild dogs? No matter if he ripped five hundred to pieces, what of the five hundred remaining? They shook their heads, sadly. It was well known that the Pharaoh feared for his throne. He had found the best way of ridding himself of a contestant. Amongst the multitudes these feelings were unvoiced. The accepted quailing before the high priests. But in higher places there were those who talked, who wished that something had been done before, as now, it was too late.

Out from the fertile fringe of valley, cutting, on the broad, straight road through the poverty-stricken settlements of the desert. Ineni had soon forgotten the sympathetic eyes of the people behind him. He kept the army marching at a strong pace and some hours after the midday rest, they reached Tharu—the last outpost of Egypt to the east. In the little fortress town, they obtained last supplies of water. To the south they could see the far distant expanse of the Red Sea, to the north the Mediterranean where it curbed inland in great, broken bays.

In this Amon-forsaken town, unsheltered from the sun, where the noseless criminals were condemned to pass their days, Ineni's men camped the night.

With the dawn, which came quickly in shades of yellow,

green and then blue, casting long, light beams over the eastern desert, the broad column of warriors set out from Tharu.

As the last vestige of civilization grew smaller and became a mere speck behind them, so the desert, vast and waste, seemed to open out like a brown, withered but nonetheless opening flower, all around them. Ahead over the great distance to Jerusalem was nothing but mile upon mile of gently undulating desert, running eventually into mountain ranges. The sun was a great, hazy force, scorching down on them as, like a column of tiny insects they left all succour, cast themselves adrift in the barren, hostile land.

Riding proudly at the head, Ineni's strong eyes surveyed the yellow sea. This was the land of fierce Bedouin tribes, who plundered and laid waste unescorted caravans and had even attacked the boundary fortresses on past occasions. They were a clever, quick-striking, fast to disappear race, sometimes combining into hordes of some thousands, sometimes making lightning night attacks in small bands. They lived frugally in this desert which they knew so well, drawing life from the sparse oases, relying on an occasional rich hoard of booty stripped from some unwary travelling column.

They were hardly likely to attack a fully armed contingent, it was true, but the prestige of the Pharaoh had sunk lower than the lowest star on the eastern horizon—and it was always possible. The Bedouin were like a starving lion: the more they starved, the more likely they were to take desperate risks.

Through the scorching wastes, the Pharaoh's army toiled. Ineni kept his men going at a good pace. Nothing was worse for morale than to feel that one's water supplies

were declining and that one was getting nowhere; much better a sharp effort over a period.

It was at the close of the second day that they saw evidence of the Bedouin. Traces at a dried up oasis, the clean-picked skeleton of a goat. And then towards sunset far out on the waves of sand and stone, riding slowly, parallel with the army, little figures on horseback.

Ineni sent out scouts, but the men had ridden off and been swallowed in the great undulating mounds of sand and dried scrub. There was no sign of a large party.

The column pressed on after nightfall, surrounded by far-flung scouts, until, at last Ineni called a halt.

The tents of the army went up under a crescent moon. Many slept against their horses; all slept with weapons at their hand. Scouts were maintained throughout the night and guards did short shifts to ensure alertness.

It was just before dawn that the Bedouin attacked. Later a scout was found with his throat slit from ear to ear. The attack was a surprise.

Ineni was one of the first to react to the call of the guards. Grabbing his bow, he saw in the pale moonlight, the broad fan of the Bedouin surging over the dunes at an arrows length. He was surprised at the size of the party, but as his orders rang loudly in the still night, the men were already aligned and as the raiders neared so that the snorting of their horses was a thunder, a thick volley of arrows met them—and then another, the arrows which had rightly made the arches of Egypt feared from ages past.

Badly hit by the rapid organization of their intended victims, the accuracy of their fire, the front ranks of the bandits would have dispersed, but they were carried forward under the impetus of those behind to meet a fusillade of spears from Ineni's spearmen. There was the clash of

27

meeting and then the Bedouin, momentarily at an advantage from the superiority of their horses, were swept into by a small force of chariotry led by Ineni. Sheltered with their bronze shields, smiting with their heavy axes, the charioteers wreaked havoc in the badly depleted Bedouin tangle. And as the eastern sky lighted to a dull gray before the dawn, the raiders wheeled and, leaving a host of dead, galloped off into the wastes.

The attack had failed completely. The Bedouin force—no more than a sixth of Ineni's number—had expected to reap an overwhelming benefit from surprise.

It was clear from the fact that they had attacked at all that the nomadic tribes were hungry. In their hunger they were likely to attack again, probably with reinforcements. Surveying his few wounded, Ineni issued quick orders and within a short time, as the first streaks of colour pierced clefts on the horizon a force of several hundred horseman set out at speed after the retreating Bedouin.

The hasty tracks were settling, the dust clouds fading back into the desert surface from their tell-tale flurry, but with the speed of their horses, Ineni's men were able to keep the traces in sight as far as a small range of hills on which the early sun was beating as they approached.

Up over the first low hummocks in a swift, hot-headed rush and there were the Bedouin tents below, with the women feeding their babies and the returned warriors quietening their sweating horses. The swiftness of the counter-attack—not anticipated at all—took the Bedouin completely unawares. There was no time, even to shout a general warning or remount before Ineni's force was upon them. The slaughter was complete. And after the slaughter of the men—the rape of the women.

Weary of the monotony of the march, thirsting, as with

all armies, for women, the Pharaoh's men fell on the wives and daughters of the Bedouin. Many of them were half naked already, some with big breasts exposed as they fed their babies. Their remaining stitches were torn from them, those other weapons of the Egyptian army produced and the women made to feel the wrath of reprisal in a different way from their men.

Ineni made no attempt to stop the ravishing. It would have been hopeless—and this was part of the fortune of war. For a while he watched the lustful scene. Not a woman escaped having her legs forced wide and a massive mace of flesh thrust up into her belly. Wiry and strong, many fought like wildcats. Some were held by two men while another satiated his lust between her legs and then the positions were reversed on a rota system. Some women were gouged by four pulsing rods or more within the next half hour.

It was while he watched that Ineni noticed a slight flutter on the nearby hillside. His hand gripped tightly around his axe and he moved forward on his horse to sound the alarm. But then his sharp eyes made out the flutter to be the white cloak of a woman. She had taken advantage of the general slaughter and lustful preoccupation of Ineni's band, to escape into the surrounding hills. It was unfortunate for her, Ineni mused grimly, that he had refrained from the brutal orgy and been in a position to see her.

Leaving his men to their pleasure, he spurred his horse in a fierce burst across the flat space to the slope of the hill. Straining, the horse took the slope in a strong gallop, topped one ridge, climbed again and looked down a long slope to see the woman running swiftly without a backward glance.

Ineni raced the horse down on her and she turned in her stride, long slim legs firm below the raised cloak. Her proud features as she turned and faced the oncoming prince bore the aristocratic beauty of the pure arab descent of the fierce Bedouins. She was obviously the daughter of a chieftain.

From the folds of her cloak she withdrew a silver dagger and waited for the onslaught. The cloak hid her strong, firm lines, but Ineni was well aware of the wiry beauty of these women and instead of riding her down, splitting her skull with his axe, he pulled up and dismounted several paces from her.

He walked slowly, warily towards her. He was aware, too, of the cunning of these women.

"My poor little desert flower," he called to her. "You'd better throw down that little toy and surrender that sweet treasure under your cloak or I shall be forced to take it by force."

"Take it if you can," she snarled back at him, dark eyes flashing in fierce warning.

"Is the jewel you guard between your legs of such importance that you would refuse it in return for your life," he goaded her as he moved around her.

Her brown eyes seemed red with fire as she watched him. Her slim lips were tight, her thin aquiline nose breathing nervously like a delicate animal.

"If my father, the chief Harkush had not been slain in the back by your cowardly brood, he would have dashed you in pieces to these rocks," she flared at him.

"Then he would have been a braver, stronger man than I'm ever likely to encounter," Ineni retorted. "But yet I shall have the pleasure of testing his qualities in his daughter. I shall judge how well she makes love."

The girl spat at him venomously and he moved quickly at her.

Silver dagger flashed, glinting in the sun. Ineni moved quickly but even so it grazed his arm in a stinging cut. Then her wrist was enclosed in his strong hand and she was jerked against him, back to him, caught round the neck by his other arm, pinioned against his body, so that he could feel her buttocks, bare under the cloak, writhing against his loins as she struggled.

"Better still your trembling," he teased. "You feel how it makes my passion rise against you."

The girl struggled violently, kicking his shins with her sandalled feet, writhing with unexpected strength, the dagger still in her hand.

"I shall cut off your frail tool," she swore at him. "And then in your impotence, the women will cast you in scorn from the harem."

"Oh, brave, rash words." Ineni laughed fiercely, feeling the sexual surge the woman's fierce spirit sent through him. "When it has filled your loins you'll have no strength left for such an operation."

His strong fingers forced hers apart so that gradually they relaxed and the silver dagger clattered to the stone and sand.

She continued to struggle, lashing at him with feet and elbows. She was stronger he reflected than even the Palestinian woman of his harem, stronger by far. These women became like whipcord in their elemental, hard, desert existence.

His hand released her wrist and tore at her cloak. He couldn't risk taking her while she still wore these concealing folds. Who knew what secret weapon they might conceal? Half released for a moment, the girl lashed at his

31

stomach and pulled away as he swayed from her. In a swift movement her leg flicked out at his loins, but Ineni was quicker. As the hard little foot rammed towards his testicles with killing intent, he twisted aside, caught the ankle and heaved.

The girl went down on her back, winded, a yard away, cloak billowing up around her thighs.

Truly the daughter of a chief, Ineni thought. Her legs contained none of the skinniness of the poorer of her countrywomen; firm and wiry, but shapely they were, strong and supple. This I shall enjoy, he decided.

Unbeaten yet, the girl rolled over and sprang to her feet as he was on her again. Another dagger had appeared in her hand as if by magic and it ripped his tunic and ground against his own concealed daggers as she thrust.

A sharp downward flick of his arm and the dagger had flown from the girl's hand. She seemed not to feel the bruising pain of the blow from such a muscular arm, but flung herself at Ineni, nails searching for his eyes, face devilish in its aroused desert fury.

This time, he caught her firmly in his arms, raised her bodily from the ground and then flung her with a twist down on her belly on the sand. He had become impatient for the hot pleasure of entering her.

Before she could twist aside, he had flung himself on her, knees pinning her shoulders. His strong hands caught the collar of her cloak and pulled. The material ripped, peeling away from her body. She screamed in fury and he knelt on the small of her back, ripping still. The garment tore and split away from her and he flung it aside.

Underneath, her dark, hard body was nude. He knelt on her as she struggled, shattering him with oaths. Her shoulders were quite broad for a woman and strong, body

tapering to a slim waist and then rounding out again in slim, lightly flesh-covered hips. Her buttocks were proudly jutting and dimpled and her long thighs tapered in slim, hard lines. Her body bespoke the wiry training of the hills and hardship, the trials of a man—but they had served only to beautify her woman's body.

Wanting to see her breasts he forced her over on her back, mentally recoiling at the fury of her face. Her breasts were big, like all the desert women's—always ready for suckling the profusion of expected young. The nipples, too, were big. The jutting mounds overpowering the comparative slimness of hips, narrow waist. Her legs writhed under him, sending long sinuous ripples along their slimly muscular lengths.

"If you touch me I shall live to kill you," she breathed through almost closed teeth.

"Your threats are a waste of words," Ineni said, smiling mockingly. "You may as well spread your legs now and guide me in or you will make your fate only more painful."

The girl renewed her struggles, jerking her body under him, trying to toss him from her. She twisted over onto her face in her efforts and in that position, Ineni, his own tunic now flung from him, so that they were both bathed nakedly in the merciless sun, forced his arms under hers and then clasped his hands around the back of her neck in a half-nelson, forcing her face down into the sand so that, trying to ease the pain, she had to raise her hips, climb up onto her knees.

With his thighs he levered hers apart, while she mouthed curses at him and wriggled furiously. He forced her neck down, making her arch her back and involuntarily rear her hips up. Her delicious little buttocks were spread, defenceless

33

and so, too, between the wiry thighs, on which the slim muscles now stood out in strain, was her proud cleft. Her legs were wide. She could do nothing. Her threats and struggles had come to nothing. She was about to be raped by a prince of Egypt.

His great penis raging like the vibrant roars of the sacred bulls, Ineni relished the moment: the proud daughter of a chieftain forced to bending submission before him, passage unprotected and out-thrust so that he could see its fleshy crease.

With a last pressure on her neck so that she cried out, tears forcing their way from her eyes in spite of her proud efforts, Ineni jabbed his penis into the soft folds. The folds opened, involuntarily, it seemed, and against their wishes. With a gasp of passion, Ineni screwed his knob into the girl's treasured ravine.

She cried out and his thick penis met with some resistance. With a shock he realised she was a virgin. Of course, an untouched daughter of a chief. She must be younger than she appeared.

Appetite whetted, he prodded firmly in, felt the give, the warmth of blood, ignored the girl's further screams and began to thrust tightly, unmercifully into her.

"I had no idea I had an untouched flower," he breathed, thorugh clenched teeth. "You have a vagina worthy of a chief's daughter my pretty bird. And your little bottom is a delight to my eye as I feel your flesh clasping mine."

Overcome with the pain, the shame and the insults, the girl made no reply but a low moan.

Ineni moved into her, shuffling his knees between her widespread thighs, flexing his hips at her bottom, relaxing, flexing again, each flexing bursting his penis with a size and thickness the girl had never known, or perhaps dreamed

of, into her soft channel, up, up into the intimate recesses of her belly, the soft inner sweetness of the outward smoothness of muscle and sinew.

The girl moaned incessantly now. All fierce proudness had fled. She was subdued, cowed to the genital ruggedness of her master.

Ineni slid in and in, deeper, deeper. Her passage contracted like a tight glove around his long arm of stiff flesh. It squeezed and pulverized his penis within its narrow confines. In a way, punishing him as he was punishing her.

With each thrust he seemed to find new depths although his organ had long disappeared to its utmost limit into her body. His penis, within her, was painful and heavy, thickening, expanding, seeming to swell to incredible size as he ground and swivelled. His arms clasped her slim hips, hands occasionally slipping along her smooth, firm flesh to grasp in handfuls her large, hanging bosom.

Feeling the urgency, mouth awry with the furious pulling at his penis, he forced her neck lower, placing his hands now on the small of her back, she yielding, making no effort to struggle, quite broken.

His hips rammed into her bottom, rebounded from its firm rounded flesh and were drawn in again, sucked in by the contraction of her passage as it seemed to cling voraciously to his throbbing tube.

Her thighs were forced out to a wide angle, juices ran, mingling with the blood down the inside of her thighs. And as he pistoned in with growing rapidity, shorter, sharper strokes, Ineni felt the passage widen into a great gulf and heard the girl moan and cry out in despair. She had reached her orgasm! Raped and a virgin she had gone the whole distance of desire!

But Ineni had little time to consider the girl's capacity for, lost in the maw of her initiated abyss, his own hot, prickling stem was moving inexorably to its orgasm.

He pulled the girl back at him now as he screwed, feeling the flesh pulling painfully back on his penis, feeling the darts building up to shoot themselves into her belly. His head tensed back on his neck, veins standing out on his powerful neck, arms clasping her in a paroxysm and then the darts were releasing themselves one after the other in a fusillade into her soft depths. In and in, each with a painful release of the bow and then he had sunk over her and she was kneeling before him, with his thick, hot penis still in her, making no effort to escape as she had, so violently, at the start.

After a while he came out of her and, rising, donned his tunic. She writhed over and looked at him, fierceness dissipated, a miserable lassitude in its place. Later, he thought, the fierceness would return and with it, a certain wild, remembered pleasure. Certainly, as her spirit returned, she would crave vengeance. He would sleep uneasily in his tent while still in this area.

She lay where he had left her, all lithe limbs and supple body, looking at him, wondering what he would do.

Ineni indicated her daggers, glinting at some distance in the sand.

"I will leave you with your weapons," he told her. "You had better shroud yourself in the remnants of your cloak or you will inflame the desert dogs with passion."

She watched as he walked away and mounted his quietly waiting horse. Later she would join her womenfolk and lead them—hardy desert women—to a fresh Bedouin village to become the wife of some fierce Bedouin pillager.

Ineni cantered his steed away from where she was now reaching for her daggers, pulling her cloak around her.

Back at the Bedouin camp his men were resting, recovering their strength after the rapine. The women were strewn in huddled groups, cringing their stinging loins into the sand. The older of them rocked gently, old, inscrutable eyes watching, waiting for the storm to abate. Some wept at the thought of their lost menfolk, others at the thought of their lost maidenheads.

Ineni was quick to re-organize his men. They had already spent too long on this crushing vengeance. Such a skirmish was but an appetizer for the warriors of the greater plunder they might find on their route.

In swirling clouds of dust and the deep rushing of hooves, the Pharaoh's men swept out of the foothills, leaving their victims mourning, burying their dead, regathering their forces for the journey they would have to make to safety.

Back across, the still, burning expanse of yellow, the warriors streamed, well-satisfied with their coup. And soon the tents of the main army were regained, camp was struck and the column was moving on once more to Palestine.

Ineni was well pleased with the turn of events. He had suffered a few, not badly wounded men in return for a successful counter to a surprise attack and a complete annihilation of the enemy. It was a small thing. But he was aware of the enormous effect on the morale of his troops. Even those who had not enjoyed the fierce power of the fight, the lustful plunder, were fired by the stories recounted by their luckier comrades: stories of the cutting down of the enemy, stories of long, soft limbs, of breasts, of a length of woman under the hard rigidity of the assault. The contingent moved on at a good, rejuvenated speed.

On the fourth day, they could make out the far, blue and purple ridges of the mountainous hills of Palestine and some days later still, they were moving swiftly along the foothills which ran northward to Jerusalem.

They had, so far, kept clear of the outpost towns and had seen no enemy—although it was probable that news of their coming had leaked through to the cities which were maligning the Pharaoh's name and, probably, even now bristling with arms and reinforcements ready to defy openly the might which they knew was no longer Egypt's.

The unhindered march continued for a day or two until scouts reported brief skirmishes with advance scouts of the king of Arad—first of the cities to be punished. By now the news of the approaching army would be spreading throughout Palestine and up into Syria where the Hittites waited like an unleashed bow. It was probable that the approximate strength of the punishing party was also being noised in the hills and across the plains, to be the laughing stock of the kings of the Asian dynasties, counting as they did on the vast weight of the supporting hordes of the north.

Many miles from Arad, Ineni detached a third of his troops, leading them himself into the hills, marching them parallel with his troops on the plain. These troops on the plain, he brought nearer to the hills so that a few hundred yards only separated them from the rocky towering piles.

With scouts interspersed, he took his own force deeper into the hills where they became more craggy and mountainous and the column proceeded with slow difficulty. But his tactics reaped reward.

After some hours of painful progress, in which the troops on the plain moved slowly on in a state of extreme vigilance, hill scouts reported to Ineni that a force of some

thousands of the King of Arad's men—doubtless reinforced from the followers of sympathetic monarchs of
surrounding cities—were drawn up in battle array in a
declivity of the hills some half an hour hence. Their
archers overlooked the road on which the Pharaoh's men
were marching and their horse and spearmen were waiting
to follow the first volleys of arrows which they hoped
would spread confusion in the ranks of the approaching
army.

By a backward route, Ineni despatched the scout, with
orders, to his commanders on the plain. He moved on with
care towards the unsuspecting ambush.

Soon he was looking down on the massed troops of
Arad. There were, perhaps a few hundred more men than
his whole force. Slightly below the main body, aligned on
a jutting ridge, the archers waited, thick as the sands, to
deliver the wounding blow.

From his vantage point Ineni could see the clouds of
dust on the desert below, hazing over the thickly grouped
dots of his main, advancing force. Quietly he brought up
his archers and spearmen. They descended softly through
the ravines to within an arrow-length of the wholly unsuspecting enemy below. The King of Arad, on horse at
the head of his several hundred horse behind his archers,
was, like them, concentrating with a blind fixity on the
men on the plain.

The manoeuvre was swift and neat. Several hundred of
Ineni's archers made a thick tier behind the tier of the
archers of Arad. Behind them, ready to surge over the
sheltering slope, Ineni and his horsemen waited for the
moment to charge into the ranks of the ambuscade.

Below, the archers of Arad were tensing; the contingent
of Egypt had almost reached the spot, moving, unaware, it

seemed into a trap of death and destruction. The head of the bowmen, drew taut his bow—and then like the sudden flood of rain in the hills which swelled the mighty Nile overnight, Ineni's arrrows reaped their harvest.

Stabbed from the rear, the archers slumped, cascaded over their protecting ridge, sprawled down the loose slopes in clouds of dust to the sands below.

The King of Arad whirled in confusion; his waiting men spun and flailed on their horses, seeking escape from the rain of arrows which was now directed at them.

And then with fierce cries, Ineni and his men were thundering over the slopes, descending at breakneck speed like a horde of locusts. The ambush wheeled, turning for escape to the desert. But there, strung out in a thick, impenetrable line, the Pharaoh's chariotry was sweeping, spearmen racing on foot behind.

The Palestinian troops were seized with panic and as they turned again, they were cut down from behind by the rush of horses from the hills. They fought with the wild power of desperation, but desperation was to no avail against their hopeless position. As they rallied against Ineni's horsemen, so the chariots from the desert had entered the declivity behind them. They were surrounded, herded in twisted confusion.

It was a matter of some fifteen minutes and the whole force was either slain or bound in capture, their weapons piled on the Pharaoh's train, rich robes torn from the chieftain's bodies.

So it was, in triumph, leading his prisoners, who included the King of Arad, that Ineni marched, without struggle into Arad. The people bowed before him, officials came to pay him homage and swear their allegiance to the

Pharaoh. An unexpected force had come out of Egypt to subject their rebellion once more.

Supplies replenished, Ineni camped outside the city. He was aware of the effect of the inevitable carousal on his men if they were allowed to stay within the city walls.

But it would have been a mistake had he not allowed his men the spoils of war and he had certain quantities of wine and food brought out to them and a number of women were presented for their pleasure by the officials of the city.

In a circle of camp fires, with his guards doubled and strong on the camp perimeter, Ineni, to maintain his troops' lusty spirits, had a novel punishment organised for the King of Arad.

From her palace in the city his queen, the head of his harem, was brought, frightened, but trying to maintain her dignity, into the midst of surrounding ranks of Ineni's men, where they massed in ribaldry.

The fires were stoked up so that they flared in gigantic fingers, flooding the clearing in the camp like a reflection of the sun, darting long flickerings on the shadowed tents, lighting up the fierce, eager faces of the laughing, joking men.

On the outskirts, quiet, in the deeper shadow of the moonlight, away from the central fires, the guards patrolled in silence.

Into the midst of the men, the Queen of Arad was brought and exhibited, like a glorious slave, with the diadems sparkling in her hair and the bangles flaming on her brown bare arms as she pulled her robe closer around her. She was a proud beauty, paler than the daughters of Egypt, but with dark eyes which gleamed in the flames like the proudest beauty of the Pharaoh's harem.

41

While she stood, the focus of all eyes, the King of Arad was brought, bound and helpless into the clearing and stood with a guard on either side at several paces from his queen. He looked at her with a fierce look of possession and her returning glance contained a hint of anguish.

Then, from the forward fringes of the crowd, two Egyptian warriors came. Picked for their size and rugged strength, they were veritable giants. Their tough bodies were quite naked and the firelight cast depths of shadow on the creased muscles of their frames as they approached the queen. The penis of each dangled, long and thickset, already thicker—although still comparatively limp—from the thought of the prize. For them, ordinary soldiers as they were, the soft, scented, never-seen body of a queen was something out of the world of Gods and man.

The queen drew back as they came close to her, her eyes betraying her fear of their hard, lustful eyes. She clasped her robe tightly around her body as if it would give her protection against these infidel hands. The ranks of warriors were gripped in a concentrated silence, only the heavy breathing a reminder of the inflamed passions that were contained in their clustered rows.

The two warriors had reached the queen and laid heavy hands upon her shrinking body. As one grasped her robe at its crossed front, she turned to draw away, but the other held her arms firmly, and her movement ripped the flowing garment from her back.

From her slim, feminine shoulders, her back slipped slenderly into a whittled waist, light, hardly visible muscles, tensing in the firelight. The crowds held their breath, passions rising in thick power against their tunics. And then the warrior had tugged again and the robe came away completely, slipping to her ankles, revealing like a peeling

42

fruit, her hips, rounding out into full, firm buttocks, rounding in again into long thighs, tapering to slim knees and calves.

The queen turned with a scream, horrified at her nakedness in front of these thousands of rough men and the flickering flames, leaping high over her and her two tormentors threw deep, voluptuous shadows on her breasts and belly, shadowing their outlines, lightening their round inner surfaces as if a dark hand was offering them to the crowd.

She pulled away to where her king stood, powerless and overcome with horror, her buttocks, thighs, calves tensing with her step as she moved.

But before she had taken three steps, both men were on her, like birds of prey on a small desert creature. Rough great hands had seized her tender flesh and two great, nude bodies were mauling her to the ground. She struggled, fighting to keep from her the two enormous erections which seemed to vie with each other for size and power as they dug at her in the struggle.

And then she had collapsed, a slim reed of luxurious flesh, to the warm, shadowed sand between the fires and the men had fallen on her like wild beasts.

For a moment, while heads strained and tunics strained, taking the strain of protesting penises, it was impossible to see what was happening, but then the men fell away from her, forcing her over onto her side, one in front, one behind her. The one in front caressed and kneaded her soft buttocks, the one behind, pinched and fingered her taut, thrusting breasts.

The queen was sobbing, moving her head from side to side as if she were engaged in a horrible, delirious nightmare from which she might yet awaken unscathed.

There was the panting intake of breath around the verges of the surrounding circle. Men moved involuntarily closer, to see what was happening.

On the hot heap amidst the fires, before the wild eyes of the King of Arad, the warrior lying along the warm belly of the queen, raised her upper leg with his arm, forcing it apart from the other, in spite of her efforts to cross them in defence. Rolling over at her, his great, fleshy erection visible, he pulled her other leg under his hip so that both legs jutted across his waist, one over, one under him and then, spreading her secret, voluptuous fold, the folds of a queen which only a king should have known, he inserted his penis tip into the split of flesh between her legs, insinuated, held, re-established, and then rammed in.

On the queen's scream of anguish, there were those in the serried ranks, who were unable to contain their bursting loins despite the lack of contact, and the King of Arad turned his face away.

Clear to those who continued to stare, the long rod of the warrior continued to delve and thrust deeper and deeper into the queenly nest of privacy, moist and enlarging at the barbaric pressure.

From behind her then, where he had continued to squeeze her nipples and pinch the firm skin of her breasts, the other warrior drew back his hips and ranged his cudgel, red and burning, against her bottom. His hand left her teats, transferred in a trembling anticipation to her buttocks and roughly pulled the soft creases of flesh apart. As he spread her, so that the flesh lobed outwards, the crease became a central, dark, pivotal hole, he moved his hips in towards her, directing his penis at her little black anus. Her behind was already thrust out in offering from her position as she was being ravished by the other of the Pharaoh's men. This

further spreading of the orbs of flesh, stretched the back passage so that with a sudden thrust, withdrawal and thrust again, the probing member at her rear had formed a bridge-head in the soft, puckered, yielding skin of the tight aperture.

The queen cried out. The shame was overwhelming; raped on the sand by an uncouth soldier before her king and a thousand or two of commoners and now she was having her bottom raided to crown the ignominy. She was being plundered at both openings of her body for the amusement of the lewd, conquering Egyptians. Tears of shame and pain, rolled down her lovely, anguish-ridden cheeks.

On either side of her, the two great men jockeyed her, riding up and up between her splayed-out legs. Entering her in twin shafts of thick violation at the soft, dark, sweating junction of her legs.

The watching army could see the two great stems withdrawing, thrusting in again, their full lengths, appearing almost to rub together, so near were the holes they 'entered.

The queen, squirmed and wriggled, trying to escape the raping pain of her front only to find herself further impaled at her behind until it seemed as if twin points of fire were sweeping up into her belly, denuding it of entrails, filling it with a fiery furnace of pain. She was filled, completely filled as if a great tree were being forced up between her legs until her vagina would split with the pressure. Behind, sore and aching, her whole rectum seemed subjected to a darting animal which explored further and further into narrower more painful places at every surge.

In the crowds, men were openly masturbating, if they hadn't involuntarily spilled their load already onto the

silvery desert sand. Every face was hot and passionate; every body longing to grab the women who had been brought into the camp, but determined to see the finale of the spectacle.

The two warriors had accidentally formed a rhythm. Each entered in his separate orifice at the same time, so that in having her legs forced up as her front passage was plundered, the queen also gave a deeper field to the incoming sword at her rump's opening. The trio formed a wild, passionate, sexual rhythm, while the King of Arad stared in mute, helpless frenzy.

The queen was sobbing hysterically, as the appearing and disappearing arrows of flesh grew redder and more pronounced. The warriors began to bellow with great roaring sounds, thrusting so hard that the queen was forced onto the chest of one and then rocked back onto the chest of the other with each stabbing blow.

The audience became tense, strained, eyes bulging, hearts pounding, faces and penises hot and throbbing as the climax was sensed.

The two warriors were writhing into the noble queen, twisting their limbs into an agony of movement, searching further and further into the exquisite, high-born flesh.

And then with a mighty gasping roar the possessor of her vagina slowed, ground into her with a slow skewering push, and, as the breath was torn from him in an excruciating, grating groan, his great reserve of sperm flooded from its coarse peasant reservoir into the noble, widened aperture of the Queen of Arad.

The queen gasped, eyes closed and wrinkled in pain as it seemed the point and the flood pierced her belly, entering up into the deep regions below her breasts.

But she was not, even now, to be spared. For with his

comrade's fading passion, the warrior at her rectum was becoming wildly, deliriously inflamed. His pulsing extremity advanced, broadening the bridgehead into a great retreating battlefield with every gasping thrust. He forced the queen's legs up further in front of her as his companion rolled away and struck into the brown, soft depths of her royal bottom, in and in, wiggling his hips, spiralling his penis in fierce, lip-biting tension. A tornado of passion whirling like a sandstorm inside him as the queen cried and cried with the pain of a ravished behind and then with a shattering which seemed to burst the knob of his weapon into smithereens, he spattered into her a volley after volley, wet, warm liquid shooting up into her unused, inexperienced back passage. The man's hips crashed at her buttocks with bruising force as he flooded her body. The queen's eyes were dull with horror as she felt his great, thick, probing climax, the hot jets of liquid scorching the sensitive depths of her rectum.

As his thrusts tailed off into nothing, she jerked away from him and he let her go. She staggered to her feet and stumbled in the clearing, reeling from the hot eyes which watched her in hundreds on all sides. Frantically she searched for an avenue of escape, somewhere to hide from the men who had witnessed the shameful using of her body, had seen her, raped, buggered, degraded. But there was nowhere and in desperation she lunged, weeping into the ranks of the men trying ridiculously to force her way through the ranks.

Hot eyes surrounded her, hot hands mauled her as she pushed. She was caught. Hands were holding her breasts, pulling at her thighs, slapping her buttocks, digging between her legs, into her bottom; a penis was pressed against her, trying to find the spot between her caught legs,

47

another was rubbing the crease of her buttocks in emulation of the spectacle. She screamed and wept. And then the guards were forcing their way into the crowd on orders from Ineni and dragging her to safety from the mob, to escort her to the captives' quarters. On the way she swooned and had to be carried by the guards, who secretly fondled her queenly treasures.

With the violent, incensing close of the exhibition, the men fell upon the women who had been brought for them, drawing lots to decide their order of turn. Some women were ravished more than a dozen times by different masters during the night. Ineni contented himself with supervising the guard and ensuring that the night's events did not get out of hand with their boisterousness.

The following day more lords and kings from far places arrived at Ineni's camp to bring gifts for the Pharaoh and declare their loyalty. Truly Ineni had made a triumphal entry into Asia. But it was only an entry and he was well aware that the very kings now fawning before him were probably playing for time until the full strength of the Hittites could be mustered and brought south to meet him. As always they were vassals of the momentarily strongest; as always, hoping eventually to throw off all yoke and, perhaps, become powerful enough themselves to expand into distant lands, to forge an empire to equal that of Egypt.

Throughout the midday sun the camp stirred little, recovering from the night's activity, but when the sun was waning from its zenith, the contingent moved northwards up the valley from Arad. Up through the valley through Jerusalem to Damascus and back down the coast through Tyre, Sidon and Gezer, the news of the Pharaoh's victory preceded him, his strength of numbers even, was exagger-

ated and the rebellious, but weak vassal kings sent gifts to his train from far off.

At each town was a fresh triumphal entry with the gates thrown wide. It would have seemed that the Pharaoh was beloved in Palestine, that revolt was far from the minds of his vassals. But inevitably the coming storm grew. The deciding conflict approached. Word came that a vast Hittite army was marching south through Syria to join the forces of Egypt in battle.

The vassal kings, their own army routed by Ineni, awaited in simulated friendship, his annihilation at the hands of the Hittite hordes.

Ineni's men, growing strong and more cohesive from their skirmishes were in a good state of morale, but it was obvious to him that morale would be useless if reports of the size of the Hittite army were true. It was not yet clear to him how best to deploy his meagre forces against the northern adversary. Time would have to reveal if there was to be one way better than another out of the lion's mouth into which the little Egyptian contingent was daily wending its way.

All around were the Hittite spies, the more plentiful as the advance moved more to the north. A daily account of the Pharaoh's companies doubtless found its way into the tent of Hartason, fierce, bearded king of the Hittites.

As the estimated gap between the two armies dwindled to a day's march, Ineni pitched camp in the desert several hours south of the strong city of Kadesh on the Orontes. It was here, at Kadesh, that his valiant ancestor Ramses II had fought himself with a magnificent courage out of a desperate situation in his war with the Asiatics and returned to Egypt crowned in glory.

During the day the men slept. It appeared to an observer

that they were gathering their strength to meet the Hittite onslaught at this spot.

But with nightfall the whole column moved on with a great rapidity, crossed the bend in the river and under cover of darkness, approached Kadesh. The city—whose allegiance at this stage was doubtful—was entered almost without a struggle and taken over in comparative quiet and efficiency. The whole of Ineni's army moved in and was enclosed within its walls.

It was long before the dawn that the Hittite scouts were met by the cowed leaders of the city to be told that no sign of the Pharaoh's petty forces had been sighted, that it was reported the Egyptian camp was firmly entrenched far south near the bend of the river at Shabtuna.

Watching in the pale light of the stars, the broad line of the Hittites approaching from the far white gleam of the sands, Ineni felt a thrill of apprehension lest things should go wrong.

The vanguard was a mighty stretch of gleaming spears behind which the chariots rumbled and glinted. The hordes seemed to stretch as far as the eye could see east and west from Kadesh, so that it seemed that the whole city would be swept away in the oncoming tide of men.

In the city, Egypt's suicide forces waited, each man armed from head to foot in his own and captured weapons. There seemed a hush on the desert air. In the quiet stillness of the cool night under a high stencil of stars, massive events were shaping. Perhaps the destiny of Egypt.

Now it was all or nothing. The Hittite swarms were too close for flight, seeming now to envelop the city in a great sea of glinting axes, spear-heads and thousand upon thousands of fierce, bearded, heavily armed men being led to drive the Pharaoh once and for all from Asia, to crush

completely his dwindling power, perhaps, even to invade and lay waste the fertile valley at the empire's source. But who thought of flight? The blood-lust was in Egypt's sons. They had faith in Ineni's leadership. They were prepared to die for Egypt. Even the mercenaries had found a leader they would follow with thoughts of honour and glory as well as the reward of spoil.

From the heights of the city's wall the desert was alive with the soft, all-surrounding swooshing of ten thousand footfalls, sounding eerily like the ghostly rustle of a woman's robe magnified many millions of times.

The army must have been ten thousand strong, Ineni estimated, looking out over the heads of the enemy. He had expected far worse. The Hittites had sent no more than they expected to need to destroy the impudent invader of what they doubtless considered almost their minor states.

At the northern wall of the city the huge army halted. Orders rang on the night air; there was a general unloading, a pitching of tents, hobbling of horses. With the city of Kadesh a bastion between them and the Pharaoh's army—according to report—the Hittites were preparing to settle down for the remaining hours of darkness. They were arranging guards, lying down for sleep under the very wall from which Ineni surveyed them!

From the thick, stone ramparts of the city which had withstood siege after siege through history, Ineni watched while the Hittite camp settled slowly, like a great bird descending, drawing in its wings.

In the pale moonlight, the guards began their lonely tour, casting long, pale shadows over the silver sand, shooting gigantically up the lower reaches of the city walls. A soft silence fell over the forest of tents—the great silence of an army asleep.

Ineni's face showed no emotion as, with his lieutenants he gazed down from his commanding height. But within him a prayer to Amon was whispering quietly through all his fibers; a prayer of hope and thankfulness. Amon had indeed been good to him. It was as if the God himself recognised the corruption of his high priests.

In a silence still more profound than that without, the Egyptian army waited. The men, too, uttered soft prayers to Amon.

Apart from the quiet footfall of a guard, the snort of a horse, an odd murmur, the desert was as quiet and unmoving as its great, empty wastes to the far south and east.

It was in this silence that the cautious whisper of activity began within the city. Half-heard whispers like the sound of a beggar praying, a stream rustling, people moving, making love within the thin walls of their homes. The army of the Pharaoh was preparing.

Up on the heights of the walls, protected by the ramparts, the archers poured, each man with a vast stock of arrows, each ready to loose a stream of death into the sleeping tents below.

Behind the bastion of the northern gate, the chariotry, the spearmen massed, preparing to stream out into the desert over the tents of the enemy, trampling them underfoot, crushing the sleeping Hittite troops as they awakened in horror from their slumber.

In the chariots fresh archers stood behind the drivers, spears and axes in their belts for the moment when their arrows ran out. Strung from the iron frame of every chariot a dozen quivers full of arrows to replenish the hungry bows as the horses weaved amongst the tents.

Below the ramparts low fires were kindled; torches for the arrows to complete their death-blow.

High above the city in which the inhabitants dozed and awakened, waiting for the storm they knew would come, Ineni took a last look over the dense rows of Hittite shelters.

The desert was a great, bleak beauty, quiet and majestic in its awe-inspiring grandeur, the Hittite tents myriad unmoving ants on its surface. The desert would become a fiery demon, a blazing, roaring, hysterical charnel house. He raised his hand.

The archers tensed. Picked men drew on the strolling guards within arrowshot. Five hundred bows drawn taut to breaking point.

The arm fell.

A single magnified sound of release, a fierce rushing of air like birds unseen in the night and the Hittite guards were collapsing below the city wall, the tents becoming suddenly pierced as pin cushions. Amongst the shafts a short stream of fire blazed, curling out into the night, dropping in a shower of sparks, seemed to explode into a great flame—and the tents were blazing.

As the tents billowed and swayed, filled with the muffled sound of cries, the gates of Kadesh had opened and the chariotry was sweeping out, racing at fierce speed through the lines of now unguarded tents, transfixing the humps of confusion with arrow after arrow, spear after spear.

Ineni waited no longer. His archers on the battlements had struck their deadly initial blow. His chariot was below. As he careened out into the desert, through the settling clouds of dust his archers followed on fleet foot, spears and axes in hands.

As he thundered down on the Hittite tents in the wake of his men, the walls of Kadesh were dancing in the fierce

firelight of a hundred blazing hides. The flames dwarfed the running figures of men, crawling from collapsed imprisoning folds beneath which their comrades lay thickly dead, trying vainly to fight and then fleeing out into the unsheltered desert to be cut down by the swift Egyptian chariotry.

Ineni raced through rows of flattened tents from which the limbs of the dead protruded. On the far side of the camp he could hear the sounds of more determined battle, but here, under the city's shade, the Hittites had been crushed into the sands before they could stir. The air reeked with the smell of burning flesh as the fire raced from one tent to another, like the floodwaters flowing from one irrigation channel to another in the Nile valley.

As he swerved his horses through the funeral pyres, Ineni felt the glow of triumph already in his breast. The battle had been almost won before the Hittites were awake. Almost half their number must have been struck down in their sleep or waking moments and now the remainder were in disorderly confusion, fleeing, stumbling, running blindly in the confused, swirling shadows of the fire.

At one point there was a stand, elsewhere the chariots were streaking, golden inlays gleaming, flashing fiercely yellow from the flames, driving down, crushing under them the terrified, helpless enemy, cracking skull after skull with the blow of an axe, pounding body after body under the flying feet of the horses.

It was at the point farthest from Kadesh that the opposition had had time to gather in a rough, half-organised circle of defence. Here, where Ineni hurled himself into the struggle, there was hand to hand combat with Hittite maces and spears crashing on Egyptian shields.

Into this vast mob of thousands, the Egyptian chariotry followed Ineni. The Hittites, their horses gone, terrified by

the fire, into the desert, fell back before the greater speed and protection of their enemy.

The bearded Asians fought with desperate courage—a small taste of the short shrift the Pharaoh's men would have received in a straight, open battle—but the odds were overwhelmingly against them.

Ineni gave them no moment for breath. A quick withdrawal of his infantry, while the chariotry continued to keep the Hittites fighting for their lives; another quick withdrawal of the chariotry—and a great sheet of arrows from Egypt's deadly bowmen once more spattered the field with dead and wounded.

In again swept the chariots. There was no quarter. The Hittites found themselves in a fast-moving hell in which they fought until their arms grew weary and leaden against a host of relentless demons, who struck them down from beyond their reach and thundered by.

Courage was theirs, but beyond, against the walls of Kadesh from which the people now watched the massacre, their camp was an inferno; here, with the dead already piling a wall of flesh around and amongst them, they were surrounded and hopeless. The weariness of their day's march, the sudden horror of the enemy upon their tents, the lost cause was too much. They began to throw down their arms in hope of salvation. The movement caught, like the fire amongst the tents and soon the piles of Hittite arms had topped the piles of dead.

Out in the desert where they had tried hopelessly to flee, the remainder of the northern army were laying down their arms. The battle was over.

Ineni, riding amongst his men, supervising the herding of the prisoners, was overwhelmed by the complete success of his strategy. As far as he could judge he had

suffered only a few hundred casualties while probably three-quarters of the Hittite forces were dead and dying, the remainder captive. Amon had made it clear that he did not favour the high priests.

Hartason, fierce leader of the Hittite forces had killed himself rather than be taken alive as prisoner, when he saw his men throwing down their arms around him. But, nonetheless, Ineni reflected, the enormous number of prisoners would make re-entry into Egypt an affair of glory. The high priests would find themselves in some difficulty.

The Hittites, weary-eyed, beards sagging to their chests, were marched into Kadesh while the ruins of their camp smouldered and flickered behind them. There they were herded tightly into the underground dungeons to await the journey's start the next day. A strong Egyptian guard was placed over them while the main Egyptian force made camp outside the city to the south.

The Pharaoh's men were tired, but happy with the flush of victory. They settled down, with the dawn, to a few hour's sleep before the long trek to the south.

In the streets of the city odd groups of people still moved and talked uneasily, disturbed, thrown out of their routine of sleep by the night's events.

Riding amongst the last signs of life, touring the city on horse for any sign of trouble, Ineni was suddenly aware of two shadowy figures walking along the foot of the great wall of a noble's house, far from the poor quarter of the city. He galloped his horse towards the faint movement in the shadow and saw two women stepping quickly along towards the entrance of the house.

In the moonlight, he could see that one was well advanced into middle age, the other—taller and slimmer—a mere girl. The older woman appeared not to hear as he

approached, but the girl turned while still walking and looked back. Her robe, close around her, tautened into long, suggestive folds, bulging over her breasts, falling away in slim lines to her hips, tightening around her shoulders and buttocks in a twisted clasp.

Ineni drew up his horse alongside them and the old woman drew back in fear. The younger had a sweet, almost child-like face, with a small nose, a pouting lower lip and large soulful eyes, which looked, now, at the Egyptian with nothing but curiosity.

"Where are you going?" Ineni demanded of the elder woman.

She looked pale and frightened as she answered, her voice little more than a whisper.

"We have been watching your glorious troops in action," she said. "Now we are retiring in thankfulness that the battle was short and saved us from the northern invader."

"You have worked your fawning subservience to a nicety," Ineni said, scornfully. "Had I been the king of the Hittites you would have been licking my feet here. As it is I suspect you would be glad to thrust a knife between my shoulders."

"No my lord, that is not true." The woman was almost in tears in her fear. "Both I and my daughter here abhor the barbarity of the Hittites."

It was clear the woman was one of the noble's harem— probably the daughter, too, Ineni decided, as he looked them over. The woman continued to shift uneasily as if she were likely to dart away through the gates at any moment. Her daughter—large undulation of her breasts under the robe, clearer now—continued to gaze at Ineni with a curiosity which amounted almost to boldness. She was a very pretty creature.

"Your lies do not become you, woman," Ineni said sternly. "But although I could have you raped and slaughtered, I shall bid you quietly goodnight if you will tell your daughter that she is to come with me."

The woman clutched the girl's hand, seeming to grow suddenly bolder in protection of her young. The girl's slim fingers twined around her mother's but she didn't take her eyes from the Egyptian prince.

"Oh my lord, she is very young and yet a virgin," she whispered.

Ineni raised his eyebrows in surprise.

"Indeed the harems must be well filled if a place could not be found for such a dainty morsel," he said. "She has, indeed, the face of a child, but her body, I would say, is that of a woman. Tonight she shall behave as befits a woman."

"My lord, I beg you. I will bring you other more beautiful women if only you will not harm my daughter," the woman pleaded.

"Why this concern?" Ineni asked with a laugh. "Your daughter will not be harmed, woman. She will learn what all daughters must learn—how to take a man's weight on her hips, his spear between her legs."

As he said this, Ineni looked straight at the girl, but her eyes showed no trace of her feelings. The older woman was clutching her arm now. Tears shone in her eyes.

"My lord, I will give you anything within my power if you will not take her. She is my only daughter and she is not yet fourteen." A tear flowed gently down the woman's face as Ineni regarded the girl again with surprise.

"A woman, indeed for fourteen years," he said. "But how do you feel, my daughter at the thought of making love to the leader of the Pharaoh's army?"

The girl spoke, for the first time, quietly, in a voice which made her seem suddenly more mature.

"My fate is in my lord's hands," she said.

"Words of wisdom, my child. I am sorry for your mother's fears, but they are groundless and I cannot deprive myself of such a pleasant hour or two on their account."

So saying, Ineni leaned suddenly from his horse, caught the girl around her slender waist, feeling the warm, living flesh against his arm, and whisked her onto the horse in front of him. Her mother, almost pulled off her feet as her daughter was dragged away from her, gazed at them in mute horror, tears coursing down her cheeks, unmoving, as if she knew the futility of movement.

Beginning to trot gently away, Ineni called back softly to the woman. "Don't worry, I will bring her back, safe and happy in a few hours time."

Jogging back through the city—deserted and quiet now except for the Egyptian guards on the walls—Ineni pulled the girl's dark head back against his lips, feeling its almost liquid texture. He kissed the back of her neck and she moved it against him, completely acquiescent. His free hand, held her against him, moving strongly over the outline of her breasts and ribs, tracing with a fierce tense hand, their firm, springy contours.

Her body, under the robe was wonderful to the touch. It sent a thrill through his fingertips so that his body gave an involuntary shudder of anticipation.

"Such a virgin," he whispered to her as they rode. "Your mother must be mad to withold you from your destiny."

"It was not my wish, my lord," the girl said, softly. "I

59

have longed for the moment although now I am half afraid.''

"Don't be afraid," Ineni whispered gently. "You could have no better tutor.''

The girl nestled contentedly against him, breathing slightly, aloud, through parted lips as his lips caressed her hair and his hand her body outside the robe.

Soon they had reached the Egyptian tents and with the bright rays of light splintering the eastern horizon, Ineni pushed the girl gently ahead of him into his nightly shelter.

His heart was thumping fiercely and his hand found an echoing tremble in the girl's quivering flesh. Now that the moment was upon her, she was very frightened.

Ineni turned her and pulled her to him. Her soulful eyes were deep and giving, her body trembling slightly like a felt but unseen ripple on a pool. His hands moved over her, intently feeling her body with its warm vibrations, sensing the roundnesses, the fleshy weight of breasts and buttocks through every pore. He kissed her, thrusting his tongue into her mouth, forcing apart her unwary lips, penetrating her for the first time. In his arms she was like a soft shifting of desert sand, light, slipping and moving in little eddies.

He pressed his hips in against her, clamping them to hers and through hers in a strong, relentless movement. Her loins, for a moment, seemed hesitant and unsure and then his pressure was answered. The soft, hot flesh of thighs and hips pushed against his so that he could feel their tubular imprint, could feel it flattened and spread by his own strong force. And in the centre of this pressure where their central cores seemed soldered together was his pulsing, hot pyramid, which crushed and bent against her

triangle of junction; crushed until it was so painful that he had to ease back for a moment to relieve it.

The girl's hands were tentatively pressed on his arms now, moving slowly like searching, timid animals, feeling the long, hard lines of muscles which tensed and relaxed as he moved her against him. Her tongue was answering his, learning readily, flickering softly over his lips and in with a swift determination.

Gently, with hands which she could hardly feel, Ineni eased off her robe. She made no effort to help him, seeming, now, overcome with a stomach-clutching tension which allowed her only to breathe with difficulty. Her body when it rested, nude, in his arms, was shivering.

Again he brushed his hands over her, heat seeming to leap from flesh to flesh at every spot his hand touched. Her buttocks were full—quite fleshy for one so slim—and as his hands explored them, fingers probing gently against the sensitive flesh between them, she tensed them, swaying them involuntarily away from his hand, so that her hips pressed in against his.

He slipped his hands lightly over her back and shoulders, drawing it over her flesh to the front of her body where her breasts, large and fragile-feeling, like enormous rain-drops, also trembled at his touch. The nipples were small and hard and as he moved his lips from her neck to kiss them, she gasped, made to push his head away with her hands, but then clasped it closer, wriggling her breast against his mouth as he nipped her gently with his teeth.

Ineni piloted the girl across the room to his bed of hides, leaning her gently backward so that she collapsed on her back on them, soft arms moving automatically around his shoulders as he sank down beside her. Lying on his side against her, he stroked the whole of her body with his

hand, running his fingertips down from her shoulders out over the breasts, in again to her waist and then across the slight, smooth bulge of her lower belly.

As his finger explored the outer fringes of the soft hair which dwindled down to a point at the junction of her closed legs she began to wriggle her bottom uneasily. Slight, strangled whimpers choked in her throat.

At her leg junction, Ineni pressed his hand along the flesh of her thighs which felt like the skin of a grape. As he forced his fingers through between her thighs, she involuntarily pressed them closer together so that his hand was caught in a vice of flesh, unable to move up to its goal. But then her legs relaxed and he moved up a little before, involuntarily again, they tightened. Thus his hand continued its interrupted progression until, with the girl straining in thrilled fear, his fingers were brushing the warm, wet flesh of the lips of her vagina. She pushed a hand down at his arm, holding it away, reluctantly, not really wanting to hold it away, but afraid. And then he bent his face down on hers and kissed her passionately, losing his tongue in the depths of her mouth. She gave a little groan, there was a tremor of relaxation—and then his fingers had pushed up and into the hot, moist aperture as the girl gave a gasp of pain.

In the first moments, she jerked her hips away from him, afraid of being hurt, afraid of unknown mysteries. But as, moaning quietly, she became used to the intruding pressure, she allowed her legs to be opened so that his hand no longer brushed against the inside surfaces of her thighs as he dug into her farther.

For some time, Ineni coaxed her, getting her used to the feeling of a strange flesh inside her passage and then, face

and body flaming, he released her for a moment and slipped out of his tunic.

His body compared with hers was huge and rugged and his over-strained penis soared out from his loins like a temple obelisk.

He had risen to climb out of his clothes and he stood above the girl, looking down on her so that she would see the secret body of a man in all its splendour for the first time.

The girl, slim body rising and falling slightly with her disturbed breathing, looked through half-frightened, half-desiring eyes at the rugged nakedness before her. Her gaze swept down his body to the all-important source at his leg junction and there rested in wonder and fear on the great, thick, rigid rod which jutted out at her and over her.

Exploring, timidly, her eyes ranged over the large, dangling testicles, half lost in the shaggy covering of black hair and then her eyes moved up again to meet Ineni's with a look which plainly showed her mixture of willingness and fear.

Quickly he lay down against her once more, running his hand in fluid movements over her body so that she began to tremble. Then he caught her hand and pulled it against his penis, closing her fingers around the stiff, bursting flesh. For a second or two her hand remained limply where he had placed it, making a hot fusion between them and then she began gently to slip her fingers up and down and round the organ, feeling it, squeezing it, wondering at it. Bolder she moved on to his testicles, drawing her finger tips over them in an intuitive recognition.

Ineni, lying taut against her, felt his great projection raging as if it were water boiling and sizzling over a fire.

His whole body was alive with thrills and skewers. He could wait for her no longer.

Raising himself, he moved one leg over her, lowering it between hers and then he moved his body onto hers drawing over his other leg in the same movement so that his hips were between the girl's thighs.

Her hands pressed against his chest for a fraction of a second as if she would try to push him away, but then they relaxed again and moved around his neck, pulling his face down to hers so that, she in turn, could dart her moist little tongue into his mouth.

With that indication of her readiness, Ineni raised his hips onto hers, feeling her hot and waiting beneath him. With her smooth, little face pressed against his, cheek to cheek, looking over his shoulder into the gloomy shadows of the tent roof, tensely waiting, he reached down to her leg junction. A soft movement spread her legs a little more so that she was completely exposed and then he had guided his pulsing spear at the moistened cavity. For a moment, in which life seemed to stand still for the girl, he hesitated—and then he thrust into her, holding her tightly in his arms so that she could not wriggle away as he did so.

The girl screamed and squirmed as the mountain of flesh burst into her, but she was firmly caught against his body and he drove into her again.

"Oh, oh, you're hurting me," she screamed, trying to sway her hips from under the anchoring weight of his. But Ineni's body was now a great yearning, down at his penis the hot, moist relief for the yearning—a hot, jellied feeling—so that he began to grunt and his breath grated in his throat. He held the girl with all his force, crushing her, rendering her body helpless. Her upper body was unable to

move, only her legs could writhe and struggle and her central opening slip and jerk against the rigid pain.

Ineni ignored completely her whispered gasps for mercy, her tears. And in a short time the gasps had changed, mellowed into gasps of pure yielding and joining and enjoying as the pain, too, changed and mellowed.

He reached down, grasping a slim, smooth thigh with each hand and drew her legs apart and up around him, plunging deeper into her abdomen. There was to be nothing timid and too-gentle about this union. The girl would remember the first time in a sharp, clear image for the rest of her life.

Her hips wriggled and swayed under him, crinkling the flesh of her belly in little, momentary ridges. Her thighs clasped him as if she would hold him in her for ever. Her moans became the fuller, deeper moans of accepted challenge. Her eyes were closed as her fingers stroked down over his cheeks and drew his face onto hers for his mouth to make an outlet for her searching, giving tongue.

With quick, furious movements of his hips, Ineni thrust into her and into her again, regulating the speed to ensure her satisfaction.

His penis seemed to be burning as if it were on fire and in the tight, tender grasping of her channel he was pushing always against a slight force which agonisingly forced back his skin, contracted around the knob in a painful embrace.

The girl's whimpers became, suddenly, a greater, more prolonged consistent moaning and she caught at his thighs where they pressed against the undersides of hers, pulling them at her while her mouth opened as if she were gasping for air. Her whole tender frame began to writhe and twist in an agony and in the rushes of air which burst from her

throat, Ineni sensed rather than heard whispered pleadings for speed as she felt the enormity of sweet pain building up, inevitably, in the soft, marshy regions of her genitals.

In turn he felt the pain, as if he were trying, agonizingly, to urinate and couldn't. His breath exploded from his stomach in fierce, coughing gasps and he slowly swept his penis in a great, bulging crush in and in with a painful grinding, forcing it more slowly and more slowly into depths which felt strangely solid as if he were reaching the flesh of other openings.

And with a sudden, continuous, high-pitched moaning, the girl found words: "Quick, quick, quick, quick, ooooh!" in a cascade of incoherent emotion. Her hands clutched him with the force of a madman, digging into his shoulders, her knees stretched back, so that her buttocks were wriggling under his thighs, her face contorted and then her whole body was wracked and tormented in a series of convulsions and her mouth opened in a great "Aaaaaaaaah . . ." as her soft passage reached the extreme of sensation and the liquid juices exploded as the breath was drawn from her body in a furious, aching sigh.

As he had felt the channel grow big around his penis, Ineni forced himself into the girl, holding her, pressing and grinding against her for seconds without jerking his hips, his head swaying in ecstasy on his shoulders and then he withdrew, thrust slowly in again—and again—and with a last deep surge, his entrails seemed to break through his penis and spatter in swift floods high up in the girl's body. He rammed in and into her, gasping, with her pulling his thighs to her, until the very last of his emotion had been dragged from him and then he settled slowly down on her hot, soft body and lay, crushing her breasts and belly with his weight until the immediate exhaustion had dissipated.

He rolled off the girl and stroked her belly gently. There was blood on the hides.

The girl smiled at him through deep, grateful eyes which knew, now, all of the world that she had not known before.

"You were very cruel to me at first," she whispered with a smile. "But I am glad you were. It was a sweet pain."

Ineni kissed her, stroking her full breasts and she looked down at his penis with a curiosity which contained now, little embarrassment. It was thick and heavy even now and she traced a vein with her finger tip, glancing up at his eyes with a quick, child-like smile.

"Now I am fit for the best harem," she said with an air of satisfaction.

"There are many things you have yet to learn," Ineni replied with amusement. "You must be ready to obey your lord's every whim, his every perversion, to give him the fullest enjoyment no matter what he demands."

"Is there more he might demand?" the girl asked, raising dark eyebrows, while her hand moved gently, possessively almost, around the thickening penis.

"You sweet innocent. He might demand of you three score positions, or your mouth, perhaps, or your tender behind."

"What would he want with my behind?" the girl asked in surprised.

"If you like I will teach you," Ineni said.

The girl looked at him uncertainly, large brown eyes troubled.

"I am a little afraid," she said. "But I want to be taught."

Her slender fingers had continued to caress Ineni's penis,

which had swung in gentle stages to a fully rampant position. As he kissed the girl, his organ was crushed, vertically, against the soft flesh of her belly, indenting it with the pressure. He slid his hand down her back, brushing lightly the firm, stretched skin until his hand soared out over the twin smoothe mounds of her buttocks. They were full and voluptuously bulbous to the touch and he cupped his hands around them, stroking them, kneading them. He rubbed his hand in little circular motions over the deep inturned join and the girl began to wriggle a little so that her buttocks moved and tautened under his hand, brushing against his palm.

"Turn over onto your belly," he whispered. And after a moment's hesitation, she rolled gently away from him and over, face flat on the hides, turned to one side watching him, waiting.

Her bottom rounded out below him like a full water bottle and he continued to stroke it, his penis beginning to throb in its heat. His fingers moved gently into the hot ravine and the girl involuntarily tightened her buttocks into taut melons, trapping his fingers between them.

He dug the softer, inside flesh with his finger tips and waited for her to relax. When he felt her muscles loosen again, her brushed his fingers down into the depth of the crease, while the girl squirmed with tiny, rippling movements of her hips which creased her buttocks in sinuous hollows and rounded them out again into full moons of flesh.

She began to breathe heavily and Ineni felt with his finger tip for the tight little pucker in the flesh. He found it and began to press. The girl seemed to hold her breath for a moment, but then relaxed again and he insinuated his finger carefully and slowly into the loosening bud which

was gradually becoming an aperture. His finger moved in and the firm, gristly flesh clasped him like a strong elastic band. As he thrust in, the girl's body flexed rigidly and he eased the pressure for a moment, but continued relentlessly as she slumped again. Soon his finger up to the first joint was warmly enclosed in the tight, rubbery core of her squirming rump, pressing, digging, enlarging in preparation for the greater intrusion.

The girl's face was hot and flushed, pressed tightly into the hides. Her eyes were closed and she breathed heavily and unevenly through open lips.

Ineni's eyes feasted on the creasing flesh of the slim, writhing body as his finger plunged unmercifully into the depths of the girl's bottom. Her breasts were crushed and half flattened against the hides and her hands slowly clutched and unclutched the material as he entered her.

With his penis rigid and pulsing at the very feel of the soft, springy texture of her behind, Ineni felt a surge of power sweep through him. With a sharp movement, he forced another finger into the girl's anus, crushing it in with the first so suddenly that she gave a little squeal and jerked away. But his fierce insistence allowed her no escape and soon she was moaning quietly at the thick ravaging so close to her aching vagina.

Judging the time right and, in fact, unable to restrain himself any longer, Ineni withdrew his fingers and slithered onto the warm skin of the girl's back. His penis rode up vertically between the spheres of her buttocks and he pressed against her for a moment, revelling sensually in the squeezing pressure as she flexed them containing his penis in the deep crease.

"Spread your legs," he whispered fiercely.

The girl obeyed after a little hesitation. Her thighs slithered

out below his hips until they made an obtuse angle with each other, extended on either side of him in quivering anticipation.

Quietly, Ineni guided his penis down to her anus, raising his hips so that his body pivoted against her on the arm of flesh. He moved her buttocks apart with his hands and prodded gently against the spot.

For some time he lay on her, jerking up and down in little movements while the knob searched, vaguely and without penetration, against a surround of flesh. And then he began to feel a give in the fleshy resistance, a sharp feeling of containment.

The girl gave a gasp, tautened her buttocks and pulled away from him slightly.

He kissed the back of her neck, stroking her hot face with his fingers.

"It will not hurt in a moment," he whispered.

The girl relaxed again and he resumed the gentle pressure.

This time as he felt the tight containment, the sudden, defined solidity of feeling at the very extreme of his penis, the girl uttered an "Oooooh!" but did not pull away. Her buttocks went rigid, but relaxed in a moment and he continued prodding gently at the bridgehead. The tiny entrance was clasping at his organ in an agonising grip and he longed to plunge straight into the depths; but he bore the slowness with patience, consolidating gradually for the sake of the girl.

Her anus was broadening, loosening slightly as she became used to the intrusion and although she uttered agonized gasps from time to time, she relaxed almost immediately and Ineni was soon acutely aware of a small section of his penis rubbing in a tight friction well inside the opening.

He pulled her thighs towards a right angle from under his body so that she was stretched away from him in three directions at the latter end of which he was joined to her through the small posterior aperture, leaning more and more heavily onto her bottom with his hips.

The girl began to breathe heavily, lips apart, eyes closed as he explored the outer cavern of her rectum. Her buttocks began to wriggle, apart from her, it seemed, in small intense movements, alive under him, excited by the intimate thickness of him on her and in her.

"Kneel up," he said in a voice broken with the fierce carnal emotion of the sucking of his organ.

The girl complied, pulling her thighs in a slithering movement under her, arching her back in a concave and then a convex as she thrust her buttocks up for him.

Now she sloped away before him, from where his great, throbbing rod surged roughly into her back channel, rounding in from her taut, stretched buttocks to her slim, firm waist on which the top part of her body swayed in an agony of half-pain and pleasure, from side to side on the bed of hides.

Her face was crushed in hot helplessness of unseeing, her breasts brushed against the surface below her as she swayed.

Ineni had also moved up between her legs as she knelt and was now firmly pressed against her doubled over buttocks, watching his penis slipping in and out of her anus.

The outer skin slipped like some, thin, sensitive peel on the inner piston as he jerked in and out and the knob, when he occasionally withdrew it completely, or when the girl jerked forward involuntarily at a sudden further pressure, was a furious, outraged red.

71

Grasping her firmly on either side of her waist, where the flesh creased in thin superfluous folds from her bending, Ineni was overcome with the sheer physical necessity of plunging into her completely, of losing his penis in her so that his whole body, the whole weight of his hips could ram against her, the full length of his rod be clasped to its base in the slim, tight passage.

Squirming her anus on the end of his organ, the girl writhed unaware of the length yet to go. Her breath was issuing in what was almost a continuous thin, low croon at the new experience.

Ineni's grip on her waist tightened. His mouth twisted with the passionate anticipation of his thrust—and then he rammed into her, splitting, like a knife through canvas into the depths of her behind, his penis surging forward like a great, inevitable wave, slower as the thicker base reached the opening, but inexorable and unable to be denied.

The girl screamed at the sharp, painful entry.

Her bottom writhed like an animal trying but unable to reach the spear in its back.

"Oh—oh, it's too much—oh, oh!" The words could hardly form themselves as she tried to escape the pain.

But Ineni held her in a grip against which she flailed in vain. His face, strained back on his neck, was furrowed in passion, his thighs rigidly tensed with his hips as he thrust into her again and again.

The narrowness was agonisingly sensual, seeming to crush his penis, to be tearing the skin from it, leaving it doubly naked and sensitive. His hips pistoned backwards and forwards with increasing rapidity, his penis drawing out and then rushing forward the whole length of her back passage so that she cried out with each hot, furious in-thrust.

Deep in his belly, Ineni was half-conscious of the fierce,

unbearable sucking of his entrails. His penis seemed heavy, fully-laden, its very fiber whirling in sharp painful spirals. He rammed his hips against the buttocks of the girl and held them there, crushing against her, wriggling from side to side, while his penis moved in different angles in the depths of her rectum so that she seemed to be almost swooning.

Her anus was larger, easier, now, and between her gasps she was breathing words, indistinct and half-formed.

"Yes, yes . . . hurts . . . wonder . . . oh . . . oh!" They came to him like a far echo in a temple as his head felt tight and crawling.

His hands moved fiercely along the girl's body, grasped her breasts cruelly, clutched them in handfuls, pinched the nipples, returned again to her hips, where they dug deeply into the firm flesh as his hips danced a passionate dance against her behind.

The sucking in his belly had spread like a growing fire until it seemed that his whole body below his waist was being drawn into the girl, as if the whole of him would disappear into the soft, dark regions of her black passage.

At his penis was the extreme heat of the fire, a painful, burning furnace against which he was helpless, a furnace impossible, now to extinguish, a furnace which he could only go on stoking and stoking in abandoned, willing slavery.

In, in, in he jerked, with his penis expanding and expanding, his mouth opening and closing, eyes fixedly on the face of the girl. Her face, too, was a mask of passion; her buttocks swayed in fury on the end of him; her anus had become a gaping hole into which he had no difficulty of access. He was lost in it to the hilt as his hip movements reached a peak of rapidity, his penis bursting in

73

quick explosions into the waiting sheath, each explosion coming more quickly on the last until they were almost a continuous stream, so that it must have seemed to the girl she was filled without respite with a great thing which was splitting her bottom in two.

His breath was an explosion of gasps. His penis was poised on the brink. The girl was ramming her buttocks back at him. Her mouth saying "Go on, go on!" His belly was flooding down to his extreme projection. There was a pause of agony in which the world stood still. And then his organ was undulating in great squeezing jerks which drew sperm in quick jets as when a water-bottle was squeezed.

Ineni went on ramming into her for some time with his penis so concentrated in sensation that it hurt. A gasp accompanied each fresh sucked out release of liquid into her.

As his thrusts dwindled and the dregs of his passion spurted weakly into her bottom, the girl was almost weeping with passion, still thrusting back her hips as if she wanted more.

Ineni withdrew from her at last and rolled over, exhausted, onto his back. His penis slumped, deflated, against his thigh. For some time the girl lay, buttocks crushed together, moving slightly on the hides and then she wriggled towards him, lay her head on his chest and gave a great sigh.

Half an hour later, Ineni, as good as his word, was riding back to the city, with the girl sitting in front of him. She was quiet and thoughtful.

"You have learned well," Ineni told her with a smile. "You gave me more pleasure than many an experienced woman of the harem."

"My lord it was wonderful for me," the girl whispered.

74

She looked at him sadly. Her hands and lips were trembling.

"What is the matter my sweet little flower?" Ineni asked.

A tear flowed down the girl's cheek and when she answered, the words were a mere, frightened whisper.

"My lord I cannot bear the thought that you are going. I want to stay with you."

Ineni smiled in surprise, touched by the girl's concern.

"But I promised your mother I would bring you back," he said gently.

"I don't care. I don't care." There was a desperation in the girl's voice which troubled him. "I want to stay with you. Oh, please take me into your harem. Take me with you to Egypt."

Ineni stroked his chin. This was an unexpected result of his passion. Of course, the girl had been a virgin. She had just endured feelings she had never dreamt of before.

"I want to learn," the girl went on, desperately. "I want to learn how to please you, how to use my mouth, how to make those other positions. But only with you."

Ineni stroked her hair, his mind a-chuckle. Certainly the girl was wonderful in sex. Possibilities began to occur to him. He could easily take her amongst the captives back to Memphis, of course. But what of the mother to whom he had made a promise?

"Do you not care for your mother?" he asked the girl.

"Of course," she replied. "But are we not all in your hands? Could you not take her, too?"

He laughed aloud at her audacity—and her desperate searching for a solution to dispel his doubt.

"Your mother is a little old for my harem?" he said with a smile.

"She is no doubt more worthy than I," the girl said archly. "But could you not give her other work?"

"I could give her the work of a servant," Ineni answered. "But your mother is of noble blood."

"She would do anything to stay with me," the girl said confidently, "as you will see if you will let me stay with you."

They rode in silence for a while, the girl, twisted on the horse in front of him, gazing all the while into his face, trying to read his thoughts there.

"Well we shall see what your mother has to say," Ineni said, finally.

Before they had reached the house where he had found the girl, Ineni saw her mother coming towards them. It occurred to him that she had probably been waiting there for most of their absence.

He lowered the girl from his horse and the mother clasped her in her arms. Her eyes as she saw the tear stains on her daughter's face were anguished, but the girl gave her no time to indulge in flights of fancy as to the tortures undergone.

"Mother we must go to Egypt," she said in a tone which mixed love with defiance.

Her mother stared at her and then at Ineni. For a moment she was completely uncomprehending and then she burst into tears. It was as if she understood everything with a sudden shaft of recognition and knew the uselessness of trying to dissuade her daughter.

The girl held her mother gently, but there was no consternation on her face at the reaction—only determination to conclude the persuasion.

"We are not happy here, mother," she pleaded. "And I

am so happy with this prince. We are his captives. He will take us to Egypt and I shall join his harem.''

"Oh my daughter—and what will become of me?'' her mother sobbed.

"Our lord is kind,'' her daughter continued with rapid conviction. "He will give you work in his house and you will be happy.''

The mother continued to sob, but her tears were already those of resignation.

"What—what of our clothes, our belongings,'' she stammered eventually.

"They will be taken care of,'' Ineni assured her. "I will send my men for you.''

"We—we must think, my daughter.'' The mother put her hands to her eyes overcome with indecision.

"You have no choice,'' Ineni said. "My men will be here within minutes.'' He had recognised the woman's need to be pushed into action. He admired her daughter. She was a clever girl.

When, in the late afternoon, with the greatest heat of the sun long past, the Pharaoh's army began to move south from the scene of their victory, the girl and her mother were among the ranks of the loot and captives.

As the triumphal caravan wended its way south through regions which bowed low before it and cities which sent out gifts of homage to add to the overflowing train, Ineni taught his new concubine all that she desired to know of the delights which her body could give and receive.

The journey south was slow, due to the increased weight of numbers and material, and relaxing. News of the return went before the army; reports of its victories—hardly exaggerated—were talked of throughout the empire. In Egypt the prestige of the commander was immense—so

77

immense and unexpected that the hierarchies at Memphis and Thebes were disquieted.

Across the wastes of Sinai, Ineni encountered no hostile Bedouins. It was in peace and glory that he and his soldiers rode into Tharu—eastern bastion of the Pharaoh's land. From there into the land whose history resounded with the names of previous commander-kings, Ineni, a noble of the court, was feted.

At Heliopolis, he was received with joy by the governor; the peasants left their work in the cornfields to cheer him; the nobles bowed in recognition of his prowess.

Along the road from Heliopolis to Memphis, the loot and captives were gazed at in admiration by thousands who, in their lifetime had seen no such similar spectacle. Ineni was a national hero.

At the royal court in Memphis, he was received by the Pharaoh, who gave a feast in his honour to which the high priests came. It was during the feast that Ramses made it known that he intended to allocate nearly all the spoils of battle to the High Priest for the endowment of the temples.

Ineni, incensed, expressed the hope that the people might also share in the distribution of the freshly-gained wealth. His tone was controlled and respectful in spite of his anger, but his attitude was seized on by the High Priest.

"Would our brother wish the people to grow fat before hommage is paid to our lord Amon?" he asked with a sneer.

"I would wish Amon to be judge of what was best for our land—and not the High Priest!" Ineni snapped in a burst of rage.

The High Priest was cool, knowing his power, baiting the trap.

"But," he replied in mock surprise, "it is our Lord the

King who decrees that Amon shall rightly have acknowl-edgement. I, the High Priest am but the servant to his wishes."

Ineni was silent. He dared say no more.

"Does our brother wish to quarrel with his King?" the High Priest pursued, his voice slimy, menacing.

"I say that the priests are fat enough already," Ineni flared, eyes blazing.

"You are speaking treason, brother." There was gleam of triumph in his eyes. He looked meaningly towards the Pharaoh who had been silent witness of the outburst.

"It is not treason against Egypt that I speak," Ineni said.

Around him were the hostile faces of the priests. The great hall of the palace where the feast was taking place had gone suddenly quiet. Armed men had appeared under the colonnaded roof on all four sides. Ineni's hand moved under the folds of his tunic for his dagger.

The Pharaoh drew his eyes away from those of the High Priest which stared into his with a look of invitation which was almost command.

"I declare that you are speaking treason," he said stern-ly, without emotion. "It grieves me that after such a fine campaign your ambition should so overthrow your judgment."

He signalled, motioning with his hand without looking round and the armed men advanced from all sides to where Ineni glanced fiercely around him. He rose, pulling his dagger from his tunic and several of his lieutenants rose, nobly, with him.

The struggle was brief. The priests sat in safe, sneering silence while the small band of rebels was quietly and

inevitably overpowered. As they were led from the palace hall the High Priest said loudly:

"All plotters against His Majesty must be made an example of."

The Pharaoh said nothing. He did not look round as Ineni disappeared.

The prince and his small band of loyal followers—high officers of the army—were shrouded with cloaks and taken quietly to one of the lesser-used temples on the outskirts of the city. Here they were separated and flung into the little stone cells reserved for potential sacrifice.

The whole thing was done quietly and efficiently by the band of ambitious officers who expected promotion and favours from the ruling priests in return for their loyalty. These men would take charge of the army, there would be no fuss. Another "ambitious" commander would have disappeared. Ineni's name would be mentioned no more.

Sitting on the bed of hides in a corner of the otherwise bare cell, Ineni cursed his lack of foresight. He should have made promises to his army and marched into Memphis not as returning hero, but as a conquering revolutionary. He would have had the populace behind him and probably a large portion of the army which had never left the capital would have joined him. Such things depended on choice of the right moment. Now it was too late. There was nobody to organise his sympathisers. The high priests were in complete control, with the Pharaoh as their mouth-piece.

He got up and moved to the door—a great oak seal barred with an iron bar on the outside.

At eye level was a small square hole, too small for a hand to pass through, sufficient for the prisoner to look out and the guards to look in. Outside in the small hall from which steps led to the upper regions of the temple, the

guards were chatting. They sat on a low, rush divan, beside which their spears were idly propped. There were two of them. They did not glance at the door while he looked.

The hall, like the cell, was gloomy. The only light for either flooded down the narrow stone stairway opposite Ineni's eyes. It was as he peered silently into the outer chamber, that the High Priest, accompanied by two others came down the steps. The guard stood up.

As he came across the dim space towards the cell, the High Priest's eyes stared into Ineni's through the aperture.

"Look well on the outside world, brother," he sneered. "You have little time remaining for this life—and be sure that when your heart is weighed in the land beyond, Osiris will find you wanting."

"In the next life," Ineni retorted, "your earthly power will be as useless as a broken spear. You will answer not only for your sins but for the sins of others such as our King whom you have corrupted."

"Brave words, indeed." The High Priest had not lost his sneer. "And can you not afford to be brave at this time. There is nothing more to lose."

"Wickedness and indulgence cannot reign forever," Ineni said. "Had I but thought a little while ago, your power now would be tottering like the army of the Hittites. But others will rise against your corruption before I have joined the gods."

The High Priest regarded Ineni for several moments while the guards kept their heads averted as if the very act of overhearing such sacrilege was a heinous crime. At last he spoke, softly, controlling himself with difficulty.

"So my proud prince, we shall see. We shall watch on the morrow the collapse of this haughty disdain. We shall

watch with pleasure your reaction to the delights we have in store for you before the altar of Amon. Amon, himself, will be struck by the novelty of your punishment.''

His eyes continued to blaze at the prince through the little cut-out square while his face regained the composure it had all but lost completely.

"In the meantime, brother," he added in biting mockery. "You shall enjoy the delights of the flesh. You will be wined and dined afresh, you can choose whom you wish from your harem."

He smiled, slowly, gloating over his victim.

"May your appetite be well satisfied, brother. Tomorrow Amon shall have his fill."

Ineni watched him go, yearning for a single spear or dagger to hurl at the straight, all-powerful back as it disappeared up the steps to the porticoed court above. The guards relaxed, glanced half fearfully in his direction and then sat silently on the divan.

Withdrawing into the gloom of his dungeon, Ineni walked slowly the few steps around the walls. His mind was lost in bitter thoughts, which, for the moment even clouded thoughts of survival and escape. If only . . . But what sort of commander thought after the event "if only". He clenched his fists in fury.

Looking again through the aperture, he felt the immediate hopelessness of his position. All weapons had been taken from him. He had nothing but his tunic and his two hands. The prison was impregnable. The guards were incorruptible in face of the might of the High Priest.

There had, of course, been talk of his harem. He returned to the bed and waited.

Some time later, the slight drone of the guards' voices

stopped and there was the sound of soft footsteps beyond the oak door.

Ineni stood up and stepped swiftly to the aperture. Down the stairway, led by an officer of the guard, came his harem, anxious and afraid.

In the chamber they were halted and the guards were ordered to search them. Ineni watched the heavy hands of the guards moving over the soft bodies of the women outside their thin robes. Hands violated even between their legs and buttocks over the slight protection of the robes. The officer stood by to see that no impropriety beyond the embarrassment of the search, took place. These women were the harem of a nobleman—most of them of high rank themselves.

The officer called out in the gloom to the blank door.

"The women are here for your pleasure, my lord. Is it your desire that all should enter?"

Ineni surveyed them from his eye-hole. They were all there: the Palestinian, a dozen others and, looking unhappy and forlorn amongst them, his recent acquisition from Kadesh.

"The dimensions of my chamber would not permit of such lavish hospitality," he called back. "Have enter but one: the young Syrian girl on the end of the line."

The guards immediately seized the girl, whose eyes darted, quick and frightened from one to the other as once more rough hands mauled her. This time, the officer, too, approached after the examination by the men, had the girl remove her robe and looked at her more thoroughly. His eyes were dull, inscrutable as he surveyed her pronounced charms, but the eyes of the guards, forgetful of the proximity of the girl's master, lit up with lust at the sight of such beautiful flesh, so thinly covered, it seemed, with a taut,

83

filmy skin. As the officer's hand, searched in turn between the girl's legs, one of the rough men licked his lips involuntarily.

"Right, she may enter," the officer declared after a moment. "Should she leave before the morning you will keep her here with you. On no account must she be allowed to gossip before the sacrifices are completed."

The eyes of the guards were riveted on the girl while he spoke. They saw in her an image of sweet, innocent beauty so much intensified from her noble standing and her uncovering before them.

One of them moved with the girl to the door, eyes still fixed on the profile of her face so near to him as, re-clad in her robe, she waited for the door to be opened. The iron bar was withdrawn with an effort and with a grunting tug, the door was swung outwards and the girl slipped into the cell.

She stood just inside in the gloom, staring uncertainly towards the dim shape of Ineni, while the door was re-barred and the sound of the officer's footsteps dwindled. For a moment the guard stood outside the door, staring in through the aperture. But then he decided discretion was necessary from one of his lowly station, even in face of a condemned man. There was the creaking of the rushes on the divan and a low resumption of conversation.

Ineni moved towards the girl who meekly waited. As he reached her and caught her in his arms, she suddenly clasped him with a furious pressure.

He drew her to the bed, pulling her down alongside him in the gloom. Only their vague outline could be seen from the door.

The girl's hands moved tenderly over his face, her eyes looked bewildered; lovely and bewildered in the twilight.

"What has happened?" she breathed at last and there was unbelief in her voice. "Why are you here?"

With his lips close to the smooth warmth of her forehead, Ineni spoke quickly and quietly. The girl listened, her fingers digging in continual little pressures into his shoulder.

"The high priests are corrupt," he explained quietly, intensely. "They are afraid of my power with the people. They know that I hate their corruption. When I met you in Kadesh, I had been sent on a war mission which it was thought could end only in my destruction. But I returned and they were afraid. So I am here. Nobody knows I am here. But tomorrow I shall be sacrificed to the god Amon and corruption will continue unopposed in Egypt."

"But—but what of the Pharaoh?" the girl asked. "His name flies throughout Syria. Is he not the lord of Egypt?"

"In name only," Ineni whispered in reply. "He is the tool of the priests. Their word is law and they could overthrow him with ease if he tried to shake off their yoke."

The girl was silent for some time. Tears welled in her eyes and she tried to force them back, but failed, so that they suddenly flowed in profusion over her slim cheeks.

"I—I just don't understand?" she said. "You were all-powerful in Kadesh. Everyone spoke in awe of your power. And here you are thrown, like a common thief into a cell."

"The ways of corruption," breathed Ineni. "But keep your voice down or the guards will hear."

"But what can we do—what can we do?" She clung to him with a desperate longing.

"Whatever is to be done," Ineni whispered, "it will be very risky with only a small chance of success."

"But we must do something?" the girl breathed intensely.

"I should die if you were killed. My life would be worth nothing."

"A plan occurred to me as I watched the guards searching you," Ineni went on quickly. "It involves you and will mean death if it fails. It will also be unpleasant for you—but it is the only chance."

"I will do anything," the girl said firmly. "If you die I shall not want to live anyway."

Ineni kissed her gently and wiped away her tears with a corner of the hides.

"In a few moments we must pretend to make love," he whispered. "But it would be better if we didn't make love in fact so that we shall preserve all our energy.

"After this pretence, I shall send you away. The guards have orders to keep you with them if you leave."

He hesitated for a moment, searching for the best words to explain his plan. The girl's body was pressed against him, her face pressed against his as she listened.

"Normally they wouldn't dream of touching you, no matter how acute their desire. You are a noblewoman and the wrath of the nobles and the priests would have them slain. But if, while you sit with them on the divan, you make advances towards them they will, if I am not mistaken, have great difficulty in controlling their desires."

He paused again. The girl's breath was sounding slightly, close to his ear. She said nothing.

"This plan," Ineni continued tersely, "is our only chance and you must forgive me the indignity I suggest. You must try to force them to make love to you—and not much force should be necessary.

"One of them has a dagger in his belt. He must be made to see the necessity of keeping his tunic on in case some-

body comes. In his passion you must withdraw the dagger from the belt and kill him.''

The girl's grip on his shoulder tightened to a long slow squeeze and Ineni was afraid she would be unable to carry out his plan—unable through her unwillingness. But when she spoke, her words made him grip her with a burst of love and continue.

"What shall I do with the other man—there are two?" she asked softly.

"That is the difficulty," Ineni said quietly. "I can think of only one solution. In order to stab them both you must have them both very close to you, both off their guard. They must both make love to you at the same time."

There was silence and then the girl said: "Yes, I see."

"It will be unpleasant for you," Ineni added, brushing his lips along her brow, "and I cannot force you to do it. But it is my only chance of escape."

"And what after they are dead?" the girl asked.

Ineni felt a surge of hope pass through him at the certainty in the girl's voice.

"Then you will have to pull back the bar and we can escape together through the temple," he whispered. "There will be more guards in the temple, but I shall be free and armed. Once out of this cell we shall escape."

"Where shall we go?" the girl continued her relentless questioning. "How can we hide?"

"That we shall have to decide in due course," Ineni replied. "We will have most of the night before discovery and I know where we can get horses. Can you ride?"

"I was taught by my father."

"Right. Enough talk. Now we must pretend."

Outside the door, shadowing through the hole, was a flickering of light. Ineni got up and crept over. A brazier

had been lighted in the outer chamber and the guards were sitting quietly on the divan. They appeared to be listening. They are hoping to bear aural witness to the passion of a prince, Ineni thought with grim humour. They shall not be disappointed.

He tiptoed back to the girl and removed her robe. He in turn took off his tunic and lay alongside her. Their bodies were fused together and his penis rose in spite of him, pressing with rigid pain against her thighs. The girl breathed heavily.

"Could we not make love?" she pleaded in a whisper. "The plan may fail."

"It will not fail," Ineni said, quietly. "It must not fail. We shall need all our wits and strength and one becomes listless after passion is spent. It is better that we deny ourselves until we are safe."

"I shall long for our safety with all my heart," the girl said.

"So be it," Ineni echoed.

For the next half-hour they pantomimed the act of love. Lying in the gloom where their movements would be now undiscernable from the door. The rustlings of the hides, the heavy breathing, the muttered exclamations, the moanings, the whinings, the groan after groan of growing passion, the convulsive explosion of fulfilment. All were there for the benefit of the guards, quietly listening outside, picturing afresh the lush curves of the girl they had seen searched in her nudity.

After the final gasping of the act, they lay silent for some time. Then both dressed quietly.

"Tell them I am asleep," Ineni whispered. "And you must act as if you really desire them, as if you mean every

88

movement of your body, every word of encouragement. My life—and yours if you fail—depends upon it."

"I will do all I can," the girl whispered back. "And I shall be thinking of you with every act I make."

"Amon be with you," Ineni said.

The girl breathed a prayer and then walked to the door. She banged on the inside and a guard came over.

"My lord has bid me leave him. He is asleep," she said.

The guard tried to peer past her into the cell but could see nothing. He called out to his companion.

"Our lady wishes to leave. Be ready with your spear."

The other covered the door from a slight distance, spear raised. His companion eased back the bar and the girl slipped out into the chamber, the light from the brazier shadowing over her, outlining the creases around the fleshy parts of her body, where the robe clasped and offered them. The bolt slid back into place.

"You had better sit on the divan, my lady. It is more comfortable and we have been ordered to keep you here for the night," one of the guards said, gruffly, embarrassed in the presence of a noblewoman.

The girl thanked them and sat on the divan, while the two soldiers drew away and squatted on the floor at the foot of it.

Very quietly Ineni rose from the hides and crept to the door. He stood back a few inches from the aperture so that he had a good view of the outside, but could not in turn be seen. No light came down the steps from above. It was full night.

Ineni's heart kept up a continued, abnormal thumping as he prepared himself for the events which would end in life or death for him.

The girl had surreptitiously eased up the hem of her robe and she leaned back against the wall, legs apart so the material stretched tightly across her thighs, revealing their bareness under the skirt of her covering up to the gloom of her crutch.

The guards sat with their eyes on the ground, afraid, perhaps, to look at the lightly protected beauty of the girl.

"How boring it must be for you to have to sit in this chamber all night."

The men looked round. She had succeeded in attracting their attention to herself.

"It gives us no great pleasure, my lady," one of them replied—and his eyes fell on the open, revealed gulf of her legs under the robe. His companion, too had seen the uncovered intimacy. Their eyes became glued on the dark, firm, muscled flesh of her thighs—and were stuck there. Neither, it seemed to Ineni, had the physical power to remove his eyes from the tempting view.

The girl pretended to be unaware of their lustful eyes, the colour which had flamed to their faces.

"Are no women ever brought to give you a little distraction?" she asked.

She moved her position slightly as if she were uncomfortable—and succeeded in presenting the men with an even fuller view of the secrets under her skirt. Her thighs, wide under the robe were now all visible and to the furtively searching eyes of the guards, the soft lips of her vagina were there in sight. Their heads, on the level of the divan, were directly in line with her legs and their eyes feasted ravenously—and now almost openly—on the object they would have given their lives to possess.

"Never such luck," one of them answered. And his

voice came out gruffly and uncertainly in his passion so that he had to cough to hide his feelings.

"How inconsiderate of your commanders," the girl continued.

She rose as if to stretch her legs and strolled around the chamber, clasping her robe about her, outlining her buttocks as she walked away from them. Her bottom seemed contained like a firm pudding in a thin cloth and at its extremities it rippled out against the cloth.

The men exchanged glances and stared with fixed eyes at the buttocks which rounded and creased like live things before their eyes. The fire threw shadow and light on the ripples of flesh so that they seemed even accentuated.

The girl turned back towards them and in walking appeared to find something wrong with a sandal. A few paces from them she paused and bent in front of them, jostling her sandal with her hand. At her bosom, the loose robe opened out and fell forward so that the guards found themselves looking down a long ravine of cleavage, their hungry eyes roaming over almost completely revealed mounds of round, firm breast-flesh.

Ineni, watching them closely was aware how hard put to it they were not to leap to their feet and start the rape of the girl, in spite of the penalties which would follow. So far she was playing her role well.

"I always feel a great sympathy for guards," the girl continued. "They have no fun, while frequently their prisoner has everything he could desire. It seems so unfair."

"We are not the privileged, my lady," replied one, tongue slithering over dry lips.

"But nonetheless you have probably more power and capacity then those in higher places."

The girl, churned up with nervousness inside, as Ineni

well knew, was giving no indication of anything but complete self-possession far beyond her years.

For a moment the guards stared at her, racking their brains for meaning to put to her words, unable to believe the obvious.

"My lord within there, for instance," the girl continued relentlessly, nodding towards the door behind which Ineni watched. "He has no more power than to satisfy himself and leave me unsatisfied—and now he sleeps while I can only regret."

Slow grins appeared on the faces of the guards, grins they were prepared to wipe off at the slightest sign. Now they were sure—but one could not be completely sure with a noblewoman.

The bulges at the loins of their tunics were unmistakeable. The girl sat once more on the divan, robe drawn up to reveal several inches of smooth, silky thigh, and motioned to the men to sit with her.

"Is it not ridiculous?" she asked with a smile. "Two fine men like you, unable to have a woman and a woman like me left unsatisfied because of my lord's weakness. And here we are able to do nothing but sit and dream and wish."

Her slim fingers played with her thigh, as if absently and her big, doe-eyes swept the two men.

"It is a great pity, my lady," one of the men replied. "And anyone who could not spend a whole night with you but must needs send you off at its beginning is no man in my view."

He had risked all on his remark. The other guard looked at the floor.

The girl eyed the man.

"You would not have done so?" she asked. "You would have kept me the whole night?"

"And several more besides if it were my choice."

The other guard had not yet looked up from the floor. They were playing with dynamite.

"Then you would seem to be the man for me," the girl replied.

The other guard looked up at last. He grinned. They both grinned. This was a noblewoman with a difference. One could laugh and joke and talk intimately with her. But yet neither consciously dared suggest—not even hope—for more.

"You are so beautiful that I should probably have kept you for life," the guard added, warming to his compliments.

"Am I so beautiful?" the girl asked, raising an eyebrow and smiling provocatively.

"More beautiful than the lotus blossom," declared the guard who had not spoken up to this point.

"Ah. You, too, are a man of taste." The girl encompassed him in her smile.

"But surely you have seen more beautiful women?" She addressed them both.

"I have seen some as beautiful of face and a very few as beautiful as body, but never one of such virtue in both," the first guard said, boldly.

"And how can you be sure that my body is so beautiful?" the girl asked with a smile.

"My lady, you cannot hide your beauty—and was it not revealed to us when you were searched?"

Both men were now getting obvious pleasure out of simply making suggestive remarks to such a beautiful and noble woman. The bulges in their tunics were enormous

and they made no fruitless attempt to hide these gauges of passion from the girl.

"But that was for only a moment. You had no time to judge," the girl laughed.

"It was enough, but indeed we could have wished for more," the first guard said, with a ring of passion in his voice.

"Then you shall have it," the girl declared.

And before the lustful eyes of the men—hardly able to believe what was happening—the girl slithered off the divan and slowly divested herself of her robe. It peeled from off her breasts, which soared into view like great balls of ivory, strongly pointed at their uttermost protrusion by the expanse of nipple. Down from her slim ribs and slimmer waist the garment slipped, clasped her tightly around the broader flesh of her hips a moment and then with an extra tug and wriggle, had flowed off her hips so that her delicately rounded abdomen shot into view, the little muff of dark hair at her pelvis and then the broad, tapering-to-slimness thighs.

The robe slumped to the stone floor in a soft swoosh.

Bending before them so that her breasts hung vertically like the suspended, heavy fruit of a tree, the girl drew the robe from off her sandals and stepped out of it altogether.

"Now you can judge," she said, with a deep lustful look at the men.

She came closer to them, as they sat, mouths open, breath escaping in painful jerks, bodies heaving irregularly with their efforts to control their breath.

Close in front of them she spun around. The firelight flickered on her flesh, shadowing the rounds and hollows of her buttocks, her breasts, her belly as she turned,

throwing into relief the lightly moving muscles as they tensed sinuously in her arms and thighs.

So close were the two men that they were aware of the flesh as if the skin was throwing off a light, radiant heat which reached them. They could see the light down on her body, feel in their minds, the texture of the taut, soft-looking skin.

Still they did not move.

"Tell me now am I not beautiful?" the girl asked, gazing down at them.

"My lady, you are so beautiful that you come near to tempting us to sin against our duty, which bids us quietly guard the prisoner, and our class which bids us not to touch a lady of noble birth—save in the spoils of war."

"Would you like to touch me?" the girl asked, flaunting her hips.

There was a moment's hesitation.

"I should like to stuff my rod into the very depths of you." The words came out quickly in the coarse expression which was all the soldier knew. The girl smiled at him invitingly.

"And I told you how unsatisfied my lord left me—I give you that right. Stuff me, stuff me with all your might until you are exhausted."

Both men squirmed with passion at her words—but neither moved.

"We would be killed if we were discovered," one whispered after a while.

From his hiding place Ineni held his breath. Would their fear overcome their lust and ruin everything?

But the girl had moved up to the men where they sat, open-legged on the divan, great branches thrusting out

from between their legs, lifting their tunics in a great undulation.

With a swift movement she knelt in front of them and grasped each great penis in a hand through the cloth, squeezing it, fondling it.

"I need to be satisfied," she said passionately, "And now you need to be. I offer you my body—a body such as you have never had. I offer you the nectar between my legs. I offer you anything you want of me. It is past midnight. Nobody will come now until the morning. You will never have this chance again."

At the feel of her hands both men had writhed their hips uncontrollably and now the first guard, helpless against himself, leaned forward and pulled her roughly onto him, hands running voraciously, fiercely, over her body.

The girl pursued her bridgehead. Her hand slid under the guards' tunics, up their hairy thighs and then clasped, gently, the thick stiff organs she found there, clasped them and then drew soft, cool fingers up their hot lengths.

The other guard, too, not wishing to be left out, had moved in and was feeling the girl all over from a side position.

Her hands slid, relentless, down from their rods to the hot, soft expanses of their testicles. Both men groaned and wriggled in delirium.

"Come on, come on," the girl entreated.

"Just a moment."

The first guard tore himself away with an effort, snatched a blazing torch from the brazier and moved towards the cell door. Ineni moved swiftly and quietly back to the bed, lay down and feigned sleep. The torch flickered for a moment or two at the aperture, while the guard endeavoured to peer through the inner gloom. After a moment,

96

satisfied, he moved away and the light receded from the door with him. Ineni rose quietly again and moved once more to the aperture.

The first guard had returned to the divan and was pawing the girl. He pulled her at him and crushed his lips on hers. From his grunt, Ineni could tell that she had slipped her little, lean tongue into his mouth. The man's hands caressed her breasts, clutching them so tightly that they bulged out around his fingers and red marks appeared on the skin as he slid over the smooth expanse.

The other man had, now, boldly slipped his hand between her open legs from behind and was fingering the slim folds of flesh, searching between them for the spot. His other hand stroked and pressed the firm, bamboo-texture of her buttocks.

For some minutes they continued thus, all three breathing fiercely.

And then the girl cried out in passion:

"Oh, put it in me. Quick, put it in me."

She rolled off the man and flung herself down on the divan, legs wide apart. Both men moved, tunics rolled up above their loins, to get on her as she lay with eyes closed, moaning through open mouth.

Each tried to elbow the other away. Neither succeeded.

"Oh, don't fight over it," the girl begged, voice broken with passion. "If one of you can't wait, you can have me together."

The men looked at her in surprise.

Quickly she rolled onto her side, reached behind her and spread the cheeks of her bottom with her hands.

"One of you must have my behind," she said.

The two men were in no mood to argue about details.

Each simply wanted to embed himself in this beautiful woman without delay.

"All right, I'll have her ass," the second guard said through his thick breathing.

Falling over each other in their hot desire, each with an enormous penis sawing the air, they fell onto the divan on either side of the girl.

As the first guard, taking the more normal passage, pulled her legs on either side of his hips, Ineni, watching with a turbulent pang of upset in his stomach, thought: shades of the Queen of Arad—but what different circumstances and how much more depends on it.

Both men were coarse and brutal. There was no waiting, no question of finesse. Behind her, while his comrade arranged the girls legs, the other—all reserve of class gone now—pulled apart her buttocks, spreading them with a great pull on either hand, pressing the anus open with his thumbs. An aiming. And then his fleshy organ barraged against the hole, rebounded on the first attempt, stuck on the second and with a third thrust had seared into her soft back channel to her cry of pain. He showed no gentleness, but, face screwed up in passion and fury, shagged with wild, rapid movements straight into her rectum, bursting in, with a few strokes, to the full length of his organ regardless of the girl's cries.

Meanwhile his companion, slower to get started, had succeeded in drawing up the girl's thighs on either side of him, so that one was crushed under him in the crook of his waist, the other strung limply over his hip.

Without more ado he caught her cool hand and placed it on his penis for to place it in her vagina for him.

The girl seized it bravely and directed it into the opening of the aperture. Feeling the moist warmth around its tip,

the guard heaved upwards with a flexing of his hips and his penis in turn burst into the girl in one great, gluttonous movement, forcing up and up, determined to feel the tight, painful pressure on his organ in one movement before the channel had adapted itself to his intrusion.

Another cry was drawn from the girl, but she held her own and was soon forcing her hips back at the spearing of her behind, forward at the penetration of her vagina with alternate squirms.

Her hands moved around and the broad back of the first guard as he buried his organ of pulsing pleasure into her. Her arms encircled him, pulling him into her, thighs clasped him, cradling him warmly against her soft secret. Her hands roamed over his back, down to the belt until they rested on the leather sheath in which the dagger was enclosed.

For a moment, while Ineni stared in a sort of hypnotised horror, she fumbled with the sheath, but was unable to unfasten it for fear of attracting attention.

Behind her, the second guard was well taken care of. Forcing his way in and in and in her tight back-passage which clasped his penis in a soft vice, he had no thought in his head but the sensual, almost unendurable pain down there at the protrusion of his loins.

The girl concentrated on the first guard, while her hand rested lightly on the dagger sheath.

"Come on, come on," she pleaded. "Stuff me as you said you would. Kill me, shove it in further, further."

Goaded on, loins alight with the thrill of her coarse words, the guard stuffed and stuffed. His movements grew faster and faster until his body seemed out of control and his face was furrowed all over, his neck stretched and taut

with veins standing out on it as if he were about to burst at any moment.

"Oh how wonderful! You're so thick and filling me! I can't stand it! Go on thrust your knob home."

The girl's wild, coarse words assailed his ear, sharpening his passion, pointing it to a razor edge until it seemed that razor edges were flicking the tender extremity of his penis and then his mouth had opened in a great rough bellow as his loins opened and his juices flooded out through the phallic canal into the soft receptacle of her body.

Ineni muttered to himself, spurring the girl on. What was she doing? In a moment it would be too late. Sweat stood on his brow and his jaw was taut as he watched.

But the girl had chosen the only moment in which success was inevitable. As the hot discharge shot in bullets into her opening and the guard's head and thoughts were filled with nothing but a furious, all-pervading thunder of release, she undid the clasp with deft fingers, drew out the knife and plunged it deep into his back all in one movement.

He gave an extra jerk which could easily have been one of passion, and let out a sharp cry of pain, which mingled with his roars of filfilment.

The girl, her face set, eyes filled with horror, but determined in her horror, pulled out the dagger and thrust it into his back again.

Watching, his heart pounding, biting his lips, Ineni saw the little drama enacted fully. Saw the incongruity of a beautiful girl being buggered furiously while the recent possessor of her vagina, penis still in her, clasped in her legs, gave his last twitches all unknown to his comrade. The blood flowed down from his back onto the divan while the girl wriggled uneasily free of the body. The great

penis, wet and slippery with the dregs of sperm, dangled limply to the rush surface on which the body lay.

The girl held the dagger, dripping blood, in front of her. The body had swayed over onto its back. It might have been exhausted from the violent intercourse.

The girl held the dagger tightly, waiting. She didn't want to risk a false blow at the man behind her. In the meantime Ineni could see his great shaft appearing and disappearing with startling rapidity. His hands moved around to the soft belly of the girl, grasping fiercely the soft flesh, clasping and unclasping the slim folds of her abdomen.

His thighs moved up and under her, clasped her hips as his hips smashed at her in quick undulations, his penis skewering into her bottom from all angles, splitting her buttocks apart, still bringing little shrieks of sensual pain from her lips.

His mouth was open. He bit her neck so that she cried out. His hands moved up, almost in a paroxysm to her breasts, pinching them, twisting them, digging into the nipples. His thighs twined and untwined, his hips undulated and moved in an almost rotary motion. Trying to hurry him, the girl extended her bottom at him, spreading her buttocks, straining her aperture as if she were emptying her bowels so that it met his upthrust in the middle of emptying, aiding his organ on its inward rush into her backside depths.

"Shag!" she whispered. "Harder. You're making me sore. Make me sore. Go on, lose it in me. Push, push harder!"

Her words reached Ineni as a gentle echo in the chamber and, in passing, he thought he had taught her well, that she had played the role tonight well, that she had probably half-enjoyed it after the initial moments.

101

And then he heard the guard uttering a long drawn-out moan which grew in pitch until with a sudden convulsive thrust which almost hurled the girl onto the corpse in front of her, his penis had shattered its contents into her bottom. It continued thrusting into her in long forceful strokes and a sharp gasp at each painful release, until the reserve had dwindled and drained and the man rolled away from her, his penis sucking out with him, onto his back.

The girl turned over without a moment's hesitation and plunged the dagger into the man's heart.

Leaving it buried there she rushed to the cell door, struggled with the bar a moment and then grated it back from its staples.

Ineni pushed from inside and the door swung open and he stepped out into the chamber.

The girl flung herself, sobbing into his arms, overcome with the macabre horror of the role she had played. Her nerves, stretched to breaking point had, momentarily snapped.

Ineni held her calmly, unhurriedly, while she recovered. The two corpses, naked from the waist down, lay with glazed eyes fixed at the gloomy roof of the chamber. The blood dripped steadily from them, oozing through the rushes of the divan to the floor. The dagger gleamed in the chest of one. And the naked girl was sobbing a little less, recovering, in the arms of the grim-faced prince.

After a while the girl began, quickly to pull on her robe. Ineni collected the arms of the two men: two spears and two swords plus the dagger which he pulled, all bloody, from the chest of the cooling body. He wiped the dagger on the tunic of one of the guards, decided on the futility of hiding their bodies in the cell, took the girl by the hand and led the way up to the steps, out of the chamber where

the flames from the brazier flickered long, moving shadows over the figures of the guards.

Up the gloom of the steps they crept into the pale moonlight of the temple colonnade. In the deep gloom of the colonnade they breathed the fresh air for a moment. In front of them stretched the pale, silvery expanse of courtyard. Directly opposite them was an archway leading into the outer courtyard and the desert beyond. To reach it they could follow the perimeter colonnade all the way round the inside of the temple wall.

"Ready?" Ineni whispered.

"Ready," breathed the reply.

Taking her hand, Ineni led the way in the deep gloom of the colonnade. The pillars towered gigantically around them to the great, stone roof of the portico, as like the dwarfs which had been brought back from the south in former days, they crept around the central patch of moonlight in the courtyard to the archway.

At the arch there was a break in the pillars—a narrow aisle through the colonnade.

Leaving the girl in the shadow, Ineni moved carefully to the archway and peered through. The colonnade continued around the perimeter wall as far as the main entrance to the temple on the far side. And just inside this entrance two more guards were talking, idly, while they guarded the house of Amon.

For some minutes Ineni watched them and then he drew back and whispered to the girl to stay where she was.

He watched again for a moment or two and then, like a shadow, slipped through the archway into the darkness of the second portico.

The guards continued to chat. There was never any trouble at the temples; the priests were too strong. One of

them scraped a spear in the sand to illustrate some point as, like a mountain snake, Ineni slithered through the gloom towards them. Under cover of the dark pillars he could not be seen from their position—only heard should he make any sound.

In a number of swift, silent strides he had reached a point on the same side of the temple wall as his prey beyond which he dared not go.

There, only a few yards from the guards he rested, letting his tautened nerves relax. Recovered and controlled again, he quietly raised one of the spears he had taken from his cell guards. The other he held ready for immediate transfer in his other hand. Standing back, shielded by the first line of pillars, he trained the spear on one of the guards. A slow backward movement of his strong arm, a sudden fierce flexing—and the spear had hurtled straight into the man's side.

His companion gazed, unbelievingly at the shaft for a moment—and his slowness was his undoing. For fast in the wake of the first, the second spear flew to its target. It caught the second guard full in the chest before he had even raised his eyes from his groaning fellow on the moonlit dust.

Following the two spears, Ineni ran out from the shadow, covering the distance in a couple of bounds. His sword flashed, finishing the work the spears had almost completed.

With furious energy, he hauled the two dead men back into the deep shadow of the temple wall, brushing over as best he could the traces of blood and the dragmarks which were left. He recovered his spears—and two more besides—and then, a veritable armory, slipped like a ghost back to the middle archway and beckoned the girl.

She ran to him, peering through into the outer courtyard.

"What happened?" she whispered intensely.

"It's all right. The way is clear," he replied softly.

With quiet haste they moved across the courtyard, the temple seeming to surround them like some eerie, all-knowing being.

Outside the temple nothing moved. The stretch of desert which led down to the western outskirts of the town lay pale and cool and empty.

"Now we must hurry" Ineni warned. "We may have until dawn—but that will not be too long."

In silence they raced over the sand until they were lost in the built-up sanctuary of the city. This was the poor man's quarters; to the east, along the river were the noblemen's villas.

It was well after midnight and the streets were deserted save for an odd beggar who moved and shuffled in his simple covering of hides and an emaciated dog who slunk quietly away on their approach.

"The priests have probably put a guard over my villa," Ineni said as they approached the river. "We shall have to help ourselves to horses from another's house."

Arrived at the broad, sandy walk along the serene-stretching Nile, they entered the open archway of the first villa which presented itself. Inside was dozing the watch servant, whose job it was to keep stray beggars from appropriating his master's goods while he slept.

The man sprang, startled to his feet as Ineni, followed by the girl marched boldly into the walled grounds of the house. His sleepy eyes took in the rich tunic of his visitor, alighted on the face, and then he bowed low in recognition. The news of his imprisonment had not yet been noised abroad, Ineni thought.

"I have urgent business with your lord," Ineni told the

man in a tone which brooked no refusal. "It is to his interest that I see him with the least possible delay."

"If you will wait in the lodge my lord, I will summon my master immediately," the servant assured him, indicating the small visitors' lodge to one side.

"Good," Ineni said. "I shall wait."

The man conducted them, together to the lodge and as he bent to unfasten the door, Ineni's sword crashed, flat-bladed onto his skull. The man dropped in a huddled heap, unconscious.

"A pity to be so hard with the poor fellow," Ineni murmured as he stretched the man out. "But we cannot choose to be gentle at the moment."

Without being asked, the girl swiftly tore strips from the hem of her robe and passed them to Ineni to secure the still form.

"He has a bump on his head the size of a wild duck's egg, but he will recover," Ineni said as he gagged the man firmly.

He pulled his victim into the lodge and fastened the door on him. Then, eyes darting furiously around him, led the girl to the spot behind the main villa where he knew the stables would be.

The grounds were quiet and still. There was no guard but the man on the gate. This was a time of peace in Egypt.

The villa itself was equally quiet. It could have been deserted.

At the stables, Ineni spoke softly to the horses, calming them before they had time to distrust his presence. There was an initial, startled snorting and then silence.

Quietly and with patience, Ineni led four horses out into the grounds.

His eyes watched the house warily, but there was no murmur of movement as he and the girl led the animals quietly through the grounds, past the lodge where the watch lay bound and unconscious, through the arched portal and out onto the broad bank of the Nile.

Outside, the horses moved quietly, snuffling one another, lowering heads to the sand, straightening again and nuzzling at their human leaders.

Ineni and the girl mounted and with the spare horses between them trotted, at first, along the Nile, the far bank of which could just be seen in the pale light of the moon.

Soon the southern outskirts of Memphis had dwindled and they were galloping at speed into the desert.

Along the banks of the river as they rode, the cluster of rooftops gradually disappeared behind them until the only signs of life were the occasional hovels of a fisherman and on the Nile itself his boat.

To the west the green, fertile fields of cotton and vegetables stretched in a thin blanket of foliage. Beyond them the flat desert and beyond that again the upward sweep of the distant hills.

"Would it not be better to go into the hills?" the girl asked as they rode.

"We should probably perish there," Ineni told her. "They are as barren as the desert itself—although as a last resort it may be necessary to use their shelter."

He mused for a while as the hooves of the horses thudded in soft harmony on the sand, the only sound in the great silence.

"No. Our best plan is to keep heading south. We must follow the river. It is the only life in Egypt. With luck we shall reach Nubia in a few weeks time and then we shall see."

"My poor mother will be terrified," the girl said sadly.

"You will see her again," Ineni said with determination. "When I enter Egypt again it will be to sweep the priests from their foul throne."

The girl seemed to have recovered her good spirits with the strong rhythm of the horses' movement.

"Did I do well, tonight?" she asked, knowing the answer, wanting to hear it from his lips.

"You were wonderful," Ineni answered. "No man could have failed to be seduced by you. Those poor fools gave themselves up as sacrifice the moment they set eyes on you."

"It was very painful," the girl mused. "I still feel as if I had been raped by elephants."

"Better that than to be journeying from this life so young," Ineni said.

"Better that than to see you no more," the girl echoed fervently.

"Soon we shall make amends," Ineni said with a smile. "But for the moment we must ride with all speed. A hundred of the Pharaoh's best horses would still catch us after a day's lead if we were not wary."

They galloped on through a cityless land in which the green fields still stretched on either side of the river in thin ribbons, but in which only an odd cluster of workers huts gave sign of habitation.

They were riding still, dusty and tired, when the eastern sky rent into thin shreds and a pale light flecked the desert far to the east.

The greenish hue expanded as they rode until it was lightening the broad, sluggish surface of the Nile, suffusing them in its soft, morning glow. Coldly at first the green changed to yellow and then bright rays of light were

streaking the desert, and on the horizon was a bright profusion of misty white. And then the sun had risen. The journey of the night was over and Amon was shining over his broad river, his narrow, cared-for valley and a new day of toil in the sun had commenced.

"They will have discovered now that you have gone," the girl said, a note of weariness sneaking into her voice.

"Even before now," Ineni said thoughtfully. "By now the pursuit will have started and it will not take them long to find our trail."

"We have come a long way," the girl said. "Can we rest a little, soon?"

"You are tired and what woman would not be," Ineni said. "But we must continue for a while until we find somewhere to hide. As soon as we halt the pursuit will gain on us. There are contingents of the army at every small town along the route. They will continue to hunt us while the others rest. The pursuit will be non-stop."

The girl did not speak for some time.

"I didn't realise how desperate our plight was," she said, quietly after a few minutes reflection. "For every hour we stop, they will gain a great amount of the distance we have put between them and us."

"That is so," Ineni replied grimly. "But we will win the race, never fear."

With the sun mounting in the sky and beginning its merciless battering of the life below, they passed through several large oases in which Ineni pointed out, as they travelled, the clustered mud and papyrus barracks of the local army contingent. As yet they were safe—a noble and his wife on a journey—for news had no way of reaching these little clots of life save from the hands of the Pharaoh's men as they swept south after their quarry.

"At the next town, we will sell the two horses which have born us so nobly," Ineni announced. "With the money we can buy some food. We will take a chance on resting throughout the heat of the day and then continue south."

"Will it be safe to rest?" the girl asked anxiously.

"No," Ineni replied briefly. "We must take that chance."

At the next little town, Ineni searched until he found a merchant who was interested in the horses. The man was suspicious. He did not put his feelings into words, but he could not understand why a nobleman should want to come to his little town to sell a fine pair of horses for a price which was probably less than he would get for them at Memphis or Thebes or many other bigger towns along the river.

But Ineni allayed his fears with a story of his journey to his brother in Thebes. The horses were to have been a gift to the brother but Ineni now found he had come out without his purse of gold and had no money for food on the route. So he had to sell the horses.

The story not only dispelled the man's doubts but put him in a very good humour as it was now clear to him that this nobleman must sell the horses, at no matter what loss, in order to live.

For a long time they haggled and bargained and finally Ineni let the animals go for about half what they were worth. The merchant was well aware that he could have acquired them for even less, but the price was magnificent anyway and he did not want to get too much on the wrong side of a nobleman.

In return, the fugitives received some gold and enough food to last for a day or two. On the river bank, sheltered

by a fringe of palms they ate and slept for a while. Then they bathed in the river and lay in the shade.

A few hours later, with the ring of sun still sparkling fiercely on the sands, they set out once more, refreshed and determined to recover some of the ground they had lost.

They rode thus for four days, stopping for brief intervals of a few hours only, travelling throughout the cold nights, buying fresh food with the gold. Each time they stopped they did not even take the risk of making love for fear of thus being caught unawares. The horses they fed on the same food as themselves and allowed to munch the roadside foliage at night.

So it was that they reached Thebes, the very heart of the priests' domain, the very seat of the god Amon. Here the great plain spread out, dotted with temples. Up on the western kills were the myraid cliff openings of mortuary tombs of former kings, their inner passages crossing and re-crossing in an effort to confuse the tomb robbers who from time to time committed unheard of sacrilege. In the shadow of the brown hills too were the immense stone statues, memorials to the great kings of the past.

"These are the temples in which the high priests gorge themselves," Ineni said bitterly, as he and the girl galloped across the plain. "The nourishment for the departed on which the priests grow fat, lines the tombs to their very doors but I know not a single priest who would give a crust of bread to a beggar."

The girl was silent in the face of her lord's bitterness. These were things of which she knew little.

In Thebes they rested again, but the horses were extremely weary. A short rest for them was not enough.

111

Their nostrils were foam-flecked even while resting. They were looking lean and gaunt.

"The horses will not take us much farther," Ineni announced after an examination. "We shall have to abandon them unless we can give them a much longer time for recovery."

He raised his hand to his eyes and peered over to the craggy, western hills, seeming to rise in a sheer escarpment at this distance.

"But we cannot give them a rest without the risk of being overtaken," he mused. "If our pursuit has kept going all the time we've rested, they can be only a few hours behind."

"You are thinking we should hide out in the hills for a while?" the girl prompted, a note of pleading in her voice.

"Yes. I think we had better hide out there," Ineni said slowly.

The decision was made. The horses were coaxed to their feet once more to bear their burden.

Many were the curious eyes which watched the pair ride through the city. Eyes which noted and would tell their tale to the Pharaoh's men when they swept into the city later.

For a few miles they rode on along the Nile and then, at the least inhabited spot they could find, cut through the palms and irrigation canals to the border of the green belt and out into the stretch of desert below the hills. An hour or so and their tracks would be covered by the softly shifting sand. As far as they could see no-one had observed their deviation from the obvious path.

They raced across the desert at speed despite the heat of the sun which fell on them with a heavy pressure, like a great stifling cover which prevented the air from reaching them.

The hills loomed larger, steep, inaccessible in many spots, the rough paths becoming clear at others. The tomb openings cut into the cliff face grew from pin points to great, dark holes. Many of them were now abandoned.

Soon they were in the foothills, climbing, following the rough, little-used tracks, horses slithering from slope to slope.

From a point high up, near the summit, Ineni led the way to one of the gaping caverns overlooking the plain and passed into the deep, cool shade of the interior.

The horses snorted and stood quivering from their exertion. The girl flung herself down near the entrance of the tomb.

"At last we can rest for a while in ease," she said thankfully.

Ineni had a brief inspection of the interior. Inside there were remnants of a sarcophagus. This then was one of those luckless homes of the dead which had fallen prey to the marauders. Doubtless the jewelry, weapons, all of value which had been placed with the body for its use in the next world, had been taken. Perhaps, even, the robbers had cut the rings from the king's fingers. Now the body had been moved in an attempt by his descendants to find a tranquil resting place for their departed.

Leaving the horses to quiet their heavy breathing, to start to recover the immense resources of energy they had lost on the furious southward race, Ineni lay down beside the girl in the entrance shade.

From where they lay they had a bird's-eye view of the distant temples and rooftops of Thebes. They could see the Nile gleaming and stretching back along the way they had come for some miles. From here they would be able to watch the pursuit ride into Thebes and out again.

"What shall we do if someone has seen us?" the girl said softly, putting her fears into words.

"It will be very hard for us." Ineni replied. "We shall have no choice but to ride out into the Libyan desert which lies to the west of our shelter."

The girl lay for a long time, her body pressed to the cool, sandy stone of the cave and then she said:

"I am going to sleep for a while. Will you wake me when you see them?"

Ineni put his arm around her.

"You have been very strong," he said softly. "And for it I shall make you Queen of Egypt. Sleep now."

For a long time, he kept a vigil, with the girl sleeping, warm against him. The sun was falling lower and the horses were quiet. Gazing at the monotone of desert, Ineni found his eyes closing involuntarily from time to time. It was with an effort that he kept awake.

But suddenly his fatigue left him, forgotten in an instant. He stiffened and his brow furrowed as he stared out along the bank of the Nile to the north of Thebes.

There a cloud of dust was rising, rising and growing at every minute.

Ineni detached himself from the girl and moved closer to the entrance, so that, lying flat on his stomach, he was on the very edge of the pathway to the tomb, from which the hill fell away in a sharp descent.

The girl, awakened by his movement, had slithered up beside him.

"They are here already?" she whispered.

The center of the cloud seemed to have opened out now and through it came a large body of mounted warriors, indistinct at first and then clearer so that the sun reflected on their host of bronze spears.

"There must be two hundred of them." Ineni said softly.

He felt a faint tensing in his chest at the sight of the body of men. They had ridden at great speed, the vast distance from Memphis purely to capture him, to return with him, alive or dead.

"The Pharaoh wants my blood badly," he said grimly. "The High Priest is already beset with the fear of my vengeance."

The girl's hand closed on his arm and held it with a continuous pressure.

The men, minute, but clearly discernable were now passing into Thebes. For some minutes they were lost to sight, but then they reappeared in a body on the southern outskirts.

"They are heading straight for the barracks," Ineni explained.

At the barracks, which Ineni and the girl could make out from their cache, the riders came to a stop. Odd ones dispersed in different directions, doubtless to glean information of the passing of the fugitives. The remainder dismounted and disappeared into the poor, inadequate buildings.

There was a delay of only a few minutes before the scouts were returning from their search for information. In a few minutes more fresh horses had appeared and fresh men.

And in no more than fifteen minutes in all, the party had moved on south, some of the men fresh, some of the horses fresh, but with many of the band which had just arrived.

"They are enthusiastic," Ineni said. "There must be a rich reward for my capture."

The body of soldiers disappeared, slowly, along the valley until the drift of dust in their wake was settling down once more below the tops of the palms.

The girl breathed an audible sigh of relief.

"We're safe," she whispered.

"Not yet," Ineni cautioned. "They've left many of the arrivals in the barracks to rest. A chance remark in the village by someone who many have seen us come out here, but not been questioned, and we'll be fleeing again."

"What shall we do?" the girl asked.

"We'll stay here until nightfall," Ineni answered, "And then we'll try to get a boat and follow up the river. Go to sleep again."

At sunset, with the twilight falling quickly over the valley, they climbed carefully down from their hide-out to the sands below.

They and the horses were refreshed and recovered.

"We may have to trade the horses for a boat. It would be risky to steal one," Ineni said as they rode at a canter across the desert to the outskirts of Thebes to the north, away from the military barracks.

"It will be much more pleasant in a boat," the girl said, thoughtfully, "But more difficult to escape if they locate us."

"We can keep to the far bank," Ineni explained. "We might even get some fishermen's clothes from someone. They will so little expect us to be on the bosom of the river that we will probably be much safer."

Cautiously they trotted through the palms which surrounded the northern perimeter of the city. At this point, set well apart from one another, were the houses of the merchants and, nearer the broad vista over the Nile, those of the noblemen.

116

"We shall have to take a chance," Ineni said, softly. "These villas are far enough from the river bank for their occupants not to have heard of any of the afternoon's incidents."

Quietly they rode up to the first villa and were conducted in by the gate guard. Inside they were shown into the presence of the owner of the house.

He was a fat merchant, with a belly which ballooned out as if his tunic would be unable to contain it and a fat fleshy face in which the eyes danced with merry wickedness. Around him when he received the pair were three armed men—his personal bodyguard.

Ineni restrained himself from reaching for his sword. Merchants, he remembered were the most disliked men of all classes. They needed bodyguards.

The merchant's little eyes flickered over them as he rose to meet them. His glance took in everything—the evidence of their days of fast travel, the girl's torn robe. His eyes rested on the girl as he came forward and then he was bowing before them.

"What happy chance brings a noble and his wife to my house at this hour of the night?" he fawned. "I am indeed honoured."

He ushered them to a divan before his own and ordered wine to be brought.

A few pleasantries followed while the merchant cast quick, beady glances at the girl, his eyes lingering on the pronounced fullness of her breast under the dishevelled robe.

Then Ineni broached the object of their visit, explaining that they needed the boat immediately if possible.

"You are continuing your journey tonight?" The man

raised his thick, short eyebrows. "I had hoped I might be able to offer you the poor hospitality of my house."

"No, our time is short and we must reach Assuan soon to meet an old friend before his departure," Ineni told him. "At another time your graciousness would have been most acceptable."

"My heart is very sad that you cannot stay," the merchant said, and his eyes flickered once more over the girl, dwelling on the protruding roundness of her upper breasts above the robe.

"But," he continued. "I doubt very much if I shall be able to trade with you for at this moment I have but one boat—my own. And it is worth more to me than five horses."

"I should like to see the boat," Ineni said.

"By all means."

The merchant rose from his divan and waddled heavily to the door. There he stood aside politely to allow his visitors to pass. As the girl followed Ineni through the door, the fat man's eyes gloated down on the firm thrusting jut of her bosom. As he walked after them, his eyes bored into the girl's buttocks as they twitched and rippled under the eddying folds of her robe.

The bodyguard followed as they walked in slow procession through the still, empty land to the Nile. At its bank they descended some steps in the built-up stone embankment and found themselves looking down on a neat, strong-looking craft.

It was big, presumably to take the weight of the merchant, and its cedarwood lines were well shaped for speed. There were several oars and at one end a canopy which could be taken down if necessary.

"To keep the sun off beautiful heads," the merchant said, and his eyes flickered greedily over the girl again.

"I cannot give you more than two horses," Ineni said firmly.

"Well, let me see the horses," the merchant murmured.

Slowly they trooped back to the villa.

The merchant studied the horses, running his hands over them with unsmiling face.

"They are lean," he announced. "They have been worked hard. I would need five of them. But perhaps we can discuss the matter further."

He motioned for the party to enter his house once more and, from desperation, Ineni led the girl into the villa again. He had seen no cheaper looking boat on the river.

The merchant muttered a few words and his bodyguard did not follow them into the room where they had met.

The merchant seated himself on the divan. His glance lingered on the girl's robe where it folded, creasing tightly around her hips and outlining the bulges of her thighs.

"I think we can come to an agreement," he said, raising beady, smiling eyes to Ineni. "You see I know who you are."

Ineni's hand flew to his sword. There was no point in calling the man's bluff. It did not take much deducing if he had heard reports of the chase that afternoon.

The merchant spoke sharply, quickly, but with confidence.

"No don't touch your sword, I beg of you," he said. "I am not going to give you away."

Ineni sat tensely, hand on his sword hilt and the man continued:

"Your fame has reached us from Heliopolis and I am a man after your own heart. The priests rob me whenever I bring back a cargo from the land of Punt or Nubia or our

119

empire in the east. I am not concerned that the poor would benefit from your ideas, but I am concerned that the merchants would. So you see you have in me a strong sympathizer."

He paused and Ineni did not relax his grip on his sword.

"What then do you intend to do?" he asked.

"I shall take your horses and give you the boat," the man answered. "But I shall demand one thing more of you."

"Name it," Ineni said.

"The girl with whom you have fled," the merchant replied boldly. "I would like her just for an hour—or even less."

"You miserable . . ." Ineni rose to his feet.

"No. Just consider the proposition." The merchant was calm and he motioned Ineni to his seat again. "I hold the whip hand. Outside this door are my bodyguard awaiting the least command from me. To fight with them would bring the whole neighborhood around you and there is a strong military contingent in this city. You might kill me. You might kill all three of them. But you would be hacked down by the soldiers and your lady would be mercilessly raped—not once but a score of times."

The fat merchant paused and his little eyes grinned blandly up at Ineni.

"But if you meet my wishes," he said. "Then you will have the boat and in me a man who would not breathe a whisper of your visit to anyone."

"Even if we did as you wish, how could we trust you?" Ineni snapped.

"Ah. That is the difficulty." The merchant sighed and his gross belly trembled like a jelly. "I have the reputation of driving a hard bargain, but I also have the reputation for

keeping my word once given. You would have, I'm afraid, to take my word. But really you have no alternative.''

Ineni looked down at the girl, his thoughts confused. He was not sure of the merchant. He did not want to subject the girl to further degradation. But she decided for him.

"We have no choice," she said softly. "I will do as he wishes.''

"It is the women who are wise," the merchant said to Ineni, his eyes fixed on the girl. His eyes as they roved were already gloating on the firm, rounded flesh which was soon to be his, naked in his arms. He was already undressing the girl in his mind.

Ineni turned back to the merchant, eyes narrowed.

"It is true we have no choice," he said, through clenched teeth. "But if you don't keep your word, or if you hurt her, I shall wreak my vengeance on you no matter what else befall.''

"I shall keep my word, never fear," the merchant assured him. "Now if you will leave us, my men will see that you are well dined and that the boat is filled with provisions for your journey.''

Ineni looked at him for a long moment, glanced at the girl, who kept her eyes on the ground, and then marched swiftly from the room.

Left alone with the merchant, the girl looked up at him, moist lips apart. There was no point in delaying the ordeal and she had better give him fun in case he changed his mind from disappointment.

The merchant wheezed to his feet, little eyes narrowed with desire, and came heavily towards her. He sank down on the divan beside her and pushed her onto her back, falling with her.

"You beautiful flower," he whispered.

And then his hot, pudgy hands were holding her breasts, moving over them as his breath began already to pant with desire. As if he couldn't wait for it to be under way, he began to pull at her robe, tugging the folds apart so that her breasts shot cheekily into view.

His eyes doted over the twin mounds and then his hands were on them again, pressing them, moulding them. His fat lips came down, brushing her neck as she lay, waiting, and closed over her nipples.

She felt his teeth pulling on them, lips sucking on them and a spasm which was half horror, half passion, shot through her.

But his lips had moved away and were pressing into the softness of hers, his thick tongue intruding into her mouth and below her breasts his hand was travelling hotly against her cool skin as it pushed before it the falling draperies of her robe.

She felt the robe whisking down her hips, his hand following it, hot and degrading at every new place it touched. It roved hotly over the soft mound of her abdomen and was coursing down her thighs, up and down on the silky insides of them. Suddenly his fingers had moved up between her legs and entered the intimate place. There they were scourging the flesh, moving, exploring into the depths.

The merchant moved up and looked down at her. His eyes feasted on her breasts, her hips, the whole beautiful naked length of her and then he seemed to be in delirium.

His breath had become a furious whine and he pulled at his rich tunic, tearing it from him with as little ceremony as he had disrobed the girl.

The tunic fell away and, determined to play her part as she had already played it before, the girl moved her hand

down his gross, hairy belly until her fingertips ran lightly on his great, hairy penis. It seemed strange that such an obese man could get such a large, passionate erection.

She ran her fingertips lightly over its heat and over the hairy heat of his testicles and he began to writhe his hips, caught her in a crude roughness of uncontrollable passion and pushed her forcibly over onto her face.

Lying there, face pressed into the divan with the man wheezing above her shapely, helpless buttocks, she thought that he was going to force himself into the hole between them. But as he pulled her to her knees, she realised that this was another position, that he was too fat to have her lying on top of him, that this way was easier.

He pushed her body down, hot, fat hands gripping her sides tightly, so that she felt her bottom fly up to him, had her face crushed on her hands on the divan. For a moment she was horrified at the thought of this huge, fleshy man leaning, breathing stentoriously above her back, looking down at the stretched expanse of her buttocks, the revealed little anus between.

But then he had stuffed his thick, hot rod into the cool moist channel between her legs and she gave a start at the pain.

Above her the merchant thrust in tightly. It was a long time since he had had such a young and beautiful girl and the feeling of relief at the warm foreign pressure around his organ filled the man with a crazy delirium.

He wriggled his fat, naked hips more dexterously than he would have thought himself capable and his great, fat buttocks swayed. He forced his fatness into the girl from every angle, moving his hips slightly for new and greater pressure. His throat was choked in a continuous moan of ecstasy as he felt the tight channel clamping his heat,

seeming to try to contain it in a smaller space than was possible.

He burst right into the girl up to the hilt, his fat belly resting fleshily on her buttocks as, with his hands, he spread her vagina wider under the flap of his belly and pressed with an unrelieving pressure on her slender back.

Ravished under him, the girl felt as if the whole of her belly had been scraped of entrails and filled with a great moving block of substance which was moving in fast friction to a bursting point.

She felt the man's fingers groping down between her legs, felt them pulling apart the sore lips of her vagina so that she had to groan.

The great thing inside her drew back, relieving her a little of the hot, thick heat and then it surged right into her belly again, fiercer than before, while fat thighs spread her thighs, almost knocking them under her so that they made, with her pelvis a great, obtuse V, inverted and swaying back at him as he thrust forward.

The girl closed her eyes, imagining the intrusion to be from the loins of her true master. Intuitively she realised the necessity of making the merchant feel that the union was complete. But she could not simulate passion easily.

So she wiped the image of her ravisher from her mind, placing there a picture of Ineni and she felt the stirrings swirl inside her belly.

The merchant's teeth were clenched, now, as he punished the girl with each battering-ram thrust. His loose, fat breasts jumped up and down like a woman's, his great belly flattened against his victim's bottom, oozing out and enveloping it.

He was unable to see his organ for his great paunch, could only feel the sweet sucking in the lower regions out

of sight where he and the girl met. His breath was breaking out in long wheezing gasps, his penis seeming to be pulverized as if it would be crushed to pieces by the intense sensation. His hands pushed the girl rudely in a concave as his organ seemed to thicken and grow like a blossoming flower.

Beneath him he heard the girl cry:

"Come on, come on. Now, now."

And his passion flared into a dazzling climax so that he seemed unable to see. There was a long moment of waiting. And then the warm, excruciating flowing of relief—and re-flowing. He emptied his great store of desire into her in a long, almost continuous flow, grunting and gasping with the relief.

Under him the girl breathed a sigh as she felt his brutality waning. Her half aroused desire flickered out like a spark and she was aware only of her shameful position on hands and knees, her loins raised and thrust at the obscenely gross, satiated loins of her unchosen lover.

The merchant rolled off her, flopping on his fleshy back on the divan, his great paunch heaving, tongue flicking dry lips.

The girl dressed, hoping he would not demand more of her. He lay for some time with his fat penis hanging limply between his great bulging thighs. After a while he scratched his testicles, heaved himself to his feet and began to don his tunic.

"I think the bargain was a good one," he said, grinning lewdly at the girl. "My only regret is that I am getting too old to insist on my full reward."

The girl smiled at him. She could not risk a change of heart on his part at this stage.

"Well, everything should be ready for your departure,"

he said when he had dressed. As they left the room he patted her buttocks and for a moment the girl was afraid his lust might revive, but he made no further advances.

In another room Ineni had eaten and food was given to the girl in preparation for the journey. Ineni was silent. He did not want to cross the merchant but he dared not give vent to his feelings.

At last they were ready. The merchant accompanied them down to the river where provisions had been placed in the boat and all was ready.

"How about your men?" Ineni asked, as the members of the bodyguard unmoored the craft.

"Don't worry about them," the merchant assured him. "They are absolutely loyal to me. No word of your coming will pass their lips."

A cold, dank smell arose from the almost still waters as they cast off into the broad, black stream. The merchant and his men watched them into the darkness.

Ineni rowed strongly across the flow of the current. The boat cut smoothly across the great expanse like a small, dark insect. His muscles lengthened and flexed with a steady rhythm. Neither he nor the girl spoke a word.

In silence and with a great cold silence around them, they reached the palm-fronded far bank. A few yards from it, Ineni relaxed his stroke and pulled them more gently against the current up the broad water highway to Nubia.

Between them and the barracks of the soldiers there was, now, a dark, misting stretch of water some half a mile in width. In the shadow of the palms sheltered from the moonlight they could not be seen from the far bank.

Ineni kept up a slow, steady pull so that soon he was sweating in spite of the chill. The girl shivered and pulled her robe close around her.

There was no falling off of pace and no word to break the silence until Thebes was well behind them, enveloped in the darkness.

"We must pray that the merchant keeps his word," Ineni whispered, pausing for a brief rest.

"He has every reason to," the girl said with a trace of bitterness.

"I could have killed him for his baseness," Ineni muttered fiercely. "You were very brave."

"He was disgustingly fat," the girl said with a shudder. "I hope we meet no more of his kind."

Ineni resumed his strong pull. The current against them was negligible and the boat slid through the water like a lizard through the sands.

"We will keep on for the few hours before dawn and then we will rest for a time," Ineni said. "Then during the day we must continue slowly. It will be only a matter of time before the Pharaoh's men find, from questioning villagers and townsfolk, that we have not continued along the road. Then they will be back."

"Surely they will scour the river," the girl said.

"I think that first they will decide we have fled—as in fact we did—to the western hills," Ineni said. "They will search the cliffs around Thebes for a day or more before they return in a quandary to the river route. But we shall see."

In the pale light of dawn they moored the boat at a small, wild oasis. In the shade of the riverside trees they slept for some hours.

The sun was high when they awoke.

For several hours they continued until Ineni's arms were aching continuously with the unyielding effort.

At a small town they were able to trade one of Ineni's

127

captured swords with a fisherman for a piece of cloth, a fishing net and a light fishing harpoon.

They rowed on and, at a deserted oasis, Ineni was able to build up a small mast and make a rough sail with the cloth. There was no wind that day and with the sail dragging limply, Ineni continued to row.

During the night there was a breath of wind and they were able to scud along at a good rate for some hours while Ineni kept watch and the girl slept under the canopy. By late evening they had reached Assuan and passed through it towards the first Cataract where the Nile broke up into numerous channels flecked with rocks and boulders and surrounded by wild mountainous country.

They slept again and with the dawn, Ineni was forced to row once more as the wind had dropped.

Towards the middle of morning, the girl stiffened and stared, beyond Ineni up the rough desert road running parallel with the far bank. Ineni twisted in his place and stiffened too at the pall of dust growing nearer, drifting out across the water.

He answered the girl's unspoken question.

"On their way back if I'm not mistaken."

With feverish activity he pulled the boat in to the bank, told the girl to lie quiet under the canopy and stripped off his robe. Completely nude, he strung the fishing net over the side of the boat and seized the harpoon.

As the cloud cleared and a large body of men emerged, thundering north towards Thebes, they passed a naked fisherman, lunging with his harpoon far out across the water.

The dust cloud was settling again to the north before Ineni put down the harpoon and donned his tunic. He chuckled quietly.

128

"They were slow deciding we had tricked them," he said. "It is as I had thought. They are returning to Thebes to take up the chase again from where they last had news of us."

A thought occurred to the girl.

"If they go to the house of the merchant, they may find our horses," she said.

"In that case they will slit his throat," Ineni chuckled. "But we have a good lead."

In a short time they were wending their way through the rapids of the first Cataract close to the old boundaries of Nubia. Ineni was a skilful oarsman and his skill was thoroughly tested as the boat was tossed between the jagged rocks in midstream. Despite a buffetting, however, the boat stood the strain well and they emerged into the calm but stronger current beyond.

For days, which seemed so many that Ineni and the girl lost count, the boat struggled southwards, sometimes by the strength of Ineni's arm, sometimes by the faster billowing of the sail.

During their brief rests, Ineni began to lay his plans, plans which had lain dormant in his mind since he had first decided to flee south to Nubia rather than to Libya or the Asian Empire.

The girl listened attentively while he explained his hopes to her.

Ever since the days when the Pharaoh had made his first tentative advance into the wild, southern land, many centuries ago, Nubia had borne the yoke of his sovereignty with little relish. There had been uprisings, large-scale revolutions and although now Egypt held nominal sway over nearly the whole of the southern country, the governor's position was precarious. Numerically it was well known

that Nubia was strong. All it needed was a leader with the breadth of vision to plan a conquest of Egypt.

"Nubia's sons are ever in an attitude of revolt," he told her. "The only possible reason for the present peace is that they are unaware of the weakness of Egypt at this moment. I can give them that information. I can lead them with all the knowledge they need against the half-empty arsenals of their overlord."

"I am afraid for you," the girl said, quietly. "I think I would prefer to live in a beggar's hut and be safe than endure the unrest which surrounds a throne."

"One is never safe in a beggar's hut," Ineni assured her. "One is ruled by oppression, starvation and all that the throne fails to pursue justly. It is for the beggar that I wish an overthrow in Egypt."

The girl sighed.

"I would still prefer a life of peace with the man I love," she said.

"You will be happy when it is done," Ineni said with a smile. For more than a week they rowed and sailed up the Nile through villages, towns, oases and long, bare patches of desert. Ineni's body had become tuned to the work and from under the canopy the girl watched him during the long hours of moving on into Nubia. When the food ran out, Ineni traded one of the daggers for more. All was serene and peaceful as they came nearer and nearer to their objective of war.

Towards evening, they approached the wilds of the second Cataract. And it was here, as Ineni prepared himself for the ordeal of negotiating the rapids that they passed right under the noses of a large band of Egyptian soldiers.

The country was wild, rugged and tree-covered. Amongst

130

the trees on the bank farthest from the slowly sailing boat, the soldiers were resting.

By the time the girl had seen them, the Egyptians, some fifty strong, had spotted Ineni's rich tunic.

It was too late to do anything except continue. Ineni bent his back to the oars to add to the sail power and the craft sped forward in a burst against the stream as cries and activity erupted in the Egyptian camp amongst the trees.

"They didn't all return to Thebes," Ineni panted. "We underestimated them."

The girl crouched, half-sheltered by the canopy, looking back along the far bank. She didn't speak. She realised as well as Ineni what a tough spot they were in.

Ineni's muscles bunched as he propelled the boat against the faster-flowing, foam-flecked stream. Already rough rocks were protruding near the banks on either side.

From the far edge of the river came a thundering of hooves as the enemy swarmed out in a scattered bunch from the trees. An arrow curved over the river, dropping short of the boat, and another, and another.

Ineni twisted and peered upriver. They were approaching the first low terraces of the cliffs. Although they were out of arrow-range at the moment, the river steadily narrowed between the cliffs until it was no more than a couple of hundred yards across. There they would be an easy target for the archers.

Along the river bank the fleet arab horses were fast overhauling the boat as Ineni stood up to guide it through the increasingly treacherous rocks.

"We haven't a hope if we continue," he called to the girl, over the rushing of the cascade. "We'll have to try and pull in to the near bank and hide in the hills."

The girl's eyes rose up the broken sides of the cliffs,

now almost upon them, and then dropped to the almost continuous reefs of rock barring them from the bank. She stared back at Ineni where he struggled with the oar, fending off sharp, jagged spires of stone.

"There's nowhere to land," she cried desperately.

Ineni didn't reply. His sharp eyes scanned the line of foam-washed rocks. She was right.

The Egyptian horsemen were now riding level with and ahead of them, loosing further arrows into the stream as it narrowed, coming nearer and nearer to their range.

Some spurred on their horses over the rough, broken undulations of rocky ground, ready for the ambush at the stream's narrow point.

Ineni's face was tensed in desperation.

"We'll have to turn back and try to reach the bank at a clear spot," he shouted. "Pull down the sail."

Frantically, the girl began to do as he ordered. There was no time or room to turn the boat. They began to drift back with the current, stern first.

There was a shout from the bank and downstream, behind them, a dozen horses splashed into the river where the rocks disappeared and the foam became a thick, bubbling eddy. They were trapped.

Ineni took his spear, loosened his sword and prepared to sell their lives dearly if that were possible before an arrow brought him down. There was no further hope.

And then the girl gave a shout and the Egyptians in mid-stream began to tug their horses in an arc, directing them back to the banks.

Ineni whirled on the drifting craft. Behind them, where the cliffs towered over the rocky foothills lining the river, the Pharaoh's men were falling with their horses in a thick cluster before a shower of arrows. In the cliffs above them

were odd darts of movement, seen then unseen then seen again in different places.

Ineni stared in astonishment, almost forgetting to steer the boat with his oar through the last stretch of the rapids.

The horsemen behind them had now regained the bank and were urging their steeds towards the rearguard action that their comrades were desperately and not very successfully maintaining.

"What is it? What's happened?" cried the girl, not sure whether to be afraid or delighted.

"I don't know, but it's got us out of trouble for the moment," Ineni called back.

The river bank below the cliffs was fast becoming a charnel house. The Egyptains stood no chance. They were a perfect target with no shelter from above and they were unable to see their foe for more than a brief glimpse. There was some confusion, a wild shooting of arrows up the cliff face and then the remainder—no more than twenty men, wheeled and galloped back along the bank in the same direction as Ineni.

For a few minutes there was no sign of pursuit—and then a band of Nubian horsemen, some hundred strong appeared from what looked like the entrance to a pass at some distance from the river, and streamed back in a wide arc in the wake of the fleeing Egyptians.

Ineni pulled the boat down with the stream, back to its broad stretch. There he rowed gently in to the bank farthest from the fight.

The Egyptians swept by with hardly a glance in his direction. The Nubians, yelling their war cries, cries which made their big, dark figures seem like ferocious animals, fanned after them.

Undecided, Ineni and the girl stayed in the boat. There seemed to be dangers on all sides.

While they waited there was a sudden rustling of the trees on the river bank nearest them, a mere dozen yards from where they floated. Silently watching them on the bank, as they turned in a prickly heat of awareness, were a score of Nubians, horsed and armed to the teeth.

At the same moment, from the edge of the oasis on the far bank, the triumphant band from the hills appeared at a slow trot in thick, dark ranks. The Egyptians had fled to the north.

Ineni was quick to realize that he and the girl were completely at the mercy of these dark foreigners. He was quick to realize, too, that not an arrow had been fired at them, not a spear raised.

Impassively the long rank of men on their nearest bank watched them. They seemed to be waiting.

The far contingent drew level with the boat, as Ineni, grasping his spear in a fiercely clenched hand, watched with proud, fatalistic expression. The girl crouched, quiet and terrified in the shade of the canopy.

From the far bank a rider detached himself from the main group and rode his horse without hesitation into the broad waters. He was a big, imperious-looking man with large negroid features. He directed his swimming horse towards the boat without a drawn sword. Ineni watched and waited, clasping his spear, but making no effort to raise it.

The horse and rider passed behind the boat, rising gently with the slope of the river bed until they towered, both big and black, over the boat between it and the men on the bank.

The man on the horse, obviously the leader, raised his hand and addressed Ineni in a strong, bass tone.

"Welcome, Prince Ineni," he said. "The news of your coming had preceded you through the mouths of your hunters. We have been sent by the king of the southern land to conduct you to him. I am Tabaka, commander of the southern king's army."

Still unsure of the meaning of immediate events, Ineni could do nothing but indicate his complete trust and friendship.

"I bid you welcome Tabaka," he replied. "Your coming has filled my heart with thanksgiving where otherwise an arrow would have been."

"A heart well worthy of more than an arrow," the Nubian commander replied with a smile softening his broad features. "Stories of your prowess and your hatred of the Pharaoh who oppresses us have been held in our minds for many months. We are glad to be able to welcome you so opportunely."

At the Nubian's invitation, Ineni rowed the boat, beside the commander's swimming horse, across the river to the bank where the main contingent patiently and unstirringly waited. There he and the girl were given two of the men's horses and the march into the cliffs began.

In the cliffs were more horses and men and thus, with an enormous bodyguard, Ineni and the girl, rode south, through the pass to the banks of the Nile beyond on their journey to a point beyond the great city of Napata which marked the southern boundary of the Egyptian sovereignty.

On the long journey to the seat of the king of that part of Nubia which was not under the Pharaoh's domination, Tabaka explained how he and his men had come to be in the cliffs

above the Nile at that propitious moment—and the story went back quite a long way.

In the hilly country south of Napata was the seat of Sharmab, king of all of Nubia that had not fallen to the expansion of Egypt. There, in wild country, almost inaccessible to the northern "imperialists", so used were they to the flat plain of the Nile valley, were many thousands of trained soldiers.

For several years, Sharmab, who was in touch with many followers farther north in Egyptian-controlled territory, had been laying plans to recapture his land. The annual taxes exacted from the north of Nubia by the Pharaoh were heavy. All of Nubia wanted to be free of the yoke.

So far, however, Sharmab, with centuries of remembered defeat in his country's tradition, had not considered himself strong enough to hold northern Nubia against the Pharaoh's wrath even if he succeeded in taking it over before troops could be sent from Memphis.

When news had come far south with the straying pursuit, that Ineni—whose deeds and disagreements with the Pharaoh were well known—was fleeing, Sharmab had decided that here was a strong, useful ally, who, after all, could be fleeing to Nubia with no other aim than to take shelter within his territory.

Tabaka had been dispatched in the wake of the returning Egyptian force to find Ineni and conduct him safely to his destination. With foresight, he had ridden almost within striking distance of the Egyptians over the whole distance of their retreat from his country.

It was indeed the will of Amon, Ineni decided as they rode south across the great bend of the Nile, that events had turned out thus.

He had known something of the political and military

136

attitude of Sharmab—indeed it was guessed at by the Pharaoh—but that the Nubian king should so eagerly extend a hand towards him was more than he had hoped for with such immediacy.

So they rode south and south through weakly Egyptian-controlled land, where the few contingents of the Pharaoh's soldiery made no effort to hinder them. Until, at last, in a heavily fortified town to the south of Napata, they reached the very heart of Sharmab's stronghold.

Sharmab, an elderly, but still strikingly active man, greeted Ineni with a hospitality that was festive. It seemed, in fact, that his victory against such odds in Asia, had made him a legendary figure in the ranks of the southern warriors.

In the presence of Tabaka, the two men discussed for hours, the prospects of taking over northern Nubia. It was not until Ineni had convinced the Nubian king of the improbable retaliation of the Pharaoh and the certain success of the campaign, that he launched into the plan for a complete conquest of Egypt.

Sharmab was at first incredulous, later doubtful, and the arrangements for the night's festival were held over while the three men talked.

Ineni pointed out the softness and corruption into which Egypt had long been falling, he exaggerated the probable support he would receive from the interior if he were commanding a section of the invading army, he emphasized his knowledge of local conditions and deployment of arms and troops.

Sharmab listened, doubt still in his mind, but fading to a dim shadow. He had every reason to believe Ineni's information and he was, in addition, well aware of the Egyptian prince's remarkable qualities of leadership.

"And if we conquer Egypt? What then?" the old king asked at last.

"The choice will be yours," Ineni declared. "I suggest that an Egyptian as the new Pharoh would kill in the bud any attempt at revolt by the population."

"Especially one so idolized as you," the old king replied bluntly, with a smile.

"The choice is yours," Ineni repeated.

"And what would Nubia gain with a new Egyptian Pharaoh?" the king pursued.

"Nubia would gain complete independence, a vast treasure from the over-endowment of the tombs, a firm ally against all enemies and a yearly gift which could be decided upon," Ineni replied promptly.

The old king considered for a long time, a slight smile on his face.

"You have the reputation of a just and fearless man, Ineni," he said, at last. "But I think we must leave Egypt in abeyance until we see how we fare in the northern territory which is ours."

"As you wish. You may count on me no matter what you decide," Ineni assured him.

"Good. Let us relax for tonight. Tomorrow we can prepare."

Messengers were sent out forthwith to gather all the warriors of southern Nubia to the king's headquarters and then the festivities began.

A great space was cleared in the centre of the city, great fires were kindled in the middle and the music was played on instruments which were strange and new to Ineni.

While whole oxen and sheep were roasted over the fires, the two thousand men who had gathered to take part, watched a series of fierce, savage dances, performed by

both men and women. There was chanting and a clapping of time.

Ineni and the girl watched from the seats of honour in the foreground beside Sharmab and Tabaka. The girl was a little frightened by the strange, splendid savagery. Ineni revelled in the wild splendour and the warlike potential it reflected.

During the whirling of figures to the backgrounds of shooting red and yellow flames and the pulsing rhythm of movement, the roasting animals were torn to shreds and passed through the ranks of men. Huge carriers of wine were passed from hand to hand, falling, red as the blood that would fall, to the sand.

At the height of the dark fantasia of movement came the crowning spectacle.

A large, voluptuous Nubian woman danced in amongst the fires. Her legs and body, thinly covered with a tight robe of silk, moved in large angular movements, awkwardly as if she were possessed of some strange devil. Her unharnessed breasts jumped and quivered in heavy bouncing jolts under the robe. Her buttocks forced themselves against the thin material in lithe, suddenly changing to rigid, movements so that it seemed she must split the robe right up the back.

Into the fluid, changing light of the fires a donkey was led, stepping reluctantly, dragged by several muscular men who carried long, whiskery papyrus stems. In the centre of the clearing it was forced back on its haunches and held there in a squatting position.

The eyes of the spectators, distracted for a moment, swung back to the woman who was still dancing with peculiar wooden tension which seemed to jar her whole body into sudden, buttock-flexing, breast-quivering tensions.

While greedy eyes followed the contorted lines of her body, she suddenly changed the rhythm completely. With a quick snatch she had ripped away the robe and flipped it into the flames of a fire where it shrivelled and disintegrated immediately.

With the complete revelation of her heavy-breasted, heavy-hipped body, the angularity of movement changed to a sensual quivering. Her head went back on her thick, strongly sensual neck, her arms drifted out on either side of her body and her whole fleshy frame, from neck to knees shook in a long rippling movement which seemed to move downwards like a twirled rope.

Two thousand pairs of eyes bored into her dark skin, roaming like phantom fingers over the heavily bulging contours, lingering on the broad ovals of buttocks and breasts, the subtle tremors of her belly and thighs, devouring the insides of her legs up to the shaven, vague fleshiness of the volcano between them.

The men holding the donkey began to flick him softly with the papyrus stems as the woman danced around them.

The whiskery fronds delved gently between his back legs around the discreet, heavy sheath—and then on it in dabbing, caressing traces.

The donkey's tail flicked, his foot kicked out half-pensively. The men held him fast with ropes. And then like the prow of a great boat coming out of the rushes, the dark interior rod came probing into view.

There were guffaws of ribaldry from all sides at its gross size and the woman's eyes settled on it as she danced as if she would hypnotize it into further revealed surrender.

Soon it was protruding full length, stretching up at an angle close to the perpendicular from between the shaggy limbs of the donkey.

140

The woman moved in, like a shimmer of black light. In and in towards the donkey until she was almost between its legs.

Without altering her movement, she swayed down to her knees before the animal and grasped its penis with her hand to the ribald cheers of lusty throats around her.

The donkey began to struggle, but was held and the woman, leaning between its front legs, gently tickled the long, thick, black, rubbery length of flesh.

Ropes holding the donkey were tautened and his front legs pulled back, his body straightened a little to give the women clearer access.

Without any hesitation in the continuation of her fondling, the woman turned on the balls of her feet, kneeling. With her breasts hanging, heavily and her buttocks stretched, thighs apart, she wriggled back inch by inch, still caressing with her hand behind her, towards the enormous fifth limb of the donkey.

The animal's eyes moved about, his nostrils flared. He could feel the woman's naked back now rubbing up and down against his belly.

Releasing her grip of the massive animal organ, the woman crouched, sensually feeling her way with her crotch to the great rod.

She hovered above it for a moment, thighs wide and then let herself fall backwards. The great black thing ran into her like a sword, impaling her in the one irrevocable movement of her own falling momentum.

The woman uttered a great gasp which could be heard all around the clearing and then the ravished passage had closed over the animal and her buttocks were resting on his hairy belly between his back legs.

"She must be deformed!" the girl whispered in horror to Ineni.

The donkey had snorted and tried to struggle at the sudden enclosing of his sexual tube, but the men held him, muscles bulging with veins, as they strained on the ropes.

For a few moments, the woman rested, as if recovering from a wound and then, without rising from the impaling sword, she began to wriggle her hips in little worming movements, savouring the thickness within her with eyes closed, mouth wide, body quivering.

Tongues licked dry lips in the crowd and moved around the dry insides of mouths. There was a restive fidgeting.

Slowly, resting still on the balls of her feet, the woman lifted the strain from her buttocks, raising them, drawing herself up off the donkey's thick power so that her back indulged in a gentle friction with the length of his belly as she did so.

Up she rose, flexing her thighs so that long slim lengths of shining muscle stood out and with a sudden sucking release she slipped off the huge, rounded end of the bestial penis.

Her eyes opened, the skin around them still creased in a deep mesh of desire, her mouth closed for a moment, body relaxed and then she slumped back again so that the organ embedded her up to the animal's belly and her mouth opened wide again in a great unuttered cry and her eyes closed tightly in painful ecstasy.

The donkey wriggled, trying, against the pull of the ropes to stand and mount the woman, but he was securely held.

The woman's passage, which must have been as big as a cavern, sucked the animal's organ so that he snorted as she rose again. She seemed to rest on the tip, so that it was

142

just inside her—and then in a deflated rush, she flopped back on her buttocks once more so that the enormous cudgel burst into her again.

Gradually she increased the speed, sounds issuing now in a low-pitched moan from her open mouth, drawing herself up and letting herself fall, contracting her passage around the long intruder with fierce, squeezing pressure.

The woman's body rocked from side to side, scraping the animal's belly as she rose and fell. Her hands grasped her flexed thighs with indenting force and then moved backwards, clinging to the donkey's haunches, pulling him into her.

Her moan became a permanent grating noise hurtling from her throat and sometimes she choked. But not once did she slacken the speed and force of her thrusts as she revolved backwards and forwards with the bestial sex probing, expanding, growing hot and lustful inside her.

The donkey began to snort with violence, foam flecking his nostrils and dripping to the woman's thighs below.

Moving up and down at a great rate, the woman began to mouth oaths which Ineni could not understand, no doubt goading the donkey on to greater efforts.

Her body began to twist and writhe, jumping and screwing on the smooth, fleshy spear. Her body creased in slim lines of flesh as she leaned in cortortions. The men around began to shout and eventually to chant in time with her lewd sexual rhythm. Then, as her mouth opened so wide that she seemed unable to utter sound through it, they began to clap in time with her rapid rise and fall in addition to the chant.

Her breasts leapt and flopped in passionate undulations, her buttocks were widespread as they fell against the donkey's inside hindquarters. Her face furrowed and tensed

143

with strain until with a shrill cry and a rapid falling back in a lunging movement that impaled her with a crude, brutal strength, she had widened, opened and released her sexual flood between the donkey's legs.

Head hanging and flopping like a dolls' she went on riding up and down, up and down in a mechanical fury until the donkey's nostrils flared with purpose, teeth bared and a fury of snortings flew from his snout. The woman jerked as if she had been shot, as if an arrow had found its mark on the target of her open, unprotected passage.

She jerked up and down in the last pre-exhaustion flare of energy on the donkey's rod and then signalled to the men that his great, hot discharge had dribbled away. They heaved on the ropes, pulling the animal free of the woman and she fell forward, grovelling in the dust.

Nobody moved forward. She was left there, face down heaped in a ruined, bestially ravished exhaustion.

Then, the music, which had stopped during the act of intercourse, began, softly, again.

In slow, dragging efforts, the woman pulled herself to her knees, swayed to her feet, remained a moment, legs bowed apart as if the channel running up into her body between them was too painful to permit her to move.

As the music grew in volume, seeming to become a command, the woman moved her legs painfully together, shuffled a step, acquired greater ease and shimmered into the dance with which she had begun. Her body shuddered and quivered, breasts seeming to flick from side to side with incredible rapidity as if they were palm leaves.

Reaching the inner edge of the circle where the other dancers were watching in a crouching group, she changed suddenly to the angular movements, raising her legs in wide semi-circular postures in an engulfing, erotic fury.

The music began to fade and as it faded, the woman swayed, still in the dance to her knees before the watching group of her fellows. As the music disappeared on a long lingering note, she flopped back onto her haunches as if onto another invisible organ, and then forward to rest her head on her thighs.

With the final movement, the dancers behind her sprang into a whirl of activity, flying afresh into the arena, leaping, swaying, hip-jerking, erotically pairing until the woman was fogotten and the whole spectacle seemed to have been some weird, un-real phantom.

The spectacle and festivities continued long into the night until the fires had burned low, every morsel of meat had been devoured and such wine as had not been drunk was spilled over the sands.

It was approaching dawn before Ineni took the girl to bed in the annex of the king's makeshift villa which had been prepared for them.

Late the following day Ineni with Sharmab and Tabaka began to make plans for the conquest of northern Nubia. It was a straightforward matter for which Ineni's advocacy of straightforward tactics was eventually agreed to. He was well aware that there was not the slightest difficulty. The Nubians' fear in the past had been the psychological one of fear of reprisal from Memphis. Ineni, knowing the true weakness of Egypt was able to overcome that fear.

Within the next several days the nearby thousands of Sharmab's army began to pour into the headquarters until a great camp had grown up around the original nucleus of some two thousand men. By now, Ineni estimated, the Pharaoh would have been reached by the returning band of soldiers who would have to report the escape of their quarry and the attack made upon them by the Nubian

force. The Pharaoh, he decided, would almost certainly send an army of a very few thousands to teach the impudent Nubians not to meddle in the affairs of their overlords. He gave a quiet chuckle of satisfaction as from the brow of a hill near the camp, he overlooked the massed tents of the men he would soon command. There were some fifteen thousand or more.

A few days later the whole army moved slowly north with Sharmab riding nobly at its head, with Ineni and Tabaka in the place of his two lieutenants.

In the days that followed, they encountered virtually no resistance. Napata was taken by surprise. Elsewhere the Egyptian governing forces were either wiped out or forced to flee not only before the advancing army but under the harassing attacks of the rebelling population who seized whatever crude weapons they could find when they heard of Sharmab's coming and prepared to join him.

Astonished and overjoyed at the ease of their success the Nubian avengers swept on over their former territory. From commanding positions in the hilly country they overwhelmed any town or garrison which showed the slightest inclination to join battle.

Fired with enthusiasm they swept on to the first Cataract. There was no question, now, as to whether Egypt should be conquered or not. It was tacitly agreed amongst the leaders.

At the heights above the beginning of the plateau which was the valley of Egypt proper, Amon, Ineni was sure, played fate into his hands once more.

In the far distance from the direction of Thebes an Egyptian army was marching south to punish the recalcitrant Nubians.

Preparations were made quickly and efficiently despite

the huge number of men. Born into the hilly country, the Nubian soldiers knew how to make use of every inch of cover. The army vanished. And by the time the Egyptian scouts toiled into the rough pass through the cliffs everything around was as blistering and bare as the desert from which they had come. A cursory examination of the rocky edges of the pass confirmed the opinions they had formed beforehand. One rode back to bring the Egyptian army on, the other continued through the pass.

Signalled on by their leaders, the Nubian thousands moved in towards the pass's axis. They slithered in like an unseen breeze which is sensed intuitively rather than heard or felt. The scouts rode on.

Slight movements from vantage points and the archers were tensing their bows, waiting for the signal.

In deep, almost hidden ravines cut in the slopes above the pass the horses and chariotry waited.

The Egyptian army came on in a great cloud and quivering of movement like heat waves on the sands and Ineni thought of the time when an Egyptian army had moved on with exactly the same apparent unawareness while his own party waited in the hills to strike.

The Egyptians numbered somewhere between a thousand and twice that strength. They would be the Pharaoh's loyal and trusted men, Ineni decided. Nobody suspected of having any sympathy with Ineni would be sent to the country into which he had fled. Wholescale desertion was the last thing the Pharaoh desired with his military forces in their present feeble state.

On the far side of the pass, ensconced in the heights Ineni, knowing where to look, could make out the head of Tabaka. His was the signal which all were to follow.

The hills were silent as the Egyptians marched on, chariotry on either flank.

Into the pass the chariots took the lead coming proudly, majestically to their doom. Behind them marched the archers and spearmen, flagging a little with the long march.

Tabaka waited. Ineni, watching him across the defile waited.

In a rumbling, thudding, muffled advance, the Egyptian army passed beneath until the last line of men was taken in out of the desert to be enclosed in the solid rock which was to be the mass tomb.

Watching intently, Ineni saw Tabaka's hand move. His hand moved in the following instant and almost together, from either side of the pass a great shower of arrows fell thickly into the midst of the unprotected men below.

Horses reared, fell and stampeded; shields were raised above heads as the men raced desperately for shelter leaving a trail of dead and wounded across the breadth of the pass.

From their sheltering ravines, the Nubian horsemen rode up and then charged in a dangerously mad rush down the steep slopes to cut down the confused, fleeing remnants of the enemy.

The Egyptians had stood no chance from the start. And now they found themselves hopelessly outnumbered. Those who tried to escape through the hills were pursued and shot down; the remainder surrendered.

The Nubians could hardly believe in their success and clearly ascribed their good luck to the presence of Ineni.

There were hard, astonished glances from the Egyptian commanders when they saw who had been partly responsible for their crushing defeat.

From them, by clever and careful questioning, Ineni was

able to establish that the Pharaoh had no idea that the Nubian army was marching against him and that Egypt was far from being in a state of readiness to resist invasion.

During the day that followed, the victors rested on their laurels.

And during this time Ineni evolved a plan of conquest to which the King and Tabaka eventually agreed.

With their main force, the two Nubians were to continue up the river in a direct, frontal attack. They were unlikely to encounter opposition in sufficient strength of numbers to trouble them as the vast portion of the Egyptian army was stationed in the delta area and around Memphis.

In the meantime, Ineni, with a small force of some five hundred men would follow the line of hills to the west of the Nile, travelling in their shelter for the whole distance of the land at the most rapid speed possible until opposite the delta area. Once there, he would travel alone into Memphis and on to Heliopolis to gauge what support he might expect there. If, as he hoped, it would be considerable, he would return immediately to his waiting force and storm Memphis. He would then do his best to hold it, inciting his old-established supporters to revolt, until the main Nubian army arrived.

If, however, the support were not what he hoped it to be, he would hold his men in hiding in the hills until he judged it time for the army to arrive, and then attack Memphis at the time it was preparing its army to march south.

"The confusing effect will be worth many times its weight of numbers," he declared.

It was agreed that Ineni's band should have a day's start and under cover of the hours before the following dawn,

they reached the western range of hills and began to push at speed along them.

It seemed a lifetime later that they reached a point from which they could see the distant domes of Memphis, but, in fact, they had accomplished the journey without being detected, in a remarkably short time.

Dressed in the garb of a common soldier, Ineni crossed the narrow stretch of desert which formed the fringe of the valley, skirted Memphis and entered Heliopolis.

In his old city he made his way unnoticed through the market crowds to the villa of the governor, an old friend, who had been one of the band originally to suggest that Ineni should form the centre of an overthrowing of the present regime. It was vague rumours of this plan which had resulted in him being moved to Memphis under the eyes of the priests.

Awaiting his chance, Ineni scaled the wall surrounding the villa and, after a brief glance at the grounds, dropped down amidst the grape vines. It was the heat of the day and the servants were lazily unwary. Ineni entered the villa without being challenged and flitted between walls he well knew to the room where he knew the governor would be taking his afternoon repose.

The man was incredulous at the appearance of his unexpected visitor. He ushered him quickly into an unused room before having food and wine brought and then stood over him insisting that he eat before they talked.

When, refreshed, Ineni explained the events of the past weeks, his friend was overjoyed and eager for immediate action.

"Since your flight," he said, "there has been more anger than ever against the Pharaoh and the High Priests. But there has been no-one to lead the anger and the talk

into action. There is no doubt you will have many followers here and in Memphis. If you can give me twenty-four hours I will have everything organized.''

Thus it was arranged at dusk on the following day, when Ineni besieged the barracks of Memphis and stormed the Pharaoh's palace, the interior revolt should be ready to join forces with him.

Ineni left the way he had come, skirted Memphis again and was soon back in the hills with his small force preparing them for the patient wait they had to undergo.

The time seemed to pass very slowly in the hills. From blazing sun to its red twilight glow, the sudden fall of night and then the dawn softly touching the hills again.

By now, Ineni estimated, unless he had had any serious trouble, Sharmab, with his commander Tabaka must be in the area of the Fayum south of Memphis. Word had probably reached Memphis already of his coming.

Sure enough, as dusk approached there were signs of furious preparation on the desert plain outside Memphis. From their distant perch, Ineni and his men could see the sands clouding over with the tiny figures of men and chariots—an army forming to meet an approaching foe.

Within the city a garrison would be left to deal with any emergency.

Towards the end of the afternoon, the Pharaoh's army which, numerically, Ineni estimated to be some thousands less strong than the Nubian forces, began to move south to do battle.

In the hills the the little Nubian vanguard waited. A couple of hours later when the purplish evening light was misting the desert they rode down into the desert.

Racing across the broad stretch of country to the outskirts of the city, thundering over the rich maize fields, the

band was seen, peasants scattered from their path in terrified confusion, the alarm was raised within the city.

Inside, in the streets, surprised patrols were cut down and trampled underfoot by the horses, people fled in all directions and within a few minutes the city appeared deserted.

Descending on the barracks, Ineni heard the sound of fighting. As he and his men swept into the rough square before the mud buildings, they were confronted with a minor battle which raged in full view and beyond view in the narrow corridors of the men's quarters.

At the sight of the new force many of the men threw down their weapons, others fled. The governor of Heliopolis had virtually presented Memphis to Ineni.

Leaving a lieutenant to reorganise the reinforced strength of his band, Ineni led a score of men at a gallop for the Pharaoh's palace.

They were met on the steps leading up to the colonnade surrounded by a group of armed priests. The Pharaoh, himself, would be at the head of his army marching south, but it was obvious to Ineni that these men were protecting somebody within. It could be nobody but the High Priest.

The battle on the steps was a fierce one. Ineni fought with a bitter strength and the priests countered with the strength of desperation in face of a world which was falling from under their power.

Forced back to the lines of pillars which shielded the inner court and rooms, the priests sold their lives with courage. As their numbers decreased, Ineni forced his way through to the inner court and at a run, the smaller court beyond that.

In the courtyard a brazier was burning, throwing a light as far as the surrounding portico. Ready for trouble, tensed

to receive it, Ineni heard a bow twang and flung himself on his face.

The arrow ricocheted from the stone of the archway and slapped to the dust. Almost before it had fallen, Ineni was on his feet and had hurled himself into the gloom of the portico.

For some seconds he remained crouched against the broad protection of a pillar, staring from his dark shelter to the menacing stretch of blackness shrouding the portico at the far side of the courtyard.

He could see nothing at all, was unable to tell if he had one man or a dozen to contend with.

And while he crouched, all his senses keyed to receive the slightest impression from the darkness, the High Priest's voice cut out from the long length of darkness opposite.

"Prince Ineni, are you willing to come to terms?"

Ineni's laugh echoed eerily amongst the dark pillars.

"Tomorrow Egypt will have a new Pharaoh," he called back. "There is no need for me to make terms."

"I will obey your wishes," the High Priest's voice declared from the gloom. "I will obey your wishes in all things. You may reduce the endowments, eliminate the sacrifices—do what you desire . . ."

"I desire your blood as the last sacrifice to Amon, to purge the corruption with which you have surrounded the god," Ineni cut in.

"My power would be useful to you even now," the High Priest's voice snapped back. "You would do well to consider my offer."

Listening to the words, Ineni became suddenly aware of their pointlessness and with swift decision he moved back from his pillar until he felt the wall of the courtyard against his arm. He stood there, holding his breath listening.

The High Priest's voice again crossed the lighted space between their refuges.

"Will you not answer?" he called.

As the words died in the blank emptiness of the courtyard, Ineni was aware of a faint movement close to him and a little in front, stealthily edging towards the spot from which his voice had been coming, in which he had been crouching while he answered.

Moving soundlessly, Ineni, in turn edged towards the noise until he could sense rather than see a man crouching in front of him. He heard the lightest whisper of breathing and, as his eyes peered into the gloom, he fancied he could see a patch of darkness just a little darker than the rest.

With a quick rustle his arm moved up and down. He had been right. The dagger sank between a pair of shoulder blades.

Ineni caught the man as he fell, drawing him backwards, lowering him without a sound to the floor.

Once again from the gloom, the High Priest's voice echoed.

"You would benefit greatly. There are hoards of treasures in the tombs of which only I know."

"I am not interested in . . ."

Ineni broke off, letting his words end in a strangled groan. He lifted the man at his feet and then let him fall with a thud which sounded across the court.

Immediately two young priests sprang out from different points in the portico and rushed to the spot from which Ineni's groan had issued. They came rashly and unguardedly and as they entered the gloom, Ineni cut them down with his sword one after the other.

Silence hung over the courtyard and then the High Priest called out: "Is he dead? Is it done?"

There was no answer; nothing but fresh, pregnant silence. Ineni waiting, could picture the High Priest's confusion.

"What has happened? Answer me." The voice contained a note of shrill panic.

Again silence. Within the courtyard it seemed a quiet other world which had nothing to do with the noise of continued battle beyond its walls.

"Where are you? Answer me. Answer me!" The High Priest's voice rose in brittle fury.

Swiftly Ineni stripped the daggers from the bodies around him and flitted along the portico.

Silently reaching the far side of the courtyard, he hurled one of the weapons through the darkness between the pillars to a point beyond that from which he judged the High Priest's voice to have come.

It hit the ground with a hollow clank and there was a sharp intake of breath and a soft scurry of movement in the gloom. Ineni waited for several seconds and then he flung the second dagger to a point between himself and the High Priest.

There was a muttered oath. It must have seemed to the priest that he was surrounded by demons. And then, with his tunic flapping, his bow in his hands, the High Priest had forsaken the shelter of the portico and was running across the courtyard, trying to cover all directions at once.

Watching from the darkness, unseen, Ineni raised his spear and let fly. It curved through the court, a glittering streak in the firelight.

The High Priest sensed rather than saw it coming and dropped on his face. In the same instant, Ineni, sword bare, rushed from the colonnade.

Feverishly the High Priest grabbed for his bow which had slipped from him in his fall. He found it and, unable

to take his eyes from Ineni, racing like a madman towards him, searched with clumsy fingers for his quiver of arrows. The quiver, too, had swung round his body in the fall and, as his fingers grappled madly for it, Ineni was suddenly too close for it to matter.

The High Priest lashed the bow at Ineni, rising and drawing his sword in the same moment. His face was furrowed in fear and anger. It seemed to him that Ineni was some sort of god, immune from mortal danger.

Ineni ducked from the wild sweep of the bow. At the same time, he scraped his flat-bladed sword in the dust and flicked it up into the High Priest's face. In the second for which his adversary was blinded Ineni plunged his sword into his belly. The blood gushed in a sudden flood and showed red and spreading through the man's tunic.

The face of the High Priest was, for a moment, clouded over with a look of horror and then he fell slowly forward, doubled over in the dust. The blood seeped thickly into the sand, spreading in a patch of dark wetness from under his body.

For a few minutes, Ineni stood looking down at the crumpled heap. It seemed to him that with the fall of the High Priest there was nothing truly left to conquer. It seemed that Egypt could start afresh building up the glory which it had all but lost. With the death of the High Priest, the corruption with which he had surrounded himself and entangled the whole of the land, would find itself like a line of crops without a channel of irrigation.

But Ineni was brought back to the immediate present by the sound of fighting, still, in the outer court.

He ran to the archway. In the outer court, the little band of priests were still holding their own. There were several

dead of both parties and the numbers, now, appeared to be roughly equal.

Ineni ran back to the body of the High Priest and dragged it, dripping blood, to the arch. There he gave a shout and pushed the cooling corpse through before him to send it sprawling, all bloody, in the dust.

There was a cry of dismay from the priests. Their leader was dead. They were completely unnerved. Unable, even, to fight with any zest. It seemed that they were unwilling to live and, indeed, so it was that they were slaughtered by the Nubians.

Ineni and his band quickly returned to the square outside the barracks, where they found a small army already organized and awaiting them. The vast majority of Egyptians now seemed to have come over to the invaders and there were felicitations and congratulations for the Egyptian prince from several of his former officers.

Within an hour, Ineni was making a rapid march southwards from Memphis through the desert night.

The moon had now risen and shone gently on a serene river as the third force bent on death and destruction trekked south through the palms and out into open rise and fall of desert.

For several hours they moved south in a rapid advance until in the still night air the faint sounds of battle reached them from some point beyond the intervening waves of dunes.

They pressed on with renewed energy. For those who had joined Ineni's ranks, this hour heralded, in the case of the mercenaries the possibility of reward such as they would never receive under the Pharaoh, and, in the case of native Egyptian troops, the chance to place on the throne a leader in whom they could really trust.

The faint buzz of distant noise became gradually clearer, more varied and individual in its soundings until, riding up over a final peak, Ineni saw, stretched before him in panorama a massed tangle of confusion.

It was difficult at first to make out what was happening, but, as the fresh body topped the peak behind Ineni and came into view on the horizon of those in the heat of battle, it became clear that the Pharaoh was retreating. Having dashed themselves at the wall of the Nubian forces and been beaten off, the Pharaoh's men now saw, what appeared to them to be a fair-sized army of reinforcements marching down to join them.

Watching the chariots and men streaming back towards him, Ineni ordered the Nubians in his force to stay to the rear.

Sharmab had halted his pursuing army at the sight of what appeared to him, also, to be a strong, fresh reinforcement for the Pharaoh, and now waited, regrouping his warriors.

Ineni held his archers ready. Behind them, horse and chariots tensed, waiting for the order.

The Pharaoh's retreat began in ragged flight, but, as it was seen that the adversary had halted and there was no pursuit, the Egyptians slowed and moved back in more closely-packed, more orderly fashion.

Ineni sat silently on his horse waiting as the mass became clearer more distinct in detail in the approach. Shielded from view by Egyptian horsemen, he hung on the word to fire, hoping that Sharmab and Tabaka would be quick to realise the situation.

As the chariots surged back so close that the creaking of their wheels could be heard with the actual words of the shouting warriors trotting between them, Ineni passed his

158

order along the line of archers, who would appear to the Pharaoh's retreat to be simply standing by in readiness to deal with any sudden pursuit.

At close range, the final order whipped through the air and the arrows swept, like a push from a solid hand, into the first ranks of the retreat. Amongst the Pharaoh's men there was consternation, disbelief. And then, taking them, still, off guard, the chariotry and the Nubian horsemen raged down upon them like a plague.

The sight of the Nubian warriors in the "reinforcements" was not lost on Sharmab, unhappily watching the meeting of the two Egyptian bands from some distance south.

He saw his enemy falling like reaped corn and spurred his great army-machine into rapid action.

Across the intervening distance at breakneck speed they came thundering and the Pharaoh was caught in a trap.

Weight of numbers carried portions of the retreating Egyptians through the center of Ineni's attack and Ineni fell back on either side, letting the rush pass through and then sweeping in a harassing action along the flanks, while the warriors following Sharmab and Tabaka followed quickly, too, though the cleft in a rapid overtaking slaughter.

Psychologically, numerically and positionally, the Pharaoh was at a hopeless disadvantage. Nobody saw him fall, but he, the son of the gods went down. ingloriously somewhere in the ruck of the battle. The remainder of his men, either escaped in dregs to the north and east or surrendered.

With the dawn breaking, Ineni, Tabaka and Sharmab were discussing their different experiences in the van of the great army moving north to occupy the Delta.

Ineni learned that the Nubian army had enjoyed an almost leisurely advance up the Nile, without serious opposition at all until the Pharaoh had moved to meet them.

159

Ramses' forces had proved considerably fewer in number than the Nubians, but they had fought well with lightning attack and retreat until Ineni's arrival on the scene. The Nubians were jubilant with their triumph.

"Your advice has been sound, your judgment borne out in action," Sharmab told Ineni. "We could wish for no better ally as the new king of Egypt."

In the days that followed, Ineni was hailed by the people of Egypt with the joy and thanksgiving which his reputation as a champion of the oppressed warranted. He ascended the throne with ceremony and festivity, declared Egypt Nubia's ally against aggression, made public the other conditions by which Nubia had agreed that he should become the new Pharaoh and announced various administrative changes, benefits and curtailing of endowments and human sacrifice.

If there was anyone who plotted against the new king in spite of his revolutionary take-over, it was not apparent. Egypt was on the road to restoration and recovery.

Ineni sent an escort to Napata to fetch the girl to whom he owed his escape and present glory. She would become his Queen as he had promised—a fact that should link Syria to the land of the Nile with closer bonds.

As a special gift for Sharmab and Tabaka on the eve of their departure to their own land, Ineni ordered to be brought before him several very young girls who, as virgins, had been confined for sacrifice after the fashion of the former High Priest.

He had them brought into the hall of the palace he now occupied and ordered them to dance for his guests.

The girls were no older than eleven or twelve. Already their small, round breasts were taking on the firm, fleshy shape into which they would soon fully develop. Their

limbs were firm and well-formed with the tender, lightly-muscled flesh of the young. Their little buttocks tensed like round melons as they danced. Their faces bore the small-fine-featured prettiness of the aristocratic Egyptian. They were, as Tabaka described, delicate morsels for the palates of discerning men.

They danced the charming, willowy dances they had been taught with a shy diffidence, hardly daring to glance at the great men who sat in comfort watching them so intently.

On Ineni's invitation, his two Nubian guests picked out during the course of the dance, their partners for the night of initiation. And Ineni himself made a choice.

"If they please you, you may take them back to add to your harems. If not, I will add them to harems in Memphis," he said. "It is foolish, indeed to sacrifice to the knife such sweet buds as they are about to break into the blossom."

When Ineni clapped for the girls to be taken away, the three chosen for the men's pleasure were told to remain.

Ineni indicated to his guests where they could find rooms in which to indulge their desires, but Sharmab suggested: "Why not let the private enjoyment come later. The girls are shy. They will feel better if they are taught together. And is there not something stirring in the communal moaning of young souls in the pit of pain and desire?"

Ineni laughed.

"I had no idea you had such subtleties of taste," he said. "Is Tabaka agreed?"

"Certainly," the Nubian commander replied, with a smile. "It will rid the girls of any ideas they might form of being individually persecuted."

"It will also rid them of any ideas of being individually favoured." Sharmab countered, fiery old eyes atwinkle.

Ineni directed them to divans, well-cushioned and placed in the angles of the corners of the walls and each of the men began his sensual instruction of his favoured girl.

Ineni took his girl in turn to a divan. She was a pretty, little, soft-eyed creature with, already, a passion-provoking lilt to her breasts.

Ineni made her lie on her back on the divan. The girl, almost trembling with fear of the unknown, did so without a murmur and lay with her eyes closed, breathing in sharp little heaves.

Gently he undressed her, uncovering the swelling mounds of flesh with her half-developed nipples, laying bare her slim, soft figure with the little double crease across her abdomen and the slight down of hair where her legs ran into her ripening hips.

During the process the girl did not open her eyes as if she were afraid the scene would become, suddenly, terrifingly real if she did.

Gently Ineni ran his fingers over her small breasts, tickling them softly with the tips, working up to a stronger kneading of the hardening centres. The girl's hand had moved up in an attempt to cover her bosom when she first felt his touch, but he removed them gently and firmly and eventually she made no further effort to protect her uncovered protrusions from the fondling.

Standing over her, still beside the divan, Ineni ran his hands down her body. As he reached her abdomen, savouring the soft, jellyish texture of the skin, she uttered her first little murmur and caught his hand, wriggling over onto her side at the same time.

He turned her back into her former position, held her hands in one of his and let his other hand continue its exploration of her loins. His finger moved over the light

down and she pressed her thighs tightly together. He roamed on down her thighs, tickling them with the touch of a feather and the girl gave a little squeal and tried to wriggle away.

He encompassed her calves with the palm of his hand grasping them, experiencing the pleasure of containing their firm muscle at their thickest point, within his hand.

And then he moved up again, drawing his fingers over the flesh as if it were water which he wanted to feel but not disturb.

"Open your legs," he said softly as he arrived once again at the summit of her thighs.

The girl kept them as tightly closed as her eyes and made no reply.

"Open your legs, or I shall beat you," Ineni commanded, grinning to himself.

The girl hesitated a little longer and then reluctantly opened her thighs about an inch, holding her body tense, divining that here was the source of life and pleasure and misery all in one tiny area.

Ineni's probing fingers slipped gently up the last warm inch of thigh and suddenly tickled the young lips, hardly formed as yet. The girl wriggled away in sheer panic at his touch, snapping her thighs shut once more.

"Keep your legs open," Ineni ordered in a stern whisper.

Slowly the legs opened again, just a fraction. Ineni's fingers gently caressed the soft, intimate flesh once more and the girl wriggled away again in an automatic movement.

"I—I can't bear it," she whispered, voice trembling.

"It'll be all right in a minute," Ineni assured her.

His hand followed her thighs to their new position and this time, as his fingers crept between her legs, he held her

163

Ineni, a great hot bulge throbbing beneath his robe, now, persevered with the sensual exploration of the thick rod his two fingers made. The girl's cries dwindled to soft moans whose tone changed from pain to reluctant pleasure.

Standing over her still, Ineni withdrew and pulled off his tunic.

"This is what you will have to receive inside you," he told the girl.

Her eyes slowly opened, looked at his nude, shaggy body in fear and dropped in horror on the first penis she had ever seen. It stretched out over her like a boom and she stared at it, hypnotized, unable to speak.

"Oh no," she whispered, at last. "It would be impossible."

Looking down on her small, determined, aristocratic, little mouth, Ineni leaned against the edge of the divan, turned her face sideways toward his rugged stiffness and pressed the knob against her lips.

It grazed through her lips and brushed against her clenched teeth. She tried to turn her head away with a strong twist of her neck. But Ineni forced her back.

"Open your mouth," he commanded.

Slowly the girl's jaw line relaxed and the teeth unclenched. Ineni pressed, tensing his thighs against the divan and his penis burst through, her teeth grazing it, and was moving in the moist containment of her mouth.

He pressed against her face, constricting his loins so that a prickly passionate heat was concentrated in his jogging at the girl's lips.

"Use your tongue," he commanded.

The teeth seemed to relax so that, pushing backwards and forwards, he felt the soft pull of the lips with each movement and then the smooth, loin-flaming caress of the tongue as she learnt how to lick the intruding member.

165

Continuing in this fashion for some time, Ineni began to feel the thick concentration at his organ, the fire throughout his whole loins. It was almost too late to be able to stop, but slowly he forced himself to withdraw from the girl's mouth. He had other things in store for her.

With a quick movement, he climbed onto the divan and lay down beside her, feeling the warmth of her flesh, pressing along his body, flesh to flesh in an intimate heat.

The girl's eyes were open now and she looked at him with a glance that was half-frightened, half-defiant. He smoothed his hands down her warm body, watching the flesh bulge away in front of their movement and then yield under the advance.

He moved her legs apart and kissed her mouth for the first time as he did so. The mouth was soft but unresponsive and he forced his tongue between the soft, unresponsive lips to teach them that that was no way to be. His tongue raped her mouth for a while and the softly-breathing aperture contained him submissively.

With his face crushing hers, he moved his hand up over her body, cupping her breasts, stroking their undersides with quick caresses. The girl lay quietly as if she were trying to control herself, but her breathing when he withdrew his face from hers had moved his lips down to her nipples, was in rapid little gasps.

Once more he stretched his fingers like searching lizards down over her navel, her abdomen, through the down of soft hair and into the unresisting cleft.

The girl made no effort to prevent him from pulling her thighs wide before he inserted his fingers in a fresh attack. She began to squirm, shyly, trying to control herself, in some embarrassment.

Ineni rose on his knees and slipped between the girl's

legs. As he knelt looking down on her slim, softly-curved form, she tried to close her legs, terrified now she realized the moment had arrived. But his frame was big and unmoveable and she could do nothing.

He lowered himself down onto the writhing warmth of her body, flattening her breasts into stretched disks of flesh, feeling her hips brushing, alive under his.

"No, no. Not yet. Please, not yet!" the girl begged.

He kissed her neck, brushing his lips down the long, tensed firmness. He moved his hips on her, taking sensual delight from the warmth of sliding contact between them, with his penis crushed against her belly.

Catching her thighs he drew them up, against the force of her resistance so that they were resting in a nervous pressure along his sides. He held them there, soft undersides up while the girl choked with fear.

His penis was aching with a tight, bruised sensation to which the only relief could be a hard thrust into the soft, clinging swamp of her sex.

Slithering down her, his flesh rising in damp suctions from hers, Ineni guided his organ to the point where her vagina and bottom were thrust out towards it. The girl struggled in a sudden panic, trying to lower her thighs, but he held them doubled back towards her breasts with his elbows.

He glanced down to where his massive projection cleaved the space between their genitals, making a bridge. He could see the vague, upturned redness of the moist opening between her legs, seeming very small. He hesitated. And then with an upward thrust he sank into her with a groan of relief.

The girl cried out at the thick, determined entry. Her

vaginal walls gave before the rigid battering ram, containing it like a tight sleeve.

She struggled again, but Ineni held her and screwed in with little advances and smaller withdrawals. He felt the extra warmth of blood on his flesh and pistoned in and out with gentle contractions of his hips.

Beneath him the girl's pretty face, twisted from side to side on her neck, like the grassy tuft on a reed. Her lips were drawn back, teeth clenched and deep in her throat and chest she made heaving noises as if she were overcome with sickness.

Ineni was in sweet agony. The girl's passage squeezed his penis with a tight pressure such as he hadn't known before. The rest of his body was like dead matter compared with the sizzling fury of sensation which linked his loins with hers.

For a moment, a sharp cry, reminded him of the other occupants of the room and he glanced up. In their respective corners, Tabaka and Sharmab were also grinding out their passion. He could see Tabaka's slim buttocks hollowing and relaxing between the thighs of the girl whose belly he was penetrating. In the other corner Sharmab had his young virgin kneeling and widespread before him. He was giving her painful punishment for her initiation.

Thrusting in with a smooth rhythm, Ineni slithered his hips closer against the girl's inverted thighs, kneeling up, pressing his knees against the outside swell of her buttocks, pushing her thighs farther back in a contortion which brought a groan from her lips.

He could look down on her soft body trembling, see the flesh of her hips creased with the backward bending of her legs. He pressed her thighs outward away from her body, watching, jaw fiercely set, his pulsing rod storming be-

tween her legs, disappearing up to the hair of his loins, half-reappearing again.

The girl was moaning incessantly with the pain she would have to nurse for days. Her mouth was open as if she were trying to draw in air enough to breathe and Ineni lowered himself onto her breasts once more and plunged his tongue into her mouth as he continued with mounting, unbroken rhythm.

He moved his hands under her and her thighs fell back to a more normal position, holding him on either side of his hips. His hands moved under her buttocks and sank into their soft flesh. He squeezed and massaged them, drawing them apart. His finger rummaged under her thighs, feeling the clasping rim of her vagina where he entered her, feeling his own rapid, forceful invasion of her.

Then he moved his hands back under her tensing buttocks, drew them apart once more as she moaned and caressed her little anus with his fingertips. Jerking his hips with a growing fierceness as he felt the hot concentration mounting in intensity inside her, he wriggled a finger at the rubbery entrance to her back passage. She jerked at his touch, but he continued with his posterior insinuation until the tight little band relaxed and yielded and his fingertip penetrated into her from behind.

The girl gasped, her breath breaking in little explosions around his tongue.

Ineni felt the heat from his penis blazing throughout his genitals in an expanding wave. It grew and grew, hotter and hotter and he thrust his finger in and in, in time with his penis so that the girl rocked in something close to delirium at the double entry.

Every stroke he made brought a gasp from the girl and expanded the heat of his loins. His penis formed the

spearhead of the heat as if it were a twig being rubbed and rubbed until it would burst into flame. Hotter and hotter in a searing, killing sensation, until he felt he could bear it no longer and the girl was uttering little shrieks at the harsh stabbings.

He slowed to a concentrated grinding movement, panting, face taut with the potential.

And then with a final forceful, tearing entry the flame had broken out in a great flare and was burning, hot and thick into the girl, emptying itself up into the soft regions where his penis could not reach.

The girl choked and cried out, clasping and releasing his hips with her thighs in swift, agonized alternating movements. Ineni thrust into her in a long, sustained staccato undulation of loins and her tongue, learning, already, pushed into his mouth and collapsed there.

They lay together, exhausted, unmoving for several minutes. From the other corners of the room came the sounds of approaching climax and after a while they sat on the edge of the divan and watched the Nubian leaders indulging their passion.

Having accepted the pain, now, and remembering the final enjoyment, the girl studied the entangled figures with interest. Sharmab was proving particularly energetic for a man of advanced years. With every thrust he pushed the girl along the divan on her face and then pulled her back again by her hips onto his skewer. Tabaka had his young initiate in a contorted position so that she looked like a frog lying on its back: all thighs, belly and lower regions. Both girls seemed to be in a half swoon, overcome with either pain or pleasure.

With only seconds between them, the two Nubians con-

cluded their performances with great snorts of passion and shot their loins' juices into their sweet, fleshy receptacles.

Within a little time, wine and food was brought for all six and, with the terrifying deed now done, the girls were much less shy and nervous and drank and ate with relish.

"We have decided we shall take our young brides back to our country with your permission," Sharmab said, when the rejuvenating wine had put him in a good humour. "They will be a constant reminder of the success of our entire expedition."

"They are yours," Ineni replied. "And may they develop as an example to the rest of your harem."

The girls, both of upper middle class families—the artisans and merchants—begged tearfully to be allowed to stay in Egypt, but Ineni was adamant in sticking to his promise.

The following day the Nubian forces started on their long journey back to the southernmost tip of the valley they had taken by storm, to the wild, hilly country in which they felt at home.

Small detachments of them remained in the big cities to ensure protection against a counter-revolt. Although, on the face of it, the whole Egyptian army had now come willingly under the command of Ineni.

The Egyptian people were glad to see the Nubians leaving. Even in the peasants was a traditional pride which had no sympathy for a foreigner in occupation of the country which was their birthright, into which the gods had been kind enough to have them born.

There were some who thought Ineni had been unwise and unfaithful to his heritage to allow a certain number of the invading army to remain a controlling position.

It was in the quiet heat of the afternoon following the

171

morning on which the Nubians had left Memphis that
Ineni, with a small bodyguard from the Nubian residue
walked down to the market in the poor quarter of the town.
He wanted to see just how far improvements had to go to
make such a market into a useful, profitable field for the
poor man.

With his men walking behind him, he strolled across a
small square around which mud and papyrus huts were
baking under the sun. At their doors old men and women
were squatting and dirty, little urchins playing in the dust.
As soon as he was recognised, the urchins were seized and
the peasants bowed low before him.

Ineni had nearly crossed the square when, from behind
came the soft thud of running feet followed by a rising
hubbub from the peasants. He turned and stared back.

From between two huts a tall, wild-looking man had
appeared. In his hands he clasped two spears and an axe.
His appearance was normal apart from his weapons, and
what gave him the impression of wildness was the set,
mad look of hatred contorting his face.

Realising he had been seen, he gave a wild cry and let
forth a string of yelled oaths as he raced across the square.

"The Pharaoh is evil, the Pharaoh is evil!" he was
shouting in a hoarse scream as people cleared out of their
doorways, rushing for shelter.

Ineni's bodyguard had immediately formed into a protecting line in front of him, cutting him off from the
approaching madman.

A dozen spears were raised as the man, who had not
slackened speed in the slightest, flung one of his into the
heart of the group. One of the bodyguard fell and then the
spears were flying back in return.

Several struck the man, pulling him up as he ran. He

faltered, his body looking like a pin cushion—and then he came on. He seemed hardly to be human and Ineni drew his sword in spite of the thick line of men between him and the amok.

Another of the bodyguard fell as the man found enough strength to loose his second spear.

With his eyes blazing on Ineni, he was amongst the bodyguard, blood gushing from wounds all over his body. His face was a transformed mask of hatred and he lashed blindly all around him with his sword, never taking his eyes from the new Pharaoh's face as if he were afraid that if he did he would lose sight of it for ever.

His impetus and sheer, inhuman determination took him through the bodyguard and straight on at Ineni, who stood, uncomprehending, but calmly ready.

As the man rushed, another spear hit him straight between the shoulder blades and he jerked back, his sword arm flailing the air. In that moment Ineni stepped forward and ran his sword through the man's heart.

With a last look of maniacal hatred, the madman sank slowly to the ground, collapsing on the spears which already pierced his body. He was surrounded immediately by the remainder of the Nubian bodyguard who tore him to pieces with sword and spear as if he might yet get up and fight again.

At last the furious tangle of thrusting figures stepped back, leaving the body, like that of a dead rat, soaked in its own blood in the hot sand of the square.

The bodyguard swayed, leaning on their spears, panting—and from a side road a volley of stones and a knife or two crashed into their midst.

Ineni stared at the scene, unbelievingly. What plot was this, so soon hatching behind his back?

173

In a rush the Nubians were into the road. There was the sound of running feet, a cry or two of terror, the sound of scuffle, sickening thuds and then after a few minutes silence during which time the peasants crept back to their doors, the bodyguard reappeared dragging with them the crumpled bodies of four peasants.

Ineni stared at the still, gory figure at his feet. He stared at it for a long time and then his voice bellowed throughout the square.

"Who was this man—this amok?"

At first there was no answer and his voice shook with anger as he repeated the question.

Then, from her cross-legged position in front of the hole which served her hut for a door, a half-naked old woman called: "He was Ahmed the potter. His daughters had been sent to Nubia for the King's harem."

Ineni stared at the woman, motioning to stillness a member of his bodyguard who had moved in her direction. He looked back at the tattered remains before him. And then, his mind a whirl of confusion, his heart heavy, he walked quickly from the square. His bodyguard dropped their victims to the dust and hurried after him.

Behind them, as they disappeared from view, the peasants moved silently into the square and carried the dead from the heat of the sun.

Back in his palace, Ineni sank to a divan, cursing his stupidity, wracking his brains as to what should be done. Later he realized there was nothing to be done. It was too late.

News of the incident spread like the suns rays through Memphis and beyond and Ineni never felt safe enough to go out without his bodyguard again. From that time on, fierce acts of agression were carried out against the Nubian

detachments by little bands of Egyptians, who sometimes stayed to fight and pay the penalty and at others fled after they had struck.

A few weeks later, Ineni received a deputation from the priests of a number of cities to the south, from Memphis to Thebes. They were led by the new High Priest who greeted the Pharaoh with every sign of respect and deference.

Ineni received them cautiously in his new position. He did not want to antagonize the priests unnecessarily, but there were many in their midst who had sided against him with the old Pharaoh.

"What is it that you desire?" he asked. "I trust that I may be able to grant your wish and that our relations will be smooth."

'Your Majesty, we have come to state our loyalty to yourself and our trust that our faith and goodwill may be acceptable to Your Majesty," the High Priest replied.

Ineni repeated his question as to the reason for their visit.

"We have found, Your Majesty, that those who suffered most under the hands of the invading Nubian with which Your Majesty was bound to ally himself against corruption, were the priests," the man declared. "In his trail up from the Cataracts, the invader plundered every temple he found, taking away the food and furniture, the pots and riches of the dead—even cutting the rings from their fingers. The priests are without food, the dead are without nourishment to sustain them in the journey to the other land."

Ineni considered the words. It was true the Nubians were, perhaps, even greater spoilers than the Hittites. Everything they saw they smashed and stole. He would

have to inspect the valley through which Sharmab and Tabaka had passed.

"What do you wish me to do?" he asked.

"It is common knowledge that Your Majesty has reduced the endowments to the temples," the High Priest explained. "And under normal conditions no-one could deny the wisdom of such a move, but in the light of the new knowledge that we bring, we would beg Your Majesty to reconsider this step."

"But the previous endowments were much too large," Ineni said. "Even if I partly restored them, that should be enough."

"It is not only for ourselves, we ask, Your Majesty," the High Priest continued. "The people, too, are clamouring for the return of substance and nourishment to their dead kings and nobles to the degree of the previous amounts."

He hesitated a moment and then continued, quietly, with just a shade of emphasis on the words.

"Of course, the people were unable to see the wisdom of Your Majesty's original command, but if we teach them perhaps they will listen. However, in the meantime, I have assured those who have come to me that Your Majesty has the people's wishes at heart and will not let their hopes go unheeded."

Listening to the words, Ineni felt their veiled impudence, their veiled threat. But it was only a feeling. The High Priest was regarding him respectfully with an inscrutably serious expression. With his initial disasters and lack of popularity, Ineni felt unable to risk a fresh uprising of public feeling. Later he could visit the temples and the people and judge for himself.

"I will grant your request," he said. "The endowments will be restored."

"I am sure Your Majesty will not regret the step," the High Priest replied with a smile of gratification. "You may rest assured of our loyalty."

The next day the new decree was announced.

A few days later Ineni set out on a journey south to see how the rest of the country had fared under the Nubian advance. In nearly every village he found the rebuilt huts where the old ones had been destroyed by his allies. In the bigger towns where they had camped he heard, through the priests, stories of killing and rape which ran contrary to the agreement he had made with Sharmab and Tabaka.

Accompanied by his bodyguard of Nubians—the only men he felt he could trust, Ineni rode as far south as Thebes. Everywhere he could tell that he was hardly welcome. He could read it in the people's faces as they gathered to watch him pass through. He could read it in their eyes as they looked at his Nubian entourage. It was the Nubians who had wreaked havoc amongst them. They watched the Pharaoh in the midst of the Nubians they hated and it seemed that they did not understand.

At Thebes the High Priest suggested that human sacrifices should be reinstituted.

"Apart from their placation of Amon," he said, "they would show the ignorant fools who talk against Your Majesty that he is not weak against them. They are saying you would not dare to offer human sacrifice."

"Who are *they?*" Ineni demanded.

"They are the wealthy class," the High Priest told him. "Not the nobles, but the commoners—the merchants and the money-lenders. The peasants want the sacrifices renewed. They know how necessary is the soft virgin flesh to the needs of Amon."

"I have broken one of my decrees. I will not break

177

another," Ineni decided. "The sacrifices cannot come back."

"As Your Majesty wishes," the High Priest said, coldly. "I shall try to explain to the wealthy that Your Majesty is not afraid and to the people that you are acting in their interests."

A little confused and downcast, Ineni returned to Memphis. And there fresh trouble awaited him.

Passing through that part of Memphis where Ahmed the potter had lived, two of Ineni's harem, one of them the Syrian girl who had returned from Nubia, had been stoned and beaten by a gang of local women, who had disappeared before patrols could reach the spot.

Overcome with rage at the response to what he had considered a necessary move in sending the potter's daughters to Nubia, Ineni stormed into his palace.

There, in their chambers, the two women were being tended by physicians. Both their faces were scarred with deep cuts, their bodies black with bruises.

Breathing hard with fury, Ineni knelt beside them as through bruised, swollen lips, the Syrian girl told him what had happened.

"There must have been a score of them," she said. "They hurled stones at us from all sides, knocking us down. Then they tore off our clothes and kicked us and beat us with sticks. They were calling for the men to rape us when the patrols arrived."

"Did you see any of the women? Could you recognize them?" Ineni demanded.

"It was all too quick," the girl replied. "But I'm sure they all came from the huts in the area."

Ineni stood up.

"Continue to rest," he said. "And I will show these

178

low fools what it means to dare to meddle with the Pharaoh's harem.''

Later that day he had a cordon of soldiers thrown around the area of the attack. They formed an impenetrable wall, guarding all street exists at a radius of two hundred yards from the spot. Leaving them with strict instructions to hold prisoner anyone who tried to escape from the area, Ineni took a body of some thirty Nubian soldiers and entered house after house. From them he dragged all woman who were not caught in the net of old age, all who were not children in arms.

The menfolk watched, dull-eyed, powerless against the show of force. Some of the women struggled. They were roughly handled by the intruders and pulled by their hair through the narrow, dusty alleys between the huts.

The majority allowed themselves, resignedly, to be led out from their homes. They were herded together and driven like animals along the streets.

Ineni personally led the entry into each house. Many woman were surprised in their toilet and were led, half-naked to join the rest. Behind them, the old women began a high-pitched wailing which soon filled the whole area and rang, accusingly in the ears of the Pharaoh's police as they went from house to house.

The whole district was combed until several score of women had been torn from their families, who sat with eyes downcast before the fierce strength of the Nubians.

Driving the women from the area towards the temples, the soldiers left behind a din of wailing like the aftermath of war.

The women, stumbling and weeping, some of them struggling still, were forced through the city. Crowds gath-

ered in silence to watch them pass and were driven back by threats from the escort.

The women were admitted to the massive coolness of the temples and locked into small chambers where they were forced to stand pressed together from the lack of space.

Ineni had the High Priest summoned before him at the palace. The man came and bowed low before him.

"I have decided to reinstitute the sacrifices," Ineni announced without preliminaries. "There will be one tomorrow."

"As Your Majesty wishes," the High Priest said.

That afternoon Ineni had the women led, under strong military escort, from the temples to the barracks alongside the main square of the city. There they were jostled into the barracks while outside stakes were driven deep into the ground.

The activity attracted attention with rapidity and in a short time the whole of Memphis seemed to be congregating around the edges of the square.

From the barracks, a dozen of the women, stripped of covering, were pulled to the stakes and tied to them by their wrists which were stretched high above their heads.

Naked, muscles tensing as they hung almost on tip-toe, the women were left while a host of archers ranged themselves outside the barracks in case there was any trouble from the crowd.

A young priest was chosen to shout a word of warning to the massed watchers while Ineni stood amongst his archers, arms folded, thoughts of the treatment of his two concubines killing any feeling of compassion which might rise in his mind.

"Citizens of Memphis," the priest shouted. "This pub-

lic flogging is to serve as an example to any who contemplate any further act of violence against the Pharaoh and his house. To those who perpetrate such violence no mercy will be shown.''

The crowd received the announcement in stony silence. Not a murmur ran through their thick ranks. The priest moved back behind the shelter of the bowmen.

From the barracks, then, strode a dozen Nubian soldiers, stripped to the waist. They positioned themselves behind the captive women. Each carried in his hand a long, hide whip.

While the others stood, motionlessly waiting, one of them ranged himself behind the woman at the central stake. She had been chosen for a preliminary exhibition because her breasts, buttocks, her whole body had a lush plenitude of flesh which now quivered in fear. All the women were able to twist on their bonds and turn in any direction and the woman spun on her toes to face the Nubian, became fixed there in a paralysis of fear.

The crowd was hushed, all eyes gazing at the flexing muscles of the Nubian in fear and resentment.

His great biceps tensed. He raised the whip and cracked it once along the ground with a sickening retort which made the woman's eyes bulge in horror.

While the barbaric sound lingered in the ears of the watching multitude, the Nubian flexed his arm again. This time, with a sudden, furious movement, he lashed the whip at the woman.

She seemed as if she were standing on the brink of a chasm about to fall as she saw his movement. She could do nothing. And then the throng had caught her, biting across her breasts as she faced him, bringing forth an immediate red weal across their bulge. She cried out with

181

the pain and spun round, tugging on the rope, trying to break free.

A groan rose in a dull wave of noise from the crowd and then the whip had smashed for a second time across the space separating tormenter and tormented.

It wrapped itself in a stinging embrace around her buttocks, producing across their broad, fleshy expanse another thin red weal. The woman's hips jerked forward, crashing against the stake as if she were overcome with an urge and was moving her loins in an abandoned sexual intercourse.

The Nubian's face was contorted in a savage, sadistic desire as he raised the whip again. A third time it cracked across the woman's buttocks and another thin streak of colour appeared criss-crossing the first in a sensual pattern.

The woman screamed, spinning, sagging with all her weight on the ropes attaching her to the pole. She struggled in vain, succeeding only in cutting her wrists in her attempt to break free.

Around the square the crowd seemed alive with the vague, general noise which sprang from quick intakes of breath, groans of sympathy at the sickening lashes and fierce grunts of anger.

Again and again the lash fell, snaking around the woman's tender body, indenting it, catching as she swung first buttocks and then hips and then buttocks again and then breasts in a biting, indiscriminate caress so that her flesh became a red and brown mesh of whip-marks.

For the first strokes, the woman jerked at every one as if she had been struck by a spear. Then her body went limp and later, as the blood spouted from a twice-hit weal, she was sagging like a doll, head hanging, eyes closed unconscious.

After a dozen strokès the Nubian stopped and glared round, sweating and shining, at the crowd as if he would turn on them with the whip in his sadistic fury.

In the crowd there were hearts beating fast, men who needed only a lash from the hide to tell them whether they would run in fear or surge in fury into the square at the barbarian whose eyes held them at bay.

But, at a cry from the priest, the Nubian turned reluctantly and waved his comrades on.

It seemed that a hell had been created in the square. The other women who had been hypnotised into watching the fate of their companion, cringed in readiness and then eleven whips were twining themselves like furious, unyielding lovers around their quivering frames.

The space became a jerking mass of soft, feminine bodies, jumping like the swaying bunches of dates in the wind. Overall a growing murmur of horror and objection grew amongst the watchers.

As the thongs cut deeply into the rounded flesh of their women, the fierce possessiveness of the peasant men in the crowd grew and overflowed.

Suddenly a shower of stones cascaded onto the Nubian torturers and then the defined edges of watchers had become a broken, moving line and men and women together were surging across the square to where the sadism of the whip-wielders was abating.

From the far side of the square a storm of arrows carved great gaps into the advancing people. The Nubians turned, lashing their whips in a furious desire to inflict pain, at the advancing mass.

"Fall back! Fall back!" Ineni yelled. His men held their fire as the peasants merged with the Nubian soldiers. And then it was too late for arrows. The foreigners had been

pulled down and inextricably mingled in the crowds, whips torn from their hands and turned on them.

Trembling hands were reaching for the bonds, supporting the slumped figures of the women as Ineni gave the order to charge.

Swords and spears in their hands against the stones and fists of the people, the mixed Egyptian and Nubian troops slaughtered the revolt before it could become anything but a hysterical attempt to protect its kin.

Within minutes, the square was littered with dead and dying. Those living had fled with their cuts and bruises. The twelve women still swayed at the stakes in mockery of the crushed rescue.

Overhelmed with the cruelty which circumstances seemed to have forced him to adopt, Ineni ordered the women to be cut down and taken back to the temples, the dead to be buried.

Accompanied by his ever-present bodyguard he returned to his palace.

That night many people left Memphis. And like a slow flood, intensified by the wretchedness of wandering, homeless peasants from the capital city, the word of the Pharaoh's cruelty and oppression spread through the valley.

The following day, determined to see through what he had begun, Ineni publicly announced the resumption of the human sacrifices to Amon. It was to be the final punishment of the women whose sore, broken bodies were now lying in the cells of the temples.

In their chambers in the palace the two wounded concubines were recovering when news was brought to them of the fate of their attackers. Later when Ineni visited them, he found them sad and thoughtful.

"My lord, what have you done?" the Syrian girl cried as soon as she saw him.

"I have thoroughly punished the crime committed against you," he replied sternly.

"My lord, forgive me—but you have been too harsh. These women felt they had good reason to do harm to your property."

"I cannot have my power questioned. I have nothing but desire to improve the lot of my people. The invader might have stayed for ever. I had no choice but to treat them well."

"Please, my lord, do not sacrifice these women." Tears welled in the girl's eyes as she made the request.

Ineni's eyes blazed and his words rasped angrily through the chamber.

"They have tried to see with the eyes of the Pharaoh as to what should be done. I cannot rule Egypt unless I have power to act as I think necessary. These women must be made an example of so that thoughtless rebellion is crushed at its roots."

The girl stared at him through puffed, anguished eyes. And then she sank wearily back onto the divan where she was resting.

"So be it, my lord," she whispered.

During the night extra military patrols paced the streets; extra guards were placed on the palace and the temples. But there was no trouble.

The following day, the captive women, smarting and collapsing still under their wounds, were dragged through the streets to the main temple on the outskirts of Memphis.

There they were received by the priests. Through the great archway, flanked by the, as yet unremoved, statues

of Ramses, they were taken, through the colonnaded court-yard to the inner court.

Outside the temple in the heat of the sun, a few dozen people sat miserably on the sands, bowing their heads in the dust, muttering prayers to Amon.

In the courtyard a quietness reigned as if this was another world, far from the domain of lust and passion which filled the land of mortal men.

Around the courtyard in the gloom of the portico, the priests grouped chatting quietly, faces flushed in the excitement of anticipation of the sacrifice.

Some of the women were bound, weals showing pale under the fierce light of the sun, to the iron rings in the dust-covered flagstones. The remainder were ushered into the adjacent chambers to await their turn.

Spreadeagled in obscene positions the women were inspected by the priests. The young novices amongst them could not resist a gentle feeling with the hands of the soft mounds of flesh rawly revealed to them.

And then the spectators withdrew once more to the cool shade of the pillars. There was a flutter of movement at a chamber door—and the sacred baboons moved stiffly through the pillars into the sunlight, blinking for a moment, gazing fiercely around them.

Watching, Ineni felt a cold chill at his heart as if waters from the Nile had been flooded around it inside the outer warmth of his flesh. He stared at the baboons as they began to stalk the women, with a strange feeling of helplessness such as he had never experienced before.

The women, flesh-hidden vaginas exposed and projected towards all curious eyes, buttocks reared up, nakedly to the heavens, breasts sagging to the flagstones, remained

186

crouched in a painful fixedness of position as if their bodies were too hurt to move or even twitch.

Ineni's eyes moved through the pillars at the priests tensed in their attitudes of watching. He saw the High Priest gloating, a faint, cynical smile twisting his lips. And then he turned coldly back to the scene.

The baboons had begun to paw the women with sharp, bony fingers. Their skinny digits prodded the raw weals bringing hoarse cries, uttered with difficulty, from the throats of their victims.

The same pantomime of sniffing, noses prodding bestially up the soft inside of thighs, rummaging in the heavy creases of flesh between the widespread legs and then a clambering of possession.

Ineni saw the whole thing as if it were unreal. The long, bright red sticks of animal penis. The obscene juxtaposition of long, grey-black fur and raw pink flesh, the fusion of bodies from different stages of being.

As the probing rigidities of sex rifled the outer lips of soft, human vaginas, the priests craned forward, openmouthed with desire. As the thick bestial rods thrust in and in, in growing speed and passion, the tell-tale bulges grew under the tunics of the watchers.

A heat of debauchery seemed to shroud the sanctuary of the temple as the inhuman intercourse worked to its gasping, belly-rending close.

The raped women were led off, a fresh number brought, a new contingent of baboons. The scene was repeated until Ineni, sickened with the realization of his ruined intention, walked away through the archway, his bodyguard falling in hurriedly behind him.

As he went, the smile of the High Priest followed him.

Later the women's throats were slit and their bodies hurled into the river in the final act of sacrifice.

Throughout Egypt in the days that followed there were acts of minor rioting. Nubian guards were knifed, stones were thrown at passing chariots of the soldiery. Sometimes there was a reprisal in which several people were killed. It was difficult to say if they were the guilty or the innocent who suffered.

And then, after a period of some weeks in which Ineni had begun to feel powerless to alter the situation of unrest and alarm which had arisen from the Delta to the Cataracts, there came a lull in all acts of hostility. No more were reported for a period of time sufficiently long for the Pharaoh to wonder if he could risk despatching back to Nubia the men he had kept on Egyptian soil for so long against the wishes of his people.

Late one afternoon, the High Priest begged audience with him. Ineni had him brought. He felt a certain powerlessness against the priests. It was probable, he knew, that they sowed sedition against him—although there was no proof.

"What it it?" he asked.

"It is a matter of which Your Majesty should know," the High Priest replied. "It is reported that a young noble of Assuan is plotting to overthrow Your Majesty. He is popular and strong and is believed to have the support of many people. So far south as Assuan it is difficult to find proof of what the local lords are about. But this information comes from the reliable source of the temples."

"Is this a question of open revolt?" Ineni asked sternly.

"No Your Majesty. There have been no acts, no words that can be related. But there is a whisper which seems to spring from no source, which is spreading through the

land. The people have stopped their acts of pillage. It seems they are waiting."

"What is the name of this noble?"

"His name is Setu. His ancestry spreads far back in a noble line."

For a long time Ineni considered this news. He seemed to hear an echo of himself. And all it produced was a dark, sad anger within his breast.

At last he looked up at the long, hard features of the High Priest.

"You have done well to bring me this news," he said.

He paused for a moment as if about to change his mind and then added: "Have this man Setu brought to Memphis. Place him in the court circles and watch him closely. Later we will decide what to do with him."

The High Priest bowed. He bowed low, turned and walked away from the Pharaoh towards the papyrus-covered entrance to the inner room of the palace.

As he went, a faint, gloating smile hovered around his lips.

THE FRENCH WAY

CHAPTER I

The room was not terribly small but there was about it an overwhelming air of constriction as if once inside its walls one would never escape. Its walls were a dull buff colour streaked in places with cracks and smudges which through long existence had become indelible like the lines on a man's face. The ceiling was not low—a dozen feet above the floor—but it, too, was patterned with cracks meandering like little streams, erupting in places into a veritable lake of dull colour where a whole patch of white-wash had flaked off leaving to view the older hue of previous ceilings. There was one small window, cloudy with dust over most of its expanse, grimy round its edges where a dirty blue putty was breaking off. The window looked out onto an air shaft more constricting than the room itself, dark and dirty with pieces of newspaper from ten years back on its floor and strange vegetable messes like mixtures of decomposed potatoes and cabbages. This was the only window to the room and, even when the sun was shining, the shaft was so dark that the light had to be kept on in most of the rooms that looked onto it. The light in the room was a single 25-watt bulb, suspended naked from

the ceiling. It seemed unwilling to reach the corners, as if it were exploring unknown territory and did not trust itself to move beyond the central circle of its glow. There was a bare wooden table against the wall under the light with a broken, chipped enamel bowl on it and a stool pushed under it. There was a single cupboard with an uneven door which enabled a visitor to see a portion of shabby clothes hung inside. Apart from that the room was bare but for a narrow bed in the gloom of a far corner. On that bed a man lay staring at the shabby ceiling, unmoving, his arms inert at his sides. There was about him an air of hopelessness which immediately gave the clue to the constriction of the room. It might easily have been a prison room; in fact it was difficult to believe that in fact it was a hotel room for which guests paid and in which they lived of their own free will—more or less of their own free will.

After several minutes of complete stillness, the man on the bed rolled over onto his side and changed his unseeing stare from the ceiling to the opposite wall. His body was slim, rather small and his face flatly handsome and dark. His name was Ahmed ben Lulla, his home—if it was still there—was in Algeria. He couldn't be sure that it still existed. His people were unable to write and he had stopped sending them letters some years ago when the hopelessness had begun to set in.

After several minutes more he swung his feet heavily off the bed and sat up. He wore a pair of jeans and a dark brown shirt that looked as if it had seen several campaigns with an active army. He rubbed his hands slowly along his eyelids and blinked slowly. His hands fell back to his sides and then he stood up, pulling himself up as if each limb, each joint fought a separate, losing battle to prevent him. He crossed to the cupboard and opened it. He felt inside without looking, staring still, without seeing anything.

He pulled out a leather jacket which zipped up the front—one of the few solid possessions he had. When he had half zipped it and it clung neatly to his slim frame he went to the door of the room, turned off the switch without looking at the bulb and went out.

From the tiny, uncarpeted landing with the water tap which dripped into a fixed basin he walked heavily down the narrow, bare-boarded staircase which wound round and down, passing several other landings with three or four doors on each.

At the bottom of the staircase two prostitutes were sitting on a stair. They made way for him to pass without a word and he stepped over the threadbare mat, didn't look into the dismal office where mail, for those who ever had any, was kept in little boxes. The door at the end of the short, bare vestibule was open and in the moonlit street beyond an occasional face glanced in and eyes ran over the two prostitutes as someone passed.

He stepped out into the street with a faint feeling of relief which was only momentary and instinctive. It was a narrow street. There were two other shabby hotels in it, with signs in which some of the letters were missing; there were several more prostitutes chatting in doorways. They looked up at him and then immediately resumed their bored conversations.

The street was slightly inclined and he walked down it with a rapidity which was automatic, a reflex which had nothing to do with his mood. He passed through another street, dark and bare, with a few shuttered shops and high, shabby apartment buildings and then he was in the big boulevard where it was still dark and bare but where there were more people and a few lights and a glow some distance off which was the neon-land of Pigalle.

He began to walk towards Pigalle, passing the tiny bars

where he would normally have drunk a black coffee and chatted with acquaintances. Tonight he didn't want to see anybody, but he wanted to be surrounded by humanity, a humanity which had no relation to him, to which he was a complete stranger, a humanity that by its own, recognisable, agonised existence would, perhaps, make him feel less afraid and self-concerned.

The boulevard began to light up, as if he'd been walking through a forest getting nearer and nearer to a glade where the sun was brightest.

The bars became bigger and more frequent, throwing their brash light out across the road; neon signs had sprung up on both sides, shop windows were ablaze for night window shoppers, crowds thronged around the foyers of bigger and bigger cinemas, the traffic grew thicker and thicker, gliding along a dual carriageway; on the broad stretch of pavement and trees which separated the two roadways, people were buying the last edition of *France-Soir* from the gaudy booths; he began to hear English and German mixed with the French and the Arabic which formed the background.

In Pigalle the lights flickered in a fluid pattern like coloured fountains, distracting the eye with unexpected explosions. The bars were filled with tight-skirted, jut-buttocked whores, their low-cut blouses revealing the lack of brassieres beneath as they leaned over pinball machines and tried to pick up American GIs on leave from Fontainebleau and elsewhere. Commissionaires invited the passing crowd to see "the most daring nudes in the world" and dark doorways offered "genuine strip-teases every two hours from 3 till midnight."

Ahmed ben Lulla paused beside a bright *charcuterie* in which the multi-coloured dishes seemed almost to be alive. He studied the price tags: "*macédoine de légumes, 600 fr.*

le kilo," "cervelas, 800 fr.," "champignons grecs, 1,100 fr."
He felt saliva gather in his mouth and his throat constricted
in a small torment of frustration. He hated these expensive
little shops which stayed open late for the tourist and
charged prices which only tourists would pay. He walked
on and, at a small, steaming counter which jutted onto the
pavement from the cafe behind, he bought a small carton of
chips for 60 francs and continued to walk, eating ravenously
until there was nothing left and he could roll up the greasy
little carton and throw it in the kerb. He wiped his hands
on his jeans and turned up a side street which ran steeply
off the boulevard, up toward the Butte Montmartre.

He turned into a little bar and sat down at a small
table beside the window that looked out onto the street.
He was going to order a coffee but changed his mind and
asked for beer instead. Then he asked himself what good
a single beer would do. What good would a single
anything do?

When the beer was brought and placed before him on
a little cork mat, he sat watching the foam slowly disintegrate
until the golden liquid beneath was shadowing darkly
through the last white-veined bubbles.

Tonight they had come to his hotel. He had known
they would come, it had been inevitable. He had, of course,
made his excuses and they had, as he'd known they would,
rejected them. He put his hand in his pocket and pulled
out some coins—534 francs that was all. Of course he
would have a little more in a few days' time, his *assistance*,
for he'd been unable to find a job for several months.
But he could hardly live on that and he owed a month's
rent. And now, when at last he'd refused to pay his
contribution because he didn't want to starve and he wasn't
interested in politics anyway, they'd come and told him that
he must pay or be killed. He had two days.

It wasn't a big sum, but for him it was a lot and he wasn't interested in them. That was what hurt. *He wasn't interested in them*. Nor their murders, their "*Algérie pour les Algériens.*" He wasn't interested in politics, in revolution, in violence. He wanted a quiet, simple life with enough to eat and drink and a place to live. He'd been mistaken to come to France—all those promises of work—but now he couldn't get back and all he wanted was a quiet life with a chance of improving his lot.

So, after paying for so long, after going without food for three days in order to pay, after not being able to buy the cheap shoes he needed, to pay, after lying and begging to keep his hotel room in spite of arrears, to pay. After all that he'd decided to hell with them and he hadn't paid. And so they had come, four of them. It was hardly surprising. They had been stern but not brutal. They had simply made it clear he had to pay and it was not their concern how he found the money to pay. The National Liberation Front was bigger and more important than any individual with his petty little problems of eating and finding a roof and clothing.

Then they had gone, saying they would be back. And he had lain on his bed for three hours, dulled with hopelessness because he knew he couldn't pay and wasn't going to pay.

He sipped the beer and looked abstractedly out of the window. Opposite, a young prostitute with large, firm breasts was encouraging passers-by to take her upstairs in the hotel by the door of which she stood. Farther along a couple of older whores stood in an apparently blasé unconcern at the proximity of their more attractive neighbour. Ahmed looked back at his beer. All the bubbles had gone—lost, dead, finished. There was no hope anywhere.

CHAPTER II

Within a few streets of the cafe where Ahmed ben Lulla sat drinking his beer was another room also with its air of constriction. But this air of constriction was of a type that was much sought after by the small crowd which filled the room.

Lights were low, half-concealed in the walls. At one end of the room was a small platform on which a little, dark girl was slowly undressing to the soft, sexy rhythm of a mamba.

In the gloomy body of the room, sitting on hard wooden chairs on the pain parquet-floor, were a crowd of individuals. Some were clearly French, others had the air of knowing tourists. They all looked rich and they were all straining forward watching the girl disrobing. There were no windows and beside the heavy, red velvet curtain which hid the single door a dark man was standing, smoking and indifferently glancing from the girl to the audience.

There were women amongst the audience as well as men. Most of them were middle-aged but there were also a few

young people. They were watching one of Pigalle's clandestine exhibitions.

When the preliminary striptease had started a little while before, the girl, who had small features and short, dark hair, had been wearing a long evening gown. Now she was dressed in a sort of petticoat which swathed her slim, muscular body in quick, tentative embraces as she moved gently to the music which seemed, itself, to be a solid presence in the confining space.

The lights adorning the walls around the small dais were more numerous than those in the other parts of the room and some were so arranged that as the girl moved in front of them they shone through the thin material of her garment and outlined the dark shape of the body and limbs beneath. Every so often the girl, whose face was normally without expression, would flash a deep smile into the audience. At such times it seemed to every man there that she was looking at and smiling just for him—the way women claim that Frank Sinatra seems to be singing just for them individually.

She moved in a gentle dance rhythm which sometimes merged into the music, sometimes came out of it as if sometimes the beat dominated her and sometimes she dominated it. Swaying her hips a little, she turned her back to the audience and pulled the petticoat slowly up and over her head. The old-fashioned garment gone, she was all modern underneath—a pair of undersized briefs and the slim string of a brassiere. The briefs were not big enough to cover her buttocks fully and the audience could see where the slim, supple back with its central hollow ran into the rising mounds of her bottom. Below, the briefs arched up half-revealing each buttock where it joined the thigh. She continued to sway gently and moved along the stage with her back towards the room. Her buttocks

hollowed gently as she moved and there were dimples just above them which came and went. Her bottom, surprisingly full now that it was more or less uncovered, seemed to be on the point of bursting through the light cloth which covered it. The rounding of her buttocks was a rolling mamba of its own.

As the audience watched, flushed and desireful, she turned slowly and the brassiere which covered half her breasts seemed about to peel off. Through its flimsiness, her large, pointed nipples poked, scorching embossments, crowning points to a full weight of firm, caressable flesh.

Below the breasts which wobbled very slightly, more of a sensitive quiver, her waist was small and wiry. There was a little black hair just below her navel which ran in a thin line down over the slightly raised abdomen and disappeared under the briefs—disappeared in its detail but left its trace in the spongy protrusion at the junction of her thighs where the dark muff of hair made a dark bump. Her hips wavered back and forth to the music, inviting cool fingers to draw down over them the tiny material and slip it—reluctantly though it would leave—down over the warmth of flesh which would tremor slightly at the touch and the anticipation of what was to come.

The smile came, meaningful and inviting, and responsive bumps grew behind the fly buttons of the male watchers. Reaching up with her hands, keeping her deep, shining eyes still on the outside room, the girl snapped open the brassiere and let it fall to the floor. Freed now, her breasts swayed heavily from side to side as she moved. A hand under them could have lifted them slightly, just enough to feel their full, voluptuous weight; apart from that they were taut and high. It was as if the flesh were held in a glossy, transparent bag.

Slowly, languorously, half closing her dark eyes, the girl

ran her slender hands up her body, letting them flow lovingly over her hot flesh until they reached her breasts and held them out, nipples jutting, to the spectators. "Take them, take them," she seemed to say. "These nipples are longing for the cool relief of a mouth."

For a few minutes more she danced, turning her body completely round a couple of times while the audience watched almost without taking breath, fascinated, and then she reached down and undid a small catch on her briefs.

Mouths went dry as the little white garment fluttered away in a trembling flight which seemed to symbolize abandon. But no. A g-string still circled her hips in which the indentations of her movement were clearly marked, and a tiny cache-sex covered the smallest of triangular areas down where her thighs merged and rubbed in each other's heat.

A flowering of dark hair surrounded the clinging morsel and the full roundness of the abdomen below the small, flat belly offered itself to the gaze of the audience. Just that one crucial spot remained protected, that one point which it was so necessary to denude for the abandon to be complete.

Slowly, rotating on her toes, the girl turned, allowed herself to be seen in profile—a lovely swansneck shape with the beauty of breast lifting before and the voluptuousness of buttock hollowing out behind—and then edged round showing first the half-moon protrusion of another buttock beyond the first and then the whole of her naked behind, wobbling and tensing at the audience, a full, bursting smoothness of flesh which moved and wiggled as if it searched for something, some pressure which would make it squirm in a complete, cooperative delight.

Gradually, she bent her slim back forward, leaning away from the audience, which watched breathlessly, until the breadth of her buttocks was jutting towards them and

rotating gently as if in obscene invitation. Her thighs tensed and rippled in slim strength as she giffled on her feet and then she reached back with her dark, slender arms and gently pulled apart her buttocks with her fingers, disclosing in an even more obscene gesture the little dark hole between as if she were inviting a sharp, sodomising attack.

Around the little, revealed anus, which seemed so raw and vulnerable, a few stray, black hairs fringed. The girl's bottom rotated as if on its own axis, as if it were involved in some strange sexual intercourse with the surrounding air, rather like a cat brushing itself against a wall, except that there was no wall and no male member.

Slowly, in time with the music which continued to pulsate like blood through the room, the girl moved her hands away from her asshole and back over her ice-smooth buttocks and into her waist. She straightened, with her hands on that slim waist, and turned back gradually to face the audience again.

There was an atmosphere of slight relief in the room as if the bending offer had been too much to bear.

But now, with another flashing smile, she unclasped the g-string and let it slither down between her thighs until she was able to trample on it with rhythm-flipping feet. Where the dark moss of hair made a V with her thighs, there was a pink weight of flesh, a mound of promise and strength, a sight of which was not to be denied the spectators. Opening her legs wide, spreading her feet firmly on the wooden stage, the girl lowered herself backwards in a lithe, double-jointed posture until her hands reached the floor behind her head and her vaginal lips were presented head on to the audience. With a rubberlike dexterity, she moved her head forward between her legs until she was practically looking her audience in the face. She seemed to concentrate, stretched her thighs farther apart, concentrating, concentrat-

ing... and then the lips opened and her vagina was wide and wetly grinning at a crowd whose eyes bulged and remained transfixed.

✥

In a small back room above the striptease a group of Algerians were sitting, talking quietly. It was a quiet room, but the notes of the mamba came in very faintly as if from the depths of a lake. The music gave an aura of harmlessness to the men and their talk. But it was just an aura.

Sitting at the polished round table, with his listeners rounding in semicircles on either side of him, the chief of the National Liberation Front in Paris was talking. His name was Mahmoud Taluffah and his apparent and legitimate business was running a fairly large bar a little distance off in the Boulevard de Clichy. His bar was sufficiently profitable to cover the ostensible signs of his wealth which were numerous. But it was merely a cover for his political activities and his operation of a ring of prostitutes and "striptease clubs" in the hard, vice-ridden centre north of the Seine.

In front of him now he had a map of one of the Paris arrondissements. It had been drawn in pencil and was covered with figures, dotted lines and times. Each of the dozen men in the room had a copy and had made various notes at the side on the blank notes at the side on the blank portion of the paper.

"Now," Mahmoud Taluffah was saying, "you each know your role. Once he has been shot there must be sufficient confusion created for certain escape. Escape should not be difficult if everyone plays his part; it is really a secondary matter. What is important is that no mistake be made with the killing. It will not be enough to wound. He

must be *killed*—even if it involves the death of the killer."
He looked slowly at a thin man on his right, a man with
vicious eyes and a small, suave moustache. "Even if it
involves the death of the killer," he repeated.

"I am not afraid to die," said the man in a toneless
voice which belied the fanaticism of his eyes.

"You are a good servant of the cause," Mahmoud
Taluffah said without warmth, as if there were no other
possibility.

"Now," he continued, "that we know our roles, we must
destroy these plans."

The papers were passed to him and he burned them
slowly over a large ashtray while he continued to talk
quietly.

"We will meet here on the afternoon of Wednesday
and I will distribute arms. After the victim has been dealt
with, the arms must be returned here to avoid their loss
in the search which will follow." He paused. "This time,"
he said, "let us hope the job will be clean and successful.
Remember that we are striking terror into the cringing
heart of the metropolis, we are turning the metropolis into
a coward fearful for its life in a way that we are not.
We are bringing a free Algeria nearer with every blow
we strike."

There were murmurs of agreement and approval. The
mamba wafted into the room in the short silence which
followed.

"I think that is all," Mahmoud Taluffah concluded.
"Until Wednesday." He turned again to the man he had
addressed earlier. "Mohammed Arab, it is time for your
participation below," he said. "Enjoy her to the full. There
may be little time."

Mohammed Arab, who was to kill Police Superintendent
Jacques Lamotte in two days' time, stood up smiling, a

smile that did not remove the viciousness from his eyes. The viciousness was ineradicable.

"I shall treat her to knife practice," he said, "with my prick."

Mahmoud Taluffah guffawed and the other permitted himself a slight grunt as, alert and tense as he always was, he moved towards the door in the wake of the others.

❖❖

In the room below, the tourists continued to stare goggle-eyed as the girl swung back onto her feet and began a full-swinging dance to the mamba, revolving in front of them so that her buttocks waved and swayed and quivered and her breasts jumped and jogged and thin tremors of muscle moved down her legs like ripples on a lake. She would punctuate stages of the dance with a thrust of her abdomen, thighs widespread towards the audience, giving them a full view of her vagina. She had the Arab loose-jointedness which enabled her to manipulate her hips in an astonishing dance of their own. Their mobility gave rise to many a thought of how those hips would squirm and muscularly wriggle under a man's body when she was impaled with a stiff, searching penis.

At a point in the music where a crescendo had been reached and there was a slight lowering of pressure, Mohammed Arab came quickly through the door and onto the stage where he began to dance around the woman in a way that was charged with a sexual menace. He was naked from the waist, his legs enclosed in black, silk trousers which clung to them down to his ankles. His torso' was slim, with every muscle in it developed to a pitch of near-perfection, and his arms were hard and wiry. This was what the elderly women in the audience had come to see,

and there was a ruffle of excitement amongst them as they watched him circling his naked prey.

He and the girl danced in unison. She revolved round to face him, leaning backwards from her hips as if offering him the lower part of her body. He curved his hips in towards her as they mambaed together.

As they danced Mohammed Arab ran his eyes over the girl with a vicious eagerness. They had so often gone through this act, but although he had her so often on the stage in front of this audience, he hardly knew her well. They both did it as a job and were paid well for it. Neither had bothered to take their relationship beyond this strange, pulsating union in public. He knew nothing of what she did or how she lived. He was too busy to care. He had all he could want of her here in this room once a week. The rest of the time she did normal strip-teases. As far as he could tell, she loved being impaled by him. She was, perhaps, an exhibitionistic nymphomaniac. She usually went wild when he subjected her body to his own.

He permitted his eyes to rise beyond the girl's dark head to get a glimpse of the gloom-surrounded audience and the reassuring presence of Akbar Halin by the door. He could see women in the audience, well-preserved, attractive 40-50-year-old women.

He wondered how many of them he'd had, if there were any new beauties there tonight who would seek him out. That was often what they came for. After the exhibition they would approach Akbar Halim and a meeting would be arranged at their luxurious flats or in some discreet hotel. There he would fuck the life from them while they sobbed their helpless ecstasy. Sobbed, sobbed, sobbed from their mouths, sobbed from their cunts, sobbed, sobbed. Sometimes they wanted him to split their asses, sometimes they wanted to be whipped, all sorts of things they wanted and

he was always pleased to oblige, to viciously subject them to anything he cared to do to them—these rich, sexy cunts who paid him well. And how he punished them for being French cunts, for being rich, for having everything, for being able to indulge themselves while he had had to rise from the *bidonvilles*, while he had starved and been spurned. Not that he thought of these things in so many words. It was an abstract emotion firmly embedded in his mind. It showed in his eyes how he hated everybody. It showed in his gestures of contempt, in the way he treated the rich French cunt he got, the way he made them squirm, humiliated them in the way they wanted him to and hated themselves and him for doing.

He let his eyes fall back on the girl while the music and the tingling anticipation coursed through his veins. She was different, but in many ways she was the same. She was a proud-looking beauty and she was a stranger to him. He liked to feel his power over her, too, as she groaned and squirmed on the end of his prick.

He undid the catch at the waist of his trousers and felt from the distance the rustle of strained interest out there in the gloom. Yes, there was fresh cunt out there tonight. He'd have offers later. He'd charge them an outrageous figure and then he'd punish them for daring to pay it.

He wriggled with great dexterity from the silk trousers. Underneath he wore a small pair of pants which enclosed his genitals closely, a large, heavy bulge between his legs, hot in the confinement, wanting freedom, thick and fighting to escape from the constriction.

His legs were slim and muscular in the way that the rest of his body was muscular, perfect muscles, not over-large, which bespoke hours of development. He appeared to be in complete control of every muscle in his body as if he could give an individual order and immediately a

small strip of hard flesh in his back or his belly or his thigh would start to twitch in answer.

His penis had risen up taut under the pants, but was held down by the material, forming, nonetheless, a towerlike point protruding from the general bulge. In the audience the women's eyes were magnetised on that point while the men still ogled the curves and rotundities of the girl's voluptuous flesh.

Mohammed Arab danced around the girl, who let her eyes fall to the point of his knob. She moved in towards him and their hips joined, while their back-leaning torsos remained apart. He felt her hot belly pressing hard against the heat of his loins, quivering against the mound of his penis. She raised her eyes to his and they were deep and gleaming.

He reached down and slipped out of the pants and his prick swung up massively, cleaving the air, and he heard quick intakes of breath in the room.

Watching with supreme concentration, the spectators could see his prick, which was large, almost too heavy for his body, reaching out against the girl as he moved slightly away from her. He, too, revolved now in a dance of his own and they saw his balls swinging against his thighs, the muscles rippling and balancing beautifully all over his body, the small buttocks hollowing and tensing. His penis had a flat bludgeon of a head. Its first entry would be delicious shock. The longing in the women of the audience gathered in a torment at their loins, making them rub thighs together in agitation on their hard seats, feeling the wetness in their briefs between their legs.

Mohammed Arab turned back to the girl and the audience watched him in profile, his great boom reaching out far ahead of the rest of his body. Slowly the girl swivelled round until her back was towards him and he

could look down on those juicy, inviting, moving buttocks. He moved up behind her and they saw her slowly bend over in front of him, her legs wide apart, until her hands reached the floor and rested there supporting her.

Moving into her he saw that there was moisture on the tops of her smooth thighs. Her vagina which was loose and wet was waiting for him beneath the little disclosed anal aperture. Her buttocks were warm and roundly stretched. She was a lovely piece of flesh and he felt his teeth grit in vicious, joyous anticipation.

From the body of the room they saw him hovering over her bending, prostrate body like a bird of prey ready to swoop. They saw him move in with his great penis swooping out at her behind. They saw him mamba a little, arranging his prick against her vagina without touching her or himself. Then they watched while he reached down and grasped her little waist with his hands. They gave a long, choking gasp in harmony with hers as they saw him sink, at last, into her cunt with an agonisingly slow entry, like a great ship moving carefully along a narrow canal.

From their vantage point they had a perfect view of his entry as he slid in and out of her vagina, his body inclined back from her, reaching towards her at his loins, his buttocks hollowing as he pushed in until his prick was out of sight, buried deep in her cunt so that there was simply his body flush against hers.

The girl remained in her bent-over position, her mouth had opened and the audience could hear her low continuous murmuring. She began to rotate her behind, pushing back at him so that she was almost lifted from her feet and left dangling in the air on the length of his rigid staff.

Mohammed Arab's fingers tightened on the taut waist so that the flesh cringed in under his pressure, leaving red marks on the skin whenever he shifted his grip. He

shuffled in towards the girl so that his legs were in the arch made by her widespread thighs and all the weight of his body which focussed in his loins was forced against the soft, yielding roundness of her rump as he forced his thick prick deep, deep into her moist, contracting channel.

In and in he rubbed, bursting into her as if she were some ripe fruit, with her cunt widely relaxing before his entry and then swallowing his rod, holding it fast in a hot clutch.

There were hot faces in the audience; there were overwhelming itches and urges. A smartly dressed woman moved out her hand almost involuntarily and clasped the covered mound of penis of the strange man next to her as if she were in a trance. A man gripped a woman's knee and ran his fingers up under her skirt, finding her wet and totally naked underneath. Akbar Halim at the door discreetly doused the lights around the audience and smoked indifferently.

The dark bodies on the stage gleamed and writhed. Slim muscles tensed in the arms of the girl as she supported her weight with her hands on the floor. She was groaning helplessly and Mohammed Arab had his teeth gritted, his lips pulled back in a sadistic joy which sent shivers of fascinated horror through the women who watched and who would vie for similar treatment that night.

His prick stabbing in and out was swollen and white and each time he thrust it into the girl, pulling her back to meet the spear as he did, she gave a sobbing groan which sent cold chills coursing up the spines of the watchers. Her breasts hung down slightly and quivered like jellies with every in-thrust he gave. Her eyes closed and then opened in a lost glaze of passion. She spread her thighs wider, moving her feet apart with difficulty, sinking lower, forcing him slightly to alter his position behind her.

Surging into her, he watched her back, slimly twitching

beneath him. He knew that her position must be aching, painful, difficult to maintain without collapse. He knew, too, that she liked it that way, that the more she could feel debased and used and forced into positions of pain, the better she liked it, just like all the rich, French cunts out there who'd now be getting hot and probably inviting the old boys next to them to have a feel while they watched him as their idol.

He caught her buttocks and kneaded them in his fingers, letting the flesh flow round his fingers, digging deep, hurting, grabbing in fierce handfuls and squeezing with terrible pressure as he thrust so deep into her passage that he felt the soft solidity of its end and heard her gasp and jump with the unexpected sensation before she wriggled back on her phallic tormentor again.

He moved his hands over the smooth, glossy flesh of her ass which was sweating slightly. He pushed his knees against her thighs and rubbed his belly against the taut buttocks. He released his hold on her bottom and instead moved his hands between her thighs next to his stiff thing which lurched in so that he could feel its heat in a soft friction against the backs of his hands. He touched with his fingers the inflamed lips of her quim and pulled them apart, watching them trying to move back to clasp his prick as it battered triumphantly up into her belly. He felt a mad swirl in his loins and then he raised his hand and slashed it down across her buttocks so that she cried out, and there was a murmur of terror and ecstasy in the room.

Watching, they saw his beat her with the flat of his hand, his buttocks hollowing, his loins seeming to disappear in a fusion with her ass. They listened to every little groan she made and the hissing which escaped from between his clenched teeth. They saw his prick and they longed to hold it, to suck, to claw, to ram down on it—a spit that

crashed into their bodies in a merciless punishment. And the men watched her groaning and waggling and near-collapsing and their eyes glued on her sagging breasts and her swaying, tensing, finger-marked buttocks and they heard her passion and longed to be in her with their own hard, hot pricks which needed relief.

Unconcerned, because everybody in the tense room was unconcerned, some of them had begun to fuck. The women had raised their skirts and moved over onto the men's laps so that naked pricks could surge up into their crannies under cover of the skirts which fell back, a covering umbrella to the activity if not to the whimpers of passion which burst from the throats.

Mohammed Arab crashed into the girl and held his thickness buried into her to its greatest extremity, moving on the balls of his feet, so that he could feel his pulsating knob grazing against her soft cervix. He wanted to gouge out her insides, to split her from her pelvis to her throat, to hear her scream, to have her fight and try to get away, to have her helpless. That was what he liked. That was what made him a killer. But she liked to be killed. He would have liked her to resist.

In his loins the swirl had become a moving tide of sensation which was going to flood into her and drown her, make her gasp for breath as she struggled against it and it filled her. He strained back his head, veins standing out on his neck, his perfect controlled little muscles bulging and shimmering under his dark skin. He caught at her anus with his fingers and tore it apart, jabbing thickly into it with his hands as his penis bulged and battered in her channel. He heard her little scream, her gasping bewildered ecstasy as she felt the final, taut expansion of his stiffness in her.

He had a brief image of a sausage bursting its skin and

then he roared out a great gasp and began to drown her with his teeth biting his lips hard and he heard the gasps from the audience and then the curtain over the stage came down as he slumped back from the girl who collapsed to the floor. He didn't like his exhausted vulnerability to be seen.

He sat on the floor, staring at the woman without emotion now it was over and she lay with her eyes closed, breathing heavily. At times like this he was a little bewildered because suddenly there seemed no point in killing anybody. There seemed point only in resting and perhaps eating little dishes which could be brought to one's bedside. He felt naked and for the moment helpless.

The woman didn't move. Only her belly and breasts moved, heaving, and he noticed her thighs quivered a little as well.

He listened to the shuffling sounds outside, the people leaving. In an anteroom the women would begin outbidding one another for his favours for the next few nights —unless they, too, had had an orgasm, in which case they would probably think of him with disgust and hurry off telling themselves that they would not come again, but next week they would be back.

He stood up. The girl still didn't move. She would wait for him to go as usual. Neither of them spoke; she didn't try to cover her nakedness. He saw the semen flowing back out of her and making a viscid patch on the floor.

He felt with relief that in a short time he'd recover his normal killer instinct. He didn't like to feel so robbed.

CHAPTER III

The glass contained a tiny remnant of beer, just enough to justify not leaving the cafe. For the last hour it had held the same small amount and Ahmed ben Lulla's hands had lain idly on either side of the glass, his elbows across the table.

Nobody had come to sit opposite him at the small table. Most people stood at the counter, swallowed a beer, a glass of wine or pernod and then went off on some nocturnal pursuit. A few couples occupied tables farther back in the *salle* over which the patron, sitting in regal immobility behind the till, glanced from time to time without expression.

While he'd been sitting in the window, aimlessly watching the passing scene, the young prostitute opposite had been upstairs four times. That was good going in a couple of hours, with so much opposition, and he'd wished he could make money so easily. As far as he could see, the luck of the older whores was out tonight; nobody had taken any

notice of them. Occasionally one of them had taken a little strutting walk along the street and up the boulevard but without result.

Ahmed sat on and on. His thoughts, which had been all inturned, now fixed only on things outside himself as if his brain had rebelled and was giving itself a rest from depressive exhaustion. He noticed everything in great detail without having any particular concern about it. He watched the waitress in the tight skirt and sweater which was in keeping with the area. She was quite a dish and knew it. Once a large, handsome Frenchman had come in and they had stood talking for a moment at one end of the bar while the patron glanced at them occasionally in irritation that the girl was wasting her time, although as far as Ahmed could see, there was nothing for her to do at the time. As they parted, the man had placed his hand along the girl's full breast for a moment and pressed it, at which she had smiled at him. The incident had sent a sharp, painful despair to Ahmed's heart. It was a long time since he'd had a woman. He needed a sexual outlet, but, even more, what had pained him was the recognition of belonging one to the other that he'd read in their eyes. His thoughts moved fatefully back to the visit he'd had.

He considered telling the police. But they'd be as likely to assume that he was part of the National Liberation Front as well. They'd take his information and then beat him up and set him free. The NLF would inevitably get him. The loss of an odd killer would not make all that difference to its powerful organisation. There was no work. He would have gone anywhere that there was work, back to Algeria, even although he remembered the *bidonvilles* with even more horror-filled suffocation than when he thought of his room. Algerians were suspect and there were not enough jobs for them and for Frenchmen as well.

Life should be simpler than this. When one wanted so little, such ordinary things.

While he mused hopelessly against a background of hopelessness, a couple of policemen with Sten guns came in and looked over his papers. They also ran their hands over him for any concealed weapons. They taunted him while they searched.

"What dirty little game are you up to—dirty little Algerian?" He didn't answer. "Too stupid to talk—you'd better not be funny with us." He still had said nothing and, not finding anything, they'd gone out of the cafe and wandered off down the boulevard looking for other people to stop and search and taunt into insulting them back so that they could manhandle somebody and take him in.

His mind had hardly rid itself of the hurt pride at this latest unpleasantness when he realised the young, successful prostitute had come in and was at the bar drinking a coffee. He glanced out through the window at the hotel door to make sure he was not mistaken and then looked back at her, excited a little at the thought that this girl had recently been ridden naked on a bed by four different men one after the other in a short anonymous blaze of passionate necessity. She showed no signs of the experiences. She looked composed and sipped her coffee with slow, deliberate gulps, staring straight across the bar at her distorted reflection in the chrome coffee machine. He understood, now, why she had done such good business. She looked quite young and fresh. He thought she must be new at the game. She was quite attractive with short, blonde hair curled up over her head and blue, almond-shaped eyes. Her lips were well-shaped, neither thin and mean in tight lines which the majority of these women tried to hide with wads of ill-applied extra lipstick; nor yet too full and sagging in the vacancy which was so often the alternative. Her

nose was straight and broad at the nostrils and her chin firm and rounded with the skin drawn smoothly over her high cheekbones. She might have been an attractive schoolgirl. But her clothes were the uniform of this part of the world—a tight yellow sweater which emphasised wellshaped breasts and a tight black skirt through which the hems of slight briefs could be seen hardly protecting her nicely-rounded buttocks.

Watching her he wondered how much she was. But he thought of his 534 francs—and he'd not yet paid for his beer—and looked sadly away out of the window.

In the dark street he saw the two older whores coming across the road towards the cafe. A general strike, he thought, one would think they'd take advantage of her absence. He looked back at the girl at the bar and felt heat in his loins. He imagined her on a bed with the four men who'd had her that night. He wondered how firm her flesh was and how it felt to hold one of her buttocks in each of your hands, feeling it overflow in your fingers as you buried your despair in her and gained a brief respite from the ugly world. He wondered if she stripped entirely and what her breasts were like without clothes. And whether she just lay passively or whether she ever got excited. He wondered, finally, if she'd got syphilis or anything like that. It wouldn't take long for her to spoil, to look just like these other two old beat-up *poules* who came through the open door of the bar and scowled in her direction.

He transferred his attention to them, surprised at first by their hostile glances at the girl but understanding in a moment the fierce desperate jealousy they must feel not only for her youth and looks in a profession where they were all-important, but also in the suffering they underwent through loss of business.

They went to the other end of the bar and the girl didn't look at them although she must have realised they were there. She continued to sip her coffee and looked away from her reflexion in the coffee machine to the inside "salle." For a further instant she glanced at Ahmed sitting alone at his table, held his eyes for a minute, probably in anticipation of another customer, and then looked away again.

Ahmed gulped to relieve the constriction of his throat. She certainly *was* fresh. Why, he wondered, doesn't she get a reasonable job and live a quiet, simple, pleasant life out of this hard, gaudy, brassy tinsel of Pigalle where everything is slowly destroyed through commerce and anxiety and sometimes through a bullet or acid in the eyes or a knife in the back? He was overcome with a surge of self-pity. He felt no hope. He wished he had the cocky self-confidence which he read in the girl's face. He seemed to remember he'd had it once. But it didn't take long for a life with no work, little money and no hope to undermine the strongest morale. He wondered if he just went up and asked the girl if he could have a go for free whether she might take pity on him as she'd been so successful tonight. It was strange how, when everything else was low, when there was no hope in anything else, what he sought was a woman to help him ride the depression, as if it really made a difference to the outside reality of events... as if.

One of the older whores had moved along the bar and placed herself next to the girl. She was saying something to her quietly and he couldn't make out the words. She looked very angry and the girl looked disdainfully defiant in return.

The other woman had stayed at the far end of the bar but now she came up next to her crony, sliding her glass of beer along the counter with her.

Suddenly the young girl raised her voice.

"*Je m'en fous*," he heard her say. "*Ça ne me regarde pas.* I have my own life to live."

The anger on the face of the older woman deepened, her eyes looked hard and dangerous and her lips were a thin, unforgiving line.

"You dirty little bitch," she snapped back. "You'll clear out of this quarter or it'll be the worse for you."

"Leave me alone," the girl retorted, her breasts seeming to lift in pert defiance. "You can't frighten me, you old crone."

The older woman grabbed her by the hair without another word and swung her head down so that the girl's face was staring up at her in startled astonishment.

"Dirty little bitch," she rasped again. "I'll fix you."

The girl kicked out then and the woman shrieked but didn't let go of her hair. The other whore, her face wrinkled with hatred, downed her beer with a single gulp and smashed the glass on the counter.

The patron started to move round the bar but he would have been too late to save the girl's face. It was Ahmed who, propelled as if by some nervous reflex, found himself between them, knocking the glass from the woman's hand so that it smashed in a hundred splinters behind the bar and then hauling the other whore off the girl, forcing her to release her by a quick twist of her free arm.

The patron was between them too, then, and roughly pushing the older women away. A few passers-by—so quick to sense a drama—had stopped outside and were gathering in a small crowd to watch.

"Get out of here," the patron barked. "I don't want the police in here—and you'd better watch out for yourselves."

"Throw out that dirty bitch—that cutthroat little pig," one of the whores shouted as she nonetheless allowed

herself to be pushed from the bar. Her companion shouted a few filthy words and spat at the crowd which hastily made way for them.

The patron came back and looked at Ahmed and the girl without smiling.

"You'd better get out, too," he said. "It's better if you've all gone by the time the police get here."

"I'll come with you," Ahmed said to the girl. "It'll be safer for you."

"All right," she said. "Thanks."

They went out in the street together. The two whores, still cursing and swearing, had wandered back towards their hotel. The crowd made way afresh for Ahmed and his companion and then began to drift off when they realised there was nothing further to see. Farther along the street, two policemen, attracted by the sight of the small crowd, were making their way quickly towards the scene.

Ahmed began to cross the road which led on from Pigalle towards Clichy. The girl glanced down at the two women who'd attacked her and then walked after him.

"I'd better not go back there tonight," she said frankly. "Tomorrow I'll have to get some protection."

Ahmed felt wet heat on his hand and glanced down at it. There were thin streaks of blood where he'd cut himself on the jagged edge of the glass.

The girl saw it too and caught hold of his hand to look.

"C'est pas grave," she said. "We can go to my place and I'll fix it for you."

"It's not important," he said. "I don't want to put you to that trouble."

"Do you think I'm attractive?" the girl asked.

Ahmed was taken aback. Was she trying to solicit him?

"Very," he said.

"Well I wouldn't be any longer if it hadn't been for you," she said. "Come on, let's go."

They walked on through the bustle of the Boulevard de Clichy, where the noise of traffic made talking unnecessary, and turned off to the left into a quieter street.

"I thought you lived in the other hotel?" Ahmed said.

"No," she said. "That's my office."

He followed her into a quiet-looking hotel with a staircase beyond the *cour*. The hotel-keeper didn't bother to give them a glance as they passed his lodge.

"Very nice," Ahmed permitted himself as he took in the dark shape of a single tree in a bed of earth in the centre of the cobbled courtyard.

The girl said nothing and he followed her into a small foyer and up a flight of stairs with a narrow carpet running up their centre. His eyes were just below the level of her buttocks as he followed some steps behind. Her legs were flawless and shapely and the buttocks so pert and firm-looking that he longed to reach out and touch them.

They went up to the second floor and the girl took a key from under the mat.

"They're informal here," she said. "We don't have to hang our keys on a nail like a lot of schoolchildren." She unlocked the door and switched on a light.

Ahmed followed her across the threshold into a room which was twice the size of his, better-furnished and improved by various little evidences of the personality of its tenant. On a sort of washstand in a corner was an electric ring, which meant she cooked for herself. Ahmed felt hungry at the sight of the ring.

The girl walked to the end of the room and pulled back a curtain which he'd taken to be a makeshift closet. Beyond it was a washbasin with hot and cold taps. It was a long time since he'd seen such luxury.

"Come here," the girl said. "You can wash your hand first and then I'll bandage it."

He washed his hands, delighted at the warm caress of the water. The cuts were long but very superficial. He let the blood run in the water and suddenly remembered that he was under what amounted to sentence of death. He supposed it was the incredibility of the situation which enabled him to dismiss it from his mind so easily.

The girl straightened up from a small cabinet under the washbasin. She had a length of bandage in her hand and she stood looking at him, waiting for him to finish the cleaning. They had spoken very little.

She took his hand and he let her take it and hold it and bandage it, not because he thought a bandage necessary, but to feel her human warmth against his, to sink into an agreeable acceptance of someone else actually occupying herself in doing him a kindness. He couldn't remember the last time someone had actually done something for him as if he were a brother or even as if he meant anything at all.

Neatly, the girl tore the end of the bandage, splitting it into two thin laces and then she tied them gently around his hand, looking at him to see if it was all right or whether perhaps it was too tight.

He watched her concentrating on the task of bandaging and suddenly remembered the four men who'd sweated with her within the last few hours. The thought gave him a strange little chill in the pit of his stomach. Close up he saw that her skin was just as soft and smooth as it looked from a distance and that her features were, indeed, those of a high-school girl. He found that he no longer felt an urge towards her which was purely sexual. He wished they could spend a day in the country, lying in some field near a stream.

"There," she said. "That's the best I can do."

37

"Thank you," he said. "The cuts are really nothing." There was a short silence. Neither seemed to know whether they should now end the brief relationship which had sprung up. Each seemed a little shy.

Ahmed looked away round the room and remarked on what a nice little place it was. The girl followed his eyes as if she'd never really looked at the room herself before and agreed that it was pleasant enough.

"Would you like a cup of coffee?" she asked as he made no move to leave.

"But you must be tired," he said. "I don't want to trouble you."

She gave him a quick glance from her almond-shaped eyes. She sensed a trace of sarcasm in his voice, but she wasn't quite sure.

"It's not all that tiring to lie on your back and have things done to you," she said, as if to show him that she wasn't ashamed of what she did.

He held her glance and then smiled.

"Well in that case—yes, I'd like some coffee," he said.

She reached up and opened the top section of a cupboard, standing on tiptoe so that the muscle of her calf contracted and stood out and the skirt pulled tighter around her buttocks which hollowed obviously through the material. He envied all four of the men who'd had her.

Inside the cupboard when it swung open he saw packets of *biscottes*, a few tins of things and several eggs. He licked his lips, hunger rising up in him in a tormenting wave. The girl turned round with a tin of *Nescafé* in her hand and saw his eyes, aching and fixed on the food.

"Are you hungry?" she asked, in surprise.

"Yes," he said, simply.

She reached up again and brought down some of the eggs and a packet of *biscottes*.

38

"There's really not much here at the moment," she said. "But if you really want something to eat this will keep away the worst pangs."

He sat down on her bed and she busied herself with preparations for a scratchy meal. He supposed that if they'd messed up her face she would really have lost all hope of future business for a time. It was a small thing for her to fry him a few eggs.

"When did you eat?" she asked.

"Oh I have some bread and *paté* most days," he said, not answering her question directly. "And often I buy some chips and a sausage."

Arranging a small saucepan on the heater, she glanced round at him briefly as if she were reconsidering him.

"No work?"

"No," he said. "Not for some time."

"What were you doing?"

"I worked in several factories but there were always too many Frenchmen looking for jobs."

She nodded sympathetically.

"That's what got me," she said. "There were always too many women looking for jobs—and what wretched jobs, for what wretched pittances."

"I guess you make quite a bit now."

She straightened up from buttering a couple of *biscottes* and looked him straight in the eyes. When people asked questions like that they were usually wondering how much they could make out of you. It hadn't taken her long to find out what a hard, selfish world it was. He looked back at her, knowing what she thought. He'd had the same thought himself so often.

"I don't want to know," he said. "It's just that it's fascinating to see someone being successful at anything on the level on which we operate."

"I don't do too badly," she said, relaxing. "But I have to pay some of it to the syndicate."

"Uh-huh." He didn't want to sound interested any longer.

"Still," she said, "it would be much more difficult without them. They'll give me protection tomorrow from those old crones."

She made the coffee and put a small frying pan on the heater. Soon an oily aroma of eggs was steaming through the room. She sat down next to him on the bed and they both sipped the coffee from cups without saucers. She sat in a relaxed, not unfriendly manner. She seemed to begin to feel quite pleased that he was there and she had someone to talk to. Her commerce with men enabled her, when the mask of invitation was rejected, to talk to him quite naturally and without coquettry as she might have done with another woman.

"When will you get work?" she asked.

"Who knows," he said. "I try all the time."

"It must be difficult to live."

He shrugged at the understatement. He didn't really feel like discussing it and he remembered. now, the shadow which hung over him.

"It's not a very pleasant life," he said. "But when the NLF begin to get tough it makes everything else seem a trivial trial."

She took the eggs off the heater and reached up to the cupboard for plates. Her breasts rose up tautly under the sweater and a loose fold of skirt furrowed above the protrusion of the buttocks.

"You owe them money."

"Yes."

"What happens if you can't pay?"

He ran his hand across his throat.

40

"Really," she said. "Even if you just *can't* pay?"

"They're quite happy if some people can't pay," he said. "It gives them a reason for liquidating them and that keeps everybody else in order."

She passed him a plate with two eggs and a thickly buttered *biscotte*. Her eyes were clouded with disgust.

"Will you be able to pay?"

He shook his head slowly.

"I had my last warning today," he said. "There's nothing to be done. I can't pay them."

"Can't you get away?"

"Where? How? On what? My only chance of work is here. Elsewhere I'd have no hope but slow starvation."

"But the police?..."

"Perhaps you'll get to know the police some day. But for your sake I hope not."

"How much do they want from you?"

"Three thousand francs."

After a minute or two of silence she said: "It's such a small sum really."

He didn't answer. He was tired of it. He didn't want to think about it.

"So what are you going to do?"

He shrugged again. He didn't know what he was going to do. He had never thought of himself as a fatalist, but there was a great streak of it in him.

"How can you just wait for them to kill you?" she said, with a little burst of vehemence.

"There's nothing I can do," he said. "Perhaps they won't kill me after all." He didn't add what was after all an unformed thought in his mind: that life gets to such a pitch of dull hopelessness and monotony that giving it up does not seem such a terrible thing.

"I'll give you the money."

She said it in a matter-of-fact, undramatic way, this, that simply sweeping away the difference of life and death for him. He was surprised that he felt no emotion except one of pleasure that *she* was willing to give him the money. Some perversity in him even brought out an argument.

"But can you afford that much—and why should you do this for me?"

"Good God," she said. "You don't place your life very highly."

"I've lost most of the feeling I ever had about life. It doesn't seem to amount to very much."

She reached out involuntarily and touched his hand, a light touch which she withdrew immediately as if ashamed of showing any emotion.

"I will give you the money," she said. "And you can eat here with me every day..." she petered out searching for a reason to explain what she'd just heard herself say. "It's terrible... it's... inhuman not to care about life."

Ahmed ben Lulla was astonished to hear her talking in this way and to recognise that she had conceived a sudden overwhelming pity for him. He felt unworthy of pity. He felt in no sense tragic; his existence had just become a sordid headache.

"You are very kind," he said. "It will be a great burden on you..."

"It will be nothing of the sort," she said. "I happen to think that human life is... is sacred. We do lots of things which are not very nice, but to throw away life for a few thousand francs... it's too terrible to even think about."

He sat there, staring at her. It was on his lips to say: "I've never heard a prostitute so concerned with her fellow men before," but he stifled the words in his throat and said nothing.

She stood up, reaching again into the cupboard, and he found his eyes drawn yet again to the curve of her bottom. Now that she had become definitely involved with him of her own free will, he saw possession of those buttocks as a distinct possibility. He looked away, suddenly a little ashamed of his secret thoughts which were so hard and selfish compared with hers.

She tipped a little pile of fruit onto the bed—bananas and oranges.

"Help yourself—and peel me an orange," she said. "I have to clean up."

He skinned a banana and then began to peel an orange, biting first through the skin and then levering the thick peel away with his thumbnail. The girl stepped into the small alcove where the washbasin was and pulled off her sweater. Ahmed stared, his heart quickening, as, completely unconcerned about his presence, she turned on taps and gathered things from a little cabinet below. Her brassiere covered her breasts fully, but it was made of a strong-looking but very thin material through which he thought he could see the colour of her skin. Certainly there was a darker patch where her nipple stabbed out.

Ahmed had let the half-peeled orange fall into his lap. He was guiltily unable to take his eyes from the girl. When she had arranged the things she needed—talcum powder, perfume, soap on a small shelf below the mirror above the basin—she turned to pull the curtain across and caught his eyes. It took a second or two for her to realise that he was staring at her and then she glanced quickly down at her breasts and up at him again as if a recognition of their sexual difference had only just occurred to her. She pulled the curtain across with a slow, thoughtful movement and he could no longer see her.

Slowly he ate the banana. He studied the room, the long

window, the little table with some cinema magazines on it and a French-English phrase-book. The phrase-book reminded him that she made her money by opening her thighs. He wondered how many GIs she'd entertained and how many words she managed to say to them in English. He noticed that she even had a small radio and he wondered again how much she charged.

His eyes wandered back to the alcove. He could hear her slithering out of her skirt. She was getting rid of the sweat and semen of the past hours, he thought, freshening up after the day's work. He stared at the curtain as if he'd pierce it with his eyes, but he couldn't see anything, except its occasional movement as she brushed against it.

After several minutes she said to him: "There's a dressing gown in the cupboard. Will you pass it to me?"

He opened the cupboard and saw the thick dressing gown on a hook in a line of skirts and sweaters and blouses and one decent-looking suit.

The girl extended a long bare arm between the curtain and the edge of the alcove and he put the dressing gown over it. After a few minutes more, she came out with the dressing gown swathed around her, knotted tightly by the cord around her waist. In her hands she carried the skirt and sweater and some underclothes which she flung into the bottom of the cupboard. She seemed very unconcerned about her nudity under the dressing gown, but Ahmed felt a little shiver tremble through his chest.

She sat down on the edge of the bed and took the orange which he held out to her.

"God, what a relief," she said. "I feel a new person."

"You look fine," he said. Any trace of tiredness seemed to have been washed away. Her eyes looked softer as if they had relaxed with her body, her face had a slight flush from washing. She hadn't bothered to put on any cos-

metics and now he saw that her skin was fresh and school-girlish. She still looked good without any makeup. It was difficult to think of her as a prostitute.

She glanced quickly at him over a bite of orange. It was as if any hint of sexual reference took her by surprise, as if she hadn't yet quite equated them as man and woman.

"Are you still hungry?" she asked.

"No."

She had asked the question as if she wanted to avoid a silence after his compliment and he answered her as if he preferred the silence to remain.

They sat looking at each other without speaking. Her lips embraced and then swallowed quarters of orange which she chewed gently, her cheeks hollowing, her eyes thoughtful.

"You really look fine," he repeated.

She looked at him warily. He couldn't understand what thoughts she was hiding behind the alert watchfulness in her eyes. She seemed purposely ready to set up a barrier and he said with a sudden passionate bitterness: "But you'll lose it all before you realise what's happening."

"Oh, nonsense," she said, as if she'd often had this argument with other people, or perhaps with herself.

"You've seen them," he said. "You've seen their slack bodies, their pockmarked faces, those worn faces and dull eyes. It's inevitable."

"It's just that they're stupid," she said. "They don't know how to look after themselves and they don't bother either. It's quite unnecessary to become an old slut at 30—in any case I'm not going to be lectured by you or anyone else."

He relapsed into silence, surprised at his own vehemence. Thinking about what she was and how she'd be was like standing by and watching some beautiful bird dashing itself

against the bars of a cage until it was reduced to a straggling mess of feathers.

Goaded by his sad eyes looking at her, the girl added: "I want money. I want to have enough money to buy the things I want and this is the only way I can get it. Nobody forced me into this and I had a good, ordinary job with no prospects before I started it." Her voice seemed to fan out like a cat's back bristling.

"I can get 3,000 francs a time and I give a thousand to the syndicate. I've made 8,000 francs for myself tonight and I can do twice as well as that. How else could anyone my age be getting that sort of money? I'm not Françoise Sagan and I'm not Brigitte Bardot and there's no other way to make it."

"It's your life," Ahmed said. "It's just that I find you so attractive that—maybe I feel a little jealous."

"Jealous!" she said.

"But if I had 3,000 francs," he went on, "I'd be wanting to go to bed with you, so that wouldn't exactly be consistent with the tone of what I've just said."

"Is that how you'd think of it, too?" she asked. "You'd give me 3,000 francs and then use my body and forget about it?"

"Is that exactly how it seems to you with all the rest of them?" he countered.

"Oh, the first few times I was nervous and I got excited," she said, frankly. "But afterwards it became just something I did without caring. It's really very easy not to be moved by the whole thing."

"I suppose it is," he said. "I wouldn't like it that way. I'd prefer to spend 3,000 francs on beer if I knew you were going to be as indifferent as that."

"Why should it matter to you?"

46

"I like things like that to be a little more human," he said. "Like you, I have ideas about human life."

She studied his face, searching it with her blue, almond eyes. A fleeting trace of something close to longing fled across her face and then she seemed to snuff it out.

She stood up and went to the basin to rinse her fingers under the tap and after watching her for a moment he got up too and stood behind her, looking at her in the mirror. He felt all of a sudden an inevitability about their having met. It moved him to a feeling of closeness with her which he wanted more than anything to communicate, but which he knew was made so difficult by what she was and what she expected in the attitudes of men towards her.

She saw him in the glass and stared back at him for a long moment. Then she turned slowly to face him, looking up at his eyes as if again trying to read his thoughts. The longing had moved into her eyes again and was not yet, this time, snuffed out.

"I could fall in love with you," he said.

She went on looking at him, her eyes questioning and a little sad and then he leaned forward and kissed her. For a moment she made no response and he took his mouth from hers and said: "If you don't believe me or if it doesn't matter to you I'll go now."

And then she moved in towards him and kissed him and her lips swallowed his and seemed to draw the soul of his feelings out through his mouth. He put his arms around her and pulled her body gently in against his so that he could feel her warmth along him. They didn't use their tongues as if in this first moment they each wanted to show that there was something more than just sexuality in their action.

When their faces moved apart she smiled at him.

"It's so—so different to hear you say that," she said.

"I don't care if you don't really feel it, just as long as I can feel that for once somebody feels something."

He kissed her again and then ran his lips over her face as if they were sensitive fingers tracing the lines of her features. She slipped her hands round him and linked them in the small of his back as she searched out his lips and locked them with her mouth. And this time he moved his lips, sucking on hers, and her tongue slithered out into his mouth and he felt a growing weight in his loins.

"Do you feel like it?" he said. "Or are you tired?"

"I feel more like it than I ever have before," she said softly.

He felt now a vague jealousy for all those other times she'd been had that very night. He wanted to ask her questions: "Did you have an orgasm? Did you get excited? How does this feel different? Did you undress completely? Did you put your tongue in their mouths? What did their groans of passion sound like? Did any of them hurt you?..." But instead the questions joined in an unvoiced whiplash to his own passion; as if with his lovemaking he wanted to wipe away all memory she might have of previous occasions.

He ran his lips down her neck, drawing little red marks from her soft skin. He saw a bruise already there and the sight of it made him want to get into her immediately, almost to punish her with his love for the bruise she had allowed to be given her in the heat of someone else's passion and perhaps her own.

He reached down to the cord of her dressing gown and unknotted it so that it fell open and her bare skin was pressed against his body. He slipped it from her shoulders and she slithered her arms out of it, letting it drop to the floor. He ran his hands over her back and down to her bottom, letting his fingers revel on the firm skin, his loins

48

tingling, his whole body trembling at the feel of her nakedness, so firm and resilient.

He moved his face down her body, finding her breasts which were as firm and full as he'd expected and which responded to his kissing with a tautening of the nipples. He drew his fingers gently along their bulging sides, from her ribs round to the nipple, just his fingertips. And then he bit her smudge of nipple gently so that she gasped and clasped his head.

With a pulsing in his jeans, he pushed her back to the bed and slithered down her body as she sat back on the edge of the bed. He thought again of those who had possessed her within the last few hours. Those who had done what he was doing, perhaps produced the same reactions in her, and he ran his lips over the flat, little belly and down between her thighs, which she opened with a little moan.

Between them he found the warm lips and licked them with a tongue which, too, seemed to tremble and tingle. His tongue entered her, its moisture mingling with her own and she slipped forward on the bed, moaning and held his head against her crotch.

He licked and sucked and found her clitoris moving up to erection. He fastened on it and she began to wriggle her hips in little, contracting movements as if she was trying to control her passion.

Her quim had opened and there was a perfumed moisture on his tongue. She smelt of perfumed soap and her skin, the skin of her thighs which clasped his face in a gently, never-still embrace, was soft and sweet-smelling.

He felt her hands on his head, trying to pull him up. She wanted him now and he stood up, quickly, stripping off his clothes. She lay back on the bed with her eyes closed, her body wracked with heaving breath. Her body was just

as lovely as it seemed in her sweater and that tight skirt. They didn't lie. She was firm and youthful and her body was full of vigour and passion.

Naked, he moved over and knelt beside her, running his hands over her breasts, her stomach, her thighs, up and down over her nakedness with trembling hands which brought out a response of gasping and quivering from her.

She opened her eyes and pulled his head down on hers, her tongue searching immediately with a strong, rigid pressure as if she wanted him to emulate her movement with his penis in her.

"Now darling, now," she breathed.

Again he saw the bruise on her neck and it made his stiff prick a hot pulsation which throbbed against her thigh so that she could feel its scorching heat like a stick of hot metal.

He ran his hands over her and rummaged between her thighs which opened to admit him and stayed open, moving continuously in a little passionate tremulation.

"It was never like this," she whispered, choking on her words.

Her words seemed to ease the painfulness of his desire to punish her for the existence of the bruise and he moved over, slithering on her body, feeling it warm and springy under him, feeling it quiver helplessly.

She reached down under her thighs which she drew up gently and he felt her cool hand on his prick. Her hand stabbed a shock into his rigid flesh and his uncircumcised foreskin ripped back and she gently guided him at her vagina until she could feel the moist, fleshy warmth against his prick waiting for its entry.

"Darling, darling!" she whispered, losing the words in a groan which broadened and deepened as he thrust into her.

Her moist heat clamped him like a warm, resisting jelly,

and he barked a gasp out into the room and began to give quick, aching thrusts up into her vagina, thrusts which slowed and lengthened as he filled her yielding passage to greater and greater depth.

Under him her body quivered and trembled and her nipples pushed into him with a pointed, erect pressure; her warm belly brushed against his and her thighs clamped and unclamped, holding and releasing him in waves of flesh-warmth and air-coolness.

"Oh—oh," he groaned as he felt her quim squeezing along the length of his cock which seemed to expand and maintain a point just below bursting point.

"Darling, darling," she whispered over and over again as she bucked and writhed under him. Her face moved from side to side, marks appeared on her lips where she bit them and every so often her mouth came against his and her teeth bit into him and she sucked his tongue and forced her own between his lips, panting warm breath into his throat.

With her pinioned by his arm of thick flesh, he thought again of the others who'd had her in just this way, holding her with big, horny hands, digging up into her most intimate core with big, blunt pricks, producing from her just such gasps and perhaps movement while they groaned and sobbed out their coarse male passion into her slim, delicate girl body.

He felt a chill course down his spine at the thought and gave an extra hard thrust which seared into her and brought forth a throat-rasping groan: "Ooooh! Yes, darling... please."

Did she ask them when they fucked her "Ooooh yes darling... please?" He lunged again, stabbing in in a bludgeoning thrust which tore roughly deep into her cunt and she groaned and murmured: "Oh God! God!"

He slipped his hands down her sides and slid them under her moving buttocks, clasping them one in each hand, remembering that that was the very thought he'd had, of holding her buttocks, bare, in his hands.

They were tensing and untensing, firm, hollowed and then relaxed and oozing around his fingers which he dug into their orbs with fierce pressure. Her pulled her hips against him as he inthrust and felt her pull back her thighs a little more.

He slipped his fingers over the taut, stretched flesh of her rump and found the unconcealed anus, smooth and hot and working itself as she tensed and relaxed.

He dug it with a finger and it yielded and his finger, a replica of his rod, moved into soft, warm depths, bringing new gasps and exclamations from her ever-working lips. He intruded another and felt the tight resistance slowly give as she screwed her anus back on his fingers and soon both were moving and circling in her and she was impaled in both her orifices and wriggling in abandon under the dual rifling.

Her legs, on either side of his impaling, were jerking and writhing like puppet legs in abandon. He felt their warm fleshy pressure as they held him tight and then they would move off and she would pull them up to her shoulders or fling them out at right angles to her hips, moaning and gasping continuously.

Her eyes were closed; all the time her mouth worked and trembled and her neck was strained as she thrust back her head in the intensity of her feeling.

Ahmed was aware of no part of his body but his heavy, too-full prick which moved deeply in and out of her, lovingly clasped in the excruciating warmth of her. He moved his fingers from her rectum, sliding them down through her crotch, tracing where buttocks ran into thighs and then

feeling the soft folds of flesh and his own prick moving into her, making those folds yield and give way as they held his organ in a tight, contracting grip.

He stroked and pinched the folds and she jerked and cried out afresh. She was almost whining and the heat from her body seemed to envelop him.

"Oh, darling, darling!" she moaned. Her voice rose on a high, gasping note. "Now, now... coming... coming... *j'arrive!*" she groaned and choked.

He felt the sudden widening of her hole, the relaxing of the pressure of his penis and then the liquid surrounding him as if he were stabbing his rod into a lake.

Hot and pulsating, he quickened the rate of his thrusts as she continued to moan, more gently. He felt his own passion reaching up to a pin-point of highly-defined sensation at the very tip of his prick, all gathering in the aching knob of his organ.

For the last time he thought of those others who had reached this stage, about to pump their heart into her quim, with her lying under them, accepting their passion, their semen with widespread legs and breasts which dug warmly into their hairy chests.

He gripped her buttocks and squeezed with a pulverising pressure, feeling her cringe, wanting in a strange way to hurt her as he reached up and up to that culminating point.

"Oh—oh—oh—oh!" He grunted and groaned and slowed his stroke, grinding slowly and deep so that his abdomen smacked firmly against the flanges of her sex and his stiffness reached to its farthest point in the recesses of her body. He felt himself coming and pulled back her thighs to her shoulders, hearing her moan and applying all the pressure of his body down there at his loins and the long aching finger which drove into her.

"Daaaaarling!"

With a sudden wet, warm relief which was too much to bear he shot into her and he shot and shot and shot into her all the pent-up emotion of weeks in a great, overwhelming relief which her body encouraged him in.

Trembling, he relaxed on her and she put her arms around him and lay there against him, neither of them speaking for several minutes.

"It was never—never—like that," she whispered.

His passion relieved, he no longer cared about the bruise on her neck which was somebody else's doing. He felt comfortable and pleasant lying close to her other human warmth.

"I'm glad," he said. "I don't want it ever to be like that for you with anyone else."

When they both fell asleep it was without any worry shadowing their dreams. Their difficulties for the moment seemed not to exist. Such is the moment of discovering another human being.

CHAPTER IV

Detective-Inspector Pierre Raimond cut himself another piece of Munster. With the air of a man enjoying something he really liked for the last time, he dabbed the soft, runny cheese into a little pile of carraway seeds.

His young wife sat opposite watching him with a smile. A smile which covered the anxiety which gripped her heart like the premonition of death.

Raimond looked up at her over savouring the mouthful of cheese.

"Those seeds make all the difference," he said, and, without altering his tone at all, added: "There's nothing to worry about, Michele. It's not much more than a routine patrol."

Her beautiful, pale face with its aristocratic air of determination looked less sure and determined than he'd ever seen it before. She'd eaten hardly anything and seemed almost unable to do anything but smile at him weakly. He reached across the table and took her hand. There were tears in her eyes.

"It's nothing, darling," he said. "There's really little danger."

"Oh, Pierre," she said. "Whatever you say, please don't treat me like a child. There *is* danger. Everybody knows there *is* danger. They're well armed and they wouldn't hesitate to shoot anyone who was after them."

"But I only have to do the location work, darling," he said. "I find out where they are and how to get them and then the security police move in and take over when the shooting starts."

"Darling, I wish they'd given the job to someone else."

"Now, is that any way to speak of an honour that's been done your husband?"

He grinned at her cheerfully and she smiled back wanly and nibbled at a piece of bread as if she didn't even realise what she was eating.

Pierre Raimond was young for a detective-inspector. He was a detective-inspector because he was one of the most brilliant young men in the force—and this job of rooting out the NLF in Paris, of discovering who and where they were, had been entrusted to him because he was the best man for the job. It was, of course, a highly dangerous job and he knew that his wife knew this. But he went on minimising it just to show that he didn't consider it to be anything too tough for him. As long as he didn't show any anxiety it would to some small extent prevent her own from overcoming her.

He wiped his fingers on his napkin and dabbed his mouth. It was a tough job all right. The situation had been getting worse and worse and there was no hope of improvement until the hard core of Algerian nationalists in the city were rounded up and put out of harm's way. There was reason to believe they were quite few in number, the real fanatics, but their fanaticism and the manner in which they terrorised the rest of the Muslim population in Paris made them a force to be reckoned with.

In recent weeks more Algerians had been killed in the city than had lost their lives for several months before: those who wouldn't pay their contribution towards nationalist funds, those who wanted to remain French, one after another they'd been shot up in bars, knifed in their shabby hotel rooms, found dumped on wasteland on the outskirts of Paris. And not only Algerians. Passers-by had been wounded in broad daylight through happening to be in a particular spot at the particular time when somebody walking nearby or drinking at their elbow had been scheduled to return to his Maker.

And, more and more serious from the point of view of law and order and the confidence of the civilian population, no fewer than six policemen who had got involved in hunting down the killers had themselves been shot and killed.

Large-scale manhunts and *ratissages* had produced no solid result. Hundreds of Algerians had been taken in for questioning. Police patrols had been doubled in affected areas and a *prime de risque* had been agreed for police working in dangerous spots.

But the killers and their leaders remained at large, hidden in a veil of silence. Those who knew would say nothing, afraid of revenge. Others who might have given information knew nothing worth telling.

So Pierre Raimond, former parachutist lieutenant in Algeria, where he'd mastered Arabic, and now bright young member of the metropolitan police, was to be given an opportunity to root out information which his colleagues had failed to wring out of months of questioning suspects and believed sympathisers.

He left his wife pouring the coffee and went through to the bedroom of their small, comfortable apartment near Raspail. When he reappeared he was dressed like a typical

lorry driver, porter, working man. There remained about him no vestige of his profession.

He sipped his coffee and watched his tall, lovely wife clearing away the debris from their meal. She had long, perfect legs and trim, oval-shaped buttocks with a slim torso not overburdened by neat, high breasts. He wished he could stay with her tonight. He always had these feelings when off on some mission, always the thought that after all one never knew when the end was coming.

When he'd finished his coffee he stood up and looked round the familiar room. His wife came towards him and put her arms around him, her head against his neck. He held her to him, feeling tender and wanting to rid her mind of the worry he knew filled it.

"Darling—don't take any unnecessary risks," she begged. "Leave that to the others. You said you only have to find them."

He gave a little laugh to reassure her.

"I told you it's not even dangerous," he said. "There's nothing to worry about at all. I'll be back in the morning and I'll probably have spent my whole night just sitting around in bars."

She made a brave attempt at humour.

"Well, don't go to bed with any strange whores," she said.

He tipped her head back and kissed her hard.

"They couldn't hope to measure up to you," he said.

"Well, don't try to find out," she said.

He patted her bottom gently, feeling the hard round summit under his hand, wanting her now, but having to go.

He drove in his little Simca through the tree-shaded boulevard, past the brightly-lit restaurants of St. Germain-

des-Prés where conversation was endless in the cafes and each elegant woman tried to show a little more of her figure than her neighbour.

Over the great, moving chasm which was the Seine, muddy and fast-flowing from earlier floods. Up the broad sweep of the Avenue de l'Opéra where all the windows were alive with light and posters beckoned to lazy islands and bullfights and Roman sunshine and temples in the Far East. In the Café de la Paix the tourists were watching the steady flow of traffic and reading *La Vie Parisienne*.

He stopped with the lights, proceeded with the flow of this traffic, waited for pedestrians to cross. He might have been going to visit a friend.

Soon he was moving slightly uphill amidst myriad bars and clubs where a lemonade cost 400 francs and platinum blondes leaned on the door with breasts the equal of Jayne Mansfield's and twice as showing. Inside, as doors swung open and shut quickly letting in a shirt-sleeved GI, there was glimpse of strong-thighed negresses at the bar.

These little streets were jammed with cars and he had difficulty finding somewhere to park. He left the car and walked up onto the main boulevard, dominated by the lights of the Moulin Rouge and several large cinemas. He turned right towards Chapelle and the comparative darkness. Underneath his left arm he could feel the reassuring coldness of his little automatic. He hoped it wouldn't be necessary to use it.

For half a mile or so he followed the overhead *métro*, a dark, giant scaffolding running along the centre of the broad boulevard with every so often a little train running with rumbling brightness along it like some noisy glowworm.

The bars became gloomier and shabbier and both streets and cafes swarmed with a larger proportion of Arabs than

any other nationality. The monotonous, strange wail of Arab music came from doorways and he passed policemen walking slowly and carefully in groups of three, watched by ugly prostitutes sitting hopelessly in the doorways of dim, cheap hotels.

As he passed the bars he glanced in through the smoky windows. Some were almost empty, others crowded almost exclusively with Algerians. He chose one from which music came and in which he could see a group of men and women nudging a pinball machine and pushed open the door.

CHAPTER V

This was another busy night area. Around the commissariat people were strolling towards their favourite cafes. In the kerbside several barrows, from which vendors were selling bananas, dates and oranges, were perched. The commissariat was surrounded with a number of small, winding streets in which the dustbins had already been placed along the kerb for cats to start their scavanging. In the windows of the crumbling apartments which rose like cliffs on either side of the narrow streets lights were shining through washing which hung on miniature balconies. Concierges were chatting in dilapidated courtyards or sitting smoking at their windows. There was an air of quiet, everynight animation.

Outside the commissariat was a familiar blue *panier à salade*, a capacious police van. A man in uniform was sitting at the wheel waiting, yawning occasionally. In the back were two more uniformed men with Sten guns, indifferently staring out through the dark windows.

In a doorway just across the street from the commissariat, Mohammed Arab was standing back in the deep shadow, his eyes fixed on the door of the commissariat. Occasionally he glanced at different points nearby, particularly noting a

large, empty barrow which a vendor was slowly trundling towards the commissariat some distance away.

Above the unobtrusive, stone building, a tricolor hung limply while people passed laughing and talking and seeing neither the police van, nor the dark figure in the doorway.

As the minutes ticked by, Mohammed Arab eased the revolver out of his pocket. His hand was as steady as a knife, his face was a vicious mask.

Along the street, the barrow was trundling nearer. It had been impossible to time exactly as there was no regular schedule to go by.

There was a sudden stir in the doorway of the commissariat and a broad, squat man with grey hair and a hard face came walking quickly out with a younger man in uniform beside him.

Mohammed Arab stepped quickly from the doorway with the revolver hanging by his side, holding it close in against his leg. He stepped into the road and began to cross as the man at the wheel of the van opened the door. The vendor with the barrow came level, hurrying his last steps. As Mohammed Arab raised his arm and fired in a quick, smooth movement, the vendor gave his barrow a push which sent it crashing in front of the van and then took to his heels.

Mohammed Arab ran quickly too, fading into the darkness, pushing through astonished, bewildered passers-by as police came running from the building and the two guards with Sten guns leapt down from the disabled van to be met with a volley of shots from several points.

Round the nearby corner, Mohammed Arab sat low in the back of a car which sped off from the kerbside.

"Did you get him?" a voice asked.

He gave a single nod and his mouth twisted in a smile of triumph.

CHAPTER VI

Ahmed ben Lulla lay on his own bed in his own hotel room which now seemed so much less of a prison. He chuckled to himself happily. He was in love with a prostitute whose name, he'd discovered, was Françoise Louvier and she was in love with him. He'd paid his contribution to the NLF and he had no more serious money troubles. Every day he ate a good meal and he'd paid off his hotel arrears. That was on the credit side. On the debit side, and the chuckle muted in his throat as he thought of it, was the fact that she was still taking her stance outside her "office" and being solidly shagged by several men every night, the fact that he still couldn't find a job, the fact that they were both tied to their present situation by their need of money.

For the first day or two after the night they'd spent together at her hotel, he'd sat in the same bar watching her, cringing, losing his stomach every time a man stopped and spoke to her, aching in his soul when he saw her turn

and lead a man into the hotel. He'd see a light go on overlooking the street three storeys up and it would remain on sometimes for as long as 25 minutes, sometimes just for ten. Then there would be darkness and the man would come out of the hotel, look round as if to prove that he wasn't embarrassed and then walk briskly away, his lust satiated. A minute or two later she would come out, just as if nothing had happened, and glance over at the cafe where he sat. After a little of the watching he'd felt too sick to do it any more and had removed himself to another cafe or spent the hours in his hotel room waiting for the early morning when he'd see her.

She had decided, although he hadn't really understood the necessity, that he should keep his own room and not move in with her completely. There might be trouble with the protection, she'd said. It was better if she didn't appear to have any attachments.

Reluctantly he'd agreed. They had talked for a long time about what they could do. She said it meant nothing to her to continue her "profession." It was the most certain way that they could go on making money. Besides, she'd agreed to stay in the protection ring for a year at least and she was afraid they might get nasty if she tried to withdraw. They'd slashed some negress who'd tried to get out to marry a paratrooper. And in any case they had no other way to live.

Now she was on the job, being fucked at this very moment probably. Even as he lay here on his bed gazing up at the cracked ceiling, she was groaning under the weight of some gasping stranger, her legs all awry while he thrust up into her belly to rid himself of the weight of desire in his loins. He caught his breath. This couldn't go on.

He glanced at the newspaper beside him on the bed with

its headlines about the assassination of the police super-intendent. There was no escape once you'd been marked by the nationalists. If a police chief was unsafe, what chance did a lone Algerian have against the secret forces of Algeria for the Algerians.

It was an astonishing business. There was a lot of talk in the newspaper of special police measures, of the city being unsafe for the general public, even suggestion of the deportation wholesale of the Algerians in the metropolis. But there was always so much talk and never any con-clusive action. Ahmed knew that Algeria for the Algerians would eventually become a reality. The sweep of nationalism from Syria to Morocco was undeniable. But he didn't see how much in Algeria would change because of it. Algeria would still be no place to make a fortune in—but it might become a place where the *bidonvilles* were replaced with the decent sort of apartments that even the poorer French population occupied.

In the meantime—a police chief! The reign of terror in Paris, designed to push the government to making con-cessions to the nationalists elsewhere, was taking a dangerous shape.

And its effect on the Algerian population of Paris would be considerable. There would be no defaulters in the payment of contribution for the funds to create a new nation.

His thoughts wandered off politics and a brave new North Africa to his comparative happiness of the last few days. She loved him. It was the first time she, too, had considered a man as a person in whom she would find sympathy and a desire which was not purely to tear down her knickers and shag. But in bed she was warm and sweet and a relieving shelter from all their uncertainty. Every time he threaded gently into her warm, receptive body he felt at peace and

could forget all events and anxieties beyond the moment in which they joined to share a fleeting movement together which convulsed them in a vacuum of pleasure which involved only themselves.

But when he made love to her at the end of the night or in the early morning or sometimes later, even, during the day, he suffered from the knowledge of those who had so recently made love to her before him, even though she claimed that it meant nothing to her, that the girl in bed with them was a different person without feeling, thinking only of the time when she would see him again and of the money she was accumulating which would be of use to them.

He was interrupted from his reverie by a sharp tap on the door. He moved slowly off the bed. For some reason the tap had seemed to contain a menace. But he'd paid his contribution. What sort of menace could there possibly be?

He stepped across to the door and opened it without calling out to ask who was there. Three men sidled into the room, pushing him in front of them and closing the door behind them. All three were Algerians. Two of them had collected his contribution to the funds only a day ago.

"What's this?" he said. A coldness seeped inside him, surrounding his heart like ice water.

None of the men replied. One placed himself in front of the door, another moved over between Ahmed and the window and the third pushed him back onto the bed and looked at him with a vicious smile. Ahmed had never seen a killer before, but looking at this man he knew that killing was his job and his chest began to flutter with horror.

The smile on the man's face broadened and managed to become more vicious. His teeth were startlingly white where

one might have expected them to be dirty and decayed. He had a feline air of nervous energy, perfectly controlled. Ahmed's voice dried up; he felt drained of life itself.

After a long, intimidating silence, the man in front of him spoke.

"You are a good boy," he said, with a sneer in his voice. "You managed recently to pay your contribution to the movement in spite of difficult circumstances. These circumstances did not, of course, provide any more reason for you not to pay. It's of no interest whether you can pay or not—no personal interest to us, you understand. But the fact that you paid shows you are a good boy, which we recognise..."

His voice droned on and, after a few seconds of astonishment that they seemed so aware of his circumstances, Ahmed hardly heard the words. He stared into the dark vicious eyes of his visitor, fascinated as by a cobra. Occasionally the words swam back into his consciousness and then he lost them again, becoming aware, this time, only of the man's cruel lips, moving slightly as he talked.

"...Françoise Louvier is the property of the—of certain people who protect her," the voice came through, startling him with the mention of her name and pulling him together at the thought that she, too, might be involved with these men. "She can, thus, not be permitted to become too intimate with others who are nothing to do with the protection. She might get ideas."

He paused and in the next second Ahmed saw that there was a long, slim knife in his hand. It had appeared there as if he'd pulled it out of the air like a professional conjuror. He balanced it casually on the flat of his hand while he talked.

"We can, therefore, not allow such an insignificant part of humanity as you to interfere in her life and consequently

in the life of the organisation behind her. You will, there-fore, not see her again and not contact her in any way."

The indication in the words that at least he was not at this moment to be killed out of hand, reacted so strongly, so reassuringly in Ahmed's mind that he voiced a small protest.

"But we are in love with each other," he said. "It would be impossible..."

The man's hand slashed through the air and lashed him full across the face, not only numbing him with pain, but knocking him sideways down on the bed with its unexpected force.

The grin on his face became, if it were possible, even more vicious than before.

"You have been warned," he said, pricking the point of the knife against Ahmed's throat. "You know what it is to disobey."

Ahmed said nothing. Here he sensed his life hung on a thread.

The man withdrew the knife and slipped it away inside his dark jacket. He motioned to the man near the window, who crossed the room. He grinned at Ahmed and said softly: "Don't make us have to see you again."

And then the door opened and, one after the other with movements so swift that they seemed to move out like one person, they left.

Ahmed lay where he'd been knocked, for several seconds without moving, and then he raised his fingers to his face, where he could now feel the stinging pain. His heart was beating like a train shunting. The whole interview had lasted only a few minutes. They had come and gone like phantoms walking out of a dream, not belonging to the material world one knew and recognised.

After several minutes more his thoughts began to clarify

and rushed to Françoise, who, even now, unaware of the danger he'd just—for the moment—survived, was submitting to a stranger's lovemaking in a hotel a few blocks away. The thought that he would obey, would not see her again, never occurred to him. His mind was simply flooded with thoughts on how to evade this embargo. He stood up and went to the airshaft, stared down into its gloomy depths which seemed an abyss as dark and endless as the future.

CHAPTER VII

Françoise let herself into her room, rather surprised to
find that Ahmed was not there. She felt tired and rather
sick with the evening's business. Perhaps it was just as
well if he'd fallen asleep in his own hotel and would not
be round until late the next day.

Things had taken a slightly different shape today. Clients
who hitherto had been content with straightforward fucking
had begun to want to experiment. Two of them had wanted
to thrust their pricks up her asshole. She'd refused at
first; she wasn't used to the idea of that sort of thing. But
the first one had offered her double and after some hesitation
she'd been unable to refuse. The act had proved painful in
spite of the lubricant and had at one point made her feel
sick. She'd been on the point a number of times of trying
to wriggle away and refuse to go on, so considerable had
been the pain in her rectum and the sweeping waves of
disgust which had consumed her. But each time the grip in
which she was held as her customer stuffed her anus and
the thought of the money had choked the words in her

throat, drowning them in her moans. When he'd finished she'd lain, bottom uncovered, face buried in the bed, until, with a few inappropriately cheerful words of what a tight little back-crack she had and how much he'd enjoyed it, the monster had gone. At last she'd got up and washed and gone down again to take up her stance.

When the whole procedure had been repeated she'd been torn once again between refusing outright and permitting what, after all, was no longer a horrible novelty. It had been easier the second time although it had made her twice as sore and left her feeling as if she were walking about with a hole the size of a bomb crater between her buttocks.

She undressed slowly and began to wash again. Now it would become part of the night's activities—to be buggered between fucks. Then they would be wanting her to suck them off and God knew what else would follow. She bathed her anus, tenderly, and tried to see it in her mirror. It felt inflamed and it seemed, strangely, like a dark secret she must keep from Ahmed. If only there were another way of making so much money…

Recently she'd found her attitude modifying slightly. She was no longer the girl who had left her home in Marseilles to take a job with a business firm in Paris, knowing that she was going to make money by her looks, whatever the cost. Several weeks of being presented so nude and intimate for the pleasures of strangers, some of them ugly with bad breath, coarse tongues and dirty bodies, had made her feel that perhaps she could manage with less money. If only Ahmed could get a job, she felt almost inclined to become a normal housewife, staying in and doing the shopping and washing his clothes and being able to lavish all her love, emotional and physical, on him alone.

She pulled her dressing gown over her nakedness, not bothering to tie it with the cord, and then she lay on the

bed, aware still of the tender heat at the core of her bottom.

She had dozed off when the knock came on the door. It took a second for the noise to penetrate the haze of sleep which inundated her and the knock was repeated before she began to swing her legs off the bed to open the door for Ahmed.

Outside, when she unlocked the door, three strange men were standing, men who pushed immediately into the room without being asked and locked the door behind them.

So sure had she been that it was her lover that she'd not bothered to pull the dressing-gown around her and her breasts and down to her feet had been uncovered in a long panel of nudity as the men moved in. Now, too astonished to protest, she became aware of their eyes rifling her form, her nakedness, and instinctively pulled the gown tightly around her. She was too frightened to cry out and she simply stared at them with her large, almond-shaped eyes filled with terror as one of them, with the most vicious expression she'd ever seen, began to speak.

"We're here from the protection organisation," he said. "We've come to tell you what a naughty little girl you're being and how much those who have your interests at heart disapprove."

A certain streak of indignation began to merge with her fright after the initial shock. After all, this was a hotel in the centre of civilised Paris.

"What do you mean?" she said. "And how do I know who you are?"

"There is no need for any discussion," the man said, his eyes moving over the curves of her body where they indented and pushed out the dressing gown. "This man, Ahmed ben Lulla—you've been giving him money?"

A new fright gripped her at the mention of his name. Had they seen him? What had happened? Her instinct

told her to deny that she knew him or that she'd ever given him anything, but then reason asserted itself.

"Yes," she said. "I've given him money."

The man smiled, an extremely unpleasant expression.

"You will give him no more," he said. "And, as from now, the organisation will take two instead of one-third of what you make in the exercise of your—uh—talents." He continued to look at her appreciatively and glanced away to her clothes which hung flimsily over a chair. Neither of the other two men had spoken. They stood with slight smiles which were replicas of their spokesman's. She felt as if she were surrounded by tigers. But her indignation bridled at the injustice of what they had threatened.

"The money I've given him was my own," she said. "I gave it him as a present and nobody has any right to tell me what to do with my money."

With a movement which took her totally by surprise, the man caught her wrist and twisted her arm behind her back so that she twisted involuntarily round and fell against him, back towards him. Her dressing gown fell open and, even with the sudden pain which shot through her arm, she was more aware of his eyes looking down at her breasts which poked whitely, pointedly out of the open gown. The other two men moved a little so that they could look at that naked, rounded, front view of her body.

"Little girls like you do not try to argue with the organisation," the man who held her said softly. "You obey or you..."

With a shock which ran like ice-cold water down her spine she felt the flat of a knife blade drawn across her throat. Her immediate reaction was to cry out. He clamped a hand over her mouth and she bit it wildly, hearing his oath and the order that he barked to the other two to leave the bitch to him.

She was flung onto the bed and the dressing gown ripped effortlessly off her. She tried to cover her nakedness with a sheet but then the breath was knocked out of her as his fist sank into her stomach and then the flat of his hand smacked her cheek with such force that for a moment she felt nothing. She rocked back as a blow lashed her other cheek and then his hands were slashing her breasts and she was rolling over the bed, trying to escape while blows lashed across her shoulders, her buttocks, everywhere with stinging power, and she was held by other hands so that her punishment could be effected without resistance.

Mohammed Arab stood back after a few minutes and motioned to the other two to let her go. She lay before them, slim and voluptuously rounded and fresh-looking. She seemed for the moment to be dazed. There were angry red marks on her white body. He was excited by the beating he'd just administered. The soft yielding of the flesh under his hand, its warmth and resilience, had moved a weight to his loins and his penis was bulging out against his tight trousers.

Françoise lay face down, trembling, not looking round at her tormentors. And then she felt thin, wiry hands on her shoulders, with fingers that dug into her flesh like pincers.

"How many times have you been fucked tonight?" asked the sneering voice which seemed to be gloating as well.

She didn't answer and the fingers tightened until she cried out and said: "I don't remember—five."

"Well now we're all going to fuck you to help put up your average—or maybe the boys would rather do other things with you."

The other two laughed softly, menacingly, and then the hands were forcing her down on the bed, pushing her shoulders onto the counterpane. She began to struggle, fighting and kicking, but she was held so firmly that she

couldn't even turn round and a few curses were all the result she got.

Her shoulders were held tight against the counterpane and knees had forced her own knees apart with a rough pressure.

"Kneel up," his voice commanded. She tried to force herself flatly onto the bed. She was crying as much with rage as fear. The hands moved off her shoulders, making them feel free as if they'd been sheathed in iron. One of them grabbed her arm and twisted it up behind her shoulder-blades; the other reached under her loins and hauled them up bodily. The strength used against her was frighteningly great. She felt like an almost lifeless teddy bear in the hands of a hefty child even though she continued to struggle and swing her bottom in an effort to escape.

"A wildcat," she heard one of the henchmen say. They were all around her, looking at her naked body, gloating over their satisfaction which was to come.

The twisting of her arm forced her face down hard against the bedcover and her hips seemed to be lifted high up into the air while she swayed and struggled punily.

She gasped with pain as, suddenly, there was a thick intrusion which felt as if a log was being pushed into her dry, unwanting vagina. She screamed out for them to stop; tears smarted against her cheeks. But the intrusion grew and she felt her thighs swept wide apart, the heavy weight of loins crashing against her buttocks pushing her face hard into the bed with every hot pain which seared her vagina. Her vaginal passage felt on fire. The great penis penetrating it felt like sandpaper. She ached and her back ached from bending. She felt hands, many hands, the other men's hands running over her behind. Someone stuck several thicknesses of finger up her ass, which was still so sore from the sodomy she'd been subjected to earlier.

Little screams of breath broke from her lips. Her passage felt as if its walls were being chafed and pared of their skin. Then she began to lubricate a little and the pain was a little less but the penetration greater and she felt as if her whole belly were being split open, as if someone were levering apart her thighs until her body would split all the way up from her pelvis right through a line between her naked breasts which were being squeezed and kneaded brutally.

Kneeling behind her prostrate body, Mohammed Arab gritted his teeth and fucked in and out with great lunges which began from his toes and quivered up through his strong, wiry thighs to reach a zenith of sensation in his tough, iron-hard prick which burst into her, pushing her flesh in all directions, making a path for entry as if his phallus were a bulldozer tunnelling through the earth.

His hands gripped her body, squeezing with sadistic force, hurting her, making her cry out and wriggle helplessly with pain.

His balls itched with desire and his prick tingled. He ran his hands over the tormented flesh which, unwilling but helpless, was at his mercy. He tore the buttocks apart, spreading them obscenely, revealing the little, hard anus which he noticed was red and raw-looking and into which his fingers slipped without too much difficulty. His prick buried itself into her up to the hilt, encountering a certain resistance over the last inch. Her channel was pulverisingly tight around his rigidity and its squeezing clasp brought forth oaths and gasps of pleasure from his thin lips.

Françoise, shamed and aching, her face sideways against the bedcover, felt only a great heat and splitting at her loins. She felt super-naked and every part of her seemed

to be at that great hole which grew and grew between her legs as if it were some forest pathway being broadened, having its undergrowth swept away by some irresistible tornado.

Her lips opened and closed in torment. Occasionally she tried to flatten her hips or draw her buttocks in to contain the pain of her anus. But then she was aware only of the tightening of her vagina and the extra pain which ensued from his brusque entry.

Suddenly there were fingers at her lips, opening her mouth and then a spongy, stiff substance rubbing against her lips. She opened her eyes and saw, close under them, a prick some eight inches long and thick in proportion. One of the other men was lying alongside her, forcing his penis into her mouth. She resisted from a moment, sickened, but then he held her nose between finger and thumb and, as she gasped for breath, the thick sword of flesh rammed in, crushing through her soft, moist lips, between her even teeth and into the moist saliva of her mouth. She felt it on her tongue, this great blunt, hot thing, tearing her attention in brief spasms from the continuous piercing of her vagina and the blunt solidity which crashed against her cervix and made her jerk forward with pain.

The trouser-covered hips behind the prick began to undulate in towards her and the fat prick to slide in and out of her mouth, never quite withdrawing, always leaving an inch or two beyond her lips in the warm shelter of her mouth.

She saw where it came, broad and searching out from the trouser flies. There were a few black hairs straggling out with it. It grew broader towards the knob and the skin was drawn back in a series of little ridges like narrow olive terraces.

She closed her eyes. Saliva seemed to fill her mouth—all of her mouth that was left after the great rod expanding within it had rammed down towards her tonsils.

Once or twice she coughed and spluttered but then she grew accustomed to the asphyxiating entry and let it move in and out with ever increasing vigour, ramming at a faster pace than its brother which gouged her quim.

Mohammed Arab felt himself coming. He squeezed her flesh in his hands so that it grew up in great ridges—small, artificial buttocks embossed on her real buttocks. When he released her, the ridges settled back slowly into her flesh, leaving angry red marks, fringed with a white bloodlessness on her skin.

Every time he thrust now, pushing his loins forward, his pelvic area in the avant-garde of the thrust, he felt the imminence of his orgasm grow greater until there was a heavy weight of blood hanging in the knob of his penis.

While he thrust he saw her tender lips clasping the growing, whitening prick of one of his cronies who was writhing his hips as he forced her to suck him.

Françoise, obeying the command of the fingers which forced her mouth to follow, sucked and licked the great tree-like being in her mouth. Her torture had gone on and on. She prayed for it to end and so she sucked to end it quickly.

The glans in her mouth was slimy with her saliva and suddenly the moisture was thicker with a seaweedy taste. She felt his loins crush into her face, tensing in great, trembling movements. His hands gripped her cheeks and then her hair and he seemed to be trying to push his cock down her throat to meet the other coming up in her cunt. She felt at this moment totally debased, as if her body were just a piece of putty-like flesh which these men were using

79

for masturbation, as if she had no rights, no soul, no humanity, as if she were some stuffed dummy exclusively for their pleasure.

The man lying beside her gasped, once, twice, three times and then crushed his hips into her face so that she was suffocated and fought for breath. And as she fought for breath, her mouth was flooded with a great undamming of hot, thick liquid, which choked her and slithered automatically down her throat. At the same time, the organ in her mouth, after its rigid ejaculations, began to lose its size and weight and his loins moved away and she was able to breathe again and she opened her mouth and spat out some of the sperm which still remained around her tongue and on her palate.

She became aware again, exclusively, of the filling of her cunt, the never-ending object which barraged into her belly untiringly and which seemed as broad and deep as her loins. No feeling came to her except the hot chafing where his prick grazed her vaginal wall. But his orgasm, too, was coming. She heard him panting, faster and faster and he forced her thighs so wide with his knees that she was almost flat on the bed with her hips and her pelvis aching with the stretching. His fingers gripped the tops of her thighs with a pressure which didn't relax, now, but became greater and greater as his panting became more and more agitated and deep.

She heard him gasp out some words in Arabic which she didn't understand and then he thrust into her so hard and seemed to go so deep with the long thrust that it actually seemed as if his penis had been transformed into a spear which wounded her and made her moan in pain. She felt his convulsive jerks against her ass and then he too fell back from her and there was suddenly cool air entering her unstoppered hole and she fell forward on

the bed, crying bitterly and aching all over as if her body had been cramped in a tiny tomb for hours on end.

While she lay, sobbing, the men began to recover.

From their joking remarks it was apparent that the third member, who'd held only a watching brief on the whole proceeding, preferred young men. She was too curvaceous for him even to think of buggering her and pretending her name was Françoise.

But now he was urged by the others to complete what they referred to as her punishment.

Françoise lay on the bed, sobbing, aware only partially of what was going on between them, prostrate, not trying to move or protect herself from further assault.

Above her the third member of the trio began to remove his belt. His teeth were drawn back from his teeth in a vicious grin. It was difficult to say which of them looked more vicious than the others.

The belt was of thin, shiny leather. He held it at the buckle end and motioned to the others to hold the girl. Mohammed Arab sat on her feet and the other held her shoulders. Both of them kept well back from her body, leaving it free.

The man with the belt looked down on her pummelled body, which still bore faint, dying traces of her previous mishandling. This time he'd leave more permanent traces. His chest tingled with excitement. The thought of watching his belt bite into that woman-flesh, woman-flesh that he disliked so intensely, filled him with sadistic delight.

He raised the belt and lashed it down across her buttocks. She screamed exhaustedly and her body jackknifed but was firmly held by the others. The belt rose and descended again in the same thin line and then it flashed up and down, up and down until her back from thighs to shoulders

was a grill of weals and her body was squirming as if in death throes.

Finally he lowered his arm and began to buckle the belt around his waist once again. Mohammed Arab looked at her body. She didn't look too attractive now. He grinned meanly, showing his teeth.

"Let's go now," he said to the others.

On the way out, he said to the almost still body on the bed:

"Don't be a naughty girl and nothing serious will happen to you."

CHAPTER VIII

A day of hanging around the dirty little bars of La
Chapelle and the surrounding area had brought only a thin
slip of information to Detective-Inspector Raimond. Dressed
in his blues, he listened to Arabs chatting, had sometimes
chatted with them himself in French, assuming a broad,
lower-Parisian accent.

Nobody had recognised him as a *flic*. He was able to
gauge all reactions to himself by simply listening to the
remarks in Arabic which interspersed any conversation he
had with any Algerians, none of whom assumed that he
could understand.

It was simply by standing at an almost empty bar listening
that he got the little scrap of information he now intended
to use for what it was worth. And, certainly, the assassination of the superintendent in what one would have
thought of as impossible circumstances enlarged the value
of any bit of information which might give the slightest
lead.

He was walking casually along the centre pavement
which divided the dual carriageway. He was looking for

the next hotel and appearing not to. Already he had called at four and each time had drawn a blank. There had been no Ahmed ben Lulla and nobody had heard of him and nobody sounded as if they'd admit it even if they had, harmless though the inspector looked in his workingman's clothes.

It was an hour ago that he'd picked up the name. There had been just himself and two Arabs standing at the *comptoir* with the patron away in a backroom for most of the time.

He had listened to them quietly discussing the latest political moves in the French political switchback and then his ears had spread wide when he heard mention of somebody who had almost refused to pay his "contribution" but had changed his mind at the last minute.

With quiet, expressive gestures one of the men had explained to the other what his nodding acquaintance, Ahmed ben Lulla, had narrowly missed becoming—a corpse in a back street.

Pierre Raimond had made up his mind immediately that this would be followed up. Vainly he listened for information on the whereabouts of the Algerian whose name he'd heard mentioned, but all he'd been able to gather was that it was in a sidestreet off the main boulevard that his hotel was located.

He was tired of this area; almost beginning to feel that he was one of the lonely, helpless, misfit Arabs who lived here. He wanted some action and he was determined to wring whatever he possibly could from this tiny and perhaps dead-end clue.

He crossed the road, dodging the fast-moving traffic and headed into the next side-street. Like most of the others he'd been in it gave an impression of movement just under a dark façade—rather like the sensed movement of fish in

84

murky water. There were prostitutes in doorways who whispered invitations at him as he passed—each trying to outdo the last in offers of what exquisite or peculiar pleasures were in store for him if he cared to entrust himself to her imagination.

He tried the first two grimy hotels without any luck. He could sense the inevitable repetition. The street was full of uneven doorways leading blackly off the pavement, with battered signs swaying over some, nothing but a street number over others.

The third one was even grimier than the others. There were two whores sitting on the stairway and they both looked at him in startled expectancy and one of them got up and smoothed her sweater over her breasts.

He looked in at the office, which was less an office than a dismal little room where the hotel manager lived and hung his dirty clothes in a pile over a clotheshorse and stacked his dirty plates on a table as if he were never going to wash them up but just wait until the room was full and then move out.

The prostitute reached him as he knocked on the door and invited him upstairs, catching hold of his hand in encouragement.

"I just want to see someone here," he said, grinning pleasantly, "that's all."

"I'm the only person worth seeing here," she said and placed his hand on her big breast as if that proved what she said.

Raimond removed his hand after giving her teat an appreciative squeeze.

"I really only want to see this fellow," he said. "Some other time."

He knocked on the door again. There didn't seem to be anyone at home. The girl beside him moved back a

pace and pulled her skirt up to the tops of her thighs to show him how beautiful her legs were. They weren't bad at all.

"Isn't anyone ever here?" he asked.

"He went out an hour ago," the girl said. "He's in the bar down the street."

She put her hand down between the inspector's legs and felt for his penis, pressing her thigh against him.

"You can have anything you want for a thousand francs," she said. "All my openings are available."

"Is there anyone called Ahmed ben Lulla here?" he asked.

She gave his prick, which responded a little even if he was on business, a hearty squeeze and thrust her breasts into his chest.

"He won't go away," she said. "You'll have time to see him after. I'll give you a quick suck for 500 francs."

"He lives here, then," Raimond said, trying to keep the quick interest out of his voice. "Which room is he in?"

"How would I know," she said. "He's too poor to invite me in. You needn't go afterwards—I'll let you have an hour for a thousand francs. You could make it three times in that."

"You tell me which room he's in and I'll give you 500 francs just for the information," he said.

She looked at him suspiciously.

"Let me see the money," she said.

"I'm in a hurry to find him," he said, "otherwise I wouldn't be throwing away tomorrow's dinner money."

He pulled out a note from a suitably battered purse and held it towards her.

"It's room 38 on the fourth," she said. "You must want to see him bad."

She took the money and smiled up at him suddenly, as

if she had only just believed he was really going to give it to her.

She patted him on the bottom as he walked past her.

"If you want to see me on the way down," she said. "You've got 500 francs credit."

The other whore made way for him on the stairs. She was wearing a blouse with nothing underneath and she'd undone enough buttons for the whole of her left breast to show. She thrust it towards him.

"If she hasn't got what you want—I have," she said.

He patted her on the bottom to even up the pattings and felt her little animal buttocks bridle against his hand and then he was going up the stairs two at a time. He heard them laughing down below him.

Ahmed ben Lulla had not yet made up his mind what to do when the second knock of the night sounded on his door. He stiffened, like a dog seeing some phantom thing in an empty room. Nervously his mind ticked over. He hadn't yet been out. He could have done nothing to offend them. Had they had second thoughts?

He moved up close to the door and listened. Then he said unsteadily:

"Who's there?"

"A friend," said a voice in French.

"Who are you?"

There was a second's silence and then the voice said:

"I can help you if you let me speak to you."

Again Ahmed's mind raced. If it was the NLF, he reasoned, there was no escaping them and he would merely antagonise them by being difficult.

He opened the door a little and saw a big lorry driver. It looked like a lorry driver. He opened the door farther.

"What do you want?"

The man pushed open the door and came into the room past him.

"Shut the door," he said, with an air of command which Ahmed mechanically obeyed.

The man sat down on the bed and looked at Ahmed pleasantly. He seemed completely at ease and his face was frank and determined. Ahmed felt relieved but wary.

"Who are you?" he said.

"How much do you pay the NLF?" his visitor countered.

Ahmed scrutinised him carefully and said nothing.

"I know you pay and I know you recently were unable to," the man went on. "I can help you if you help me."

"A *flic*," Ahmed said, as if to himself.

"I know how you're forced to pay," the man went on. "You have nothing to fear; you have only help to gain."

Ahmed sat on the bed and looked at his unexpected visitor. Various ideas were turning over in confusion in his head. If the man was a *flic*, as he was, he could get tough and Ahmed would have no recourse to the forces of law and order. Here was the force of law and order. At least here was the force. But could no dare to give any information. Who had seen this fellow come into the hotel? And what information had he to give, except perhaps a description or two? It was true that a description could be all-important.

"I know nothing," he said.

"You could give me any information about these men who collect the money from you—what they look like, when they come."

"It's more than my life is worth."

"If you give me information that leads to my getting hold of these men, you can be sure of police protection."

"Police protection," Ahmed said, with a hint of sarcasm in his tone. "For how long, against what reprisals." He

pointed to the newspaper. "You saw what happened to the police superintendent. Nobody is safe."

Pierre Raimond looked down at his hands and then up into the eyes of the young Algerian.

"What sort of life do you have?" he asked. "Work?"

Ahmed shook his head.

"And you hand over money to these fanatics? That means you don't eat, you don't drink, you don't go to a cinema, you're in arrears with your hotel money. What sort of life is that?"

Ahmed shook his head again.

"It is nothing—but it is life," he said. "It is not death, which is the alternative if you refuse to pay or if you inform. There's no..."

There was a light tap on the door and Ahmed stood up as if someone had jabbed him with a needle. He looked at the policeman on his bed in horror.

"They saw you come!" he whispered.

Pierre Raimond went to the door, motioned Ahmed back and, standing to one side, called: "Who's there?"

A woman's voice answered.

"If you think it's a joke climbing all these flights of stairs and me with bad legs and no money to see the doctor and willing to do a kindness even if it does waste my time and put me out and make my heart bad, as if it isn't weak enough already..."

Gently Raimond opened the door. An old woman stood outside. She was carrying a tray of violets and she was red-faced and puffing so much that it was amazing that she could talk at the same time.

"What do you want here?" Ahmed asked from behind Raimond.

"Which of you gentlemen is Monsieur Ahmed ben

Lulla?" the old woman asked, peering shortsightedly at them.

Ahmed moved forward in front of Raimond.

"I am," he said.

The old woman reached into a tattered pocket and fished out a small envelope with no name on it.

"Young lady stopped me in the street, gave me this for you," she said.

Ahmed took the envelope. Raimond watched him open it, read it once quickly, pale and read it again more slowly.

"Where was she?" Ahmed said.

"Right near the *métro* at Anvers," the old woman said. "Very nervous she was. Didn't explain nothing, but begged me so hard I couldn't say no."

"God," Ahmed said. "God!" He swayed away from the door and sank onto the bed. Raimond held out his hand for the note, knowing it would be given, and Ahmed handed it to him without a word.

The note said:

> "*Darling, oh darling, What have they done to you? Are you all right? I daren't come. They came to my hotel and did things to me and told me not to see you again. But I'm all right. Only we mustn't see each other for some time. Send back a note with the old woman and I'll get it from her, but don't try to see me or talk to me. I'm afraid for us both.*"

The note was signed with an "F."

"Come in," Raimond said to the old woman. He turned to Ahmed, lying dazed on the bed.

"Girl friend?"

Ahmed nodded.

"They? Same people who came to see you?"

"Protection organisation—same people."

"Oh—indeed." Raimond's mind was racing, putting facts together, drawing conclusions. Things were looking up, he decided.

"Will you help me now if I help you?" he said.

Ahmed stood up and confronted the old woman.

"How was she?" he said, intensely. "How was the girl who gave you the note?"

"How was she?"

"How did she seem?"

"How did she seem?"

"Oh God," Ahmed snapped, his voice rising dangerously. He stepped towards the old woman and Raimond caught hold of him. "Take it easy," he said and added to the old woman, "Did she have any sign of injury?"

"Oh no," the woman said, looking from one to the other, startled. "Oh no. She seemed very nervous, kept looking round and telling me not to let anyone see me with the note. Oh no—no injury. Least I couldn't see any."

Raimond looked down at Ahmed.

"Send her back a note," he said. "Telling her that a friend of yours will get in touch with her."

Obediently Ahmed took a pencil out of hs pocket. Raimond found him a piece of paper from his wallet while the old woman continued to stare at both of them in wonderment.

"You will get in touch with her for me?" Ahmed asked.

"Yes—tell her to give me any information I want."

"How will I know what information you want?"

"It shouldn't worry you now."

After a second's hesitation, Ahmed began to scribble on the piece of paper and then handed it to Raimond, who read it rapidly and then handed it to the old woman, giving her 500 francs at the same time.

"You know where to find the young lady?"

"She said she'd be watching out for me—but that I was to tell the gentleman not to try to see her."

"Right. Off you go."

Raimond closed the door behind her and looked at Ahmed, setting dejectedly on the bed.

"Now let's hear what you have to say," he said.

CHAPTER IX

Along the street, outside the hotel door, Françoise was standing in her usual encouraging stance.

From the point under the boulevard trees where they stood, Ahmed and Raimond could see her clearly. Ahmed's face was strained and longing, but he kept back out of sight and occasionally he glanced quickly in either direction along the boulevard, or up at the dim-lit windows over it.

"Somebody'll be watching from somewhere," he said. "They may even have seen us already."

"I hope not," Raimond said. "And I doubt it. They'll be watching her from close up."

They stood silently for a minute or two and then Raimond added: "Well, I'll go. Walk up the street a bit and I'll look for you."

Ahmed watched the big man stroll off and head up the street towards Françoise. He hoped this was going to work out all right. It was all much deeper than he cared to think about. From now on their lives were in real danger until such time as the gamble of taking sides paid off.

Raimond strolled along the street, looking at each of the whores who lined it, in turn. Some he spoke to for a few seconds, some he argued with and always he walked on as if disatisfied until he came to Françoise.

What a pretty one, he thought. What the devil is she doing in this racket? Even as she smiled at him and he approached her the sadness of the relationships people like these clung on to filled him. He thought of his own wife and imagined his own thoughts if she were forced to take up prostitution as a living.

He remembered just after the war, when things had been so difficult, how she had gone to a hotel with an American in exchange for some tinned goods he'd promised her. They'd all done that, even the nicest, most virtuous girls had done that, rather than see their families short of food in the terrible shortage there had been after the Germans had retreated. She'd told him about that in her honesty and he'd felt agonies for some time, imagining her in the arms of that American, submitting her intimacies to him for a tin of *cassoulet*. She'd been so young, so alive, so beautiful. He hated that American who tasted her beauty so cheaply. But he'd recovered. Time healed that sort of wound like everything else and, after all, he'd had plenty of women before he'd met Michele. But how did this young Algerian accept that his girl friend should submit to so many strange embraces every night? How could he bear the idea? Did one become accustomed to it? Was it like facing the necessity in the same way that Michele had faced it that time when the American had dangled such bait in front of her lovely eyes?

"*Je t'emmène?*"

He turned to the girl, seeing her smile, knowing what darkness and horror the smile hid.

"How much?" he said.

"Three thousand francs," she said.

"All right."

She led the way quickly, almost eagerly, into the hotel and up the narrow staircase. She was a shapely creature, he thought; under different circumstances...

She opened the door into a small room with just a bed and washing facilities and a small chair to put clothes on.

She began to strip immediately and he let her for a moment to see the sweater whisk off, the bare, unbrassiered flesh beneath and then the skirt, also with nothing underneath. He saw her pert, rounded nudity and felt a movement in his loins. But he was here on business.

"Don't bother," he said. "I'm a friend of Ahmed's."

Her eyes sparked with wild interest and she forgot to cover her body as she turned toward him. Seeing his eyes drop to the lightly-haired triangle at her loins, she began quickly to pull on her clothes as she questioned him.

"Where is he? How is he? What's happened?"

He chuckled at her eagerness and took a note out of his pocket that he'd bought for her. When she'd finished eagerly, joyfully reading it, she looked up at him slowly.

"A *flic*...! But what can you do?"

"Ensure that you people have a life which isn't run by fear. I want a description of the men who came to you and anything else useful you can tell me. Then I'll take a note for Ahmed from you and maybe you'll be seeing him in peace and security before very long."

She looked at the note from her lover again. Normally, informing a *flic* was the last thing she would have dreamed of doing. But Ahmed urged her to. It was their only chance of seeing each other again in safety, he said, if the NLF were smashed. He also said this man seemed a good man and had been very nice to him. He was, perhaps, a man they could trust.

She looked up into Raimond's straight-staring eyes and remembered that he'd let her get undressed before he'd told her. In certain directions, she reflected, no man could be trusted.

"All right," she said. "I'll tell you what I know—but we must be quick. I don't usually take too long with my ...my clients, and they'll be watching from across the street."

Quickly she described to him the three men who'd visited her, paying particular attention to the vicious-eyed ring-leader. She then told him about the protection ring, whose connections with Algerian nationalist organisations she only vaguely knew about. As she was so young and attractive, she'd been taken to a man named Mahmoud Taluffah, who had told her what she must pay to the protection ring. He'd also made it clear she had no alternative. He'd then forced his attentions upon her—which was the reason why she'd been brought to him instead of being interviewed by one of his lieutenants. This man, then, seemed to be the chief of the protection ring and was probably well up in the nationalist hierarchy, as the two activities seemed to be running hand in hand.

"Where is he, this man?" Raimond asked.

"I don't know much about him at all," she said. "But he runs all sorts of clubs and bars. He likes to live well, everybody says. He often spends some time in his bars around Pigalle, but there is another near Clichy where he presents his legitimate front—I can't remember the name of it."

"Apart from this you know nothing about his activities —meeting-places, where he lives, etc?"

"No. He has a girl friend. She dances in one of the Pigalle places and sings. She was there when I was taken to him and he sent her off when he wanted to... be alone

with me. They say she has a roving eye herself and doesn't care too much what he does."

"What does she look like?"

"She has black hair with a bleached, gold-silver streak running back from the front. Her hair's long—down to her shoulders. She's about up to your shoulder and very curvaceous. She has big, dark eyes, a rather small nose and a small mouth with a large, pouting bottom lip. I don't know about any peculiarities. I really didn't have time to study her. He called her 'Rolande.'"

Raimond let these details sink into his brain.

"Write your note for the boy. friend," he said, then: "I've got to get moving."

CHAPTER X

Later that same night, dressed now in a smart suit, Raimond made a tour of the bars on the sloping streets running south from Pigalle.

The streets were crawling with American servicemen, some on foot, some creeping around in enormous cars, all looking for women. And women were there in plenty—French, negresses, Arab women, all sorts—standing on the street corners, peering from bars, disappearing into hotel doorways with a catch, climbing into cars to make whoopee with four men together. The bars were named with every invitation likely to appeal to a woman hunter: "Sexy Club," "Strip Club," "Le Trou Mademoiselle." From them all came the sound of music and occasional dancing. It was a gaudy, garish glitter which to anybody who preferred home comforts was almost frightening, Raimond thought as he walked slowly from bar to bar, peering in at the doors, being immediately accosted by several painted women who "invited" him in for a drink. Some looked as if they might have entertainment at some time, others looked hope-

less. He made a note to return to some if he didn't find what he was looking for. He didn't want to ask any questions unless he absolutely had to.

At last he found what he was looking for. It was rather quieter, more luxurious-looking than most. Somehow the cheap effect of the other bars which surrounded it didn't touch this one. You could tell as you approached that you needed to have even more money than a GI on leave to be able to hang around in its plush interior.

There were, however, some score of people inside, sitting at tables and on stools against the bar. They were drinking, but not, at the moment, talking. They were listening to the soft, sexy voice of a woman who was sitting informally at the far end of the bar, singing into a little microphone. Her voice was quite something. It seemed to curl into the corners of the room, feeling for anybody who might be trying to escape its effect, and then to turn lazily back and whisper amongst its captives.

Raimond went to a table from which he could see the woman clearly. A first glance had shown him the long, blonde-silver streak running back from her forehead. He asked for Scotch and the white-smocked waiter brought it and slipped away. Raimond hoped his expense account would hold good.

He surveyed the woman and mentally raised his eyebrows. She really was some dish. There was about her an un-ashamed air of a willing playgirl who managed to extract the utmost enjoyment out of living dangerously on the edge of vice, and managed to keep her own special sexy vitality without getting jaded.

She was wearing an amber-coloured dress which was cut very low on her full breasts, revealing them as she leaned forward almost to the nipples. The dress was caught up in the front in a couple of long folds which stretched over

her thighs just below the point where they ran into her hips, and attached in a bow on either hip. She wore very high-heeled, pointed, gold shoes which made her long, slender legs appear even more slender and her arms were covered in silver bracelets, matching the sequins all over the dress. She really seemed to be worth somebody's discovering.

Raimond had no doubt this was the girl he was looking for: the description fitted. He wondered just how easy it would be to get to know her and then how difficult it would be to get the information he needed from her. He was prepared to go to any lengths to get it, in fact he rather fancied going to any lengths. There were some aspects of this job it would be better not to tell his wife about.

He pulled his gaze off the girl and glanced discreetly around the club. Most of the people in there seemed just to be visitors enjoying the night life, mostly French, although there were one or two American tourists dressed in pale suits and having the air of successful business men on the one trip of their lives to faraway Europe. After two days in Paris they'd rush to Berlin for two days and then down to Rome for two days and then Nice for three and then perhaps Spain for a non-stop week's tour and then back to Paris and then on to London for a day. At the moment they looked a little drunk, so they might find themselves staying for more days than they'd anticipated in Paris.

At a corner table were two rich-looking Algerians. They were sipping iced whiskies and generally taking in the scene with pleasant, patronising expressions. They obviously belonged. But neither of them fitted any of the descriptions he'd been given.

The room was very dim—just a few wall lights—and it was some time before he realised that the music was coming

from a little trio set back in an alcove at the far end of the room opposite where the girl was siting at the bar. It was quite a slick setup. He wondered why people who owned or ran such a business needed to go around frightening the daylights out of down-and-out brethren for a few thousand francs of their public assistance.

The girl came to the end of her song and there was a reaction of untensing, as if everybody had been hypnotised up till that point.

A restrained but appreciative clapping followed and then, as the trio took up another number, the girl slipped off her stool and began to dance an exotic and somewhat erotic little business in front of the tables, between them and the bar.

She slid out of her dress as if it was part of the dance, as smooth as poking out a tongue.

Underneath, she was dressed in a tiny pair of gold, matching pants, and, to the general astonishment, as she'd appeared to be naked in that area, a couple of little circles of gold cloth which just covered her nipples, resting on them like coolie hats on a head, hiding nothing of the finely-shaped teat behind.

She really was something, Raimond decided once and for all... Her body was sinuous and yet not lacking in flesh in the right places. She looked quite athletic as if she'd be a superbly active companion in bed. Her buttocks as she moved in a slow circle were not too large, but compact and very firm-looking, her legs slender and flawless under their brown makeup. Her hips, swaying to the music, were long and well-moulded, with hints of hollows just above the thighs showing through the gold cloth. When she stretched her slender, firm arms, there were faint bevellings of her ribs marking the flesh of her body and her

breasts, reached up below a slender, unlined neck, seemed to fight against being lifted and then remained stretched and swaying heavily as she moved.

She didn't take off anything else—at least she didn't take off the one real garment that was left—and that was part of her superb attraction. Just that something that they weren't going to see, that something hidden which heightened her sexiness threefold.

Her body as she danced seemed to respond with exact, controlled rhythm to her slightest thought. It was like a long, slender instrument in perfect coordination, a fine, sleek piece of material with nothing superfluous about it, resolving and dissolving in a series of sexy movements which emphasised breasts and then buttocks and then her hips and then the whole of her body merging and submerging into an instrument of love and offering.

The audience watched spellbound as the lights moved over her extremities, rotundities, sensuousness, voluptuousness. It was excruciating, they found, that they couldn't run their hands over that live, moving, inviting flesh; it was a pain which became almost unbearable.

Raimond watched, too, experiencing the same sensations. He thought of his wife, who was really just as attractive as this girl. He remembered how he'd first watched her at the tennis club, her skirts swishing up as she served, revealing a lacy piece of panties covering buttocks which stretched hard against the tight, confining material; how, facing her, waiting for her service, he'd been fascinated, to the point of losing his concentration, on the way her breast rose darkly up against her blouse as her racquet arm swept up over her head. And then those first passionate moments, kissing, petting in the car and at dances until the summer and the cartrips out to the country where he'd had her finally in a field in the long grass with cars going by on the

road 200 metres away and they'd kept their clothes on with just her panties lying beside them as he waved his hips up and down above her and she held him tight and seemed dazedly lost by her own passion. He loved her just as much now, more, and she still filled him with desire, but now it was muted. One had to accept that it became muted and that one could sit here and watch this dark, sexy figure undulating and desire it with a sharp edge which one never felt any more with more familiar limbs and breasts... To know that this sharp, excited, overpoweringly desireful sensation was never again to be fully experienced and satisfied was a crushing disappointment, which made one all the more joyful when, in the course of one's duty—necessitated even to fulfil one's duty—one had to try to take this new, exciting body to bed.

This number, too, came to a yearning end and the applause was mixed with some polite whistles of appreciation. The girl curtsied, took her dress from the bar and disappeared into a back room. Raimond sat on, waiting to see if she came back, keeping an eye on the two Algerians who had taken out cigars and begun to smoke.

The little orchestra began to play some soft dance music and a couple got up and started to dance, to be followed by several more. A couple more lights were doused and a low hum of animated chatter began with a fresh ordering of drinks. A few more people came in from the street and filled up the remaining tables and then, at last, the girl, in a dress like the last only emerald, came out from the back room and went to the bar.

Raimond reached her just as she finished arranging herself comfortably on the well-upholstered stool.

He congratulated her quietly on her voice and her dance and offered her a drink. She accepted and took a champagne cocktail. The barman maintained a suave, unmoved exterior,

but he must have seen this so often that it was a wonder he could resist a smile.

The girl gave Raimond a quick, appraising glance as he gave the order and took another Scotch himself. It was a long time since she'd had an "adventure." Mahmoud had been rather jealous lately and so she'd eased off as she didn't want to offend him to the point where he might have her pushed under a train. But the desire was there. She liked variety, she liked excitement, she liked love and glamour and having a good time. And things had been getting just so stick-in-the-mud she felt she could go to bed with a smelly old *clochard* and get a kick out of it. Raimond was the best-looking man she'd seen in some time and he had an air about him of—difficult to define—well, just being a real man.

"*A votre santé*," he said, raising his glass towards her, "and may that dance get even sexier, in which case you'll have to have a grating between you and the audience."

"Is that how it made you feel?" she asked, smiling.

"Worse than that," he said.

Yes, all the description fitted: pouting lower lip, dark eyes and small nose and, above all, the hair.

"Some people seem to think it would be sexier if I took off the pants," she said. She smiled into his eyes. Her voice was a taunting suggestion. She wanted a risqué conversation. Even if she couldn't have a risqué relationship, she'd have a risqué conversation, just to send a tickle of frustrated anticipation up her spine.

"I'd certainly like to see that," Raimond said, falling in with the game. "Normally, of course, concealment adds something to the attraction, but I'd say that with a figure like yours you'd look so hot without anything that nobody'd be able to stay in his seat."

"That wouldn't be a good idea," she said. "I can only take one at a time and I'm very, *very selective*."

"What sort of qualities pass the selection board?"

She raised her eyes from his, looking from the top of his head down his long, wiry frame with the coolest invitation he'd ever come across.

"I'd say about your build, probably, and good looking in a manly way, intelligent, a good lover, good company and preferably with enough money not to have to worry about which bars, as candidates, they drink in."

"Must take quite a time to decide who has all those qualities."

"Well, one can start with the obvious and then allow a bit of time to find out about the others."

"I'd like to offer myself as a candidate—and no bar is too expensive."

She smiled at him cat-like and for a moment he thought he'd been wrong and that she was now going to tell him where to get off, like the bitch she might be. But instead she said:

"On a superficial view you have the right qualities, but I don't know what the rest of the selection board would say." Still smiling, she glanced casually over at the two Algerians, who didn't seem to be taking the slightest interest in her activities.

"Perhaps they wouldn't have to know anything about it," Raimond said, "or do they sleep in your room?"

She grinned at him and behind the grin was the excited glimmer of readiness to take this farther than she thought wise.

"They might report to my boss," she said. "I'm not supposed to play with the other boys. On the other hand they're getting rather slack and they might not even care to mention that they don't know where I got to for a while."

106

"Your boss must be a real hard taskmaster. Though I don't blame him for being concerned about his merchandise."

"He's variable. But don't let's talk about him. I have another number to do in about half an hour. Then I'll meet you outside. Have you got a car?"

"A black Simca in the Rue La Bruyère."

"Go and sit in it after my next number and I'll join you within ten minutes."

"All right," he said. "What's the name of my fellow conspirator?"

"Rolande," he said, "and yours?"

"Pierre."

She sipped the last of her cocktail and smiled at him, letting her eyes linger on his as if in promise of what was in store for him.

"Don't get mixed up with any other girls in the meantime," she said.

"I wouldn't miss the chance of seeing those pants off," he said, grinning.

She pursed her lips in a little mock reproach and slid off the stool to take up her perch at the end of the bar beside the microphone.

Raimond went on sipping his whisky, listening to that sexy voice which was soon going to be whispering in his ear, watching that athletic body which, he hoped, was soon going to be joined with his. He never glanced at the two Algerians again.

CHAPTER XI

They sat close together at one end of the chic, elegant hotel bar just off the Champs-Elysées. It was two hours and several drinks later and the girl was glowing with generosity. She wanted to give and give and give herself. Now, Raimond thought, is the time to take off for a hotel. So far he had extracted no information. There had been small talk and a certain amount of talk about life and living and what people wanted and why. There had been a lot of sexy innuendo and virtual promise of what she was like in bed. He was clearly a very successful candidate. He'd passed himself off as an advertiser. The small Simca was passed off as his little gad-about used for narrow streets and at times when he risked not seeing quite straight enough to avoid the lampposts.

His Oldsmobile was for country weekends and trips to Spain and Italy.

The bar was quiet, but had just enough customers to drown their conversation and make them not embarrassingly noticeable. She was sitting close, looking into his face.

Her skin was good and her perfume, which was slight, not overwhelming, dusted in his nostrils, making him think of all of her body as a scented flower. She seemed to like him very much. It was partly the drink, but, he thought, she's been cooped up too long for a woman of her promiscuous passion.

"How's the selection board getting along with making up its mind?" he asked.

"The selection board? Oh, the selection board's taken a trip," she said. "A dictator's taken over and he's all for you."

"So I'll see those pants off yet."

"You're very audacious," she said, smiling and running her tongue over her pouting bottom lip. "Let's go and find somewhere where you'll see what you want to."

Raimond felt the breath catch in his throat and checked himself. He remembered his wife fast asleep at home or perhaps worrying about him and unable to sleep and he reminded himself that he was on business, big business.

"We'd better go to a hotel," he said. "I've got a boss, too."

"Oh, you have." She seemed on the verge of disappointment for some reason but then her eyes twinkled wickedly at him.

"Well, well—that puts us both in the same boat."

"And in the same hotel," he said.

"What does your boss look like with *her* pants off?"

"Wonderful," he said.

"Let's go," she said. "I want you to see that there's always something better."

They walked from the bar and heads turned discreetly to glance after her firm curves which moved tantalisingly in the sack dress into which she'd changed from her entertainment costume.

CHAPTER XII

She was moving about the room in pink, almost transparent underwear. The room was white and pale grey with green fittings in the adjoining bathroom. The bed was broad enough for a whole orgy. The broad windows looked down onto the street where an occasional neon light flashed like a spear of lightning. The Champs-Elysées was not very far away, but the street below was sufficiently narrow to be fairly quiet.

Slowly undressing, Raimond looked at her appreciatively and thought, "I won't try and pump her until afterwards; I might as well enjoy myself in the meantime."

She moved towards him and twirled round in a little pirouette in front of him.

"How's that?" she said.

Through the tight, high-holding brassiere he could see the sharp points of her nipples, darker than the surrounding skin which pushed it outwards in balloon-like tautness. The little, pink panties held her buttocks in a tight embrace like another layer of skin, revealing half of the orbs, and through the front of them he saw the dark muff of hair

with the protrusion of flesh behind it, pushing out the material.

"Lovely," he said. "But I wanted to see them off."

"Am I making you hot?" she asked with a little laugh.

He stripped off his own pants and his penis shot up into the air.

"You're really quite an athlete," she said, looking over his body and then letting her dark eyes rest on his stiff member. "I hope you're capable of a good athletic performance."

He moved towards her and said: "You're so exciting even with them still on, I hope seeing them off doesn't induce a curtailment of the performance."

"Better not," she said.

He reached her and she moved into his arms, hot and sweet-smelling. She was one of those women who, as soon as a man touches her, seems to melt to a jelly, to tremble and whimper with excitement. He felt her body shivering against him as he unhooked the brassiere and he heard her murmur with passion.

The bra came away and fell to the floor and now he felt her resistant breasts hot, too, against him with the pointed nipples heavy and digging in his chest.

"Oh—oh," she murmured as he ran his hands in a long quick caress over her back, bringing his fingertips up her spine and then moving them round to feel her teats, bulbous and bursting under the palms of his hands. He squeezed them gently and massaged the nipples, which grew long and erect under his gentle manipulation.

"Oh darling," she whispered. She was trembling from head to foot. He could feel her thighs trembling against him and his prick, riding up between them, snuggled against the soft heat of her flesh, was tingling along its length like a sharp pins and needles.

He ran his hands down her back and gently pushed and pulled the pants down over her buttocks, feeling them slide reluctantly off her hips. She gave a little wriggle of help and then shook her thighs so that they slipped down and fell to the floor. Gasping a little, she stepped out of them, leaving them in a pink, crumpled pile on the floor.

He rubbed her bottom gently in little, round, exciting gestures over the crack which separated the two. She began to wriggle against him and put her arms around his neck, murmuring little animal noises all the time.

Cupping her buttocks in his hands, feeling their weight and form and texture, raising them and her slightly up his body, he moved his fingers between her legs from behind, revelling in the moist flesh he found there.

"Oh—I can't stand it!" she said, quickly.

She pulled his face down and crushed her lips with bruising force against his mouth, opening her lips wide, and after an instant's extreme tension, hurtling her tongue with a silvery movement into his mouth. She gave little whimpers all the time as he pressed and rubbed himself against her. Her tongue seemed to fill his mouth, reaching down to his throat.

With an effort, he withdrew his lips from her and moved his mouth down onto her neck, bruising it with bites and kisses. She threw her head back and the full neck strained against his mouth and her loins pushed hard against him.

"Let's see how you look with them off, now," he said, softly.

After a second or two, she moved away from him, still trembling and shaken and turned in another pirouette. His eyes feasted on her lush curves. The sight of her breasts and buttocks moving with lives of their own, of her sinuous lack of superfluity rounding to fullness at her most exciting points, made his penis thrill.

113

"Yes—you do look better with them off," he said. "You should never wear those pants again."

She waggled her bottom at him.

"Do you like my bottom?" she asked. "Do you really think I have a nice body?"

Her words excited him almost beyond endurance.

"I've never seen one so good," he said.

"Do you think you're lucky to have it for yourself—to do you want with it?"

"A man never had such good fortune. I can't wait to show how much I appreciate it. But you'll know as soon as we start to make love."

She glided quickly towards him and wound herself around him, mouthing little cries, her eyes closed, her body in a fluid torment all around him. It was more than he'd expected.

Kissing her, wildly, he felt her hand slither down to his aching prick and touch it, sending sparks along its thick fatness. She stroked it gently, with little nervous, fluttering gestures and then held it firmly and squeezed it hard so that her hand crushed into its resistant, spongy tissue and made him gasp.

He picked her up, putting his arms around her, lifting her by her buttocks. She wound her legs, warm and smooth, around his hips as he carried her to the bed. She reached under her ass as he carried her and placed his prick against her vagina. She was groaning and murmuring incoherently. Then she wriggled down and slumped on his rigid member so that it shot into her with a strong bridgehead which made her gasp and go wild and clamped around his glans so moistly and firmly that he had to restrain himself from falling with her onto the floor and fucking her there.

They reached the bed with her jogging on the end of his organ with every step they took.

114

He lowered her onto the bed and moved straight in to lie between her widespread thighs which invited him not to linger. He fell between them in the same movement as he placed her on the bed and immediately began to screw into her, gritting his teeth with passion. Her body began to move with wild abandon.

"Oh, oh, oh!" she groaned as if in agony, digging her nails hard into his shoulders, waving her crotch wildly at his prick, scraping her buttocks along the counterpane and flinging her thighs in all directions.

"Oh—c'est bon—c'est bon!"

He wriggled his long wrist of rigidity up and up, delving into her like an exploring party in a cavern, farther and farther, deeper and deeper into darkness and moisture and a clawing grip which pulled at his loins, at his very bowels.

Her whole body twitched and writhed and she groaned incessantly, her face contorted with passion, mouth working, neck straining, nostrils flared, a light sweat breaking out on her forehead under the now tangled dark hair.

He felt the smooth, raw flesh of her vagina holding him in, breaking and pulling all around his hot, bursting prick. He pushed into her from his very toes and sent the last inch of his thickness plundering up her hole, pulling a fresh, ecstatic groan from her lips, making her open her eyes to look at him with a wild, desireful, glazed look.

"Oh, oh—wonderful, wonder-aaah!" She gasped as he grabbed her buttocks and raised them off the bed, raising his own body slightly for greater leverage, squirming into her with all the strength of his hips and thighs.

His loins moved in and out at her pelvis, her broad pelvis with that chasm at its centre, pistoning in with strong, muscular regularity. His own breath was short and the sight of her breasts, swaying over sideways towards the bed on either side of her, with her still erect nipples, made him

give an involuntary extra thrust which moved her up the bed slightly and made her arch her neck with the sudden sensation.

He watched her face, drawing different expressions of passion from it as he moved his hands over her, as if she were an instrument which produced fresh sounds as he moved his fingers over its notes. He moved his fingertips gently into the little hard area of smooth, crinkle-edged flesh which was her anus, felt it tightly resist and then give way so that his finger moved softly, persistently, sawing into softer depths, and cries broke from her lips in a consistent stream.

His loins were aflame, consumed with a fierce burning which swept through him in gusts of heat from his bowels. He gasped and quivered as he fucked, revelling in her flesh, flesh of this beautiful sexy girl whom he'd never seen before tonight.

He ran his hands from her buttocks down her thighs to feel his own chafing prick ramming in and out, to feel the clinging lips of flesh which held it firmly in and were now running with moisture which overflowed stickily down her thighs.

Her arms, which had been moving jerkily around her head like a puppet's, fists closing and opening spasmodically, swept down now and held his own buttocks as they tensed and thrust at her.

"Oh, oh, oh—darling, hard, hard!" she begged, gasping as if she'd burst something in her throat. She was nearing her climax and her body had become something demoniac, hardly human as she twisted and contorted, spreading her legs wide apart and then pulling them up to her shoulders, bending them at the knees, urging him on.

Her body was hot. Her head moved wildly from side to side, that full lower lip thrust out still further, her mouth

open in abandon. She swung her soft thighs up and clasped his waist in a scissors grip with her calves, winding her legs right round his body, tightening her grip on him, waving her ass from side to side, spiralling her quim down at his searching, hotly expanded cock.

"I'm coming!" she gasped suddenly with a sharp, shrill, intense passion. "I'm COMING—aaaaah…" She grabbed his face as she came and bit his mouth at the same time as her body from breasts to thighs arched convulsively into his and held there with the intensity of a sudden cramp and her orgasmic fluid escaped around his still hard-probing prick and ran down her smooth thighs, flooding his balls, too, as they brushed against her vaginal lips.

The intensity of her reaction was like a spur to his own potential climax. He dug deeply into her, forcing her legs up almost to her neck, doubling her over, screwing into her like an electric drill, crashing up to her cervix with his pulsating near-bursting rod. She continued to gasp and pant with little fluttering movements of her belly and thighs. She was still highly excited and followed his directions, however he wanted her to move, with a wild, eager passion.

"Darling," she murmured. "It's good, it's good. Fill me now, fuck me hard, let me have it." So she encouraged him, filling him with sharp, ecstatic pains in the region of his loins so that his prick grew and grew until he could hardly stand it and the breath was choking with difficulty through his open lips and his hands clasped and dug into her buttocks convulsively.

"Kill me with it, darling," she murmured. "That's—ah —a—ah!" She gasped as he thrust savagely high and hard, searing up through her passage, resting at the apex of his drive and jogging there for a second before withdrawing a little for another thrust and another.

He could feel he was on the verge of the break-through.

117

It was unbearable, it had to come now or he would die. He gasped, groaned, felt the bursting, heard her moan a little and hold him tightly round his shoulders and ther. with a long, toe-shaking groan which went on and on reverberating round the room he shattered into her, shooting his sperm high up into her open, receptive channel towards her womb.

.

Much later, after he'd had her twice more in different positions, each time with the same trembling abandon on her part and the same bone-shaking orgasm on his, she said to him:

"I don't know why you want to display such curiosity in my boy friend at a time like this."

She played with his penis and kissed his neck as she talked and he found himself tempted just to go on fucking her and forget everything else, but instead he said: "Naturally I'm interested in my rival. In any case I've heard he's quite a big man around."

She raised an eyebrow at him, slithered down and took the glans of his penis in her mouth to give it a little sucking nibble.

"He's not as big as this," she said.

He grinned and felt his prick move, the fibres tighten. She was insatiable. What a woman to have on safari.

"I meant in his activities."

"He doesn't like too many people to know about his activities. Anyway how do you know about him?"

"Oh, one hears about these things around the bars. It's of no interest, really, except that I wonder what sort of man attracts you."

"You do, darling," she said, licking his ear.

"I mean as a permanent or semi-permanent proposition."

"You do, darling," she repeated.

"Come, come," he said, pretending to be scandalised. "Nobody would think you're almost a married woman."

"Or you, my sweet," she retorted. "Sex is always better out of wedlock, though. Maybe it's better if we just have a long, lingering affair."

"Is that easy for you—wouldn't your boy friend wonder?"

"Oh, he's pretty busy. It's just a question of avoiding the spies he has on me without appearing to be avoiding them."

"What's he so busy at that he hasn't enough time to get you in bed at every opportunity?"

"Oh, he does that, don't worry."

"Does he prefer you to dance with your pants on or off?"

"He likes me to start one way and finish the other—so that I'm ready for the kill, as it were."

"I think I'll kill you again in a minute."

"Please—I love you to kill me like that."

"But I still can't understand what could be so important as to keep him away from you. Maybe he's having an affair *you* don't know about."

"Not him. He's spending tonight at Martha's."

"Martha's?"

"Yes. It's a striptease joint just off Pigalle—very ordinary, but it has a special show in a backroom once a week for people who don't think the usual show's up to much."

"I see. He's so discontented with you that he actually has to go to sex shows to get an orgasm."

She laughed and poked her tongue out to run it over his lips.

"He never even looks in. He has mysterious meetings in a room up above."

"Aha—that's where has has his orgy. It's probably a

one-way view ceiling so that he can watch what's happening below at the same time."

"No, they're all men up in that room."

He laughed uproariously.

"My God, this gets better and better. You'll be losing him soon for some young man from the Fiacre."

She grinned.

"Wrong again. They have some sort of political meeting…" she stopped as if she remembered that caution was really the best policy, and then said: "I don't want to talk about that, anyway. Let's make love again. I'll make you really wild this time."

So saying, she wriggled down his body and stroked his prick up to a tree-like attention. While she rubbed it gently with the palms of both hands, she began to suck voraciously.

Lying back, letting her work him up, Raimond decided he had all the information he needed. Now he might as well see the night through and enjoy her in every way possible.

CHAPTER XIII

Mahmoud Taluffah looked down viciously at the naked girl lying at his feet. She was bruised and cut and sobbing. He had beaten her so brutally that she'd fought him savagely afterwards when he'd started to have her and he'd had to rape her without mercy. He'd put real brutality into his pounding of her cunt, paying her for her infidelity which his spies had implied and which she'd confessed under pressure.

His feeling toward her was a mixture of wanting and hating her lying in the arms of another man. He'd fucked her, thinking all the time of her nakedness and the abandon he knew her capable of while the other man shagged her in delight. It had put his heart in a vice and constricted his chest. He was the boss. No woman of his was going to monkey around with him in that way.

He kicked her up her bare behind with his foot and she rolled over and lay there still sobbing. She was beaten and she'd think twice before she indulged her passion with

a strange body again. He'd been about to kick her in the quim but then he'd thought of his own future pleasures and restrained himself. He didn't mind giving her pain, but he didn't want to ruin his own sadistic enjoyment.

"You don't do anything I don't know about," he spat at her, glaring at her rounded nudity quivering and heaving at his feet. "Now you've had your punishment and he's going to get his."

They'd seen Raimond and the girl on their way back to Pigalle, driving without caution. They'd been looking for her all night, these two bodyguards who'd got anxious after she hadn't reappeared in the bar. It would be all right by them if it was a put-up job with no fear of their boss knowing and if they could have got their reward for blindness in kind from her body. But she'd purposely given them the slip and at any time he was likely to summon them or come looking for her. It was more than their lives were worth to keep quiet. As it was they'd got a bawling out which had made them tremble. But then he'd been viciously happy when at last they'd found her and taken her to him, keeping an eye on the man she'd been with as well.

They remembered him from the bar, of course, a big, good-looking fellow who might have been any sort of well-kept, successful business man. Little, doubtless, had he known he was messing around with the mistress of someone as powerful as Mahmoud Taluffah. He soon would.

When it came to a little *règlement de comptes* like this, the victim was followed and kept under observation until such time as the night was dark enough and the spot quiet

enough to enable a beating up to take place without the necessity of a kidnapping to precede it. That was how it was to be with Raimond.

He'd been followed to his home—even his wife had been noted for future reference if necessary—and had been trailed ever since. True, he seemed to lead an odd sort of existence, but it didn't occur to his shadowers that he was a *flic*. He was, perhaps, just what he seemed to be, a man who didn't need to work, who lived in a very respectable but not millionaire quarter, who could take days off from his office if he wished, who could persuade his wife that he had a lot of business to occupy him and thus spend nights away from her, hanging around the bright lights, picking up beautiful or not-so-beautiful women to seduce or be seduced by and then return home as if nothing had happened. The sort of rich, idle Frenchman whom they disliked, these Algerians, although their turn was yet to come and then perhaps they'd show themselves capable of just the same idleness. At the moment, of course, they had the fire of a cause to cover their idleness and destroy it even with the occasional supreme work of a murder.

At this moment there was no idleness. A piece of work was afoot. Raimond had decided to pay a preliminary visit to Martha's just to give it a once-over in preparation for something more in the line of a field day. He was walking, now, through the narrow streets which led to it off from the bright glare and noise of the boulevard.

Except for the bright blaze of light from a cafe every few doors down the street, the street itself was quiet. From the cafes came the explosive noise of pinball machines, juke-boxes, drunken talk and laughter. There was nobody in the street at all.

Raimond was alert; the three men who watched him from the doorway of a courtyard which he was destined to pass

couldn't know that he was alert, of course. In the first place they had no idea he was a policeman and in the second they had no idea he was on business and preparing himself for trouble.

The pavement made soft contact with his rubber soles as he walked. He was wondering how he could possibly find out what nights they had these meetings she'd told him about. That would really be a coup to catch them all together, like laying a net for the fish.

This area really swarmed with Algerians, he thought. And not one of them, officially, ever saw anything that went on. People were killed in these streets and when the trouble started the crowds which had been listening and playing and talking and drinking disappeared like forest animals at the sound of a human footfall.

The arm grabbed him from the doorway, closing around his neck and, without even thinking, he rammed back with his elbow. He heard the gasp of pain, moved quickly and felt a blow from what felt like the butt of a pistol graze down the side of his head numbing the path it took on his skull. He kicked out and saw a dark figure recoil as another sprang at him.

He was too quick, much too quick. The side of his hand lashed with a sharp flinging movement at the throat of his adversary, hitting the Adam's apple at the point of full impact.

At the same instant he pulled out his automatic, catching the dull glint of another as he fired at point-blank range. A body fell against him, heavy and clinging in the near-darkness. He pushed it back into the courtyard, catching sight of a little black moustache on the swarthy features.

The other two had gone—just like that. He saw them scuttling round a corner as he himself began to run quickly.

Windows were opening, throwing dull oblongs of light

onto the street below, but the noise in the bars was so great that nobody had heard a thing. Nobody rushed into the street to try and stop him.

Round the second quick corner he stopped running. He was slightly shaken and out of breath. The graze on his head felt hot and, putting his hand up, he felt the slight wet patch through his hair.

Now he walked at a good pace, but without any appearance of hurrying. He kept his hand tightly on his automatic in his pocket and watched each doorway and entrance to the street like a hawk as he headed back to the main boulevard. He didn't want to get mixed up in this. There was nothing to be learned from it except that they were up to his game. It was far better that he retained whatever anonymity he still possessed.

Once on the boulevard he crossed to the central island and sat down for a moment on a seat, never once relaxing his vigilance. He wiped his head with his handkerchief and wondered how they knew about him. Then he thought of the girl, Rolande, and wondered if they did, in fact, know everything. There was, perhaps, one way to find out.

He walked fast along the boulevard towards Chapelle until he came to a small, but heavily guarded commissariat on a corner. He looked up and down the boulevard once or twice and then crossed quickly and went in through the doors. He heard the hee-hawing warning of the police van just going off to where he'd come from.

The Algerian had taken the bullet in the shoulder. They'd bandaged him up in the commissariat and Raimond and his chief had left him in the hands of those specially trained to wring any secrets from him. They were waiting,

smoking outside a little room from which muffled noises came. They were both fairly humane men in the normal way of things, but this was no time to be squeamish.

After several minutes a man in his shirtsleeves came out and told them that the prisoner had said they had been ordered to beat up Raimond because he'd seduced the girl friend of a man named Mahmoud Taluffah. They had not been ordered to kill him and had had no intention of killing him.

"Would you like to question him yourself, sir?" asked the shirtsleeved man, and the chief looked at Raimond with a query in his brows.

"No," Raimond said. "Won't be necessary."

"We could bring him in on that," the chief said, taking him aside. "It speaks for itself."

"Trouble is, sir, that his two cronies have spilled the beans by now and he'll be hiding out. Better that they don't know who I am and are allowed to think that we don't know anything about them. Do you think that Arab was telling the truth?"

"Never fails by our methods."

"Well I won't be able to do much for a day except keep in touch with contacts. Better let them think there's no reason to get scared."

CHAPTER XIV

Mahmoud Taluffah was very angry. In the flat in which he'd taken refuge, he and Rolande were listening to the shamefaced account of the attempted beat-up by the two would-be beaters who narrowly escaped becoming victims.

"How would a man like that have a gun?" he snapped, immediately on the crucial point, after the resumé had been made.

"He said he was in advertising," said the girl. "Those big business men usually have something to protect themselves, particularly hanging around these quarters."

Mahmoud Taluffah sneered at her.

"They need to protect themselves from incensed cuckolds," he snapped, forgetting in a fresh pang of wrath the presence of the two men.

The girl went silent and he turned his gaze slowly back to the two men, the sneer still on his lips.

"I didn't think I'd have to use Mohammed Arab just for a beating-up," he said. "But I see that nobody else is to be entrusted with any task set them, however simple."

"He was like lightning," one of the men said. "We weren't expecting that."

"Three to one," Mahmoud Taluffah murmured, as if to

himself, and then he added in a louder voice: "Was Benabed dead?"

Neither of them knew, although it was probable, they said, at that range.

"He'd better be," Taluffah said softly. "But we'd better stay here for a day or two."

He remained thoughtful for several minutes while they all kept silent, waiting for him to speak. Then he said: "He's not getting away with this. Keep a watch on his home. Tomorrow he'll see that he can't meddle with me and get away with it."

The two men left and Mahmoud Taluffah sat in a meditative silence for a while. He'd been told the man's wife was lovely. He smiled to himself. An eye for an eye...

Then he took hold of Rolande and led her submissively into the bedroom. She'd caused him more trouble than he'd ever expected. The knowledge of that made him angry and the memory of how it had started made him want to keep fucking her until he'd wiped away the infidelity of hers, as if it would take so many times of making love to erase the traces of her one-night lover.

When he got the other woman tomorrow he'd show her an old Arab custom which her husband probably hadn't taught her. In the meantime he'd have to wreak his vengeance by proxy on Rolande.

He pushed her down roughly on the bed, let her lie there while he stripped and then pulled up her skirt and thrust into her without further ado. For some time she lay under his drubbing, simply gasping with pain as he chafed into her, but after a time her sexiness overcame her desire to remain cold and aloof and she began to buck with him, moaning with a growing passion. After all, the fuck was the thing, she told herself. Nothing else really mattered.

CHAPTER XV

Pierre Raimond was sitting once again in the prison-like room which belonged to Ahmed ben Lulla.

"So you haven't seen her at all in the days since you were warned?" he said.

"No," Ahmed replied. "We exchange notes—that much is easy. But we both think it better to wait until they have forgotten us and relaxed."

"You think that day will come?"

Ahmed shrugged his shoulders. It seemed to him more than ever that life held nothing, could never hold anything, all the promise turning to hopeless frustration as soon as it formed.

"We can only hope."

"Ahmed. When they ask you for the next contribution I want you to refuse. Tell them you have reasons and that you want to be tried by their court."

Ahmed stared at him as if he were crazy. He said nothing. There was no point in talking to a madman.

"Will you do it?"

"You are not serious."

"Perfectly serious and I'll give you the reasons."

"But there is only one decision from their court. Nobody lives."

Raimond nodded. It was common knowledge that the NLF held these mock courts, generally before execution. Like revolutionary purge courts there could be only one result. They were held for men who had already been condemned just to give a false semblance of justice to murder. To ask to go before such a court would mean that you were committing suicide, because it meant that you would never pay.

"You will not actually be tried by the court," he said. "It's just a question of getting the main people all together. We know where they meet; we want to get them there. You'll go in with them and the place will be surrounded by police in plain clothes with a hundred uniformed men standing by. We'll see that they're there and then we'll go in to get them."

"And me. I shall be with them—in their hands."

"If we act quickly they won't have any hands to have you in. I can give you a gun and show you how to use it if you think it'll do any good. It's unlikely they'll suspect you. They'll think it's a raid on the striptease joint. It shouldn't be too difficult for you to get away in the confusion."

Ahmed shook his head. He didn't fancy acting as bait. The whole thing seemed childishly dangerous.

"Naturally," Raimond went on, "you'll have done some service to the Republic and you'll be suitably rewarded."

Ahmed studied him with curiosity but without belief.

"How would I be rewarded?"

"You'll get one of the new apartments going up in the

10th Arrondissement and you'll be assured of work for as long as you stay in France. I'll give it you in writing if you wish."

Ahmed looked away around the room, slowly. A few seconds ago he would have laughed the project of going before their court to scorn, but now a big doubt had set in. An apartment! A new apartment! And work guaranteed!

"You and Françoise would be able to live happily ever after," Raimond coaxed.

Ahmed saw the room, coming back into focus from his scudding thoughts. What other hope was there? Continual threat of death from the NLF if one couldn't pay. Not enough to live on. No happiness with oneself or the people who could make one happy. What was there to lose? Could you even say you were losing your life when your life represented such a living death?

"But my life may be in danger even if you succeed. There are agents in many countries who would come here."

"If we break this ring, we'll smash it completely. Nobody'll know what happened. There simply won't be any more NLF in Paris and we'll do our utmost to make sure it doesn't rise up again. You've got nothing to lose—nothing."

It was true. He thought of Françoise. He wouldn't tell her until it was done. And then she wouldn't be able to stop him. If he died, well he died and she would find out then. If he didn't they would forget all this and be happy. His eyes brimmed with tears as he thought how happy they would be in their new apartment.

"All right," he said. "I will do what you ask."

As an afterthought, as the smile of encouragement spread across Raimond's face, he added: "I would like it in writing as soon as possible."

CHAPTER XVI

Michèle Raimond had the chess book on her knee and the board and men spread out on the low table in front of her. She was really tired of going over the games of the masters, but there was so little else to do. She'd read so much that her eyes felt strained, there was no housework, no knitting or sewing and she couldn't keep on ringing up friends.

Whatever she did, thoughts of Pierre kept swimming into her mind. The injury to his head, casual though he'd been about it, had filled her with horror and foreboding. And she knew he hadn't told her the truth about how he got it. And he knew that she knew. It was part of the half-fiction which was supposed to stop her from worrying too much through keeping her ignorant of the facts. But if the facts were worse than the explanations her imagination provided for her it was all too grisly anyway.

She moved a black knight and removed a white pawn from the board. Perhaps she loved Pierre too much, just a little too much. She always had and had always thought of it as more of a fault than a virtue—when she thought of it at all.

Even from the beginning. She'd always been unable to hide the depth of feeling she had for him. She'd hidden nothing from him, even telling him what had been such a shameful secret for so long, a secret she'd sworn would always be one—about the American soldier who'd had intercourse with her in a hotel bedroom in Montparnasse just like that, a stranger, because the family needed food so badly. She shivered even now when she thought of the American, who'd been so confident, so superior in the knowledge that he could do what he liked for a package of cigarettes. She had never told Pierre how much the American had demanded, how much he'd humiliated her. Never told him that it had happened more than once—five times in fact—always with the same American before his regiment moved on. She shuddered when she remembered the way he'd treated her. She could recapture it all with such chilling clarity if she let herself. How he'd forced her to walk around the room wearing nothing but a pair of high-heeled shoes, how he'd made her kneel before him and suck his hot erection until he came in her mouth and down all over her breasts, how he'd licked her vagina and sucked her clitoris, while she hated him with every second that passed, how he'd forced her to lie face down across his knees while he spanked her because it gave him a kick to see his hand sinking into her buttocks and to feel them quiver under his blows, how he'd made her do the same to him because that was another kick he got. All that, all that with a man she hated, all because he could get food and cigarettes which the family needed so badly in the shortage. She'd read later how the same sort of thing had happened in Germany. Indeed, how the German girls had sold themselves for a single cigarette or one piece of chewing gum.

And then there had been Pierre and she had loved him

so much that she had told him and he'd been nice and understanding except that it had made him want her, insist on having her before they got married—"so that the other man didn't get anything I didn't"—whatever he had meant by that.

And so she had given herself to him with all her heart and with a chill in the pit of her stomach one day in the long grass and she'd found herself rising to a pitch of response and abandon that she'd never have believed possible. And they'd gone on and on making love every time they met until eventually they'd got married after she'd begun to doubt if he ever would really marry her. And she'd always loved him so much, more and more and never been able to hide the depth of her feelings although she'd known that his had become, to a slight extent at least, blunted. Sometimes she'd thought that perhaps she should have an affair or be a little distant just to make him a little jealous, a little more acutely desiring again. But these, she knew, were mere fantasies. She simply was too involved with Pierre even to notice another man or even to be capable of saying "I don't feel like it tonight" when he began to move his hand over her breasts...

She was interrupted in her reverie by the buzz of the doorbell. She looked up from the chess board towards the door which led to the vestibule as if she expected to see somebody standing there. She got up, wondering who on earth this could be and walked into the vestibule and from it through into the little porch to open the door.

Three men were standing outside on the broad stairway in front of the lift. The red light was still illuminated on the lift where they'd just come up.

At the sight of them she began to close the door, uncertainly. They looked evil. She'd never seen them before

in her life and she was sure that any business they had was bad business.

In the first place they were Algerian and she didn't like Algerians; in the second they had about them an air of menace which was frightening.

One of them quickly put his foot in the door as she tried to close it and, before she had time to think what was happening, far from what to do, he had thrust the door open again with a big hand and walked into the porch, followed by the other two.

"What—what's the meaning of this!" she gasped, keeping her voice firm. "Get out immediately or I'll call the police."

The big, broad man who seemed to be the leader caught hold of her wrist and a knife glinted in his other hand.

"No you won't," he said. "Or you'll get more than we really intended to give you."

She stood frozen, with his grip cutting into her wrist. Was this something to do with Pierre? She felt sick in her stomach but she said nothing to bring him into it.

One of the other men, a lean, alert animal with the most vicious eyes she'd ever seen went past them and found the telephone in the vestibule. She heard him cutting the wires and the nausea in her stomach pervaded her whole body. They were going to do something terrible.

"What do you want with me?" she managed to get out. "What have I done—who are you?"

"We've just come in to have a little friendly play," the big man said. "We just have to pay your husband out for his little play."

"Pierre? Where is he? What's happened to him?" Her voice broke, but the man's next words reassured her.

"He's all right now, but he's not going to be when he finds out that his wife's been unfaithful to him." The three men laughed. The big man had released her wrist

but still held the knife in his hand, pointing it casually at her.

Her thoughts became confused. Over everything she was aware that at least Pierre was all right. And then the words sank in. They were going to rape her! These beastly Algerians were going to rape her! She felt physically sick again at the thought and looked round instinctively for a weapon, a way of escape. The three men grinned at her and the horror of her situation overcame her and brought a scream to her lips, a scream which was stifled immediately as two of the men seized her roughly, covering her mouth, holding her struggling arms.

"We are not averse to slitting your throat," the big man said. "But if you don't struggle or try to cry out only sweet pleasures are in store for you."

She tried to bite the hand that held her mouth but it simply crushed her lips with numbing force. She was lifted bodily and carried into the bedroom where they tied a scarf around her mouth and began to take off her clothes.

"Beasts, beasts, beasts!" sobbed through her head as she kicked and struggled. Worse than the American, horrible, unthinkable what they were going to do to her. She struggled and fought until she was on the point of exhaustion, but the two men who were stripping her seemed completely unbothered by her efforts. They held her firmly on the bed while they pulled at her garments, ripping them from her if they didn't come easily. The big man watched them as he slowly took off his own clothes.

Already they had her naked down to her underclothes. She struggled feebly as one of them caught her brassiere strap and ripped the bra off her, leaving a line of pain across her.

Her breasts soared free before their eyes and she saw those eyes as, ashamed and frightened, she struggled—

vicious, avid eyes and then hands which mauled her breasts in the struggle.

"Good," said Mahmoud Taluffah, stripped now. "Pretty little duds. Let's see what else she's got." He came over, gloating, and with eyes deep in fear she saw his shaggy body and the great mast of a prick rising out from the forest of his pubic hair. She closed her eyes to cut out the sight and felt the ripping, pulling around her hips. She made a last desperate attempt to resist and then she was naked and helpless before their eager gaze. She was sick and chilled; strange sexual horrors sparked and knifed through her loins and through her heart.

Mahmoud Taluffah came right close to her while the others held her and he pulled her thighs apart with a force she couldn't resist. A tear slipped over her cheek and her head ached.

"A nice little quim, too," he said.

She felt his fingers on her vagina and she cringed her crotch away from him, but the fingers insisted and entered, filling her with dread and shame.

"Not too big," he said. "It will be very good. Turn her over."

Nakedly she resumed her struggle with a sudden lease of fresh life. It was then they hit her; a couple of punches on the back of the neck which seemed to bring bile to the back of her throat in a sickening pain and she slumped over onto her stomach, helpless, while they pinioned her arms.

"Beautiful ass," Mahmoud Taluffah said. "Just made for giving me a nice ride."

In a daze she felt their hands opening her ass, drawing the buttocks apart. She tried to tense her behind, holding the buttocks together, feeling naked, obscenely, horribly naked. But she couldn't stop the pressure and her buttocks

were stretched away from each other until she could feel the cool air on the hot, perspiring interior of them.

"Ah," she heard Mahmoud Taluffah say. "That's it—tight and smooth and hairless—lovely to fuck."

His words chilled her and them she felt his fingers exploring the tight skin of her anus until with a little painful shock she felt one of them enter her and go in up to the first knuckle joint. Mechanically she closed her buttocks, gripping his finger in her posterior hole. She heard him laugh and she relaxed again, not knowing what to do, how to keep him away.

"Tie her," he said.

They hauled her up the bed and attached her wrists with handkerchiefs to the bed posts, spreadeagling her so that her arms were stretched out in a large V across the top of the bed.

She felt garlic breath on her and then a great shaggy body rolled onto her and oozed and undulated all over her as if revelling in the contact of their flesh. She wished she could faint, but she was fully conscious and bearing the ordeal with mounting horror. She could feel an enormous prick hot against her behind and rough hands ran all over her neck, shoulders and back. She was bitten in the neck and she squealed, opening her eyes and raising her head as far as she was able. The other two men were gloating over the spectacle, vicious grins on their faces. She closed her eyes with a gasp and dropped her head back to the bed. She had never felt so humiliated.

She felt a tongue running down her spine, felt his body moving up off hers. He forced her thighs which she was trying to clasp together apart and knelt between them. She felt his face on her bum and then he bit into a buttock. She heard his voice as she winced. It was uneven and excited.

"Delicious," he said. "Like butter."

She tried to cringe her buttocks away, but she only succeeded in waggling them in what seemed like sensual invitation.

"She wants it; she can't wait," she heard one of the other men say and there were raucous guffaws of laughter.

The knees between her thighs pushed them wide, hard and painful against the soft flesh of the insides of her legs. Her thighs were wide and helpless. She knew he could have her just as he wanted and another tear forced itself from her eyes although she was trying not to show any emotion.

She felt his hands on her hips, clasping them, digging into the soft flesh and he pulled her roughly up to a kneeling position. She could feel his hairy loins and his enormous prodding penis hard against her pelvis. She pushed out her legs stiffly, trying to flatten her body and he said:

"Hold her up—the sexy bitch."

Then fresh hands grabbed her, holding her hips high up in the air, keeping her legs apart. She felt his thumbs on the tender flesh on either side of her anus. Then she felt a hard, pointed thrusting against the anus, between the thumbs which were trying to stretch it apart. She chilled with terror. "No—no!" she screamed through the gag. The words were just muffled, meaningless sounds grunting out into the room. She opened her eyes and tried to raise her head.

"Hold her," Mahmoud Taluffah barked, as she began to struggle. She was held in a vice as she felt her anus being stretched as if it would tear, by those rude fingers, as she felt the hard, thrusting thing pushing and being rebuffed and pushing again.

She began to pray, wild prayers, and she bit at the gag.

This was death, worse than death. To have this shameful thing done to her, this horrid, disgusting, unnatural thing by beasts, by strangers. Her soul cried out against the disgusting, loathsome horror of it and then she jerked wildly with pain as a red-hot iron seemed to brand her asshole with an unbearable, aching, splitting pain.

"Hold her, hold the bitch!" Mahmoud Taluffah wheezed again. And she was held, almost unable to move, her bottom high up in the air, buttocks spread, nakedly, helping his prick to enter in and bugger her and she began to sob as the pain spread and made her stomach convulse with a sickness which rose in her throat.

Her anus was splitting. It would tear into a great slit, the length of the crease of her buttocks and blood would flow and all her inner organs would flow out to be drowned in the unbearable pain which with every second she felt she could no longer bear, but somehow did. Although she struggled, trying desperately to escape from the anal impalement, not just from shame now, but because the splitting pain was so terrible, she was held fast, held still in the kneeling posture best suited to his shagging of her ass.

She could feel the enormous intrusion of his cock, pushing solidly in now, widening her back passage, chafing and rubbing to a raw pain the soft skin of her rectum.

Once, involuntarily, she farted. And even that little occurrence, forced on her by the unnatural straining of her ass against the solid, sickening ravishment, added to her shame.

She became aware of his hand gripping her hips with a numbing pressure as he sawed and throbbed into her behind. The pain went on and on and each thrust brought fresh cringing sobs from her lips until the pain and sobbing was

merged in a continuous alliance. Each time he thrust in he seemed to go deeper and to split her more as the broader base of his penis moved slowly towards the point where the entirety of his prick would be lost in the stretched, reddish hole which suffered and clung to it like a clam.

The gag was wet with her tears. She felt wounded and ruined at her behind. As it waved and jogged high up behind her flattened shoulders, she felt as if it was a great wet open wound.

He was pummelling into her with long, smooth strokes, running into her with the whole length of his member. She heard him gasping and she heard the heavy breathing of the other men who watched. She was still held stiffly in a bent position, her thighs wide and inclined slightly forward, her shoulders pressed down on the bed, her back arched in a concave curve from the rounded hips where his body dominated her.

"God—it's tight. Ugh, ugh!"

He mouthed obscenities and descriptions to the other two men, which made her fiery with humiliation. As he lunged in at her, the other two men would let go and he'd pull her back onto his prick, slipping her over it as if she were some long boot he was pulling over his leg.

Her inside was a great, fiery, painful ball of sensation in the midst of which she was aware of that white-hot, rasping block of pressure, coming and going, which was his prick. She was a prisoner, there was no escape, she just had to kneel there, bent over painfully like a slave, while he thrust his penis harder and harder, faster and faster into the soft depths of her rectum, pushing the inflamed flesh aside with each long, ramming entry and insweep.

Her breasts heaved with her sobs. She would not be able to live after this, never able to look at Pierre or anyone else.

142

She would carry this ache in her nether hole as a permanent reminder of her shame and humiliation. Even when, physically, it had gone, it would creep back like a heavy phantom throughout her life.

Her body shook and trembled and her thighs, released now that resistance was broken in her, occasionally convulsed as an extra-hard thrust seared her rectum, seeming to push his cock right up to her colon, to fill her bowels.

Above and behind her his gasps and grunts filled the air, and she hated the pleasure and gratification and sadistic pleasure she was aware of giving him.

She longed as she gasped brokenly into the counterpane for the moment when he would finish and withdraw his deflated penis from her vastly enlarged aperture. The pain would be there still, but the solid, worming presence which seemed so repulsive would be gone—and gradually, too, the pain would go.

But with this longing went an even greater one that he should not finish his orgasm in her. It would seem like the crowning point of domination over her, of her helpless, humiliated slavery to him, at that point where he discharged into her all the pent-up concentration of his brutal passion, punishing her as the fleshpot receptacle of a climax which she in no way reflected.

But, with a growing horror which even stilled her sobs and made her sway and wait for the inescapable ejaculation with stifled groans, she knew that he was coming to the point she dreaded.

His organ was like a huge, rough-edged cudgel in her behind. Like a cudgel with knots and nails sticking out from it. And now he was grating breath through his teeth and grinding slowly into her bum, joggling his prick around in her rectum once it had gone up her to the hilt—so that

143

she felt his hairy surrounds against her buttocks and the inside of her thighs.

"What an asshole!" he gasped. "God—it's here—here!"

She bit the gag with all her force and screwed up her eyes tight, trying not to think, but she couldn't maintain a vacuum in her mind and she relaxed and heard him again just at the point where he let out a long, choking gurgle and came right up in her rectum. She froze, seemed to empty of everything and as, shaking still, he emptied the last of his vicious sperm up at her colon, filling her soft passage with warm wetness, she began again to shed bitter tears.

After a while his great bulk moved off her and her rectum and anus felt as if cold gales were whirling around and through them. They felt coldly wet and aching and she felt hopeless and wanted to die or to awaken and find it had all been just some horrible dream. But instead, as she sank down on the bed, aware when she moved of the ache in her back, she heard him say: "Go ahead, Mohammed. She's all yours—what's left of her."

"I'll find something left," said one of the other men. "Even if I have to dig a fresh hole in her belly."

Her hands were untied and she was rolled over. She opened her eyes, reluctant, but afraid to leave them closed. She saw the man with the vicious eyes pulling off his pants. He came at her in a business-like way, rolled her over onto her back, slumped on her, pulling apart her thighs and slid his prick straight into her cunt, making her cry out with pain where she'd thought there could be no pain left.

She didn't bother to struggle. She was exhausted and hardly thought of herself as a person capable of resisting. When his dark, sweating face came down on hers and he

144

sucked at her mouth, she let her lips be crushed softly under his and tried to forget the moment as if it didn't exist.

His hands slid under her buttocks and when he told her to put her tongue in his mouth she obeyed mechanically, refusing to think.

She became aware of the other two watching before she closed her eyes so that there were only his mouth and his prick in her quim which seemed real.

CHAPTER XVII

At the time of his wife's ravishment, of which he was blissfully unaware, Pierre Raimond found himself giving way to an irresistible impulse. It was an impulse which, when followed, could put him in considerable danger. It was an impulse, too, which if followed really gained him nothing except a peculiar satisfaction which, analyse and rationalise it as he might, he could hardly understand.

Having got what information he could from Rolande, he'd put off any plan to see her again. He'd let her understand that he'd show up in the club where she did her turn. He now felt magnetically drawn to it. Her violent sensuality had reacted on him so powerfully that he found he wanted her again, not to get information or through any ulterior motive at all, simply to enjoy the abandoned, passionate lovemaking at which she was such a natural past master.

There was really nothing further he could do until Ahmed ben Lulla had done what was necessary for him to do. The chief was in possession of all the latest develop-

ments and a vast force of men were standing by to go into action at any time.

He had reasoned with himself that, if he went to the club and just watched her, it was highly unlikely that her two watchdogs would try anything with him on the premises; that would brand it a little too clearly. In any case he felt adequate to deal with them. Whenever he thought of her protruding, inviting bottom with those pants off he got a quiver from his toes to the crown of his head which almost made his hair stand on end. He had only to picture her body naked on the bed in the hotel and the way she trembled like a leaf in the wind as soon as he touched her and he got an erection which threatened to ruin the line of his trousers for ever. She was a sexual instrument, designed for that purpose, with all the allure which was sometimes missing from others similar.

He was touched by a little "in-loveness" towards her, a situation the ironic stupidity of which he recognised. It was superficial feeling that would past. Of that he was well aware. But at this moment it was almost unbearable and he saw no reason to smother it. He would take the risk.

He left the bar near Opéra where he'd been moodily sipping a beer at the counter and drove towards Pigalle, speedily, wanting to get there, to give himself no chance to turn back and change his mind. He parked the car, as usual some distance from the scene of operation, and walked warily through the bustling, vice-tinted streets, ignoring the perky, tight-clad whores who encouraged him or slyly offered to give him a quick suck, as he passed them.

Outside the bar he hesitated for just a second, aware that this was the moment when history was changed, that there was still time to be cautious and live happily ever after. But then he'd never been *too* concerned about living happily ever after.

He went in quickly, his eyes taking in the whole room at a glance, while his legs didn't stop moving but directed him to an empty table against the wall within easy reach of the door.

The place was half full. It always seemed to be about half full. The usual clientele by the look of it. A single Algerian was sitting at the bar, looking out over the room. But Raimond didn't recognise him. And after a cursory glance, the man looked away, obviously not recognising the newcomer either.

Raimond arranged himself behind the table, his automatic loose in his side pocket, hand in pocket, ready for any sudden eventuality. The man at the bar was probably a new watch-dog. He looked very bored with his new work.

The little trio in the alcove were playing some soft music. The people at the tables and the bar were chatting in low voices which made a general, vague hum. There was no sign of Rolande.

The waiter came. It was the same waiter. But he gave every impression of being just an employee who knew nothing of the intrigues which involved the management. He was French anyway.

Raimond took a whisky and found, when it was brought and he took a swig, that his mouth and throat had dried up as if he'd just come through a sandstorm.

The trio were playing some French popular romantic songs and conversations were being carried on with a recognition of the background atmosphere. The few couples in the room were distinctly amorous.

Raimond, taking no chances, not risking his own eval-uation of the Algerian at the bar, kept a weather eye on the man, but the object of his attention didn't look back at him again or seem to be the slightest bit aware of him.

After a time the trio changed their mood to a soft, old-fashioned blues.

Raimond began to wonder if this was, perhaps, the wrong night. Or maybe she'd been taken off this particular aspect of her entertainment value.

He finished his whisky and ordered another, making a mental note that this was to be the last. He never got drunk, nor anywhere near it. His capacity, as a regular drinker, was considerable, but he never overburdened it.

He'd taken two sips of the liquid and chilled his teeth on the ice when Rolande came in from the back room. She was dressed in the same sort of costume as before, showing her shapely calves and thighs and the same considerable swell of breast, but this time it was pink and it reflected a rose glow on her taut skin.

She didn't see him. She went and sat at the end of the bar in her usual place, waiting for her turn to sing.

Raimond watched her for several seconds, shifting his glance from her to the Algerian at the other end of the long, elegant counter.

From where he sat he could see the long, slight furrow of muscle in her calf, the rounded heart shape of her bottom on the stool. A little contraction started in his stomach and he stood up, hand still in his pocket, picked up his drink and went over.

He slipped onto the stool next to her, and, turning to glance at him, she stiffened involuntarily and her lips opened. In the next fraction of a second she became calm and smiling, all trace of anxiety gone.

"You," she said, softly, "you."

The intensity of her tone belied the calm, smiling expression, a blind for the spy who was watching them without much curiosity. It was usual for men to engage her in conversation between her turns.

"Me," he agreed. "I had to see you."

"I've been thinking about you all the time," she said. "What happened?"

"I thought you might be *au courant*."

"I know the rough outline. You're lucky to be alive."

"How about you?"

"I got smacked for being a naughty girl—nothing too serious."

"They're quite nasty—your friends."

"Well you gave them quite a shock anyway. How come that you're all prepared for that sort of thing?"

"I've had an adventurous life."

"Darling, it was dangerous for you to come here. You came just to see me?"

"What else?"

She stared at him and smiled into his eyes.

"You're even better than I thought," she said. "God I wish we could just go off to Spain or something."

"Yes," he said. "I know some nice little spots and the climate's so conducive to making love. You feel you can do it anywhere: in bed, on the beach, in the sea, in the mountains..."

She grinned.

"I can't believe that you've come just to see me after all that," she said. Her eyes were mellow and they looked at him with tenderness overlaying desire.

"I wanted to see you in those pants again—as it's not very likely I'll see them off for a bit."

Rashly, she slipped her hand against his under the bar, just a fleeting contact because she wanted to touch him.

"We must see each other," she said. She glanced casually along the bar. The Algerian was staring into his drink.

"That's the new boy," she said. "The others lost their stripes."

"We'd better wait a few days," he said. "Things may be easier in a few days."

Something in his tone made her look at him, wondering.

"No, it won't be any easier," she said. "But we'll take the risk. I'll make this one lose his stripes, too. Just give him long enough to lose his eagerness."

"You look lovely," he said.

Her fingers touched his again, for an instant.

"Don't say it," she said. "I can't bear having you say things like that and not be able to let you see how lovely I am."

"I know how lovely you are."

"You don't know all my loveliness yet."

The trio changed tempo again to a slow, modern song.

"That's for me," she said. "You'd better go and sit at a table or I'll get too emotional and start to make love to you."

"I'll go after I've seen the dance," he said. "And I'll see you again in a few days. It'll be easier then, believe me."

"It doesn't matter whether it's easy or not," she said. "It'll just *be*."

He took his drink and went back to the table. The Algerian glanced at him casually but without any expression. He sat down as she started to sing, her lower lip pouting out, her dark eyes longing. As she sang her voice took on a husky splendour of feeling and a deep silence fell on the club. She seemed to be trying not to look in his direction, but at last, as if she couldn't stand not to, she raised her eyes to his table, looking at him with a meaning intensity which she couldn't hide.

He held her eyes for several seconds, seeming to lose himself in the savage demanding of them and then he looked down at his drink. He wanted her so badly.

As the song came to a yearning end and the music went

on softly, filling the place her voice had taken, there was the whisper of a sigh of relief and applause in the room.

Raimond looked up from the drink which was mostly ice now and saw that she'd slithered off the stool and was dancing, swaying in a gentle rhythm. This part would be the worst for his nerves, he thought, seeing her in the scantiness of her underclothes yet not being able to stretch her out on a bed and fuse with her, not even be able to look forward to it.

She unclipped her dress and drew it away from her body in a smooth movement. A lump rose in his throat and stayed there. Her breasts quivered and jogged gently under the tiny pieces which covered the nipples. He could see the hollows above her hips, the neat tapering away from the breasts to the small, firm belly. When she turned he felt his prick move in his trousers at the sight of that half-shown hollowing rump which rounded out towards the spectators like a glazed basin, stretching hard against the flimsy material which clung to it and outlined each buttock separately. He fixed his eyes on the voluptuous join of the buttocks, unable to believe, now, that his hands had held them, his finger caressed her hard little anus. It was all so unbelievable: that he'd lain on that body, that he'd caressed those breasts, that that tongue had danced in his mouth while she herself writhed under him with his sex deeply embedded in her wet, excited sexual channel.

His eyes ran over the fluid curves of her moving body as if they were hands, trying to be hands so that they could feel the flesh simply by looking.

And then the innovation happened.

She caught at a couple of clips on those pants of hers and in a trice they were off and she was dancing in the nude.

The spectators craned forward in delighted astonishment.

The Algerian raised his eyebrows and then grinned. Raimond nearly wept with consuming frustration. She had done that for him, because she knew that was what he wanted to see. She even moved towards his end of the room, swaying her buttocks as if in a mamba at the faces of the audience, so that they could follow closely the delicious curves of her buttocks which tensed and hollowed and moved like two eggs rolling together. She didn't face the audience again. Strictly speaking, that was not allowed in a respectable club. She had no g-string. But the few men at the bar had a good eyeful of her down-covered loins and the heaviness of flesh which crowned them.

Raimond swallowed his drink. If this didn't stop he'd have to go. It was too much. He took another look at her long, slender back with the shoulders slightly broader than the slim waist and all that tight, bursting flesh rounding out invitingly below the waist. His eyes ran down the slender thighs which gripped so well in the act of love, the slim calves which muscled lightly as she moved. His mouth was dry, his face flushed—and then the number ended smoothly and, without looking back, she whisked up her clothes and disappeared in the back.

Raimond called the waiter. Next time he came here it would be when he was certain of the rest of the night's entertainment.

CHAPTER XVIII

Ahmed ben Lulla was nervous. He had refused and they were giving him until today to reconsider. They were coming at any moment.

There was always the possibility that they might not accede to his request to be tried before their court. Everybody knew it was a farce, and although they liked to feign a certain democratic procedure, purely for political reasons, there was nonetheless that slight chance that they might take it into their heads to finish him off there and then.

He was nervous. But at the same time he was resigned. His only regret was that he hadn't been able to see Françoise before the event. Hadn't even told her anything about in in their secret notes. He was afraid she'd react in some way that would make the whole scheme impossible. It was better if she were presented with the *fait accompli* either of his success—or of his death. His mind had been so involved with the details of this plan that he'd even forgotten to feel sick about the fact that Françoise was still being mounted and screwed, perhaps even getting an occasional orgasm herself, by other men. They were having her in a long stream, night after night, while he wasn't

even able to see her. It was too, too cruel and if it hadn't been for the overwhelming importance of his own imminent activities he'd have been near to committing suicide.

There was a tap on the door. This was it. He steeled himself and crossed to the door, opened it. It was a single man, Mohammed Arab. He came into the room, a sardonic smile on his cruel lips.

He sat on the bed casually, chattily, his appearance belying the true nature of the situation.

"You have the money?"

"I told you I can't pay."

"You have been told before what happens to those who 'can't' pay."

"I want to go before the court to defend myself."

Mohammed Arab's lips curled in a sarcastic smile. He put a hand patronisingly on Ahmed's shoulder.

"If you take my advice you will pay."

"It's impossible—I haven't got the money."

"Why haven't you got the money? What defence have you of your incapacity to help the revolution?"

"I will put my defence to the court."

Mohammed Arab's smile disappeared.

"You are being very stupid," he said, scowling.

He seemed to hesitate, glaring at Ahmed, as if he were considering taking the law into his own hands as he'd so often done before. And then he stood up and went to the door.

"You are very, very stupid," he repeated. "We shall call to take you in a day or so."

He went out, closing the door softly behind him. And Ahmed sat down with a shiver of apprehension and of relief. So far so good. But the most dangerous was to come.

CHAPTER XIX

Raimond sat in stunned silence. He had listened for a difficult, broken half hour to his wife trying to tell him of the horrible experience she'd been through. She was wearing a thick dressing gown. She had taken a number of baths since the assaults as if to wipe clean the symbolic stain. She was sore and she ached and her heart was still heavy with shame. Nonetheless she had told her husband everything that had happened and he had listened without a word, his face changing every so often, and once he had taken her hand.

Now he sat, at the end of her recital, overcome with a sense of tragic remorse. She had undergone this not because of his investigations into the nationalists as she believed, but because of his extra-marital relations with the nationalist leader's girl friend. One always had to pay for everything. Somehow one always paid. While he had been happily fucking away, plundering the bodily delights of Rolande, this situation had been building up as from his own hand by which his wife was not only raped, but buggered and beaten to exhaustion.

He stood up then and took her in his arms, speechless, and she clung to him as if she had been frightened he might have renounced her.

Pictures began to form in his mind of these greasy Algerians toying with her body, all of them naked. He saw her tied helplessly to the bed while with lewd words and gestures they thrust their dirty pricks up her cunt and her ass, hurting her, making her cry out with pain. He remembered, once again, the American of years gone by. Every "adventure" she had was one of force. He got a nasty little chill in the pit of his stomach.

"I'll kill them with my hands for this," he muttered after a time. "I want them to die slowly, in agony."

On his insistence, she reluctantly gave him a full description of each man as far as she could remember them. One of them, a vicious-eyed one, he remembered from a previous description. He pictured them well from her description and he thought of them naked as she had seen them. He began to ask more questions about the way they had treated her, what they had said, how she had struggled, how many times they'd assaulted her. The details began to make his stomach and loins contract. The thought of her being forced to submit, gasping and helpless, made him begin to flush with a self-torturing excitement.

He began to stroke her with his hands. He wanted her. He couldn't bear to think the last sexual relations she'd had had been with these violent, rapist Algerians.

He kissed her and stroked her and opened the dressing gown. They went to a divan and, unable to wait to take off his clothes, he pulled his penis out and put her hand on it.

When he started to slip gently and purposefully into her orifice, she clung to him desperately as if she, too, wanted with this act to wipe out all that had gone before.

CHAPTER XX

Before the knock which he was nervously expecting sounded sharply on the door, Ahmed ben Lulla had carefully arranged the little automatic in its tiny holster under his armpit. It seemed to him a little academic; he couldn't seriously imagine using it, hoped it wouldn't be necessary.

He opened the door as calmly as he could and confronted the three grim figures outside.

Mohammed Arab grinned in at him and Ahmed wondered if he ever had a pleasant, non-vicious thought. The man was like some black devil; his very arrival anywhere seemed to bring the possibility, the aura of death and torture into that place.

Mohammed Arab made a slight sign with his head, without speaking, and Ahmed pulled a coat over his shirt and went out, locking the door behind him.

Nobody spoke as they marched down the stairs together, one of them in front of him, the other two behind. It was like the last silent walk from the prison cell to the gallows.

He hung up the key on the hook in the office, a thing he had done so many times without a tremor of emotion.

He noticed that his hand was trembling slightly although he hadn't thought about it before.

They went out into the street, all three of them. It was broad daylight, a little before noon, not at all the sort of time for such desperate things to be happening, he thought.

"Which way?"

Mohammed Arab took his arm and guided him to the right.

"Just friends together," he said. "Follow our friend in front."

As they walked from the street to the crowded boulevard, Ahmed tried to see the watchers from the corner of his eyes. They were there all around. They must be there. The recognition of how completely he counted on that little ambush of police turned his stomach cold. Supposing they had mistaken the day, the place, anything. A chill iced his stomach. It was always such a mistake to rely on other people. And his life was at stake. But they must be there. It was as big a thing for them as for him.

But there was no sign of anybody, no hint of the scores of police in whose hands his life lay.

Along the boulevard the traffic was rumbling as usual— little Citroens, humped like frogs, sleek American cars, mobs of scooters. The sun was shining and the trees along the central walk of the boulevard dappled a pattern on the dust surface.

Even at this time of the day the whores were out in droves and tourists jostled everywhere. A few GIs were poring over the lurid covers of books called "Myra by Night" and "Ladies Alone" in the window of a shop; the newspaper booths were doing a brisk trade in papers in several languages. The dull neon signs reflected the sun every so often. A few pigeons were strutting under the trees and a small girl with white ribbons in her hair was feeding

them crumbs. Everything was bright and peaceful and normally it would be good to be alive. But there was no sign of the police network which should be in operation and Ahmed became more and more apprehensive.

They walked at an even pace through the crowds which flowed along the narrow pavement under the six-storey buildings. Other Algerians were strolling to and fro; one was selling apricots from a car in the kerbside, selling in haste, undercutting everybody else.

Later they turned off the main boulevard and off again into narrower streets. Ahmed saw no sign of police. He couldn't think where they could be hiding if in fact they were there.

So it was that they came to the striptease club. An advertisement outside, with the silhouette of an almost naked girl, said that stripteases took place from 3 p.m. onwards, admission 350 francs. This was the "innocent" striptease. Those in which Mohammed Arab participated went unpublicised.

Ahmed controlled with the utmost difficulty his desire to give a last glance out into the street in the hope that there might be some clue to the non-appearance of any sign of Raimond and the forces he had at his disposal. It occurred to him that it might be the last time he'd ever see the street.

They went into the club, through a couple of rooms, a couple of doors and then up a staircase. There were guards posted at the doors and one at each end of the stairs. Ahmed felt a flush of hopelessness steal over him. Even if the police were watching, what hope had they of reaching him before he would be shot down?

"Up there," a voice said and they began to climb the stairs. At the top was a short corridor and they opened a door off it and went in.

Inside was a round, polished wooden table. Mahmoud Taluffah occupied the central place and on either side of him, all facing or half-facing the door, were several of his lieutenants. They all looked towards the new entrants with a sort of grim satisfaction. They rather enjoyed this little farce.

Ahmed felt panic-stricken. He wished more than anything at this moment that he'd never had anything to do with this crazy idea. Right now he could be lying on his bed. Perhaps he and Françoise would have found some way to outwit these people anyway and see each other. Now escape was cut off. He'd walked willingly into a noose—and all to help some damned *flic* that he'd never even seen before a few days back.

Mahmoud Taluffah motioned for the group to approach. When they were within a few yards of the table, his bodyguard formed up in a short line behind him and Ahmed found himself alone before his judges like an officer standing in the van of his regiment.

Mahmoud Taluffah looked up at him and grinned, a nasty grin which was not unlike the speciality which Mohammed Arab had made his own.

"So you have been giving us trouble again," he said.

Ahmed tried desperately to think of something. He had to give them some story. Or perhaps he could simply say it had all been a mistake and that he'd pay his contribution immediately.

"We are very busy men," Mahmoud Taluffah went on. "And we really have no time to occupy ourselves with someone who counts as little as you. There are far more important things to be done."

"What can be more important than the individual who makes up the important things?" Ahmed heard himself saying.

Mahmoud Taluffah stared at him as if he hadn't heard aright. A mock pained look crossed his features.

"You are very naïve," he said, "and very young, or you would not ask such stupid questions. The individual counts for nothing. What counts is that our country becomes ours. Nothing else matters."

"And who cares that much?" Ahmed heard himself persist. "How many really want to go through this sort of ritual, killing and hating, just to have their country?"

Mahmoud Taluffah scowled.

"You deserve to die," he said. "Only patriots will benefit from the Algeria which we shall win and make."

"You have no feeling for human beings at all," Ahmed said. "How can you create a country in which people will want to live. You're just cut-throats. You won't know how to begin to run a country."

Mahmoud Taluffah made a sign to one of the men behind Ahmed who had been about to strike him.

"Leave the pitiful creature," he said. "We have yet to sentence him."

He looked at Ahmed with a grim dislike in his eyes.. It was a long time since anyone had spoken to him in this way. Only the police who visited him occasionally were allowed to get away with it. Amongst the Algerians of the Metropole he was top dog.

"You are a very misguided youth," he sneered. "You are the sort whose guts we hate, who have no courage, who would be of no use to the country we shall build. You would like to remain here in France living like a dog or perhaps stay in Algeria living like a pig while the fat colons beat you down and down and make their profits to build their great white houses and ride in their big blue Cadillacs. We do not like your type of person and we intend to exterminate it, just as surely as we shall

exterminate the French in Algeria until they have been forced back across the Mediterranean and our country is ours as it rightfully should be."

Since he had begun to talk, to answer back, to attack these men, Ahmed found that his fear had evaporated. He seemed to have gone beyond fear, as if it had frozen up somewhere in some part of him and he'd gone on beyond it. His mind was clear and his hand had stopped trembling. He'd forgotten the police. He felt that he was seeing these men in perspective for perhaps the first time.

"It is up to each man to decide whether he wants to build something through hate and violence or whether he simply will accept the world as he finds it and live as peaceful a life as he wants," he said. "I would like to see an independent Algeria. I would love the country that might become ours alone. But I could not hate men so much that I am prepared to hate and kill to make that country. There are things which are more important than the particular piece of land on which one lives, or whether one has a car or a house. There are things which are more important."

"You talk like a fool," Mahmoud Taluffah said. "I will not waste my time with you."

He paused. scowling still and then said:

"As there can be no reason for you not paying your contribution. I condemn you to die."

"You could not even give me the chance of giving you any reason for my not being able to pay?"

"There is no..."

Faces froze in the room and Ahmed's heart jumped.

Down below and very close was the sound of a scuffle. Not a shot had been fired. There was just the unmistakable sound of fighting and then a voice cried out in Arabic that the police were there.

CHAPTER XXI

Detective-Inspector Raimond moved into the little street with his two companions. They walked casually, chatting, but with alert, trained eyes which took in every detail, every nuance of movement.

At each end of the street, just out of·sight round each corner, van-loads of police began to pull up. Another small party of plain-clothes men followed in the inspector's wake some thirty yards behind, also chatting casually and laughing.

"I think we can go in now," Raimond said quietly to his companions. "The boys will move up as soon as we're inside."

"O.K."

"And don't use a gun until we have to. We don't want to have them all hopping out the back door."

"O.K."

They crossed the road. still talking casually, towards the striptease club. There was nobody outside. but Raimond knew there would be plenty of people just inside, waiting

for just such an emergency. He hoped they'd manage to get to whatever inner sanctuary was reserved for the "trials" before anything happened to Ahmed. He felt sorry for the boy. But it would be touch and go. He also felt a little responsible for him. He'd misled him about the lack of risk.

He reached the club door and pushed in, followed closely by his two men. The door of the club swung open. It had been left that way to look more casual.

As Raimond disappeared, so the group of plain-clothes men behind quickened their pace and began to cross the road. Down at each end of the street police began to block off the road and move along from each direction in a body. Crowds began to gather in horror and astonishment beyond the barriers way out on the boulevard.

Just inside the door of the club an Algerian was sitting on a stool. He wasn't expecting visitors. Nothing had ever happened before. Raimond's knife ran through him before he could utter a sound. Raimond lowered the body. He felt nothing. This sort of thing had become common to him during the Resistance. It was the only way to ensure that warning was not passed on. There could be no half measures.

By the time Raimond and the other two had fanned out through the rooms which led off from the vestibule, the second batch of police had entered the building and fanned out as a second line of attack.

One by one, expertly, with a minimum of noise, the Algerian guards were dealt with and quietly left behind. Sometimes there was a struggle, but nobody had a chance to utter a cry. With rapid efficiency, the police began to take over the building. It was at the foot of the stairs that there was the first real resistance. They were seen from the top of the stairs and, crying out a warning in

Arabic, the guard from the top came springing down to help his crony on the ground floor.

Both were overpowered without too much difficulty, but by that time the alarm was raised. There were sounds and voices from a corridor which could be seen leading off from the stairs.

Running up, three at a time, Raimond and his men saw a door open and a number of Arabs dressed in expensive-looking suits come racing out.

As they saw the police vanguard, they turned to run back into the room they'd just vacated, but the door slammed shut, keeping them out and, after a preliminary push, they made off along the corridor, firing revolvers back at the police as they went.

Behind the detectives, throughout the whole building now that firing had started, was the heavy sound of armed and uniformed police swarming through the room in a body.

All around the building itself, out in the street and in the houses opposite, police with Sten guns and rifles had taken up positions of waiting, their arms trained on any exist they could see. Down along the boulevard the crowd of sightseers had grown in spite of the obvious danger. Nobody knew what was going on. But everybody wanted to be in on it. As long as "in" didn't mean being involved.

CHAPTER XXII

When the scuffle sounded down below, the nationalist "judges" had forgotten about Ahmed. With one accord they'd made towards the door of the room and rushed out into the corridor.

Ahmed, momentarily left alone in the room, had understood and also moved towards the door. He'd been about to go out himself into the corridor when the unnecessary risk he would thus run came home to him.

Instead he simply slammed the door and turned the key. Then he drew out his automatic and moved over behind a big wardrobe out of range of the door.

Within seconds came the thudding pushes at the door and then the sound of shots, barking out and resounding within the walls of the building.

Ahmed stayed where he was, staring at the door which received no further battering for several minutes. The shots continued to string out, getting a little farther off, and he heard the heavy, thumping rush of many feet clumping past the room. He heard voices snapping out

orders in French and he felt a glow of relief and then a sort of shaken happiness.

It had succeeded, actually succeeded, the whole plan. Here he was quite alone in this room with the sound of battle in which he'd expected to be involved receding. He was unhurt, unscratched. He had won his end of the gamble. The nationalists must be cornered; there was no escape surely from such a building and the police would have it surrounded. Tomorrow he would be free from all anxiety. Tomorrow—no, later today—he would see Françoise, hold her in his arms, make love to her, all without fear because fear had been surrounded with his help and defeated. His eyes lit up with joy. He remembered the apartment in the 10th Arrondissement which would be his and Françoise's and the promise of work which had been made to him.

He was still overcome with wonderment at the idea when the battering at the door resumed. Gruff voices called out in French for whoever was in there to open up. Ahmed waited a few seconds until there was no doubt that the voices belonged to the police and then he went to the door and turned the key.

Several black-uniformed police immediately brushed into the room, two of them seizing him, and began a quick search, even opening the wardrobe.

"We've got another of them," a policeman said as an inspector in silver-braided cap came through the door.

"I'm Ahmed ben Lulla," Ahmed said, quickly. "It was I who laid the trap for the terrorists here. I was working with Inspector Raimond."

They eyed him narrowly. These police were not too fond of Algerians.

"Bring him along," the inspector said. "We can check his story. Better take his gun."

CHAPTER XXIII

Raimond had flung himself into a doorway with the first wild shots that sped back from the retreating figures in the top corridor.

Behind him he heard a gasp and, half turning, saw one of his men fall. He opened the door against which he was pressed, yelled to those on their way up to take cover and, using the doorway for his own shelter, sniped at the Arabs who were rushing headlong up another staircase at the end of the corridor.

"Search all the rooms on the way up," he called back. "We don't want any rear ambush."

He moved on quickly but carefully and reached the staircase. There was a door at the top. When he reached it he found it locked. The stairs were bare boards and, at a guess, Raimond thought, it led out onto the roof.

He put his shoulder to the door but it merely hurt his shoulder when he barged. A group of police gathered around him as he shot round the lock. The door opened at the first push and, motioning back the men behind him,

Raimond peered out. He was met by a little hail of bullets.

The door opened straight out onto a flat roof which climbed to other levels and was dotted with chimney stacks.

"They can't get away," Raimond snapped. "No point in risking any of our blood. Send back and tell them downstairs that they're on the roof, to make sure the place is completely surrounded and to get up on top of the buildings opposite."

"Can they get from this one onto any other?" someone asked.

"Tell them surround the whole block and to send somebody into each apartment. We'll cut off any possible means of escape."

Raimond peered through the door again to be met by several more bullets, dangerously close to his head.

"All right," he said, "we can wait for them."

He posted a large body of men on the staircase and retraced his steps down through the building and out into the street where, in the doorways on both sides, uniformed police were keeping watch.

He had a few words with a little group of officers who were staring up at the roof of the building and then he entered the apartments on the opposite side of the street. He took the lift up to the top floor. On every floor the anxious inhabitants were crowding and being calmed by police who'd taken over the building.

From the top floor he climbed the rough spiral stairway which led out onto the roof. A superintendent came over as soon as he saw him.

"Good work," he said. "I think we've got them all cooped up there. But it may take some time to break them down."

"What's happening. Can you see them?"

"There's a parapet round the front, same as this side.

We've given them a few shots but they're not wasting their ammunition. They're keeping low."

Raimond walked with the superintendent to a low wall which formed a parapet all around the roof. Crouching behind it he glanced over to the building opposite, some 30-40 feet away.

The block of buildings was not large and all the roofs were flat on different levels. There was no sign of the Algerians.

"Well, we've got them all right," he said. "But it certainly looks like a long wait. They're covering the only entrance to the roof we've found like hellfire. And I've no doubt they're covering everyone we haven't found too. There's no way of even having a straight gunfight with them and we don't want to wreck the building."

"By the way," the superintendent said. "There's an Arab being held down below says he was working with you. We found a gun on him. That's quite a new escape method."

"Ahmed ben Lulla?"

"That sounds like his name. You know him?"

"He did it."

"Did what?"

"Got them there and us here. I'll go down and see that he's all right. I suppose we'll just have to wait for them to run out of cannon fodder."

He went back across the roof and down the stairs, leaving the superintendent staring after him in astonishment. It didn't do for everybody to know everything—even if he was a superintendent.

Going down in the lift, past the crowded landings, Raimond felt quite pleased with the way things had worked out. Of course he had no illusions. National Liberation Front activities would start up again in the capital pretty

soon. But it would need fresh organisation and after this it would have to be more careful and thus less effective. It would mean a quieter time for everybody for a while and it wouldn't do much for the morale of the enemy troops in the Algerian mountains.

On the bottom floor he pulled open the wooden swing doors and undid the iron gate. He stepped out, closing the gate with a clang and went into the ground floor apartment which had its door open and was swarming with policemen. He found Ahmed ben Lulla, handcuffed and indignant, seated in a corner and guarded by two policemen who seemed quite amused at his explanation of the part he'd played in the whole business.

"Inspector Raimond," he cried out in violent relief. "Thank God you're here."

Raimond grinned.

"A misunderstanding," he said. "These are pretty hectic times."

He motioned to the two men to release their captive which they did, slowly, in an astonishment which amounted almost to disbelief.

"You'd better stay here until we've got them," Raimond said. "Be nice to him," he added to the policemen. "He deserves a medal."

In the porch of the house he stared up at the opposite building. There must be a way of getting onto the roof. At the far end of the block was a raised platform of roof with a few chimney stacks on it. It was the obvious last line of retreat, except that the Algerians couldn't get there now because it was covered from the roof opposite. Below the roof at this point were the apartment windows with their little balconies. A pattern of bas-relief designs were carved into the wall above and around them.

Raimond slipped out of the building and moved care-

fully along the street, keeping his eyes on the parapet of the roof which sheltered the prey.

In a large tunnel-like entrance to a courtyard which had become the G.H.Q. of the police forces he had a quick discussion with a number of officers and then, followed by a couple of lieutenants, edged along the street and entered the apartment building under the raised section of roof.

This was it. He knew. This was the way to get them quickly, to make a neat and effective job of the whole thing instead of having it drag on and possibly losing a man or two in the process.

They crammed into the lift, all three of them, and went up to the apartment on the top floor, as everywhere, police and anxious people mingled in the doorway, on the landing and in the apartment itself.

With a few words of explanation, Raimond led the two lieutenants onto the balcony.

Looking up the edge of the roof seemed farther than it had from opposite, but the footholds and handholds in the bas-relief were deep.

Raimond loosened his revolver from its hoister and put it in his pocket. Half held by his two aides he climbed onto the little iron railing of the balcony and searched for a suitable hold in the bas-relief... He didn't look down at all.

He found the hold and reached up for it with his hands, digging his toes into another indentation of the wall at the same time. He clung for a minute, accustoming himself to the balance and then he began to step gently, cautiously up the wall, using each crevice and clinging tightly with his fingers. The roof which overhung slightly was three feet above when he started.

The men below helped to apply inward pressure first to his back and then to his legs and finally, as his hands caught

at the ledge of the roof and eased over, they could reach only his feet.

Hanging onto the edge of the roof over the street, leaning outwards slightly with the angle, Raimond felt with one hand towards the inner edge of the parapet. He found it, gripped it and then released his hold on the outer edge with the other, sliding it over the stone to join the first.

Sweat gathered on his face and body and he felt a slight chill in his stomach as he eased his whole body outwards around the lean of the roof, levering himself with his hands and arms, letting his feet swing free. Just for a moment or two he hung there dangerously six storeys up, heaving himself over the parapet.

He heard the sound of firing. He was being covered from the opposite roof.

A final heave and he was lying along the parapet and could see down onto the roof below where the crouching figures of the Algerians filled every spot of cover.

They were not expecting attack from this quarter. They were all facing the far entrance to the roof, which, he now saw, appeared to be the only one.

Firing from the opposite roof redoubled and some intrepid marksman managed to take a few shots from the roof entrance.

Raimond leaned back over the parapet and caught the hands which were already reaching up over the parapet. He braced himself, taking their weight as the lieutenant below pushed up with his feet. In a few seconds the man was with him on the roof and behind him, the third man was passing up a couple of Sten guns.

The two men took the guns and moved quietly to the cover of a chimney stack. The enemy was spread out below. They had what was almost an aerial view.

"Right," Raimond said.

There was no time to be squeamish. The nationalists were desperate men who would give no quarter. Surprise was the only way to avoid greater bloodshed.

The two Sten guns nosed out from the chimney stacks.

"Now," Raimond said tensely.

There was sputtering fire which fizzed and ricochetted all over the roof.

It was all over in a matter of seconds. A perfect target, the Algerians collapsed under the stream of unexpected fire, without returning a shot.

When it was done and the roof was littered with bodies and police began to invade the roof from the apartment entrance, Raimond leaned heavily against the chimney, staring with his companion over the carnage.

"Quite an anticlimax," he said.

CHAPTER XXIV

In their delightful flat in the 10th Arrondissement, Ahmed ben Lulla and Françoise were lying on the bed. They were a perfect, contented couple. Ahmed had regular work and Françoise no longer propped up the doorway of a hotel to earn a living for both of them. Everything past seemed like a nightmare of several nights ago which one hardly remembered but which left a vague disquiet somewhere in the subconscious.

The only trouble was that Françoise had found that since her half dozen lovers a night had been reduced to one she took an enormous amount of satisfying. But Ahmed was doing his valiant best. It wasn't a serious complaint.

"Let's again, darling," she whispered, stroking his half-inflated penis which was still wet from the last time. He kissed her taut, demanding breasts and ran his hands over her naked body.

"I'll have to employ a stand-in," he said with a grin as, fully erect now, he slithered onto her and began to thread his hips between her thighs in a long, smooth rhythm.

∗∗

Lying alone in bed, Michele Raimond felt very proud of her husband, who'd had such universal recognition for his cracking up of the NLF. Already she'd put behind her the ghastly experience she'd undergone at their hands. After all, she'd told Pierre everything and time was covering it over like new grass growing up. She still had her secret about the American, but it was just as well to have one secret from a man when you loved him so much. She fell asleep, wishing Pierre were there to make love to her the way he'd been making love to her these past nights. What a man he was for work. She pouted to herself. But she had pleasant dreams.

∗∗

Pierre Raimond was "working" hard. Thrust, thrust, thrust—in, in, in and Rolande writhed and twisted and groaned under him in that special volcanic way of hers which filled him with such excitement. In his hands her buttocks were like footballs.

As he worked in, deep into her loins, it occurred to him that he'd really robbed the National Liberation Front of everything they possessed.

THE END

EROTIC CLASSICS FROM
CARROLL & GRAF

☐ Anonymous/AUTOBIOGRAPHY OF A FLEA	$3.95
☐ Anonymous/CAPTURED	$4.50
☐ Anonymous/CONFESSIONS OF AN ENGLISH MAID	$4.50
☐ Anonymous/THE CONSUMMATE EVELINE	$4.95
☐ Anonymous/THE EDUCATION OF A MAIDEN	$4.50
☐ Anonymous/THE EROTIC READER	$4.50
☐ Anonymous/THE EROTIC READER II	$3.95
☐ Anonymous/THE EROTIC READER III	$4.50
☐ Anonymous/THE EROTIC READER IV	$4.95
☐ Anonymous/THE EROTIC READER V	$4.95
☐ Anonymous/FALLEN WOMAN	$4.50
☐ John Cleland/FANNY HILL	$4.95
☐ Anonymous/FANNY HILL'S DAUGHTER	$3.95
☐ Anonymous/FORBIDDEN PLEASURES	$4.95
☐ Anonymous/HAREM NIGHTS	$4.95
☐ Anonymous/INDISCREET MEMOIRS	$4.50
☐ Anonymous/A LADY OF QUALITY	$3.95
☐ Anonymous/LAY OF THE LAND	$4.50
☐ Anonymous/LEDA IN BLACK ON WHITE	$4.95
☐ Anonymous/MAID AND MISTRESS	$4.50
☐ Anonymous/THE MERRY MENAGE	$4.50
☐ Anonymous/SATANIC VENUS	$4.50
☐ Anonymous/SWEET CONFESSIONS	$4.50
☐ Anonymous/TROPIC OF LUST	$4.50
☐ Anonymous/VENUS IN INDIA	$3.95
☐ Anonymous/WHITE THIGHS	$4.50

Available from fine bookstores everywhere or use this coupon for ordering.

MORE EROTIC CLASSICS FROM
CARROLL & GRAF